Pelican Books
The Rights and Wrongs of Women

Juliet Mitchell was born in New Zealand in 1940, but has
lived in London since 1944. She was a lecturer in English
literature at the Universities of Leeds and Reading. She has
written numerous essays in literary criticism and in the
political theory of women's oppression, and is one of
Britain's foremost feminist thinkers. Her published work
includes *Woman's Estate*, *Psychoanalysis and Feminism*, *The
Selected Melanie Klein* (editor), all published in Penguin,
Women: The Longest Revolution, and, with Jaqueline Rose,
Feminine Sexuality: Jacques Lacan and the école freudienne.

Juliet Mitchell is now a psychoanalyst practising in London,
where she lives with her husband and daughter.

Ann Oakley is a sociologist and since the beginning of 1985
she has been Deputy Director at the Thomas Coram
Research Unit, University of London. She has published a
number of books on the family, the position of women and
health care, including *Sex, Gender and Society* (1972), *The
Sociology of Housework* (1974), *Housewife* (Penguin, 1976),
Women Confined (1980), *Subject Women* (1981), *From Here
to Maternity* (1981, also published by Penguin), *The Captured
Womb* (1984) and, with Ann McPherson and Helen Roberts,
Miscarriage (1984).

In 1984 Ann Oakley published a personal history of her
involvement in writing and research, *Taking it Like a
Woman*. She lives in London with her three children.

EDITED AND INTRODUCED BY
JULIET MITCHELL AND ANN OAKLEY

The Rights and Wrongs of Women

PENGUIN BOOKS

PENGUIN BOOKS

Published by the Penguin Group
27 Wrights Lane, London W8 5TZ, England
Viking Penguin Inc., 40 West 23rd Street, New York, New York 10010, USA
Penguin Books Australia Ltd, Ringwood, Victoria, Australia
Penguin Books Canada Ltd, 2801 John Street, Markham, Ontario, Canada L3R 1B4
Penguin Books (NZ) Ltd, 182–190 Wairau Road, Auckland 10, New Zealand

Penguin Books Ltd, Registered Offices: Harmondsworth, Middlesex, England

First published 1976
10 9 8 7 6

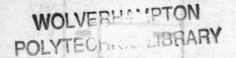

Contents

Introduction

This book originated several years ago in a publisher's suggestion for a collection of essays on women that would constitute an 'anti-text'; a text that could be set against the ideological message of orthodox literature on the position of women. Even then, the notion of an anti-text relating to women presented problems. Since that time the difficulties have multiplied, and the character of this volume illustrates both the kind of problems the original idea raised, and the particular way in which we as editors chose to confront it. In this introduction we are not speaking for our contributors but only for ourselves as editors.

The idea of an anti-text book was symptomatic of the radicalism of the second half of the sixties; it was an off-shoot of the anti-authoritarian movements which swept through universities and, to a lesser degree, other institutions such as schools, prisons and mental hospitals. At heart this movement challenged both traditional ideologies and hierarchical and disciplinarian practices. But so far as the position of women in society was concerned, the problem was one of invisibility. For those aware of women's status as a distinct social group, institutional practice regarding them was clearly discriminatory, but no one was quite sure of the forms and extent of this discrimination, nor of the subtle and complex ways in which different areas of discrimination interacted with one another. No body of empirical knowledge existed on which the case against sexism could be based. When the women's movement first began to take shape, it was almost impossible to discover the most simple facts about women's situation. In England, for instance, the school performance of girls and boys could not directly be compared, because no one saw any reason for properly breaking down the examination statistics by sex. This lack of awareness of sex/gender as a socially divisive factor did not follow from a sexually egalitarian society, but from the reality of a society so deeply unaware of social and economic inequities between male and female that the possibility of their existence could not be officially acknowledged.

If institutional practices relating to women were ill-defined, their ideological character was even less visible. Academic curricula, in line with social thinking generally, failed to see women as a defined social group, or to codify the social differences between the sexes. There was therefore no role for an anti-text, because the orthodox texts themselves did not exist.

Since then, the women's movement from the mid-sixties onwards has both uncovered some of the realities of women's situation and protested against them. The practices of sex discrimination have been revealed and ways have been sought to overcome them. The academic response to this movement from women within the universities and other educational institutions has been, in the United States and also to a lesser degree in Europe, the creation of women's studies programmes. The original concept of such programmes issued from a radical opposition to a status quo signified by the absence of women as a category warranting consideration. Women's studies courses are by definition opposed to the accepted position of women. Insofar as official texts or programmes on women now exist therefore, these are themselves anti-establishment and challenge traditional notions of woman's place. The idea of an anti-text thus gathers absurdity.

As women's studies have become increasingly accepted within higher education, the more radical elements in the women's movement have become concerned that they might come to represent 'tokenism'; that, as has been the fate of American Black studies, they would perform a function of negating the protest, a means of acknowledging and then forgetting the oppression and discrimination they had been set up to combat. A second worry is that, because feminism itself is such an eclectic thought process, its most conservative traits could be confirmed and developed within the institutional framework. Thus if women's studies do become part of the traditional non-critical educational structure, there will, presumably, in time be a place for anti-texts.

This point does not so far seem to us to have been reached. So what is the intention of the present volume? It is perhaps easier to begin with a statement of what we are not doing. It will be obvious to other women within the women's movement, but perhaps less immediately obvious to the reader outside it, that this book is not a description of the personal experience of women's oppression. The people who have written chapters for it are not arguing a personal case against sexism, nor are they listing their own encounters with the practices and ideologies of sex discrimination. *The Rights and Wrongs of Women* is not a feminist charter, and those who want to read the rallying cry for feminist revolution will have to look elsewhere.

Our aim has been to bring together a collection of original essays on the position of women, written from the perspectives of various 'academic' disciplines. The contributors include historians, English literature specialists and sociologists. The subjects are diverse, and range from women trade union activists, to Mary Wollstonecraft, Harriet Martineau and Simone de Beauvoir as three examples of bourgeois feminists; from the history of the ideology of domesticity to the liberation of Chinese women. The essays illustrate different strands of thought within feminism, but they do not offer a unified political perspective. They are all, however, informed with a feminist concern in the most general sense of the term: by this we simply mean that all the contributors subscribe to a base-line definition of feminism. They see women as a distinct and oppressed social group.

Having said what kind of book *The Rights and Wrongs of Women* is not, and having mentioned the differences in the ideological viewpoints of its contributors, we feel it is also important to define its more specific qualities so far as feminism is concerned. This involves saying something about ourselves as editors, about the problems we have encountered in getting the book together, and about our own relationship with feminism and the women's movement.

We both see ourselves as feminists yet our theoretical approaches to feminism are in many ways discrepant. Ann Oakley is a socialist and a sociologist; Juliet Mitchell is a Marxist, and after a career teaching English literature is now training to be a psychoanalyst. Ann Oakley takes her distance from theoretical Marxism and is more than a little sceptical of psychoanalysis; Juliet Mitchell has her doubts (and prejudices) about the type of 'empiricism' on which much sociology and non-Marxist socialism are based. These differences in outlook would seem to pose impossible problems for a collaboration as editors. Yet in fact, and despite many frustrations and difficulties, we have worked well and enjoyably together. How have we been able to do this? The answer has to do as much with our shared criticism of current feminism as with our endorsement of its general principles. And in turn the criticisms of feminism which we have felt emerging during our editorship have helped to shape the final form of the book.

To many women in the women's movement this volume will appear conservative both as a product and as a conception. This is because it does not appear to affirm one of the basic tenets of the women's movement – the fundamental feminist concept of sisterhood. (Our criticisms of 'sisterhood' are not by any means shared by all the contributors to this volume.) The notion of sisterhood embodies an attack on the principle of hierarchy. The argument runs thus; in a patriarchal society, male domination is assured through a structural policy of divide and rule. Women are separated from each other and from a collective awareness of their oppression as women by an enclosure within the sexist nuclear family, and by a subjection to the general principle of hierarchical (male) structure. To overcome this, they must assert their identification with one another and also their dissent from the male practice of hierarchical order. The slogan 'sisterhood is powerful' encapsulates both these statements. Among the manifestations of sisterhood has been the practice within the women's movement of eschewing the idea of leadership altogether. Both the notion of 'consciousness-raising' and of forming small, personal women's groups have been based on the idea of collective responsibility. Sometimes this is ensured by quite formal devices – i.e. the principle of each member speaking in turn, of all outside speaking engagements being undertaken by a group of women rather than individual women, and by the strict rotation of particular responsibilities and work-loads within the group. Yet the concept of sisterhood means much more than sharing work or responsibility. It involves a redefinition of the value and status of personal experience. The personal becomes the political; that is, the nature of women's oppression can be analysed through the medium of accounts of private experiences. It is argued that one of the symptoms of women's oppression is the excessive privatization of their lives; through the split between personal and public (work) life in a male-oriented culture, the personal is trivialized. It is therefore a political act for women to discover the similarities between their personal experiences and those of other women and to raise to public (political) importance these aspects of their lives.

From accounts of female childhood, marriage, housewifery, childbirth, childrearing, and other aspects of women's role, a type of panoramic description has been built up of what it feels like to be a woman in our society. Since the object of the exercise is to outline the conditions of women's oppression, it is of course the pains and the problems of femaleness that are highlighted in this literature. So there is a second tendency that counterposes the literature of degradation with songs of glory. 'I am strong, I am woman' does not simply proclaim hope for a more female-oriented society in the future; it proclaims moments of euphoria for feminists in the present and provokes a search for a golden age of matriarchy in the past.

None of this is included here. There are several reasons for this. In the first place we feel that by its very nature the statement of personal experience and the glorification of sisterhood become repetitious. They are useful as starting points but after that they act as distractions from another equally essential enterprise. It is like building up a descriptive geography of a scene; at a certain point, instead of walking the tracks for an ordnance survey map, one must get out the drawing board. Although political work is always on one level about personal lives, we feel the time for the drawing-board has come.

Secondly, we detect a move towards rigidity and inflexibility within the women's movement which we feel results from a premature codification of personal insights as political rules. It is one thing to discuss with other women the sexist attitudes of one's seven-year-old son, but quite another to demand the total rejection by feminists of their male children by forming communities which exclude them. A critical relationship to current marriage practices and to the life-styles most frequently induced by the nuclear family makes political sense. Yet no insight should blind one to the fact that the abandonment of marriage and the family may, in certain times and places, be both personally extremely painful and also politically pretty useless. This does not prevent one from asking questions about the actual practices and ideologies of people who appear to live in 'typical' nuclear family situations. In other words, we feel that the wholesale destruction of existing social practices is not necessarily to be welcomed, and a rigid insistence on the reversal of current practice may actually be disastrous. In case we should be misunderstood here, this is not the same thing as saying we do not think there should be changes here and now in the position of women. These criticisms that we have of the women's movement represent, in part, certain shifts in our thinking over the last few years.

So here we are, two women editing a conventional collection, not in content but in form, and having done so in ways that do not fit the tenets of the women's movement. We have acted in quite authoritarian ways as editors; discussing our own ideas of people's contributions with them, asking for extensive rewrites, and unfortunately rejecting some contributions. In the process of producing the book we have not forged a new concept of the feminist editor; but have, on the contrary, found ourselves behaving in a conventional manner. To some extent this may of course be because we, like many women, find we cannot easily shake off our unconscious allegiance to the traditional models of behaviour which our culture holds out to us; but we have also experienced on a conscious level certain doubts about the concept of sisterhood itself.

When the present phase of the women's movement established itself in the second part of the sixties, there was a need for a unifying ideology while ideas were being worked out or rediscovered. 'Sisterhood' served the rhetorical purpose of political under-development; it was a useful rallying-cry. But its implications were not thought out and it seems to us now to mask both an absence of any real unity beneath it and to ignore the highly problematic relationships that in itself it implies. We do live in a hierarchical world; the women's movement does not just combat structures of dominance, it is also surrounded by them and embedded in them. The ideological argument for sisterhood is that sisters must be exempt from the pernicious influence of the nuclear family; they constitute a horizontal alliance within a hierarchical structure. Potentially they have a double bond, for as girls they are being socialized into positions inferior to those of their brothers, and they are children against the domination of parents. Sisterhood can undoubtedly be a relationship of solidarity and support. On the other hand, literature and mythology, replete with misogynistic jokes against women's family roles (such as those about mothers-in-law, stepmothers and so on) has some nasty things to say about sisters too. Usually the problem is the favoured youngest sister – Cinderella or Cordelia – on whom other sisters gang up. No one would claim validity for such misogynistic tales *per se*, but we should remember that ideology not only reflects but also influences social reality.

The sisterhood of feminism cannot, in other words, be an instant and transcendent unification of women; it must to some extent repeat the terms of women's social relationships with one another – relationships that, as with all relationships in a family-oriented society, are based on the family situation. The unity of sisterhood may have magic as a political slogan, but we do not have the ability to conjure it up at will: unity is unity of purpose, the sharing of ideas. The problems of the way in which women relate to one another remain and must be recognized.

This book, then, does not represent the collective or sororal enterprise of sisterhood. Because of our scepticism about the meaning of sisterhood in the women's movement at this particular point in time, and because of our feelings that its literature is repetitious, there are no programmatic articles included; none of the pieces speak directly from or to the practice of the women's movement. Yet the essays are, as we said earlier, informed by a feminist perspective. The relationship to feminism we have experienced during the process of working on the book has been both positive and negative. Our disagreements have already been mentioned; so what do we feel confirmed in?

When we talk of returning to the drawing-board, we are referring to the enterprise of rewriting history; of re-interpreting the social world, both past and present, from a perspective which includes women. It is often said these days that most of what has been presented to us as history is the history of men through men's eyes: that all academic disciplines have a central bias towards the masculine perspective. But we feel that not only is it important to say this, to incorporate the insight into the network of realizations about ourselves and our society that feminism has implicated us in; it is also essential to carry out a major reworking of these disciplines from a feminist perspective.

Although Marxist theoretical work tends to escape censure, there is a considerable amount of scepticism within the women's movement about the value of other theoretical or even academic work. Perhaps all political movements are bound to develop certain characteristic intolerances, but we believe that part of the success of feminism will consist in the rewriting of history, sociology, psychology, economics, and so forth from a stand-point which is sensitive to the situation of women as a distinct social group.

Although the balance of the book is towards a historical perspective, the enterprise of reworking our knowledge of the social world is not only the province of historians. Feminism is a method of analysis as well as a discovery of new material. It asks new questions as well as coming up with new answers. Its central concern is with the social distinction between men and women, with the fact of this distinction, with its meaning, and with its causes and consequences. Insofar as it initiates a system of thought, feminism transforms the ideological notion that there is a biological opposition between the sexes which determines social life, and says instead that there is a contradiction in the social relations between men and women. This contradiction is never static as a biological opposition would be, but it shifts, moves and is moved and is therefore one force among others that effects social change and the movement of human history. Feminism is about this social structuring along sex lines; it is involved not only with the accumulation of information on this theme but also with the development of an understanding of the social structure itself. Such an understanding asks for a re-examination of art and ideology as well as, more obviously, of questions of history and sociology. It necessitates a new understanding not only of the social system but also of the system of thought one is using for the inquiry in the first place.

The essays in this volume do not pretend to comprehensiveness; they are a response to the demands of a feminist perspective. They make new information accessible, re-examine old ideologies and uncover previously hidden ones. Some look at the history and position of women; others at the history and status of feminism. It is difficult to separate them into categories, since their themes are interlocking. However they vary in their concern with the private or public worlds of femininity; in their concentration on theoretical analyses of feminism as opposed to the collection of empirical data on women's situation; and in the extent to which their subject matter is highly specific or, instead, relates to very general aspects of the social relations between the sexes. In differing ways all the essays imply an urgent need for social change; but they insist, too, that this need must not overshadow analytical understanding. Both reformists and revolutionaries have to contend with the fact of a class-antagonistic society; and feminists must similarly realize that the oppressive social division between men and women, though not a class division, at the very least represents a fissure in the groundplan of human society which must be charted before it can be bridged.

1

Wisewoman and Medicine Man: Changes in the Management of Childbirth

ANN OAKLEY

The ideas contained in this chapter were developed during preliminary reading for a sociological study of childbirth in modern
society. They are speculative and exploratory and are offered in
that spirit. Although the concern of the chapter is with social and
medical changes in the handling of childbirth over the last
century or so, the aim is not to provide a thorough account of
these changes, but rather to sketch out some connections between
changes in childbirth on the one hand, and the position of women
on the other. This approach takes the inquiry further back
historically: it entails important questions about the role of
women in community health care, and about the origins and
development of the reproductive care system. While the chapter
is *specifically* concerned with the changing treatment of women
in childbirth, it is therefore also *generally* about the historical
place of women as practitioners of medical care.

From Female Control to Male Control

The major transformation in the management of childbirth with
which this chapter is concerned is identified in the following
anecdote, taken from an account of childbirth in rural India
written in 1962:

One day an elderly lady came to call on Surjeeto's mother, Mohindro.
She said she was a health visitor employed by the government and from
now on would come once a month to the village to examine and advise
all pregnant women. She asked Mohindro to send Surjeeto for a

checkup. Mohindro looked surprised and said, 'but what is wrong with my Surjeeto?' She was told that pregnant women required a checkup now and then to see if all was well. They also needed advice about diet and had to be taught childcare. Mohindro looked at the health visitor in amazement and said 'but I can teach my child how to care for her children, and what advice about diet can you give? We have plenty of milk, butter, dal, atta. What more is needed? And, as for a checkup, why I have had five children and never had a checkup for any of them. The village midwife, Akki, came when it was time for me to deliver.' The health visitor said that Akki was alright, but she had had no training. Mohindro was more amazed than ever, and asked how any person could be untrained if she had delivered babies all her life?[1]

Here we have a direct confrontation between two systems. The first, to which Surjeeto's mother refers, is based on an attitude which sees reproduction as a normal process, and on an empiricism which values experience rather than 'professional' training. The second, represented by the health visitor, views reproduction as a medical condition fraught with all sorts of dangers: a condition that can only be 'cured' by the authoritarian benevolence of professionalized medicine. But the two systems do not simply oppose empiricism to professionalization: a 'natural' to a 'medicalized' definition of childbirth. There is also a sex difference in the structure of control. Although the health visitor is a woman, she is sent to educate the female community by a male-dominated medical authority.

The main change in the social and medical management of childbirth and reproductive care in industrialized cultures over the last century has been the transition from a structure of control located in a community of untrained women, to one based on a profession of formally trained men. Thus, a process of professionalization has been accompanied by a transfer of control from women to men. Whilst the development of medicine as a profession, and changes in the medical management of childbirth have been studied, this exchange of control between the sexes has received little attention. Clearly the vesting of control with one sex group rather than the other is only of potential significance if the social situations of men and women are generally differentiated. A particularly crucial factor is whether or not the ideologies held by each sex group with respect to gender roles are also dissimilar. The existence of both these types of distinction between femininity and masculinity in contemporary industrial society is documented elsewhere.[2] Just how the change of control over childbirth has affected women of course remains problematic, even if this basic premise of gender differentiation is accepted; this question is explored further later in the chapter.

Childbirth, contraception and abortion are aspects of women's reproductive life. In most cultures of the world and throughout most of history it is women who have controlled their own reproductive function. That is, the management of reproduction has been restricted to women, and regarded as part of the feminine role. Such knowledge of anatomy, physiology, pharmacology and delivery techniques as exists is vested in women as a group. This control is usually informal, often invisible and concealed. It operates through a system of cooperative mutual aid, and with a body of practical knowledge and beliefs which is transmitted from one generation of women to another. There are methods of preventing conception, and ways of ensuring abortion if unwanted conception has occurred. When a child is ready to be born it is a woman or group of women who deliver it, and who care for both mother and child in the postnatal period. Women are the experts. Men are not involved, or are only marginally involved.

Europe and America before industrialization, and for some time after this, possessed indigenous female-controlled reproductive care systems. These systems were analogous to those described by anthropologists as existing in small-scale societies today.[3]

Among the Navajo Indians, for example, the midwife is usually a person related to the parturient woman's family. The word for midwife in Navajo language means literally 'the woman who pulls the baby out'. (This is the earlier and original meaning of the English term: 'woman who is with the mother at birth' is a later meaning.) The midwife's first duty on being called to a confinement is to prepare the home, by cleaning it and tidying it, and arranging an area within it where the mother can give birth.

An important task is to hang up the 'squaw belt', a handwoven sash which is fastened to the roof and on which the labouring woman pulls to deliver the baby. Delivery is carried out in the kneeling position, with the midwife in front of the mother, and an assistant positioned behind her pressing on her abdomen. If the baby is in the wrong position to be born, midwives are usually able to correct this. The midwife cuts the umbilical cord with a sharp knife and ties it with string. She waits for the placenta and, if this is delayed, she tickles the woman's nose with the end of her mocassin strings in an attempt to make her sneeze. (Modern professionally trained midwives often ask the mother to cough for the same reason.) If sneezing fails to produce the placenta, the midwife extracts it manually. It is then her duty to examine it and to bury it.

In this account, the skills of midwifery are combined with cleaning and caring functions, whereas the modern tendency is to separate these. Among the Navajo and many other peoples the act of birth occurs in a familiar social context. Its management is continuous with, rather than separated from, the support of the pregnant woman and the care of the new mother and her child.

In the culture of the D'Entrecasteaux Islands off Australia, another instance of a female-controlled reproductive care system, a very clear distinction is made between pregnancy and childbirth, which are seen as normal conditions, and any kind of disease or injury, which is regarded as serious and attributed to supernatural causes. The care of the sick is in the hands of 'medicine men', but birth is supervised by the women of the community. At the approach of labour the husband departs. Attendance is confined to near relatives, mothers and sisters preferably. The woman sits to deliver the baby, with one woman behind her, supporting her by the hips, and others at the sides, holding her knees. During a contraction they hold her tightly. Another woman kneels in front and watches the progress of the infant's head. When the head is about to be born, she may separate the labia, but otherwise no manipulations occur. The baby is touched only when it is received on the ground, and then the cord is severed with a sharp shell or piece of glass. No attempt is made to hasten delivery of the placenta. The woman's mother, who is the most usual person to act as midwife, then washes baby and mother and remains in attendance on them for the postpartum period. Aside from the control of childbirth, women in this culture are said to prevent conception by drinking herbal potions and to cause abortion through violent treatment of the abdomen.[4]

The management of reproduction in modern industrialized societies presents a strong contrast to these examples from small-scale societies. Control is ultimately vested not in the lay woman, but in the male professional. Although the role of women as subsidiary workers in the health care system is considerable, their professional skills are defined predominantly in relation to the expertise and omniscience of the male professional. Contraception is a scientific matter and is part of a male-dominated medical technology.[5] Abortion is properly the concern of doctors only. Childbirth is increasingly hospitalized, and in hospital the woman enters a structure of control which invests the male obstetrician with ultimate power over her parturition.

Information about what it is like to experience childbirth in modern Britain or America is scanty. There is no study of child-birth from the woman's point of view; there are only personal accounts and impressions. Here is an extract from one:

Everyone is telling us to forget. They say 'you have a beautiful son. The birth is over. Put it out of your mind'. I'd like to but I can't.

Every time I nurse my baby, I rerun the scenes of his birth, trying in fantasy to deliver him my way rather than the doctor's way . . .

The doctors on the floor were worried about the baby's heart, so they decided to monitor it. When they inserted the monitoring device in the middle of a contraction and I swore, the nurse said 'language!' and slapped my wrist . . .

Then it was time for the delivery room . . . They lowered the stirrups and tied my legs in; I demanded they take them out. More assistants were called to hold me down, they tied my wrists to the table in leather thongs, and when I struggled to sit up, they laughed at me. The doctor told me to push before I was fully dilated, and he manipulated my cervix manually (gross obstetrics by any standards). It was just plain hell. The staff did everything possible to undermine my control and then inferred that because women can't control themselves in labour, they have to be strapped down.[6]

This contrast between female-controlled and male-controlled systems blurs a number of outlines. Thus, for example, in modern industrialized societies some doctors are women: to juxtapose the two categories of 'lay woman' and 'male professional' omits a third, the female professional obstetrician or gynaecologist. (26 per cent of obstetricians and gynaecologists in England and Wales are women, but only 12 per cent of consultants in this field are female. If the percentage of female consultants is taken as a criterion, obstetrics and gynaecology comes only tenth in a rank order of 'feminine' specialties within medicine.) Secondly, in Britain and other countries the midwife has retained an important role which she has lost elsewhere, for instance, in America. The important issue is that of *control*: later on in this chapter I shall try to show how both the female doctor and the professional midwife have been incorporated into a male-dominated control structure.

Two ideas or concepts need to be more precisely defined. These are the concept of a 'reproductive care system' and the concept of 'control'. I use 'reproductive care system' to refer broadly to the procedures generally employed within, or by, any particular culture in the treatment and management of childbirth (including antenatal and postnatal periods), abortion and contraception. Although the general argument of the paper relates to reproductive care in its widest sense, I shall throughout restrict myself principally to discussing childbirth. 'Control' is less easy to define. The essential conditions for the exercise of control resting with any social or occupational group are, firstly, that the group in question should have exclusive command over relevant resources, and, secondly, that its practice of this control should be legitimated (regarded as valid) by society at large. In the case of any kind of medical care, 'resources' include technical knowledge, skills, together with diagnostic and therapeutic procedures, and also the important resource of the personnel who aid in the work of caring and/or healing. The term 'control' implies not only command over resources, but also the 'exclusive competence' to determine and evaluate these resources. So far as social validation goes, a public belief in the right of certain people to control certain areas of life is (in modern society) usually based on law. The legal charters of professional organizations provide the most important means of recognizing or assigning competence; before these were established, the right to exclusive competence (in any occupation) derived much more directly from personal charisma and/or general public esteem.[7]

The changeover from a female-controlled to a male-controlled reproductive care system poses two sets of questions. The first set concern the reasons for the changeover; the processes and events which enabled it to take place. The second set of questions concern the relative gains and losses for women of these developments. Modern conventional wisdom has it that an essential part of women's emancipation from their traditional subservient role is their liberation from the burdens and casualties of the reproductive function under a professionalized, male-dominated medical system and its attendant technology. How true is this? The two questions – how did it happen, and what does it mean for women – are intimately connected.

The Wisewoman and the Doctor

Etymologically and historically, four words or roles have been closely related. These are woman, witch, midwife and healer. In the transition from female control to male control, two periods stand out as landmarks. From the fourteenth to the seventeenth centuries in Europe medicine emerged as a predominantly male professional discipline, and the traditional female lay healer was suppressed. In the nineteenth and twentieth centuries the female control of reproduction, which had largely persisted despite the rise of male medicine, was eroded with the inclusion of obstetrics in the curricula of professional medical training. There are thus two 'takeovers'. One concerns general medicine, the other obstetrics specifically. In the case of both takeovers, the change first affected the upper and middle classes and only slowly permeated downwards to working-class culture.

Women have a long history as community healers in pre-industrial Europe and colonial America. The 'good woman', 'cunning woman' or 'wisewoman' was the person to whom people turned in times of illness; she represented the chief medical practitioner available to a community living in constant poverty and disease. In the literature of the period male healers are not mentioned nearly so frequently as female healers; the bulk of lay healing was done by women.[8] There is good reason for this. The role of housewife in pre-industrial society encompassed a much wider range of functions than it does today. Healing the sick was work that devolved not only upon the upper-class ladies of households, but also upon the lower-class wives of the community.[9] In their role as healers these women had knowledge of anatomy, astronomy, psychotherapy, and pharmacology. They knew and used pain-killers, digestive aids, anti-inflammatory agents, ergot (an important midwifery drug), belladonna and digitalis (today still used in the treatment of heart disease).[10] Moreover, their work was highly valued. In pre-industrial England the female practitioner was widely trusted above her male counterpart, whose main treatment consisted of letting blood. 'Also for Goddys sake be war what medesyns ye take of any fysissyans at London; I shal never trust to hem' wrote Margaret Paston to her husband. Sir Ralph Verney gave his wife similar advice, telling her to 'give the child no phisick but such as midwives and old women . . . doe prescribe; for assure yourself they by experience know better than any physition how to treat such infants'.[11] Such references to lay female healers occur frequently in letters and diaries of the period. Doubtless this attitude favouring the female healer also made sound economic sense; the services of male doctors were more expensive.

The care of infants and of women in childbirth was an integral part of the female healing role. As Alice Clark, in her account of seventeenth-century working women, describes the rural English practice:

> It was customary, when travail began, to send for all the neighbours who were responsible women, partly with the object of securing enough witnesses to the child's birth, partly because it was important to spread the understanding of midwifery as widely as possible because any woman might be called upon to render assistance in an emergency.[12]

Women of all classes depended upon the lay midwife to see them safely through childbirth. Midwifery skills were acquired by experience and informal apprenticeship in much the same way as general medical skills. In some cases the occupation was passed on from mother to daughter. Although there were those midwives who lacked any systematic instruction, some entered long apprenticeships (among London midwives, a seven-year training was sometimes undertaken). In these instances payment would be made to the instructing midwife – in the 1690s a three-year apprenticeship cost £5.

Practising wisewomen–midwives had a generally respectable, and sometimes high, status among the people they served.[13] The negative appellation 'witch' was fostered by the medieval Church, to whom disease was a God-given affliction, and thus a phenomenon which had to be under strict religious control. Also, of course, the female healer challenged the male hegemony of the Church. There are two problems here. The first concerns how/why the association between witchcraft and the female healing/midwifery function came to be established. The second problem is a statistical one: to what extent *were* women healer–midwives suspected, accused and punished as witches? Neither of these issues seems to be tackled directly in existing studies. Sociological/anthropological interpretations of witchcraft and its persecution cite sexual hostility (of the community), economic marginality (of the accused) in a period torn by the opposed forces of charity and individualism, and the conservative position and social power of village women in a rapidly segmenting society.[14] Most European witches *were* women. In the series of Essex witch-accusations studied by Macfarlane, for example, 268 (92 per cent) of a total of 291 accused witches were women (and eleven of the men were either married to an accused witch or appeared in a joint indictment with a woman). A similar pattern emerges in a re-analysis of data on the Salem witch trials in New England, where 120 (74 per cent) of 162 accused witches were female, the typical witch was a married or widowed woman aged between forty-one and sixty, and most of the males accused of witchcraft were either the children or husbands of female witches.[15] The women accused of witchcraft in England and elsewhere tended to be married or widowed, to be middle-aged or old, and to be of low socio-economic status.

Three hierarchies corresponded; church over laity, man over woman, landlord over peasant. The existence of the woman–midwife–witch–healer challenged all three of these hierarchies. She undermined the supremacy of the Church, men and the landed classes. She represented a lay peasant subculture and she symbolized the actual or potential power that a minority group possesses: it is a threat to the established order. Women/peasants posed this kind of threat. The Church's claim was not that witches or wisewomen were unable to cure illness (or that curing illness was itself wrong) but rather that their success was a consequence of an alliance with the Devil, a temptation to which the feminine temperament was held to be peculiarly suspect. In practice neither the lay practitioners of medicine nor their clients distinguished clearly between 'natural' remedies (herbal ointments, potions, etc), and supernatural or symbolic ones. The Church frowned on magic, but the people believed in it. The assumption of control by the Church in the sixteenth century over the licensing of midwives followed from ecclesiastical anxiety about the popular belief in magic (although other motives were involved, including a desire to clamp down on incompetent medical practice, and the aim of raising money). Until about the middle of the sixteenth century, a distinction was maintained between the 'good' or 'white' witch and the 'bad' or 'black' witch. In 1548, an English Witchcraft Act specifically listed the 'good' witch as an unlicensed practitioner of medicine, and distinguished between her activities and the necessarily evil acts of the 'bad' witch. A later Act (of 1563) abolished this distinction and declared that 'witchness' was a condition of the accused person.

The midwife's role in childbirth came in for particular attack. Any midwife was liable to be accused of being a witch, but particularly the unsuccessful among them. The *Malleus Maleficarium*, a famous medieval witch-hunting text, charged the witch–midwife with various reproductive crimes, including destroying the unborn child and causing an abortion. 'No one' said the authors 'does more harm to the Catholic Faith than midwives.' Witches were thought not only to kill and eat children (the idea of the

Black Mass) but also to cause barrenness, abortion and lactation failure; according to Henry Boguet, writing in 1590:

> Those midwives and wisewomen who are witches are in the habit of offering to Satan the little children which they deliver, and then of killing them, before they have been baptised, by thrusting a large pin into their brains. There have been those who have confessed to having killed more than forty children in this way. They do even worse; for they kill them while they are still in their mothers' wombs.[16]

Behind these dramatic accusations lies a germ of truth. The medieval wisewoman in her role as lay healer and obstetrician almost certainly tried to help women carrying unwanted babies. Midwives in small-scale societies perform the same role today, and in our modern industrialized culture, it is still common for women to offer other women advice on how to bring about the miscarriage of an unwanted baby. The illegal backstreet abortionist, operating with her knitting needles or soap-and-water, can be seen as the direct descendant of the medieval midwife–witch. Professional opinion has done its best to label as evil the untrained woman who performs any reproductive care activity (one sign of this is the low opinion of untrained midwives which is reflected in much of the medical-historical literature). But in a sex-divided society, an ethic of 'we women must help each other' often flourishes, and may be as applicable to reproductive care as to those other essentially feminine activities – housework and childcare – where its existence has been established.[17]

Witch-healers and midwives were the practitioners and experts of a female-controlled reproductive care system – a system which had probably been in existence for a very long time. The force of the initial attack upon it was very great; integral to the Church's hostility to lay healing was a misogyny which led easily into an alliance with sexism and capitalism. The fifteenth and sixteenth centuries were a period when the position of women *vis-à-vis* men was in a state of flux. In a growing commercialistic society, women had proved their independence and business efficiency. This practical equality challenged the law which was sex-discriminatory. Much popular discussion and pamphleteering concerned the breakdown in old conventions of masculine and feminine behaviour and what should be done about it: the independent woman evoked fear and a backlash of patriarchal assertiveness. The antifeminism of the Church, symbolic of, and connected with, patriarchal authority generally, had a particular alliance with the oppressive power of the landed classes.

Behind this attitude lay a double standard. Whilst the poor had to endure their suffering, medical care for the upper classes was acceptable, and this was male medical care. Between the eleventh and thirteenth centuries European medicine began its career as a secular science and a profession, with an impetus gained from contact with the Arab world. Until the thirteenth century medical practice was open to all; the only formal qualification available was a licence gained from a university education. But almost without exception women were barred from the universities, and with the development of barber–surgeons' guilds during the thirteenth century, medicine began to close its doors to those without a university licence.[18] Other groups, including the apothecaries, also created professional associations and demanded exclusive rights to practise. Through this kind of monopolistic procedure, the male doctor discredited and disadvantaged the urban literate woman healer.

The early 'professionalization' of medicine was strictly controlled by the Church. In England an Act of 1512 – the first attempt by the State to regulate medical practice – left the responsibility for surveying the competence of medical practitioners to the Church authorities. University-trained physicians could, in theory, only practise with the advice of a priest, and were not supposed to treat patients who refused confession. In the medieval witch trials the male doctor was the 'expert' called in by the Church: it was he who determined who should be burnt as a witch. The *Malleus Maleficarium* (whose authors were appointed by Pope Innocent VIII to root out witchcraft in Germany) explicitly defined the role of the doctor in the witch-hunts and associated the status of doctor with the possession of formal training: 'If a woman dare to cure without having studied' they pronounced 'she is a witch and must die'. A corollary to the 1512 Act included midwives in the Church licensing system, and a condition of the licence was that the midwife agree not to practise any form of witchcraft. (Many midwives, particularly in isolated rural areas, remained unlicensed; a licence was expensive and a woman could still practise as a midwife's 'deputy' without a licence.) The attempted suppression of women healers followed directly from the association between Church doctrine, university-trained medical men and the ruling classes. Male medicine became a fashionable habit. Female medicine was stereotyped as evil magic. A pamphleteer, writing about London in the seventeenth century, noted that there was 'scarce a pissing place about the City' which was not decorated with advertisements by lay healers; but the constant barrage of anti-women legislation and pronouncements from Church and State undoubtedly had an effect. The popular status and authority of the female healer was gradually eroded.

The practice of the early male doctors was very different from the practice of the traditional female healer. Superstition and irrational beliefs played a far greater part in male medicine than in female medicine. Medical students, like other scholarly young gentlemen, devoted a large part of their study to Plato, Aristotle and Christian theology. Medical theory was almost wholly restricted to the work of Galen, the ancient Roman physician, who maintained the theory of 'complexions' or 'temperaments' of men. While wisewomen operated empirically, trusting the evidence of their senses, using trial and error, and believing in cause and effect, male medicine was highly theological and anti-empirical: hence its acceptability to the Church.

Chaucer characterizes the fourteenth century 'Doctour of Phisyk' as a pretentious charlatan in *The Canterbury Tales:*

> In all this world ne was ther noon him lyk
> To speke of phisyk and of surgerye;
> For he was grounded in astronomye . . .
> He knew the cause of everich maladye
> Were it of hoot, or cold, or moyste, or drye
> And where engendred and of what humour;
> He was a verray parfit practisour.

A broad hint of irony is dropped in this last line. As well as his book-learning, Chaucer's Doctor was rather fond of money: he made a small fortune during plague epidemics. The portrait compares unfavourably with the empirical approach to illness adopted by Pertelote in *The Nun's Priest's Tale;* Pertelote represents the good housewife whose domestic skills included a comprehensive knowledge of herbal medicine.

Not surprisingly, modern histories of medicine do not acknowledge its female beginnings. Instead, they trace a direct descent from the Hippocratic physicians of ancient Greece. The witch-healer is dismissed as an undiagnosed hysteric.[19] No doubt once witch-hunting was under way, witchcraft did acquire the function of feminine protest (although of course the label 'hysteric' remains highly political). But the witch's healing role did not in the first instance evolve as feminist rebellion. Interestingly, the so-called hippocratic oath, which is part of the official code of medicine today, probably itself contains a reference to the woman-healer–midwife. The clause 'I will not give to a woman an abortive remedy' has always puzzled historians because it contradicts the liberal abortion policy prevailing in Greece at that time (the fourth century B.C.). The alternative explanation is suggested by one medical historian, Noel Poynter; he suggests that the abortion clause is in fact an admission of a restrictive practice aimed at avoiding demarcation disputes. Obstetrics and gynaecology was the province of female midwives in Greek society, and some of these midwives were highly trained physicians and surgeons. Literary evidence indicates that they were skilled abortionists and also knowledgeable about effective contraception.[20]

Until the seventeenth century, liberal attitudes to abortion persisted in Europe. Abortion in the first six to twelve weeks of foetal life was sanctioned by the Church, since theological doctrine did not allow the foetus a soul at conception, but only some time after (opinion varied as to the exact time). In 1620, a male doctor published a book called *On the Formation of the Foetus* in which he argued that a baby's rational soul enters it in the three days after conception. The legal and religious objections to abortion in many countries date from this time, and in others there was a hardening of anti-abortion opinion.

Childbirth Pollutes; the Beginnings of the Obstetrical Takeover

Considering the extent of their exclusion from university-based medicine, women retained control over the practice of obstetrics for an amazingly long time. The official attitude of the male medical profession until late in the nineteenth century was that 'proper' doctors had no business with midwifery. It was an activity, said the President of the British Royal College of Physicians in 1827, 'foreign to the habits of a gentleman of enlarged academic education'. Not until the 1850s were lectures on midwifery given in British medical schools, and not until 1886 was proficiency in midwifery a necessary qualification for a medical practitioner. In America certainly, and in Britain probably, the standard of medical training in obstetrics lagged behind other areas well into the twentieth century. Only in 1902 in Britain after a long struggle by interested groups (earlier elsewhere) were midwives organized and their area of practice officially delineated and controlled. The definition of the respective roles of doctor and midwife as practitioners of reproductive care took longer to evolve and still has areas of ambiguity. In 1905 one in two, and in 1918, one in five, state-registered midwives in Britain had no training at all. In 1973 the majority of all British babies were still delivered by midwives – about 70 per cent of those born in hospital and about 80 per cent of those born at home. In the United States, the midwife has suffered a virtually total eclipse; in 1964 1·5 per cent of all births were carried out by midwives. Most of these midwives were untrained and female midwifery is concentrated in the poor, nonwhite communities.

The English statistics demonstrate the continuing importance of the midwife, although of course they are uninformative on her degree of autonomy within the reproductive care system, and on her role *vis-à-vis* other practitioners. In all industrialized countries, the midwife's place in reproductive care is hedged about with restrictions and its status (compared with the status of doctor) is low. There are, hence, two processes that require explanation. Firstly, how is it that female-controlled childbirth persisted for so long – why was the male takeover in medicine not immediately followed by a male takeover of midwifery? Secondly, what accounts for the kind of role that midwives have been assigned in health care systems today?

In many traditional small-scale societies, there is a belief that childbirth pollutes.[21] This may be one facet of a general belief that the reproductive powers of women – including menstruation – are dangerous to society. The parturient woman is subject to a host of regulations which control and isolate her act of birth, so that the rest of society is not contaminated by it. Among the Adivi of Southern India, for example, a woman who is to give birth must go to a hut two hundred yards away from the village when she feels the first birth contraction. For ninety days after the birth she must remain in the hut. A midwife is allowed to deliver the baby, but if anyone else touches the woman they become social outcasts and are banned from the village for three months.[22] This is fairly typical of the kind of pollution control exercised over childbirth. Other instances which come more readily to mind are the service for the churching of women after childbirth, and the Jewish prohibition against the handling of food by menstruating women.

Often (although not invariably) this perception of childbirth as polluting is accompanied by a sanction on the control of reproduction by the female half of the community: childbirth is 'women's business'. Connections can be traced between pollution beliefs, the social role of women, and the type of reproductive care system that operates within a given culture. In some cultures, a view of childbearing women as polluters links up with their assigned function as organizers, clearers-up, and cleaners-up in domestic life. Women are the housewives and domestic servants. They care for the sick, the young and the old. In the West before the rise of the nursing profession, nurses were simply domestic servants. The set of equations runs: woman = polluter = housewife = domestic servant = nurse = midwife. A contemporary medical school joke divides labour into four stages: the fourth stage – 'clearing up' – is assigned by doctors to nurses or midwives ('we doctors leave that to the women'). In the

Punjab, the only person who may cut the umbilical cord of the newborn (and thus be a midwife) is a woman from the lower caste – the social group from which servants and other menial workers are also drawn.[23]

Something of the same kind of ideology was at work in the West from the seventeenth to the twentieth centuries and it presented a largely invisible barrier to the masculinization of midwifery. There was a strong tendency on the part of the male doctor to regard midwifery as an inferior, dirty, feminine, poor relation of 'proper' medicine. In part this was because the traditional distinction within medicine between 'Physic', 'Surgery' and 'Pharmacy' allowed no place for midwifery. Neither the College of Physicians nor the College of Surgeons were prepared to accept midwifery as a legitimate area of practice; both passed regulations preventing (male) midwives from being eligible for election to fellowships. The 1858 Medical Act, which established the framework of a national system for regulating medical practice, was silent on the subject of midwifery, confirming the current view that it was not really a valid part of medicine. When men began to take up midwifery in the seventeenth century, many of the new entrants lacked skill and experience and were motivated by the attractiveness of midwifery as an avenue to general medical practice. Once admitted to the lying-in room, the newly fashionable male practitioner could ingratiate himself with the family and build up a lucrative business. Some came from tailor's and butcher's shops; others were apothecaries with very little knowledge of childbirth. Obviously the background of these male midwives did nothing to recommend midwifery to the orthodox medical practitioner as legitimate and respectable medicine. But the stigmatization of midwifery also stemmed from an ideology which saw childbirth as an aspect of women's 'natural' domestic and reproductive care function, and hence as a domain to be avoided by the masculine practitioner of medicine proper. Pregnancy was regarded as an 'infective malady' and maternity hospitals developed apart from the general hospital movement, largely because of fears about the danger to other people's health that parturient women represented. The early lying-in hospitals (in the eighteenth century) were for poor women and for teaching, and it was argued that maternity cases had no place in hospital at all:

> The separate provision of maternity hospitals had a similar rationale to the separate provision of hospitals for smallpox and infectious diseases.[24]

In the early years of this century, many British babies were born in workhouses, apparently to mothers who were not ordinarily destitute, but who used the workhouse as a maternity hospital, thus associating birth with poverty in the public mind.[25]

The general anti-women, anti-dirt attitude had strange consequences. The 'ignorant' untrained midwife was loudly denounced by many members of the male medical profession from the seventeenth century on, but the profession was, at the same time, reluctant to extend the benefits of new developments in medical science to the parturient woman. Both anaesthesia and antisepsis when first developed were reserved for surgical operations and were not applied to midwifery, where they had obvious relevance. Anaesthesia for childbirth became respectable when Queen Victoria had chloroform for the birth of Prince Leopold in 1853. But when midwifery came under state control in the twentieth century, midwives were not at first allowed to administer anaesthetics or analgesics. At the time, chloroform was the only drug available, and not until 1932 was attention given to the development of a method easily and safely administered by midwives in the home. As the official report *Maternity in Great Britain* put it in 1948:

> There is little doubt that a suitable method could have been developed many years earlier, but the stimulus to produce it was lacking. The low standing of midwives and the remains of prejudice against analgesia may have partly accounted for this delay, but *it is not unlikely that the attitude of the medical profession was the deciding factor*.[26] (My italics)

The history of antisepsis in this context is especially interesting. In 1847, Semmelweiss in Vienna observed that the death rate of mothers in hospital wards attended by medical students was three times that in wards attended by midwives. His correct explanation of this was that medical students brought contagion with them from the post-mortem room (some of the higher incidence was probably also due to lack of hygiene in the medical students' use of forceps). Four years earlier, in America, Oliver Wendell Holmes had come to the same conclusion. Both Holmes and Semmelweiss were greeted with disbelief and outrage from their fellow doctors, who declared that 'gentlemen' 'must' have clean hands, and so could not possibly carry disease among women.

The role of pollution beliefs in the patterning of reproductive care systems is a valuable subject for future research. What we need is an extension of anthropological ideas to the history of medicine in industrialized societies. Lacking this research, it is only possible to suggest ways in which pollution beliefs have existed and been influential. Although beliefs about women and their pollution potential were one important reason why the male medical profession preserved distance between itself and the province of the female midwife, there were, of course, other processes at work.

Between the two male takeovers male medicine made one particular inroad on the female midwife's work. By the early 1600s, the English language contained a new word: man-midwife. Although midwifery remained a predominantly female occupation, and in Britain still was exclusively so until the 1975 Sex Discrimination Act made male midwives a legal possibility, the man-midwife – or accoucheur as he was more politely known – presented the female midwife with one special brand of competition. The speciality of male midwives was surgical intervention in childbirth. They were thus the direct predecessors of the modern male obstetrician. [27]

The groundwork for the equation of male midwifery and surgery was laid in the thirteenth century when the barber–surgeon guilds reserved the right to use surgical instruments exclusively for their own (male) members. Thus the surgeon early on became the specialist who was sent for by the midwife in obstructed labours. (Since forceps were not in general use until the eighteenth century, surgical intervention would have consisted of removing the child piecemeal or performing a caesarian section after the mother's death.) Episiotomy – the

cutting of the skin round the vaginal outlet to facilitate delivery –
was first recorded as carried out by a man-midwife in 1780.[28]
The use of the delivery forceps was discovered by the doctors
of the Chamberlen family in England in the seventeenth century.
The Chamberlens generated a great deal of mystique about their
invention, which they retained as a family secret for several
generations. They would arrive to deliver women in a special
carriage and carry with them a huge decorated wooden box; the
labouring woman was blindfolded and the door was locked.
This mystique probably did a great deal to elevate the status of
the male midwife – an advancement that was only partly dependent on the Chamberlens' ability to secure a favourable outcome
in (some) difficult obstetric cases.

The position of the man-midwife was an anomalous one. Most
of them belonged to the Barber–Surgeons Company, the ancestor
of the modern Royal College of Surgeons. At that time surgery
was unrecognized as a branch of medicine and regarded instead
as some disreputable distant cousin of it. (This is the reason why
surgeons today are termed 'Mr' and not 'Dr'.) The lack of
articulated connection between surgery and general medicine
was paralleled by the gap between midwifery and medicine:
midwifery was not 'proper' medicine and surgery had no accepted place in midwifery. Because the barber–surgeons were
men and the midwives were women, a sex segregation underlay
the separation between the two occupations. In the processes of
definition and specialization which occurred over the eighteenth
and nineteenth centuries, female midwifery became the area of
non-surgical obstetrics dealing with 'normal' labour. The man-
midwife turned into the obstetrician trained in the use of surgical
techniques for the management of difficult childbirth.

While in the seventeenth century, the male midwife was called
only to those confinements in which surgical intervention was
necessary, from the 1720s on, as male midwifery became more
fashionable among the upper classes, men began to compete
more directly with women for the care of normal childbirth.
The use of surgical techniques even for normal labour was a
means whereby male midwives were able to assert their superiority over the female practitioner. This exploitation of surgery for

professional advancement was a main theme in female midwives' attack on their male competitors from the seventeenth century on, and was publicly acclaimed by some male midwives themselves. In 1724, Dr John Maubray wrote:

> I know some Chirugeon-Practitioners are too much acquainted with the Use of INSTRUMENTS to lay them aside: they do not (it may be) think themselves in their *Duty*, a proper *Office*, if they have not their cruel Accoutrements in Hand.[29]

Aiding the growth of male surgical midwifery was the decreasing value of the traditional Church licence, which, so long as Church authority commanded general respect, conferred some status on the female midwife. With the waning power of the Church in the eighteenth century, the value of a Church licence was eroded. In London this had come about by the 1720s and was general by the last quarter of the century. The restriction of the female midwife to the management of normal labour was officially recognized in the Midwifery Diploma first granted by the Obstetrical Society of London in 1872; this certified the female midwife as 'competent to attend natural labours'. In fact the female midwife found herself increasingly relegated to the position of a nurse, a tendency which twentieth century developments have confirmed (for instance, in the large increase in aftercare – care of the mother and baby following a forty-eight-hour discharge from hospital). Indeed, the reinstatement of the female midwife to a definite, if highly circumscribed, position within medicine which occurred with the 1902 Midwives' Act had a great deal to do with the emergence of nursing as a respectable female occupation.

Thus a main reason why the male takeover in medicine was not immediately followed by a complete male takeover of midwifery is to be found in the redefinition of the female midwife's role which was effected during the nineteenth and twentieth centuries. This redefinition was part of a larger process. The Victorian era saw a general narrowing down of the options available to women in the occupational field. An ideology of domesticity became pre-eminent, and activities incompatible with this consequently suffered. Medicine for women was one casualty, and others included a general contraction and re-definition of women's industrial labour.[30]

Despite variations in detail, the history of the male takeover in obstetrics appears to have followed a roughly parallel course in most European countries. The alliance of surgery with male midwifery, and the exclusion of women from formal medical and surgical training, formed the basis on which female midwifery was recognized as a secondary status health profession. Gynae-cology was established as a speciality (again, originally one from which women were excluded) and coupled with obstetrics. While male-controlled childbirth and reproductive care grew in fashion among the upper classes, the traditional female-controlled system persisted among the working classes. This state of affairs was not really radically disturbed until about 1920. By this date, various developments had forced the medical profession system-atically to include in its frame of reference the welfare of the parturient woman. This meant that two areas of reproduction – 'normal' childbirth, and working-class childbirth – came directly into the male obstetrician's field of vision. Their exclusion until that time had been partly a matter of economics (there was little financial gain to be had from attending working-class mothers) and partly a matter of selective perception. On an ideological level normal childbirth and the childbirths of poor women were not seen as medical matters.

Movements for Infant and Maternal Welfare

The final male takeover in reproductive care came almost acci-dentally, as a by-product of a movement whose primary concern was the preservation of infant life. When attention later came to be paid to the mothers themselves, the motive was also child-centred: it was realized that an infant's fate depended partly on the condition of its mother during the antenatal and delivery periods. In this way, the rationale came to be established for the modern pattern of male-controlled, surgical, hospitalized, childbirth.

Over the last hundred years, the single most important con-sequence of developments in medical care has certainly been the fall in mortality rates. General mortality rates – deaths per thousand persons in the population – began to decline in Britain in the late 1870s. From 22·7 per thousand in 1875, they fell to 19·2 in 1885, and to 15·3 in 1905. Today they are 12·2 per thousand. The infant mortality rate was slower to fall, and showed no tendency to decline until the turn of the century. In 1890, 151 babies died for every thousand live births; in 1900, 154, in 1925, 75. Today the figure is 17·2. The slowest of all to benefit from modern medicine was the death rate of mothers. In 1870, there were 4·8 maternal deaths for every thousand live births; in 1935, there were 4·3. Over this period, the general tendency was for the death rate of mothers to rise slightly, especially over the period from about 1925 to 1933; this rise was experienced by many countries, including the United States. In Britain, the maternal mortality rate began to fall in 1937. Today it is 0·15 per thousand live births.

The infant welfare movement was made possible through the growth of new scientific knowledge about disease processes. Its ideological beginnings are inextricably interwoven with the sanitary reform movement, and its major protagonists were either sanitary reformers or doctors (or both). Pasteur discovered micro-organisms in 1857, and bacteriology subsequently became the main weapon in the battle for public health. Its relevance to infant mortality was simple. The 'filth' disease of 'epidemic' or 'summer' diarrhoea (gastro-enteritis) killed thousands of babies every year, and the chief culprit was unhygienic feeding methods, the likelihood of which increased as breastfeeding generally declined.[31] The first infant welfare centres were therefore concerned with the feeding of infants. In Britain and America 'milk depots', and in France 'Gouttes de Lait', were established in the 1890s with the object of encouraging breastfeeding, and, where this failed, of providing sterilized artificial milk.[32] These centres pushed the battlefront of the great war against dirt forward from factory and street into kitchen and nursery. Dirt was a general preoccupation in the early infant welfare centres. From the point of view of pollution beliefs and women, the role it was assigned by the self-professed medical educators of mothers is extremely interesting. Dirt was included with alcoholism, poor feeding, married women's work and women's ignorance about childcare in a list of causes of infant death. Advice about cleanliness in the care of infants was curiously mixed with admonitions about the domestic ignorance of working-class girls and the need to keep 'dirt' under control. The Medical Officer of Health for Manchester included a lesson on dirt in his syllabus for the Manchester Education Authority in 1906:

Lesson 2. Dirt.
Visible dirt.
Invisible dirt. Micro-organisms. Living plants, some of which growing in the body produce matters hurtful to health and dangerous to life. Demonstration of invisible dirt. Exposure of nutrient gelatine in a Petri dish . . . How dirt acts on the mouth, tonsils, bowels and lungs. How dirt is carried to food such as milk (a) from without by the air; (b) from without by flies; (c) carried into the house by feet . . .
Draughts. The floor. Dirty sofa. Need to exclude dirt and how this may be done.[33]

To keep the infant well out of dirt's way, mothers were advised to suspend it in a hammock from the ceiling.

No doubt much of this emphasis on hygiene was justified. Victorian households, even upper-class ones, concealed a great deal of dirt behind the highly polished and ornamented face they showed to the public world;[34] wealthy householders only began to face the problems of indoor sanitation when the 1870s typhoid epidemic nearly killed the Prince of Wales. Nevertheless, these 'lessons' given by doctors and others to working-class women contained attitudinal and emotional undercurrents of a strangely unscientific kind. It was as though the medical profession, having discovered dirt under the microscope, needed to wash its hands of it by affirming it as the concern of women. Health visitors played an important role in the education of mothers, and men advocated the appointment of women sanitary inspectors. Some of these women were also midwives, a not inappropriate qualification, since one of the sanitary inspector's duties was to supervise the disinfecting of nurses or midwives involved in puerperal fever cases.

While women were assigned the role of *controlling* dirt, they were also seen as being, in some sense, the *cause* of it. Medical

Officers of Health talked about the 'purification' of motherhood:

First, concentrate on the mother. What the mother is the children are. The stream is no *purer* than the source. Let us glorify, dignify and *purify* motherhood by every means in our power ... We have got to have better and *cleaner* milk than we now get. We have got to have *cleaner* homes, more sober homes ... we have got to have *cleanliness* wherever we can get it ...[35] (My italics.)

This frenzied anti-dirt campaign was definitely anti-feminist in its consequences, if not in its motivations: it reinforced upper-class notions of women's 'natural' domestic vocation, and almost certainly aided the acceptance of these ideas among working-class men and women.

Medicine, still of course predominantly male (in 1911, only 477 women doctors were in practice in Britain), and medical research, a male enclave with one or two notable exceptions, thus established a male professional understanding of disease which had to be taught to women. The need to instruct women in methods of childcare was a logical corollary. Instructions about how to feed babies were expanded into a whole system of education for motherhood. A 'School for Mothers' was opened in the St Pancras area of London in 1907, and was typical of others elsewhere in Europe. Its aim was the dissemination of 'scientific' knowledge about infant nurture, and it was described in a contemporary circular as

a novel experiment ... [in] which mothers and girls may come and learn how a baby should be clothed, fed, washed and tended, and treated in small ailments.[36]

The school included in its curriculum lectures on the making of baby clothes, 'lantern lectures on baby culture', and information about the preparation of food. Mothers who were breastfeeding received subsidized meals. The school was partially supported by The Board of Education, who gave a grant of £5 13s. 6d. to it in 1908 – the first national allocation of funds for infant welfare in Britain.

The maternal instinct had no place in this scheme; the prevailing view among doctors and other 'professionals' was that motherhood had to be learnt. The idea that the upbringing of an

infant was a science identified motherhood as an area of patriarchal control in an already patriarchal society; only science had
the cure for disease; from science, therefore, came knowledge
about the prevention of disease and about the 'proper' methods
of rearing children. The maternal instinct came into play much
later (after the Second World War) as one of a number of
strategies designed to tie women, who had tasted freedom
outside the home, more closely to their domestic function.

While bacteriology established the technological basis for the
infant welfare movement, fears of national depopulation provided
a large part of its rationale. These fears also impinged directly on
women's reproductive role. Death rates were falling, but so were
birth rates. The dread of 'race suicide'[37] was strong, especially in
France where the first institutions for infant welfare were founded.
Imperialism entailed sexism. The death rates of infants had to be
reduced, but the birth rates of mothers had to be increased;
ideologically, the consequence was a restriction of women to the
biological and social rôle of mother.[38] In practical terms, male
medicine invaded not only childcare but the large residual area of
female-controlled childbirth.

The clash of the two reproductive care systems – female-
controlled and male-controlled – was evident very early in the
development of the infant welfare movement. In May 1870, the
bodies of sixteen young babies were found in the streets and
under the railway arches of Brixton and Peckham, poor areas of
South London. Although it was then quite common to find dead
babies in London streets (a total of 276 were found in that year)
this was an unusually large number to be found in a short space
of time. The discovery sparked off a police investigation which
led to the Infant Life Protection Act of 1872, an act whose main
provisions were the compulsory registration of baby-minders,
and the compulsory notification of infant deaths among 'farmed-
out' children.

Baby-farming, overtly a system of unofficial child-fostering,
had another, hidden function: it was a female-controlled method
for the disposal of unwanted babies, analogous to the small-scale
society's custom either of killing the unwanted baby or of simply
failing to provide adequate care for it. Margaret Waters, one of

the two women convicted in connection with the South London infant deaths in 1870, wrote a fifteen-page account of her career as a baby-farmer five days before her execution. This unusual document charts her entry into the occupation of baby-farmer as an unplanned response to a real social need.[39] After her husband's death in 1864, Margaret Waters tried unsuccessfully to earn a living sewing collars for shirts. Then she began to let her house to lodgers. One of her first lodgers was a pregnant unmarried woman who, on leaving, entrusted her baby to Margaret Waters' care. Others followed suit. Usually Margaret Waters was paid a lump sum of around £10 and she either cared for the child herself, or put it out to another woman. She said she did her best for the children under her care, but at a time when infant deaths were high, especially in poor homes, the system was not conducive to the preservation of life. If the babies died, Margaret Waters could not afford to pay funeral expenses for them, and so she left the bodies in the streets.

Dr C. F. McCleary, one of the founders of the British infant welfare movement, commented on the case of Margaret Waters thus:

Margaret Waters had received a good education, and her statement is a remarkable document. To the last she was utterly unable to realize that she had been guilty of murder.[40]

In late Victorian society, the unmarried mother and her child were victims of acute social censure. Since women in general were regarded as agents of reproduction and little else besides, there were no official ways in which even the respectable married woman could find relief from the burden of an unwanted child. For such women, both married and unmarried, baby-farming met an undoubted need. Yet another important function of the system was that it buttressed the childrearing habits of the social class from which its critics came: it provided wet nurses for upper-class babies. Advertisements for the 'adoption' of babies by baby-farmers were carried by many respectable journals, including religious ones. In the nineteenth century, wet-nursing was one of the most profitable occupations open to a working-class woman, and breastfeeding by the mother became less and less fashionable among the upper classes throughout the century.

As late as 1905 a copy of the medical journal the *Practitioner* advocated wet-nursing, rather than bottle feeding, when a mother's own milk failed.[41] The wet nurse had 'unavoidably' to be drawn from the 'lower orders of the population' and she had preferably to be aged between twenty and thirty. In order to secure a supply of milk, these women had first to become mothers themselves. Baby-farming was a means of disposing of their infants. To the upper class and (usually) male defender of the rights of infants, the baby-farmer was an evil woman who, either by intent or neglect, 'murdered' babies. To the working-class woman in an oppressively class-divided and sexist society, baby-farming met a practical need which could not possibly be expressed in socially acceptable terms. It is interesting that strong opposition to the 1872 Act came from members of the National Society for Women's Suffrage, who thought its provisions 'would be costly and tyrannical in the case of poor women who take charge of infants for hire without sinister motives'.[42]

Other innovations of the male-controlled reproductive care system met with more veiled female opposition. In the infant welfare centres, baby-weighing was not popular and the doctors did not understand why, until someone informed them of the prevalent superstition among women that baby-weighing was unlucky. A similar obstacle, deriving from the belief structure of the traditional female-controlled reproductive care system, complicated the introduction of the 1907 and 1915 Notification of Births Acts. One of the aims of these acts was to obtain reliable statistics on infant mortality. But since the popular belief was that stillborn babies were not 'proper' babies, midwives burnt or buried them and did not register them as they did live births. Although the registration of births became compulsory on a national scale with the 1915 Act, a separate Act had to be passed in 1927 stipulating the compulsory registration of stillbirths.

It is interesting to note that today medicine still has to contend with the vestigial remnants of a female-controlled system. For example, a study carried out in the late 1960s of working-class families in Aberdeen, Scotland, found that one reason why women did not use antenatal services was because an informal 'lay referral' system already operated among these women.[43] The women's mothers were often the first people to be told about pregnancy (before husbands) and their advice to delay the first visit to the antenatal clinic until the sixth month or later was taken. The Aberdeen practice compares with that of many small-scale societies. For instance, among the Bahaya people of Tanzania, it is the custom for pregnant women to inform first of all their mother-in-law, next their mother, and last of all their husband. It is the mother-in-law's specific duty to advise about pregnancy taboos (the small-scale society's form of antenatal care).[44]

The cause of maternal welfare had become part of the official policy of the infant welfare movement in Britain by 1915. A shift in medical thinking made this possible. At the turn of the century, infant deaths from causes other than improper feeding (prematurity, congenital deformity, and so on) were regarded as non-preventable, although they accounted for many deaths. (For instance, in 1901, prematurity was responsible for twenty deaths per thousand live births.) When it became clear that improvements in infant feeding did not entirely remedy the excess mortality rates of infants, attention was turned to the physical condition of the mother herself.

Losses and Gains

In 1885, Dr William Farr, pioneer statistician to Britain's first Registrar-General, referred in a memorable phrase to the wastage of female life in childbirth as a 'deep, dark and continuous stream of mortality'.[45] Over fifty years later, in 1937, a British Government report on maternal mortality commented thus:

... it is to many a depressing anomaly that, while the work for the welfare of infants has been attended with signal success, that for the conservation of the lives of mothers ... has failed.[46]

It was a long time before male medicine brought about any improvement in this state of affairs; indeed, it was almost certainly responsible for a deterioration in the mortality record of women in childbirth.

Of three main causes of maternal death – puerperal fever, toxaemia and haemorrhage – the first showed a tendency to rise in Britain, America and other countries over the first part of this century, until the late 1930s. Puerperal fever was associated with hospitalized, doctor-controlled, childbirth.[47] Calculations of maternal mortality in Westminster, London, during the late eighteenth century juxtaposed a rate of one in 277 for the Westminster district as a whole with a rate of one in thirty-nine for the Westminster Lying-in Hospital. A century later, Dr William Farr cited the estimate of one doctor that, of women delivered at home, about one in 212 died, whereas, of those delivered in hospital, the rate was one in twenty nine.[48] The bulk of home deliveries were done by untrained midwives, but although many hospital deliveries would also have been carried out by midwives, they were subject to the supervision (and intervention) of the male doctor. The traditional untrained midwife certainly presented a much lower risk of infection to her patient than did the maternity hospitals for a long time after their inception. 'Domiciliary confinement', said the report *Maternity in Great Britain* in 1948, 'may carry a very low risk to mother and child'. The authors of this report compare death rates in home and hospital confinements (including in the 'home' group those cases which were admitted to hospital as a result of difficulties developing) among the wives of manual workers. Still birth rates were twenty-eight per thousand for home confinements and twenty-nine per thousand for hospital confinements. (This report did not calculate *maternal* mortality rates by place of confinement – an interesting omission, which reflected the persistent child-centredness of the maternal welfare movement.)

A study of childbirth management among Punjab village women in the 1960s provides some data on the safety of the 'folk midwife's' practices.[49] There were 837 deliveries in this series, but none of the mothers died of puerperal sepsis, a finding which the researchers found surprising. The babies were delivered in the village and the umbilical cord was cut either with scissors (by midwives who had undergone some rudimentary training) or with a household instrument – commonly a leather worker's knife. General infant death rates were sixty-nine per thousand (comparable with British infant death rates in the early 1930s). Use of a leather worker's knife achieved the lowest death rate of all – twenty-seven per thousand (equivalent to the British infant mortality rate in 1953).

In 1932 (when sixty-four infants died for every thousand live births) the British Ministry of Health issued a report on maternal mortality and morbidity. Reviewing a series of 5,805 cases of maternal deaths, they concluded that at least half were preventable; other medical opinion voiced at the time put the figure at three quarters. Puerperal sepsis accounted for more than a third of the deaths (in about 10 per cent of sepsis deaths infection followed a forceps delivery by a doctor).[50] Among the reasons for death, by far the most important was mismanagement on the part of the doctor; this occurred in a fifth of all deaths. The most common errors were the premature use of forceps, failure to give proper care in cases of toxaemia, and inadequate precautions against sepsis. Aside from mortality, the committee found an enormous amount of morbidity following childbirth – lacerations of the cervix, septic conditions, and so on. An American study carried out at about the same time judged 66 per cent of maternal deaths to be preventable. Doctors' errors were found to be responsible for 41 per cent of the deaths, midwives' errors, for 2 per cent. Half the deaths attributable to doctors were due to errors of judgement and half to errors in techniques 'indicating a high degree of technical incompetence'.[51] In Britain the use of forceps was encouraged by a system under which the doctor was paid more for an instrumental delivery than for a normal one. When called to a confinement in the early years of the century, District Medical Officers (doctors paid by the Poor Law Guardians to treat the poor) were customarily paid 10s., 15s., or 20s. for a simple case, but £2 if instruments were used. A group of women Poor Law Guardians carried out a study in 1902 in which they showed that the percentage of instrumental deliveries was low in areas where the doctor received an all-inclusive salary for his midwifery work, and high where he was paid more for instrumental deliveries.[52]

While the rise in the incidence of puerperal fever associated with hospitalized childbirth is now no longer in evidence, the greater use of surgery in hospital, as opposed to domiciliary, obstetrics continues to be a characteristic of childbirth today. The expansion of hospitalized childbirth, symptomatic of the transition to male control, is the most visible change in the management of childbirth this century. In 1927 hospital confinements made up 15 per cent of all live births in Britain; in 1946, the proportion had risen to 54 per cent, in 1972 to 91·2 per cent. The increase in hospitalized childbirth was faster in the United States where, by 1944, 76 per cent of all births occurred in hospital (compared with 41 per cent in 1936).[53]

The stimulus for this move towards hospital childbirth came from the medical profession, and the hospitalization policy evolved over the period from about 1910 to about 1940 in Britain. In the early 1900s it was impossible to persuade a 'respectable' woman to have her baby in hospital. After 1944, the official policy in Britain was a 70 per cent hospital confinement rate. Today all women with serious medical conditions, such as diabetes and heart disease, are advised to have a hospital confinement, as are all those with unfavourable obstetric histories – toxaemia, haemorrhage, forceps or caesarian deliveries. Complications of the present pregnancy are grounds for hospitalization; so are poor home conditions. In addition, women with three or more previous confinements, all women over thirty-five, and all women having their first babies are supposed to go into hospital.

The move towards hospitalization, and the other characteristics of male control, followed the state regulation of midwives which occurred at the turn of this century. Until midwives came under state control, normal and working-class childbirth remained beyond the pale of the male medical establishment. In the early 1900s the care of most women in childbirth was the province of the untrained midwife – or the 'handywoman' as she was known. In Glasgow in 1906, for instance, 41 per cent of all births were attended by handywomen, and the percentage was certainly far higher in rural areas.[54] The account of one woman, published in 1931, provides valuable documentation of the 'handywoman' system, in an area where accounts by the actual practitioners of reproductive care are hard to find.[55]

'Mrs Layton' was born in Bethnal Green, London, in 1855, the seventh child in a family of fourteen. Her father was a 'well-educated man, employed in a government situation'. (He wore black clothes and a silk hat to work, but was a tailor and grew vegetables in his spare time.) On washing day, Mrs Layton and her fourth sister used to stay home from school to mind the babies – this was a local custom. She and her friends hired prams for 1d. an hour and took the babies to Victoria Park, where they ate bread and treacle under the trees. At ten, she began to earn a living as a babyminder, working for a local shopkeeper. At fifteen, she went into service with a family in Kentish Town. The fifth child in this family was born when she had been there a few months, and its mother died of puerperal fever. Mrs Layton cared for it for two and a half years, and decided she wanted to be a nurse. At eighteen she was called home to attend her sister's fifth confinement:

I came in close touch with childbirth this time, as the doctor who thought me much older than I was, asked for my help. I was terribly frightened, but I have never been a coward, and did not intend to be one then, so I consented to help him . . . I did all that I could for my sister and family, with the help of an old woman who called herself a midwife.[56]

Mrs Layton was married at the age of twenty-six to a piano-maker who subsequently lost his job and obliged her to become the breadwinner. Her first child lived but her second died: 'I think if it hadn't been for a good neighbour, I should have gone under'. After a period taking in washing, a contact made through the Women's Co-operative Guild led her to her first nursing and first maternity cases. Soon she was actually delivering babies. She wanted to become a properly trained midwife, but the cost – £30 – and the necessary three months' absence from home made this impossible. A doctor she knew reflected the prevailing opinion among her cases when he said that the training would be a wicked waste of money, and that she already knew more than a hospital could teach her.

In 1902 midwives were formally organized by the State Midwives' Act: a Central Midwives Board was set up to certify midwives, and systems of instruction and examination were designed. Opposition to the Act came from various sources. One important objection was that many mothers would be deprived of the services of women like 'Mrs Layton' and unable to secure a certified midwife (these would, of course, be in extremely short supply at first). Thus the Act incorporated a clause allowing uncertified women to practise legally until 1910, and it provided for certification in the case of women who could provide evidence to the Midwives' Board of the 'bona fide' practice of midwifery. Up to 1905, the Board gave 12,521 such certificates (more than half the total number of midwives certified since the passing of the Act). 'Handywomen' persisted, and, although the shortage of registered midwives and economic hardship both favoured the traditional system, it is apparent that many women preferred it. The 1937 British Ministry of Health Report on Maternal Mortality referred to this system:

> The practice of handywomen is still extensive in some areas, particularly in rural districts ... In some of the towns in which their services are utilized, there is not a shortage of midwives.[57]

This two-tier system – midwife and handywoman – later developed into another hierarchy – doctor (de facto, predominantly male) and midwife (by law, always female). In the early 1900s doctors delivered only a minority of upper class babies. Soon after the Central Midwives Board was set up, there were signs that midwives were fighting to maintain control. Among doctors a feeling predominated that the certification of midwives was an untoward development, since it presented them with competition in an already underpaid area of work. Although the 1902 Act laid down that a midwife must advise a patient's relatives to call a doctor in difficult cases, by 1918 the onus had been put on the midwife herself to fetch medical help. This was symptomatic of many developments to follow which served to set further limits on the midwife's autonomy.

Today in Britain, domiciliary midwives are a declining group. In 1968 there were 6,482 in England: in 1973 4,855. Over this five-year period, the number of domiciliary confinements fell by 111,000, although there was an increase in the number of cases of early hospital discharge supervised by the domiciliary midwifery service.[58] Both domiciliary and hospital midwives are subject to a large number of restrictions and regulations. For example, while a midwife is permitted to perform an episiotomy, she must call a doctor to repair it. She is not allowed to perform manual removal of the placenta. If, on examining the placenta, she finds it incomplete, a doctor must be sent for. In the course of labour any abnormality of any kind also requires a doctor. Although in theory midwife and doctor collaborate in a reproductive care partnership, in practice the relationship is asymmetrical. As the 1949 working party report on midwives protested:

the doctor must accept the midwife as his fellow practitioner and not attempt either to relegate her to the station of his handmaiden or to displace her unnecessarily from the position of authority in the patient's eyes.[59]

This is difficult, when the whole trend of modern medicine favours the prestige of the male doctor. The midwife's dual role as nurse assigns her to a culturally inferior feminine role (according to the rules of the Central Midwives' Board, the midwife must undertake general nursing duties in the care of her patient).

Despite these restrictive changes, the midwife is still an important figure in Britain. In America, the opposite is true. There are many reasons for this stark contrast, not least the completely different development of the American medical care system, with its greater emphasis on professional specialization, its absence of a state health service, and its dependence on finance from (male-controlled) business enterprises. The passing of the 1902 Midwives' Act in Britain ensured a future for female midwifery; America lacked any parallel legislation, and also the kind of agitation from a variety of pressure groups which, in Britain from the 1870s on, worked towards (and was largely responsible for) effective legislation. The professional ideal that all women should be delivered by an obstetrician was formulated much earlier in America; one doctor protested in 1913 that five million dollars annually was collected by midwives, whereas it 'should be paid to physicians and nurses for doing the work properly'.[60] American midwives were less skilled than their European counterparts: the demand for midwives far exceeded the supply of competent women, since the social groups from which midwives came were generally underrepresented among immigrants to America. Midwives in America did not form the kind of pressure group found elsewhere. The male takeover in health generally has been much more complete in America, although it started later; against Britain's 17 per cent, only 8 per cent of American doctors are women. The restriction of women's opportunities in American medicine followed two movements which created a particular aura of threat (to the male medical establishment) around the figure of the woman-healer–midwife. These were the Popular Health Movement of the 1830s and 1840s and the organized feminist movement which began at about the same time. Women were the backbone of the Popular Health Movement, opposing medical élitism and advocating traditional 'people's medicine'. The class struggle intermingled with the sex struggle:

Talk about this [medicine] being the appropriate sphere for man and his alone!

said one feminist member of the Popular Health Movement in 1852,

with tenfold more plausibility and reason we say it is the appropriate sphere for woman and hers alone.[61]

The particular exclusion of women from the management of childbirth was a logical continuation of the male medical profession's misogyny, but it was also facilitated by changing economic and social conditions. The control on immigration after the First World War reduced the scale of the demand for the midwife's services; the emancipation of middle-class American women created a rejection of the 'natural' way of doing things, and a gravitation towards the more 'professional' care of the male obstetrician. The disappearance of the American midwife was not simply a consequence of her inferior performance; on the contrary, in the early years of the twentieth century, her record was superior to that of her male counterpart.[62]

Feminism and Female Control

Protests about the modern male-controlled reproductive care system are becoming increasingly common today. These protests cover such topics as the undue use of surgical abortion techniques (as opposed to the safer and less traumatic suction method), the overuse of radical as opposed to conservative surgery for breast- and reproductive-tract diseases, the resistance of doctors to hormone replacement therapy for menopausal problems, inadequate attention paid to the psychological traumata of reproductive experiences, and, perhaps most central of all, the modern male-controlled, hospitalized, and increasingly technological pattern of childbirth management.[63] Under this heading, areas of attack include the 'depersonalization' of hospitalized birth, the ritual, unnecessary use of procedures such as the shaving of pubic hair and the giving of enemas in the first stage of labour; episiotomies and the use of forceps or caesarean section in the second stage; analgesia and/or anaesthesia throughout. There are protests about the use of the horizontal supine position for delivery – a position which favours the doctor's convenience; medical research and cross-cultural practice show that the vertical position is likely to be the most effective physiologically.[64] Many hospital procedures, such as the separation of mother and child at birth, inflexible feeding schedules and the exclusion of the parturient woman's family, are rejected as inhumane and harmful. A great deal of criticism is now being focused on the procedure of clinically induced labour, which is rapidly increasing in incidence. Mothers are objecting to the dubious premises on which this procedure is sometimes based, the 'unnatural' labour that it produces, and the technological paraphernalia which often accompanies it – the oxytocin drip, the monitoring of foetal heart and uterine contraction rate, the epidural anaesthetic administered for the pain of an artificially stimulated labour, and the forceps delivery which is more likely as a result.

The relative weights of fact and fiction in these criticisms can only be discerned by careful research.[65] To date, surveys of maternal attitudes towards the experience of childbirth have revealed a fair amount of dissatisfaction with hospital confinement;[66] but these surveys provide only crude indices of women's feelings about the experience of hospitalized childbirth. We simply need a great deal more information about both patients' and doctors' feelings and attitudes, and about the physical and psychological advantages and disadvantages of modern child-birth management than we have at present.

Nevertheless, endemic to all these various protests concerning reproductive care is one common denominator: the insistence that the modern male-controlled system has a tendency to treat women not as whole, responsible people but as passive objects for surgical and general medical manipulation. This allegation that the medical profession tends to see patients as diseases ('the appendix in bed four') rather than as individuals is, of course, not sex-specific: insofar as it is a general product of medical education, both male and female patients are affected. But it is not quite enough to say that this is an overall tendency within medicine. The evidence is accumulating that the processes of medical education and professionalization generally produce an ideological formula for the treatment of women which is different from that of men.[67]

One reason for this lies in the social context. Today reproductive care is offered and utilized within the broad framework of a society which discriminates against women in many overt and subtle ways. Thus, the controllers and practitioners of reproductive care as members of a male-oriented society tend to participate in the ideology and practice of sexism.[68] It is a sexist view of women as the dependents of men which shapes such practices as the 'rule' that women must have their husband's consent before having an intrauterine device fitted, or before an operation for sterilization; the sexist ideology of contraception is that of 'family' planning. It is a belief in women's necessarily maternal function which structures the availability of abortion, the treatment of abortion patients, the choice of abortion techniques, and the whole series of rituals which process women through childbirth.[69] It is a general failure to understand the experience of womanhood which leads to the lack of concern with the psychological consequences of reproductive surgery. The inherent conservatism of the medical profession – its general resistance to change – reinforces the inflexibility of such sexist procedures.

Detailed information on the content and effect of medical ideologies is only just beginning to emerge; within the sociology of medicine it represents a relatively new subject-area. Such data is of crucial importance to the central theme of this paper: the transfer of control over reproductive care from women to men. *Should* women be in control of their reproductive care? In order fully to take command over their destinies, women must have the prior right of determining when (or if) and how, they become mothers. This is theoretically possible in a male-controlled reproductive care system, but in practice these systems have not been phrased in terms of 'a woman's right to choose'. The social context of a sexist society and its associated ideological differentiation have had an overriding influence. Since *control* of reproductive care is effectively in men's hands, the distinction is not simply between women doctors who are 'good' – i.e. sympathetic to the female demand for self-determination – and male doctors who are 'bad', who either explicitly oppose or are fundamentally uninterested in their female patients' feelings. In fact, insofar as medical education and the practice of medicine today reflect an ideological and empirical discrimination against women in society at large, both male and female doctors are likely to participate (albeit unwittingly) in this discrimination. So far as the difference between men and women doctors in the treatment situation is concerned, the argument in favour of the female doctor is, however, one about where the break with patriarchal ideology is most likely to occur. Because both women doctors and women patients share the same biological experience of femaleness, and because they also have in common the inferior social status of the feminine role, patriarchal ideology potentially receives its most fragile support within the framework of the female-doctor–female-patient relationship. This is not to say that an egalitarian ideology always flourishes within this framework; clearly it does not. Women doctors, through achieving relatively high occupational status within a male-dominated profession, may be strongly identified with masculine ideologies. Their femininity may be a handicap rather than an encouragement to sympathy with the needs of women as a group. Since experience of female reproductive biology is important,[70] it may well be the case that the major axis of differentiation in terms of the actual *treatment* of women patients is between women doctors who have experienced motherhood and other doctors who have not.

The argument that women should control their own repro-ductive care is a new statement of an old view which crops up recurrently in the history of obstetrics and gynaecology through-out the centuries – that female control (of women's medicine generally and childbirth particularly) is 'natural' (or rather that male control is 'unnatural').[71] The earliest translations of Latin gynaecological/obstetric texts were made so that women could treat and help one another. The appropriateness of female healers and midwives was part of a general code of ethics which forbade the attendance of male doctors on women for whatever reason. As Jacoba Felice, a French lay healer accused of illegal practice, said at her court hearing at the end of the thirteenth century:

> It is better and more honest that a wise and expert woman in this art visit sick women, and inquire into the secret nature of their infirmity, than a man . . . And on this there has been public sentiment . . .[72]

'Modesty' was a reason often given for the unsuitability of male doctors in gynaecological cases. This draws attention to the particular aspect of sexual politics inherent in the male gynae-cologist–female patient encounter; the existence of this sexual-political dimension is a further reason why female control is preferable.[73]

In a much more diffuse sense, the structure of reproductive care in any society cannot be divorced from the broader social context of gender role relationships. In 1964 a British psycho-analyst wrote:

> Our society is benevolent towards childbirth in its aims physically to preserve the mother and baby, to relieve the mother of physical pain and to give her rest and peace of mind. But this aim has a tendency to miscarry [sic] and there is reason to suppose that this failure derives not only from a relative ignorance of the mother's psychological needs and aims but an unacknowledged antipathy towards them.[74]

A general cultural desire to control the creativity and pollution potential of parturition may help to 'explain' the kinds of rituals which are an integral part of childbirth today. This explanation fits modern industrialized society in exactly the same way as it has been held to apply to so-called 'primitive' societies. Thus, it could be suggested that male envy of the female's procreative ability in modern Britain and America is expressed in the medical establishment's tendency to assert rigid and authoritarian control over the patterning of pregnancy, labour and delivery. The pregnant woman is a 'patient', a sick person: pregnancy is a pathological process, delivery a clinical procedure complicated by all sorts of difficulties and dangers. To say that someone is ill is one of the most effective ways of robbing them of autonomy and authority.

Perhaps there are two cultural alternatives. According to one, the care and control of reproduction – contraception, abortion, pregnancy and parturition – lies with the female community. Men are not polluted because they are not involved. Alternatively, control of reproductive care is in men's hands, and, through the creation of rules and rituals which define women as passive objects *vis-à-vis* their reproductive fate, men are able to confine and limit and curb the creativity and potentially polluting power of female procreation – and also, incidentally, the threat of female sexuality. (It is surely significant that the 'natural childbirth' movement was started by a man.) These aspects of female life are then allocated a time, a place, and a mode of expression, which in no way threatens the authority and the order of the patriarchal medical establishment.

There are thus very good reasons why the political programme of the women's movement today should include the regaining of female control over reproductive care. In the British women's liberation movement, free contraception and abortion on demand are two of the four public demands (one of the other two is also related to reproduction – free full-time nursery care for children). In addition, the feminist movement contains groups whose goal is 'self help' in reproductive care. These groups produce and circulate literature designed to inform women about reproductive processes and diseases and their control or cure, which is not normally made available to them through orthodox medical channels.[75] Other functions of these groups encompass training in simple diagnostic and therapeutic procedures (for example, pregnancy testing, self-examination for infections of the genital tract, and the Karman cannula method of menstrual extraction for painful periods or early abortion). Not surprisingly, in America, women who participate in these groups have been charged with unlicensed medical practice.[76] The confrontation is a repetition of history. Women are challenging not only the superiority of 'professional' medicine over lay, community medicine, but also the right of men to determine the level of women's knowledge about, and control over, their own bodies. A repossession of female control over reproductive care is a basic prerequisite for all other freedoms. Thus, this particular demand is, and must be, central to women's struggle for liberation today.

2

Women's Work in Nineteenth-Century London; A Study of the Years 1820–50

SALLY ALEXANDER

Introduction

Most historians define the working class *de facto* as working men. Occupations, skills, wages, relations of production, the labour process itself, are discussed as if social production were an exclusively male prerogative. Consciously or unconsciously, the world has been conceived in the image of the bourgeois family – the husband is the breadwinner and the wife remains at home attending to housework and child-care. Both the household itself, and women's domestic labour within it are presented as the unchanging backcloth to the world of real historical activity. The labour historian has ignored women as workers – on the labour market and within the household. Consequently women's contribution to production and as well to the reproduction and maintenance of the labour force has been dismissed. This is partly because the labour and economic historians who first wrote about the working class, wrote about the organized and articulate labour movement – accessible through its trade union records, its newspapers and the occasional autobiography. Only recently have the inaccessible areas of working-class life been approached, but even here the focus has remained on the working man. In every respect women's participation in history has been marginalized.[1]

Feminist history releases women from their obscurity as the wives, mothers and daughters of working men. This does not just mean that family life, housework, the reproduction of the labour force, the transmission of ideology etc. can be added to an already constituted history, but the history of production itself will be rewritten. For the history of production under capitalism, from a feminist perspective, is not simply the class struggle between the producer and the owner of the means of production. It is also the development of a particular form of the sexual division of labour in relation to that struggle.

The focus of this article is women's waged work in London in the early Victorian period. London in the period of the industrial revolution has been chosen for two reasons. Firstly, because it offers a wide survey of women's employments within a reasonably manageable geographic unit; and because it illustrates the multiple effects of industrial change on women's work, reminding us that the industrial revolution brought with it more than just machinery and the factory system. But first, a discussion of some of the limitations of the conventional sources for women's employment in the Victorian period will remind us that the labour historian is not the original villain – the problem begins with the sources themselves.

*

The working woman emerged as a 'social problem' in the thirties and forties. Indeed, it is as though the Victorians discovered her, so swiftly and urgently did she become the object of public concern. The dislocations of modern industry, the rapid increase in population, the herding of the population into the towns, dramatized class antagonisms and forced the condition of the working classes onto the attention of the propertied class as a mass of documentary evidence reveals. The effect of these dislocations upon working-class wives and children became one major focal point of this anxiety. The short-time movement (the struggle of the factory operatives in the Lancashire and Yorkshire textile mills to limit the working day), in particular Sadler's Commission of 1832, first highlighted the problem of the female factory operative. Ten years later, the Children's Employment Commission (1842–3) exposed a string of female occupations in the mines and the traditional outwork trades, where wages and conditions were no less degrading than those in the textile mill. These revelations shattered middle-class complacency and aroused the reformatory zeal of Evangelical and Utilitarian philanthropists. And it is from the philanthropists, as well as factory inspectors, that we receive most of our information on women's work.

This sense of shock at 'the condition of England', as contemporaries termed it, in particular the apparent destruction of the working-class family, cannot be understood simply from the terrible conditions in the factories alone.[2] The British Industrial Revolution did not take place in a neutral political context. Its formative years, 1790 to 1815, were years in which England was engaged in counter-revolutionary war against France. Jacobinism (the ideology of the French Revolutionaries) and industrial discontent were fused by England's rulers into an indiscriminate image of 'sedition'. Any political or industrial activity among the working classes was severely repressed. Out of this repression emerged the distinctive features of Victorian middle-class ideology – a blend of political economy and evangelicalism. The one an ideology appropriate to the 'take off' of the forces of production – the industrial revolution; the other a doctrine demonstrating the fixity of the relations of production. While political economy asserted that the laws of capitalist production were the laws of nature herself, evangelicalism sanctified the family, along with industriousness, obedience and piety, as the main bulwark against revolution. The Victorian ideal of womanhood originated in this counter-revolutionary ideology. The woman, as wife and mother, was the pivot of the family, and consequently the guardian of all Christian (and domestic) virtues. Women's waged work, therefore, was discussed insofar as it harmonized with the home, the family and domestic virtue.

Because of women's very special responsibility for society's well-being, it was the woman working outside the home who received most attention from the parliamentary commissioners, and to push through legislative reform, emphasis was placed, not on the hours of work, rates of pay, and dangers from unsafe machinery – although all these were mentioned – but on the moral and spiritual degradation said to accompany female employment; especially the mingling of the sexes and the neglect of domestic comforts. 'In the male the moral effects of the system are very sad, but in the female they are infinitely worse', Lord Shaftesbury solemnly declared to a silent House of Lords, at the end of his two-hour speech advocating the abolition of women and children's work in the mines ... 'not alone upon themselves, but upon their families, upon society, and, I may add, upon the country itself. It is bad enough if you corrupt the man, but if you corrupt the woman, you poison the waters of life at the very fountain.'[3]

Respectable opinion echoed Lord Shaftesbury's sentiments. Both evangelicalism and political economy attributed the sufferings of the poor to their own moral pollution. Their viciousness was variously ascribed to drink, licentiousness, idleness and all manner of vice and depravity, for which religion, temperance, thrift, cleanliness, industriousness and self help were advocated as the most potent remedies. But, if there was any reason for these evils – beyond the innate moral depravity of the individuals concerned – the one that commended itself most readily was the negligence and ignorance of the working-class wife and mother. It is true that enlightened public opinion – enlightened, that is, by an acquaintance with the poor acquired through visiting them for religious or reformatory purposes – recognized that the crowded courts, tenements and rookeries of the cities, so deplored by Octavia Hill and her associates, hardly stimulated the domestic virtues nurtured in the suburban villa.[4] Nevertheless, the very squalor of working-class housing could be blamed upon the slender acquaintance with domestic economy possessed by working women whose 'want of management' drove their husbands to the alehouses and their children onto the streets. The remedy was succinctly expressed by Mrs Austin, an ardent advocate of 'industrial' education for the working girl – 'our object', she wrote in the 1850s, 'is to improve the servants of the rich, and the wives of the poor'.[5]

Every Victorian inquiry into the working class is steeped in the ideology we have been discussing. The poor were seldom allowed to speak for themselves. 'What the poor are to the poor is little known,' Dickens wrote in the 1840s, 'excepting to themselves and God.'[6] And if this was true of the poor as a whole, it was doubly true of working-class women who almost disappear under the relentless scrutiny of the middle class. It was not that the Victorians did not expect women of the lower classes to work. On the contrary, work was the sole corrective and just retribution for poverty; it was rather that only those sorts of work that coincided with a woman's natural sphere were to be encouraged. Such discrimination had little to do with the danger or unpleasantness of the work concerned. There was not much to choose for example – if our criteria is risk to life or health – between work in the mines, and work in the London dressmaking trades. But no one suggested that sweated needlework should be prohibited to women. To uncover the real situation of the working woman herself in the Victorian period, then, we have to pick our way through a labyrinth of middle-class moralism and mystification and resolve questions, not only that contemporaries did not answer, but in many cases did not even ask.

*

This applies in particular to women's employment in London. Some trades it is true, received a great deal of local attention. The declining Spitalfields silk industry was investigated as part of the national inquiries into the hand-loom weavers; dressmakers and needlewomen received the notice of a House of Lords Select Committee; while starving needlewomen and prostitutes were the subject of a host of pamphlets. But the factory girls of Manchester and the West Riding who so traumatized observers in the 1840s could have no place in London where few trades were transformed by the factory system until the twentieth century. (The high cost of rent in central London combined with the high cost of fuel and its transportation, inhibited the earlier development of the factory system.) What changes did occur in the sexual division of labour as a result of a change in the production or labour process, took place beneath the surface, in the workshop, or the home. Most women workers in London were domestic servants, washerwomen, needlewomen or occupied in some other sort of home work. Many married women worked with their husbands in his trade. These traditional forms of women's work were quite compatible with the Victorian's deification of the home, and so passed almost unnoticed.

Material proof that women's work was not just less noticeable in London but often completely overlooked is found in the

Census of 1851. The number of women over twenty who are listed as being without occupation is 432,000, i.e. 57 per cent of all women over twenty living in London. In round numbers, this figure of 432,000 is broken down as follows: 317,000 wives 'not otherwise described', 27,000 widows 'not otherwise described', 43,000 children and relatives at home 'not otherwise described', 26,000 persons of rank or property, 7,000 paupers, prisoners and vagrants, 13,000 'of no specified occupations or conditions'.[7] If we exclude the 26,000 propertied at one end, the 7,000 paupers etc., at the other, and a proportion of propertied widows and dependent relatives in between, that still leaves over 50 per cent of women 'with no occupation'. And yet among the vast majority of the working class, all members of the family were expected to contribute to the family income, for even when the wages of the male workers were relatively high they were rarely regular.[8] We know therefore that 50 per cent of adult women would not have been able to live without any independent source of income. Obviously the statistics require explanation.

There were several reasons why the occupations of working-class women might not have been declared in the Census, some more speculative than others. The work of married women for instance, was often hidden behind that of their husbands. Alice Clark, Dorothy George and Ivy Pinchbeck have shown that although the separation of workplace and home (introduced by merchant capitalism) was one of the factors reducing the opportunities for women to learn a skill or to manage a small workshop business, nevertheless, the process was gradual, especially in the numerous and diverse London trades which, well into the nineteenth century, were characteristically conducted in small workshops, often on a family basis. Some women were listed in the Census as innkeepers', shopkeepers', butchers', bakers' and shoemakers' etc. wives; but often a wife's connection with her husband's trade would not have been mentioned. Many trade societies forbad the entry of women. Also, because the head of the household filled in the Census, he – especially if he was a skilled artisan or aspiring tradesman – probably thought of his as a housewife and mother and not as a worker.[9]

of skilled workmen may be glimpsed, however, through

conversations recorded by Mayhew. Sawyers' wives and children, for instance, did not 'as a general rule . . . go *out* to work', (my italics),[10] and coachmen's wives were not in regular employ for the slop-tailors, because, as one confided in Mayhew, 'we keep our wives too respectable for that'.[11] Nevertheless, according to Mayhew, 'some few of the wives of the better class of workmen take in washing or keep small "general shops"'.[12] Taking in washing, needlework, or other sorts of outwork was the least disruptive way of supplementing the family income when extra expenses were incurred, or during the seasonal or enforced unemployment which existed in most London trades. Home work did not unnecessarily interrupt a man's domestic routine, since the wife could fit it in among her household chores; it simply meant she worked a very long day.

But only a minority of women would have been married to skilled artisans or small tradesmen. Mayhew estimated that about 10 per cent of every trade were society men, and Edward Thompson has outlined the 30s. line of privilege in London, while suggesting that Mayhew's 10 per cent was probably an exaggeration, 5 or 6 per cent being a more realistic figure.[13] Society men were becoming more and more confined to the 'honourable' sectors of every trade in the 1840s (i.e. those who produced expensive well-made goods for the luxury and West End market), whereas workers in the unorganized, dishonourable sectors were rapidly expanding in the period 1815–40, and they made a much more precarious living. Women (and children) of this class always had to contribute to the family income, indeed, in the 1830s and 1840s, a time of severe economic hardship, the London poor drew more closely together, and it was often the household and not the individual worker, or even separate families, that was the economic unit. A mixture of washing, cleaning, charring as well as various sorts of home- or slop-work, in addition to domestic labour, occupied most women throughout their working lives. The diversity and indeterminancy of this spasmodic, casual and irregular employment was not easily condensed and classified into a Census occupation.

Other women who were scarcely recorded in the Census, though we know of their existence through Mayhew, were the street traders, market workers, entertainers, scavengers, mud-larks;[14] also those who earned a few pence here and there, look-ing after a neighbour's children, running errands, minding a crossing, sweeping the streets, in fact, most of the women dis-cussed in the final section of this paper. Lastly, perhaps the most desperate source of income for women, and one which provoked a great deal of prurient debate and pious attention was prostitu-tion. This too was often intermittent and supplementary and found no place in the Census.

Despite the fact that working women emerge only fitfully through the filter of Victorian moralism; in spite of the tendency to view women as the wives and dependents of working men rather than workers in their own right; in spite of the particular problems of uncovering women's employment in London; never-theless, some distinguishing characteristics are beginning to appear.

Firstly, London offered no single staple employment for women comparable to that in the northern textile towns; secondly, in a city of skilled trades and small workshops, women, although long since excluded from formal apprenticeship, often worked with their husband in his trade; thirdly, much women's work outside small workshop production was intermittent and casual, which meant that most women's working lives were spent in a variety of partial occupations most of which escaped the rigid classifications of the Census.

These features of women's work must be looked at against the wider background of the London labour market, and the sexual division of labour within it, but first, to help fix the locality, a brief descriptive sketch of London follows.

London Topography

In 1828, Fennimore Cooper described his journey through the outskirts of London as one through a 'long maze of villages'. Even then the description was a little whimsical. London's first period of expansion had been the late sixteenth and early seven-teenth centuries, since when it had continued to extend its in-fluence as the political, commercial and manufacturing centre of England. London was also the largest single consumer market in the country. Between 1801 and 1851 London underwent another burst of expansion; her population increased 150 per cent from 900,000 to 2,360,000. Industrial and commercial innovations were affecting every aspect of its economic life. Railways were transforming not only the topography, but manners, morals, customs, the very tempo of life. London was becoming much more accessible to the rest of Britain. Finally, if industrial productivity and expansion in trade and shipping had made Britain the workshop of the world by 1851, developments in banking, shareholding and company investment were making the City its most important financial centre.

London – world centre of commerce, shipping and trade – does not correspond to the image conjured up by Fennimore Cooper, and yet there was a sense in which London was a rambling collection of hamlets. Certainly, its local government before the 1890s lent reality to that myth, if myth it was. G. L. Gomme, looking at a map of London in the 1830s, suggested it resembled an octopus, the boundary of whose body passed from Vauxhall Bridge, to Park Lane, then followed up the Edgware Road, along Marylebone Road, City Road, then southwards past Mile End, reaching the Thames at Shadwell Basin. Apart from the almost independent enclaves of Greenwich and Deptford, the south of the river began with Bermondsey – separated from Deptford by Rotherhithe. By the middle of the century, according to John Hollingshead, it 'wriggled' its way 'through the existing miles of dirt, vice and crime as far as the Lambeth marshes'. Between 1830 and 1850, London was greedily swallowing up the surrounding villages, and transforming them into the 'stuccovia, the suburbs, the terminus districts', which from the 1840s onwards, appeared with increasing frequency in the novels of Dickens.[15]

The process of incorporation was rapid, but their transformation gradual. The differences and peculiarities of London districts remained very marked. Their geographic, social and economic distinctions were more than the preservation of quaint custom. In 1830 Hampstead, Islington, Hackney and east of Bethnal Green and Stepney were rural or semi-rural. So was south of the

river beyond Southwark and Bermondsey. In the early morning
the park side of Piccadilly was crowded with women carrying
baskets of fruit and vegetables on their heads on their way to
Covent Garden from the market gardens of Hammersmith,
Fulham and Chelsea, where the river ran through fields.[30] Every
street was filled with costers on their way to market. Sophie
Wackles in *Great Expectations*, married Mr Chegg, a market
gardener from Chelsea.

Between the semi-rural outposts in the north and the north-east,
and central London, were waste districts, great tracts of suburban
Sahara, such as Dickens described in a walk from the City to the
outskirts of Holloway, 'where tiles and bricks were burnt, bones
were boiled, carpets were beat, rubbish was shot, dogs were
fought, and dust was heaped by contractors'.[16] Hector Gavin in
his 'sanitary ramblings' through Bethnal Green in the 1840s similarly found yards for the collection of dust, refuse and ash,
overflowing sewers and open drains and other 'nuisances'.
These had gradually been encroaching on the plots laid out as
gardens where he saw 'the choicest flowers', dahlias and tulips.[17]
The railway, that harbinger of progress, left chaos in its wake
in outlying parts of the East End – contributing to its general
atmosphere of desolation and disease by the destruction of streets
and alleys and the accumulation of rubbish yards and dung
heaps in their place. The summer houses belonging to the
gardens of Bethnal Green were being used for 'human habitation', and every bit of spare ground was being built on: houses
that were neither paved or boarded, lacking in sanitation and
built below ground level.

Jerry builders were busy throughout suburban London. The
hasty conversion of sheds and shacks into homes in Spitalfields,
the cheap building in these waste districts of the East End, and
on the outskirts of the City – Shoreditch, St Pancras, Agar Town
for example, once described as 'a squalid population that had first
squatted' – the rows of small houses that were built with 'mere
lathe and plaster' purely for quick profit had their central London counterparts in the decaying tenements of the City and the
West End, and south of the river in Southwark and Bermondsey.

The intervening waste lands between London and its outlying

villages were being depredated and abused on the north and north-east sides of the City – between London and Finchley for instance, or the hills and fields of north Holloway or Hackney, or the semi-rural outpost of Bethnal Green. The west and the north-west had long ago been colonized by the propertied and professional classes. As one moved from west to east, in a sort of arc from Charing Cross, fashionable society gave way to the aspiring and respectable, but definitely lower middle classes. Here, in Somers Town and Camden Town, were the clerks who toiled all day at their desks in the City or the port; whose wives kept up appearances, and whose daughters struggled in select 'seminaries' to acquire such diverse but necessary preparations for marriage as 'English composition, geography, and the use of dumb-bells . . . writing, arithmetic, dancing, music and general fascination . . . the art of needlework, marking and samplery . . .'[18] Further east, drawing inwards towards the City, lived lacemakers, drapers, embroiderers, the straw-hat and bonnet makers and the milliners of Marylebone and St Pancras, the artificial flower makers, bonnet and cap makers of Clerkenwell and St Lukes.

It is the nucleus of London which is the focus of this study: the City and its perimeter, the East End and south of the river from Rotherhithe to Lambeth. Although, in these predominently manufacturing regions of London, the polarization of classes was still far from complete – 'in the Bethnal Green and Whitechapel unions, in which are found some of the worst conditioned masses of population in the metropolis, we also find good mansions, well drained and protected, inhabited by persons in the most favourable circumstances', wrote Chadwick for instance, in his *Sanitary Report*[19] – the migration of the middle classes to the suburbs was under way.

Omnibus and rail were beginning to make possible this migration, but the principal metropolitan trades and manufactures remained in the centre – and the working classes with them. The industrial districts of London had established themselves east of the City and south of the river in the sixteenth century. During the eighteenth and early nineteenth centuries, the ground between the City and the East End had been built over; workshops and warehouses were built in and to the north and east of the City, while docks and shipyards were beginning to stretch eastwards from the Tower. Such changes had pushed many workers out of the City itself, and, between 1700 and 1831, its population dropped from 210,000 to 122,000.[20] By 1800 then, artisans and labourers were well established in the industrial belt encircling the City, and over the river in Southwark and Bermondsey. There they remained in their 'haunts of poverty' and 'pockets of vice' in the first half of the nineteenth century. Railways, docks and other 'improvements' failed to dislodge them. In Whitechapel, for instance, between 1821 and 1851 the population increased from 68,905 to 79,759, although several thousand houses and 14,000 persons had been displaced by the building of the London (1800–1805) and St Katherine's (1828) docks, together with railways and other enterprises. The result was that the 'labouring class' crowded 'themselves into those houses which were formerly occupied by respectable tradesmen and mechanics, and which are now let into tenements'.[21] Further west, the effect of pushing New Oxford Street through one of the most populous districts of St Giles was that whereas in 1840 the houses in Church Lane had twenty-four occupants each, by 1847 they had forty.[22] Indeed, with the exception of parts of Bethnal Green, Mile End Old Town, St Olave's Southwark and southern Lambeth, all the inner industrial perimeter of London was overcrowded, with between fifteen and forty houses per acre – and the population of every district in this area increased between 1831 and 1851.[23]

The overspill of the working classes in central and east London and their relative isolation from the middle classes, even within a particular district, were a source of perpetual anxiety to Victorian philanthropists and utilitarians. Separation of the classes was dangerous since it bred class hatred; proximity of the poor among themselves led to contamination; overcrowding naturally encouraged promiscuity and all manner of depravity. Nevertheless, the poor continued to crowd in on one another because they had to live near their place of work, which in the 1830s and 1840s was still largely localized in the inner industrial perimeter. There were no cheap transport facilities until the last third of the nineteenth century, and much employment was casual – that is, the worker was employed on a day-to-day or weekly basis. Every trade had its casual fringe and in many partial and improvised occupations (of which London, as a capital city, had an abundant supply), employment sometimes only amounted to a few hours a week, and even then was contingent on being immediately accessible. Even workers in the 'honourable trades' had to be 'on call' daily, which meant it was impractical to live further away from the place of work than a couple of miles.

There were working-class communities beyond the industrial perimeter of course – the potteries of Kensington, for instance, colonized by pig-keepers, and later brickmakers, in the early part of the nineteenth century. And, in every wealthy district, 'from Belgravia to Bloomsbury – from St Pancras to Bayswater' – there was

hardly a settlement of leading residences that has not its particular colony of ill-housed poor hanging onto its skirts. Behind the mansion there is generally a stable, and near the stable there is generally a maze of close streets, containing a small greengrocer's, a small dairy's, a quiet coachman's public house, and a number of houses let out in tenements. These houses shelter a large number of painters, bricklayers, carpenters, and similar labourers, with their families, and many laundresses and charwomen.[24]

But while these groups are important in so far as they serve as a reminder that London was the centre of wealth, luxury, fashion and conspicuous consumption – they were part of a different city from the East End, the City and its boundaries north and south of the river.

Within the industrial perimeter and the East End, work specializations on a local basis reinforced the separation into distinctive communities. In the 1850s, Mayhew listed, apart from the Spitalfields silk weavers, 'the tanners of Bermondsey – the watchmakers of Clerkenwell – the coachmakers of Long Acre – the marine store dealers of Saffron Hill – the old clothes men of Holywell Street and Rosemary Lane – the potters of Lambeth – the hatters of the Borough'.[25] More could be added. But the correlation between district and trade was never absolute, except perhaps in a place like Bermondsey, virtually surrounded by water and uninviting to outsiders because of the 'pungent odours' that exuded from the tanneries, glue, soap and other manufactories of the noxious trades. In general, it was poverty and common want that drew people together in the tenements of St Giles's, or parts of the East End, haunts of the poor as Dickens describes in the *Old Curiosity Shop*:

... a straggling neighbourhood, where the mean houses parcelled off in rooms, and windows patched with rags and paper, told of the populous poverty that sheltered there ... mangling women, washerwomen, cobblers, tailors, chandlers driving their trades in parlours and kitchens and back-rooms and garrets, and sometimes all of them under the same roof.[26]

The women of these districts are the subject of this essay.

London Trades and the Sexual Division of Labour

Women's waged work was not immediately conspicuous in London in the early Victorian period. Women were not found in the skilled and heavy work in shipbuilding and engineering, two of London's staple industries in the first half of the nineteenth century. Neither were they employed in the docks and warehouses, nor their subsidiary trades. There were no women in the public utilities, (gas, building etc.) or transport, nor in most semi-processing and extractive industries – sugar refining, soap manufacture, blacking, copper and lead working and the 'noxious' trades – which were London's principal factory trades in this period. Finally, women were excluded from the professions, the civil service, clerical work, the scientific trades, and had been excluded from the old guild crafts (e.g. jewellers, precious instrument makers, carriage builders etc.) since the fourteenth and fifteenth centuries. If women were not in the heavy or skilled industries, in public service or factory, in the professions or clerical work, then where were they to be found?

The 1851 Census tells us (in round numbers) that 140,000 women over twenty, (or 18 per cent of women of that age group) were employed in domestic service; 125,000 (16·3 per cent) were in clothing and shoemaking; 11,000 (1·9 per cent) were teachers and 9,000 (1·2 per cent) worked in the silk industry. The bulk of the remainder were employed either in other branches of manufacture, (artificial-flower making, straw-hat and bonnet making, tailoresses, etc.) or as licensed victuallers, shopkeepers, innkeepers and lodging-house keepers, or else they were listed as the wives of tradesmen and manufacturing workers. Bearing in mind the insufficiency of the 1851 Census as a source, we can see that women's work fell into four principal categories: firstly, all aspects of domestic and household labour – washing, cooking, charring, sewing, mending, laundry work, mangling, ironing etc; secondly, child-care, and training; thirdly, the distribution and retail of food and other articles of regular consumption; and finally, specific skills in manufacture based upon the sexual division of labour established when production (both for sale and domestic use) had been organized within the household. That is to say: the sexual division of labour on the labour market originated with, and paralleled that within the family.

This sketch of women's waged work in London is not an oversimplification. A closer examination of the Census and other sources apparently reveals a wider variety of women's work. Arthur J. Munby, for instance, a careful observer of working-class women, wrote in June 1861:

London Bridge, more than any place I know here, seems to be the great thoroughfare for young working women and girls. One meets them at every step: young women carrying large bundles of umbrella frames home to be covered; young women carrying cages full of hats, which yet want the silk and the binding, coster-girls often dirty and sordid, going to fill their empty baskets, and above all female sack-makers.[27]

And in the same year Munby met or noticed female mudlarks, brick-makers, milk-girls, shirt-collar makers, a porter, a consumptive embroiderer, a draper's shop assistant as well as servants and some agricultural labourers from the country. Mayhew also talked with women in heavy manual work: dustwomen, milk-girls, porters, market girls. Nevertheless, most women's work fitted into the categories described above. Poverty had always forced some women to seek employment in heavy, unpleasant, irregular work, especially those women outside the family, or with no male wage coming in regularly. Dorothy George wrote of women among the eighteenth-century London poor, for instance, that there is no work 'too heavy or disagreeable to be done by women provided it is also low paid'.[28] And an investigation by the Statistical Society into the poorer classes in St George's in the East, uncovered the same characteristics of women's employment in 1848. Whereas men's wages

varied as usual, with the degree of skill required in the several trades, the lowest being those of the sailors, 11s. 10d. per week beside rations, and of the mere labourers, 15s. 7d. per week, on the average; the highest those of the gunsmiths, 41s. 9d. per week; the general average being 20s. 2d. per week . . .

The average wage of single women and widows was only 6s. 10d. The average earnings of 'widows with encumbrance' was 9s. 11d. The report blamed those 'limited means' on the 'narrow range of employments available for female hands, especially if unaccompanied by a vigorous frame and habits of bodily exertion'.[29] Although the sexual division of labour was seldom static on the London labour market, the designation 'women's work' always meant work that was unskilled, overcrowded and low paid. Consequently men in the relatively highly paid skilled trades, especially in the honourable sectors, jealously resisted the entry of women into their trades and excluded them from their trade societies. Indeed, such was the force of custom and tradition in the structure of the London labour market that the appearance of women into a previously male-dominated trade or skill indicated a down-grading of the work involved, and this was generally achieved through a change in the production process itself.

The Capitalist Mode of Production and the Sexual Division of Labour

The sexual division of labour – both within and between the London trades – in the 1830s and 1840s had been established in the period of manufacture (roughly from the sixteenth to the eighteenth century). It was predetermined by the division of labour that had existed within the family when the household had been the unit of production. The epoch of modern industry, far from challenging this division further demarcated and rigidified it. Historically many steps in this process must be left to the imagination. Its progress anyway varied from trade to trade and was modified by local custom. But a schematic outline can be given of the way in which capitalist production, as it emerged and matured, structured the sexual division of labour.

Capitalist production developed within the interstices of the feudal mode of production; it emerged alongside of, but also in opposition to, small peasant agriculture and independent handicrafts. Capitalist production first manifests itself in the simultaneous employment and cooperative labour of a large number of labourers by one capitalist. Cooperation based on division of labour assumes its characteristic form in manufacture, which, as a mode of production arose from the breakdown of the handicrafts system.[30] Each step in the development of capitalist production is marked by a further refinement in the division of labour, so that what distinguishes the labour process in manufacture from that in handicrafts is that whereas the worker in the latter produces a commodity, the detail labourer in manufacture produces only part of a commodity.[31] Nevertheless, the technical basis of manufacture remains the handicraft skills. However, these skills become differentiated:

Since the collective labourer has functions, both simple and complex, both high and low, his members, the individual labour-powers, require different degrees of training, and must therefore have different values. Manufacture, therefore, develops a hierarchy of labour-powers, to which there corresponds a scale of wages. If, on the one hand, the individual labourers are appropriated and annexed for life by a limited function; on the other hand, the various operations of the hierarchy are parcelled out among the labourers according to both their natural and their acquired capabilities. Every process of production, however, requires certain simple manipulations, which every man is capable of doing. They too are now severed from their connection with the more pregnant moments of activity and ossified into exclusive functions of specially appointed labourers. Hence, Manufacture begets, in every handicraft that it seizes upon, a class of so-called unskilled labourers, a class which handicraft industry strictly excluded. If it develops a one-sided speciality into a perfection, at the expense of the absence of the whole of a man's working capacity, it also begins to make a speciality of the absence of all development. Alongside of the hierarchic gradation there steps the simple separation of the labourers into skilled and unskilled.[32]

The accumulation of capital was held back by the handicraft base of manufacture, which enabled skilled workmen to exert some control over the labour process through combination in a trade society. Entry into the trade was restricted and knowledge of the skills involved in the work process was confined to those who entered formal apprenticeship But these limited privileges were gained at the expense of the 'unskilled'. Excluded from trade societies most workers were denied a specialized training, and hence lacked bargaining power against capital. The transition from handicrafts to manufacture relegated most women to this position.

By the fifteenth century many craft guilds were excluding women, except for the wives and widows of master craftsmen. Even when women were admitted there is little to indicate that they had ever been formally trained in the technical skills of the labour process itself.[33] But the guilds had been organizations of master craftsmen. With the accumulation of capital, and demarcation of economic classes within a handicraft, the practice of a craft or trade required more capital. The proportion of masters to journeymen altered on the one hand, while, on the other, the impoverished craftsmen (masters or journeymen) practised their trade outside the jurisdiction of the guilds. As more journeymen became wage-earners at their masters' workshops, they organized themselves into societies to protect their interests, which, insofar as they preserved work customs etc., coincided with the master craftsmen against the domination of merchant capital and the encroachment of the unskilled. These journeyman societies also excluded women. Women, who were now denied access to socially recognized skills, formed a source of cheap labour power for the unskilled unorganized branches of production developing outside the corporate guilds. This pool of female labour formed one basis of the industrial reserve army, which was at once both a precondition and necessary product of the accumulation of capital.[34]

Women's vulnerability as wage-workers stemmed from their child-bearing capacity. Upon which 'natural' foundation the sexual division of labour within the family was based. Because, in its early organization (the putting-out, or domestic system), capitalism seized the household or the family as the economic and often the productive unit, the sexual division of labour was utilized and sustained as production was transferred from the family to the market-place.

The pre-industrial family had a patriarchal structure. This was true of the working-class family in the period of manufacture (sixteenth to eighteenth centuries), whether the family was employed directly on the land or in an urban craft or trade, or in a rural domestic trade. The father was head of the household, his craft or trade most often determined the family's principal source of income, and his authority was sanctioned by both the law of God and the law of Nature. Nevertheless (except among the very wealthy minority), every member of the family participated in production and contributed to the family income. A woman's work in the home was different from her husband's, but no less vital. (All women were married or widowed in the pre-industrial period except for those in service.) Her time was allocated between domestic labour and work in production for sale, according to the family's economic needs. And sometimes a woman's economic contribution to family income was considerable (especially in rural industries). But a wife's responsibility for the well-being of her husband and children always came before her work in social production, and in a patriarchal culture, this was seen to follow naturally from her role in biological reproduction.[35]

The intervention of capitalism into the sexual division of labour within the patriarchal family confirmed the economic subordination of the wife. By distinguishing between production for use and production for exchange and by progressively subordinating the former to the latter, by confining production for use to the private world of the home and female labour, and production for exchange increasingly to the workshop outside the home and male labour, capitalism ensured the economic dependence of women upon their husbands or fathers for a substantial part of their lives. In these conditions, each further step in the development of capitalist production – breakdown of the handicraft's system, division of labour, exclusion from the skilled craft guilds, separation of workshop and home, formation of trade societies – further undermined women's position on the labour market. Manufacture provided the economic conditions for the hierarchy of labour powers, but it was the transference of the sexual division of labour from the family into social production which ensured that it was women who moved into the subordinate and auxiliary positions, within it. (The other main area of women's employment, domestic and personal service, cannot be analysed in these terms, since it remained outside capitalist production proper arguably into the twentieth century. This did not prevent it however, from sharing the general characteristics of women's work, low pay and low status).

This reservoir of female labour was an immediate source of cheap labour power ready for utilization by capitalist production when a revolution in the mode of production altered the technical base of the labour process. For as long as production depended upon the workman's skilled manipulation of the instruments of labour, the capitalist could not dislodge his skilled workmen. Only the decomposition of that skill into its constituent parts, which was brought about by a revolution in the instruments of labour, could break up workmen's control over the labour process. It was this revolutionary progress in the division of labour which marked the advent of the epoch of modern industry. Machinery and the factory system abolished the material base for the traditional hierarchy of labour powers and so for the first time the possibility of the introduction of cheap unskilled labour on a large scale.

Along with the tool, the skill of the workman in handling it passes over to the machine. The capabilities of the tool are emancipated from the restraints that are inseparable from human labour-power. Thereby the technical foundation on which is based the division of labour in Manufacture, is swept away. Hence, in the place of the hierarchy of specialised workmen that characterises manufacture, there steps, in the automatic factory, a tendency to equalise and reduce to one and the same level every kind of work that has to be done by the minders of the machines; in the place of the artificially produced differentiations of the detail workmen, step the natural differences of age and sex.[36]

In this sense, modern industry was a direct challenge to the traditional sexual division of labour in social production. In the Lancashire textile industry, for instance, women and children were the earliest recruits into the factories. But in London the ways in which the labour power of women was utilized in the transition from manufacture to modern industry was more complicated, because that transition itself, when it was made at all, was made differently in each trade.

Some traditional areas of the London economy, the small, specialized and luxury trades for instance, which depended on proximity to their markets and skilled handicraftsmen, were not at all affected by modern industry. Indeed in a few cases, they had been only minimally affected by the transition from handicrafts to manufacture. There were still handfuls of women working in these skilled crafts – engraving, precious metals, instrument makers, watchmakers, etc. – who served as a reminder of the position that women had once occupied in production during the handicraft era. Yet even in the trades most directly affected by the industrial revolution there was no single process of adaption. Of those which had transferred to the factory, there were one or two in which the introduction of machinery at certain stages in the labour process was forcing a realignment in the sexual division of labour. In the Spitalfields silk industry, for example, William Wallis, a weaver, states that 'the winding is almost wholly done by machinery now consequently it is performed by girls only', and that '. . . winding under these circumstances obtains the best wage of any other branch of trade in Spitalfields'.[37] Further examples in book-binding, hatting and rope and sailcloth making are discussed in the following section. But, on the whole, those trades with a potential or actual mass market found the high costs of rent and fuel and its transportation in central London, made the introduction of machinery and factories quite impracticable. Other techniques with which to counter provincial factory and foreign competition were found. The large supply of cheap labour favoured the development of sweated outwork and other slop-work, not modern industry proper.

Industrial Change in London 1830–50: Slop-work

The slop trades produced cheap ready-made goods for retail or wholesale shops, showrooms and warehouses, in the East and West Ends of London, and the City. They were based upon the same principle as that which permitted the introduction of machinery in cotton textiles, the breakdown of the skilled labour process into its semi- or un-skilled component parts. They depended upon the unlimited exploitation of an inexhaustible supply of cheap unskilled labour. Women and children formed the local basis of this labour force, as well as the pool of casual labour that had always belonged in London. But from the end of the Napoleonic Wars, this labour pool was swelled by growing numbers of immigrants from Ireland and the agricultural districts.[38] As the men sought work in the docks and the building industries, their wives and children flooded into the slop trades. Long hours, irregular employment and wages often below subsistence were the marks of these industries, as the wholesalers or 'warehousemen' adjusted the labour supply to fit the demands of the market.[39] A host of new techniques – scamping methods – were introduced which shortened the length of time it took to produce an article. The division of labour, and lowering standards of workmanship enabled the influx of unskilled labour. A shoemaker in Bethnal Green in the 1840s describes some of the effects of slop-work in his trade:

It is probable, that independent of apprentices, 200 additional hands are added to our already over-burdened trade yearly. Sewing boys soon learn the use of the knife. Plenty of poor men will offer to finish them for a pound and a month's work; and men, for a few shillings and a few weeks' work will teach other boys to sew. There are many of the wives of chamber-masters teach girls entirely to make children's work for a pound and a few months' work, and there are many in Bethnal Green who have learnt the business in this way. These teach some other members of their families, and then actually set up in business in opposition to those who taught them, and in cutting, offer their work for sale at a much lower rate of profit; and shopkeepers in town and country, having circulars sent to solicit custom will have their goods from a warehouse that will serve them cheapest; then the warehouseman will have them cheap from the manufacturer; and he in his turn cuts down the wages of the work people, who fear to refuse offers at the warehouse price, knowing the low rate at which chamber-masters will serve the warehouse.[40]

In every slop trade, there were various middlemen between the warehouse or showroom, and the producer. The work was sub-contracted out to the lowest bidder, who was usually a small master or mistress; the sweater in tailoring and the other clothing trades, the chamber-master in men's, women's and children's shoemaking, the garret-master in dressing-case, work-box, writing-desk making and other branches of the fancy cabinet trade (which Mayhew described as among the worst trades even in Spitalfields and Bethnal Green). Outwork was an effective counter to factory competition because it saved on overheads, required small capital and isolated workers, thus preventing their effective organization. Small masters employed their wives and children, and apprentices or other workers more destitute than themselves, to assist them. By constant undercutting and all the methods of slop-work, wages sank beneath subsistence and the small master undermined his own livelihood.

This sort of 'domestic industry' had always existed beyond the skilled 'honourable' sectors of the London trades, but in the un-stable economy of the thirties and forties, even workers in the 'honourable' sectors felt threatened by the expansion of slop-work, and especially by its erosion of customary skill differen-tials. A journeyman tailor, for instance, describes the blurring of distinction between men's and women's work:

When I first began working at this branch there were but very few females employed in it; a few white waistcoats were given out to them, under the idea that women could make them cleaner than men – and so indeed they can. But since the last five years the sweaters have em-ployed females upon cloth, silk and satin waistcoats as well, and before that time the idea of a woman making a cloth waistcoat would have been scouted. But since the increase of the puffing and the sweating system, masters and sweaters have sought everywhere for such hands as would do the work below the regular ones. Hence the wife has been made to compete with the husband, and the daughter with the wife; they all learn the waistcoat business and must all get a living. If the man will not reduce the price of his labour to that of the female, why he must remain unemployed; and if the full-grown woman will not take the work at the same price as the young girl, why she must remain without any. The female hands I can confidently state, have been sought out and introduced to the business by the sweaters from a desire on their part continually to ferret out hands who will do the work cheaper than others.[41]

It is easy to see why the journeyman tailor, the shoemakers and indeed most of the workmen who spoke to Mayhew at the end of the 1840s, could attribute their lowered standard of life over the previous fifteen years to the influx of cheap labour. Many trades had bitterly fought (tailors' and woodworkers' strikes in 1834 for instance) and failed to resist the erosion of skills, work customs and wage rates in those years.[42] But their diagnosis was over-simple. The flow of unskilled labour into a trade was the *result* of the dissolution of a skill. This, and the opening up of mass markets was made possible by the strengthening and concentration of capital within a trade, generally in London in the form of the wholesale or retail warehouseman. In this way the skilled workman lost his bargaining power against capital.

But the income differential between men's and women's work did not simply measure the distance between skilled and unskilled. The idea of the family wage had been transferred onto the labour market with the male worker. Although few men's wages actually did provide for all the family, one of the marks of a 'society' man was supposed to be his ability to take home a family wage, and the *assumption* that a man had to support a family, whereas a woman did not, was echoed throughout all but the most casual reaches of the labour market. That this assumption was unjustified, is testified by the Statistical Society's inquiry in east London in 1848. There were 229 'unprotected' women compared with only 125 'single' men.

A glance at the table which shows their scanty earnings, and the numerous families which are dependent upon two thirds of them, will convey a sufficient idea of the position of moral as well as pecuniary difficulty in which they are placed. Some of the women included in this class are, indeed, widowed only by the abandonment of the husbands. All, however are living unprotected with families dependent on them.[43]

Women's casual status as an industrial reserve army for most of London's manufacturing trades was buttressed by the ideology of the family. The implications of this were far-reaching. Whereas the unskilled countrymen who flooded the slop trades were eventually organized, women workers remained almost entirely outside the trade union movement throughout the nineteenth century, and into the twentieth. Their position as home workers, slop-workers, sweated workers and cheap labour both made them difficult to organize, and reinforced the ideology which prohibited their organization. By excluding women from trade societies, men preserved their patriarchal authority at the expense of their industrial strength.

The sub-contracting and undercutting of slop-work which reduced so many London workers to near destitution in the thirties and forties, were as much part of the 'industrial revolution' then as the machinery and factories of Lancashire. And the employment of women and children at less than subsistence wages in the slop trades was as symptomatic of the concentration of capital and the maximization of profit within an industry as the mill girls in cotton textiles.

Hierarchy of the London Labour Market: Women's Skilled Work

In such a state of flux within the labour market it would be difficult to construct any hierarchy of employment. But since most women's work was lumped together at the bottom of the social and economic scale, stratifying it is almost impossible. There are none of the familiar landmarks which help us to assess the relative status of a working man on the labour market. Few women's skills had any scarcity value or socially recognized status. Most of them – food and clothing, and the service trades, for instance – had only been transferred to the market in the previous 150–200 years. They had no experience of combination, no sacrosanct customs, no tradition of formal apprenticeship – all of which established a skill.[44]

What skilled work there was for women, however, fell into three categories: the exclusively female trades; women's work in the 'honourable' sectors of men's trades, and factory work. These are the occupations which, as far as we know, required some formal training, where the wages were relatively high for women's work, and where there was the possibility of secure employment.

Dressmaking and millinery

Dressmaking and millinery, were trades traditionally in the hands of women and they remained so throughout the nineteenth century. Mayhew distinguishes between the two branches of the trade:

The dressmaker's work is confined to the making of ladies' dresses, including every kind of outwardly-worn gown or robe. The milliner's work is confined to making caps, bonnets, scarfs, and all outward attire worn by ladies other than the gown; the bonnets, however, which tax the skill of the milliners, are what are best known as 'made bonnets' – such as are constructed of velvet, satin, silk, muslin, or any other textile fabric. Straw bonnet making is carried on by a distinct class, and in separate establishments. The milliner, however, often trims a straw bonnet, affixing the ribbons, flowers, or other adornments. When the business is sufficiently large, one or more millinery hands are commonly kept solely to bonnet-making, those best skilled in that art being of course selected; but every efficient milliner so employed is expected to be expert also at cap-making, and at all the other branches of the trade. The milliner is accounted a more skilled labourer than the dressmaker.[45]

Dressmaking and millinery offered girls both a skill and respectability – a quality indispensible to the Victorian lower middle class. But when looked at more closely, we discover that the opportunities they offered were limited, and these available only to a select stratum.

No working-class household could afford the £30–50 premium which was the price of a two- to five-year apprenticeship in a respectable house. Most girls served their apprenticeship in the country and came to London to be 'improved' – a process which took another nine months to two years, and cost a further £10 to £15 fee, in a fashionable West End house. There were at least 15,000 dressmakers' and milliners' assistants employed in about 1,500 establishments in London in 1841, aged between fourteen and twenty-five. Only a few of these were indoor apprentices and 'improvers' in the first-rate houses. Mrs Eliza Hakewell, who, with her sister, had kept such an establishment at Lower Brook Street, Grosvenor Square, for the previous twenty years, employed six or seven 'improvers' (but no apprentices). She told the House of Lords Committee in 1854, that they were 'very respectable young people (who) would not like to mix with common young people. They were the daughters of clergymen and half-pay officers and of first-rate professions.' Mrs Hakewell added, 'I have had many officers' daughters, many young people of limited incomes and many who come up to learn to make their own clothes.'[46]

These girls obviously fall outside the scope of our survey. So do the first hands, showroom girls and fitters, all the women Mrs Hakewell describes as 'the first-rate talent'. But most dress-makers and milliners came from less elevated social backgrounds; they were either 'out-door apprentices' – that is, they paid no premium and received no wages; or else they were day workers employed for the season (February to July; October to Christmas) and paid perhaps £12–20 for the year. These workers, according to Mrs Hakewell were 'quite common people: little tradesmen's daughters', or even the daughters of the poor. As a young day worker who supported herself and her mother on the 7s. she earned for seven or eight months of the year (and 1s. 6d. a week average for the remainder) told Mayhew: 'There are several respectable tradesmen who get day work for their daughters, and who like that way of employing them better than in situations as assistants because their girls then sleep at home and earn nice pocket money or dress money by day work.' 'That,' she added, 'is a disadvantage to a young person like me who depends on her needle for her living.'[47]

All dressmakers' and milliners' assistants were excessively over-worked. Ill-health often forced retirement from the trade. During the season an eighteen-hour day was the norm, and it was 'the common practice', Commissioner Grainger reported, 'on particular occasions such as drawing-rooms, wedding or mourning orders for work to be continued all night'.[48] The result was that girls working at this pitch from the ages of fourteen to sixteen, suffered from 'indigestion in its most severe forms, disturbance of the uterine actions, palpitation of the heart, pulmonary affections threatening consumption and various affections of the eyes', together with fainting and distortion of the spine. Consequently, many young girls who had families to retreat to, did so. Those that survived the rigours of their teens and twenties in the fashionable West End houses (distinguished, according to Mayhew, by the fact that they 'put out the skirts and served the ladies of the nobility rather than the gentry') moved down the social scale to the third- and fourth-rate houses 'where the skirts are made at home (and they) seldom work for gentlefolk, but are supported by the wives of tradesmen and mechanics'.[49]

Long hours, ill-health, and early retirement were the rewards of many of the 6,000 young women employed in the 'better class' house. 6s. to 8s. a week for a day worker was a respectable wage for a young working girl, but the cost of lodgings were high (not all lived with their parents), and a further expense was the obligation 'to go genteel in their clothes'. In this respect, milliners and dressmakers were on a par with the upper servants, the drapers, or the haberdashers' assistants of whom it was also said that they were 'remarkable for the gentility of their appearance and manners'. Dickens humorously evoked the aspirations of some of these young women in his description of the West End cigar shop in which young men were

lounging about, on round tubs and pipe boxes, in all the dignity of whiskers and gilt watch-guards; whispering soft nothings to the young lady in amber, with the large ear-rings, who, as she sits behind the counter in a blaze of adoration and gas light, is the admiration of all the female servants in the neighbourhood, and the envy of every milliner's apprentice within two miles round.[50]

We know little about the organization or work process of women's trades other than dressmaking and millinery, in this period. Sectors of embroidery, tambouring, lacemaking and straw-hat making were among women's skills which required a recognized training. Two other apprenticed trades were pearl-stringing and haberdashery. Some laundry work was also skilled and highly paid, and small businesses were probably run by women. But the numbers of women's trades had declined. Many had passed into the hands of men in the previous hundred years. (Hairdressing, for instance, which had given 'many women in London genteel bread' in the eighteenth century, was taken over by Frenchmen by 1800.) Fewer women were able to set up in independent business because of the separation of workplace and home, and the increase in the scale of starting capital. Some sewing trades remained almost the only manufacture both managed and worked by women on any large-scale basis in the nineteenth century.

Ivy Pinchbeck describes the scope of an embroideress's business, which, she says, hardly changed between 1750 and 1850:

> ... Women in business as embroiderers were in a very different position from the sweated journeywomen who worked at home on the materials and patterns supplied to them. Sadlers, tailors and milliners were their customers as well as the general public, and for advertisement the more enterprising of them occasionally held exhibitions of all kinds of needlework, including the then popular pictures in silk and materials, for which there was a good demand in a day when needlework was so universal an occupation.[51]

Women's dressmaking and needlework trades suffered from the competition from slop-work perhaps more drastically than any other manufacturing trades. The needle was the staple employment for women in London – apart from domestic service – and remained so throughout the nineteenth century. Distressed needlewomen were a notorious problem of London life. Economic instability in the 1830s and 1840s accentuated the inherent seasonality of the work making the skilled needle-woman's living precarious. As slop-work increased, so did the numbers of out or home workers, and the embroideresses, sempstresses, tambourers, artificial flower makers, makers of fine and expensive shirts etc. could no longer rely on regular employ-ment, not even in the first-rate (fashionable West End) sectors of the trade. A saw-seller's wife who spoke to Mayhew, for instance, told him that she 'could earn 11s. and 12s.' a week when she 'got work as an embroideress', but 'at present she was at work braiding dresses for a dressmaker at 2½d. each. By hard work, and if she had not her baby to attend to, she could earn no more than 7½d. a day. As it was she did not earn 6d.'[52]

The 'Honourable' Trades

The second opportunity for women's skilled work lay in the 'honourable' sectors of the male trades. These women were very much in the minority; they were confined to a few specific skills; they were seldom, if ever, included in the trade societies; their wages were very much lower than the men's in the same trade and any encroachment on the traditional sexual division of labour within that trade was zealously resisted by the men. Women worked in the 'strong' men's trade in shoemaking, for instance, where the 'closer's work' which was 'light compared to that of maker' was principally in the hands of females, many of them wives and daughters of the workmen. Mayhew stressed that he was speaking of the workmen who 'in that part of the trade which I now treat of (the West End union trade) work at their own abodes . . .' He added that 'the most "skilled" portion of the labour is, however, almost always done by the man'.[53] In desk making, a branch of the woodworking trades, again our information comes from Mayhew;

The journeyman executes the ink range, or the portion devoted to holding ink bottles, pens, pencils, wafers, etc., and indeed every portion of the work in a desk, excepting the 'lining' or covering of the 'flaps', or sloping portion prepared for writing. This 'lining' is done by females, and their average payment is 15d. a dozen. Desks now are generally 'lap-dovetailed'; that is, the side edges of the wood are made to lap over the adjoining portion of the desk.[54]

Women in the numerous branches of tailoring were sometimes apprenticed. Women were also employed in some leather manufactories, sewing goat-skins into bags, or as sewers and folders in book-binding, and trimmers and liners in hatting. There might well have been 'honourable' sectors of other trades which employed women, but our knowledge of women's work is still incomplete.

Book-binding

Respectability and gentility were the qualities which set book-binding above domestic service or plain needlework as an occupation for girls in the nineteenth century. Commissioner Grainger approved of women's work in book-binding provided the employers complied with the demands of propriety. He found Messrs Collier & Son of Hatton Gardens, for example, a 'respectably conducted establishment', Mrs Mary Ann Golding, the forewoman, assuring him that her employer only kept on those who had been apprentices or learners as journeywomen 'if they conduct themselves properly'. The premises of Mr Horatio Riley of St John's Street on the other hand, were 'rather confined'. Nevertheless, the sexes were kept apart. 'The females work in a separate apartment', and there were 'orders that the boys should not go into this room. There is a discreet person as forewoman in the shop.' Unfortunately, there was only one privy for the whole establishment, but Mr Riley was 'convinced of the importance of having separate privies and (he intended) to make an alteration to effect that object'.[55]

Messrs Westley and Clark, of Shoemakers' Row, also received special credit for the scrupulous care they exercised in 'reference to the character and conduct of the females in their extensive establishment'. 'A single act of levity, or even a look indicative of a light disposition', according to one authority,[56] was 'sure to be followed by the dismissal of the party.' Fortunately for the girls employed in other book-binding houses, this same scrupulous regard was apparently not to be met with everywhere.

Messrs Westley and Clark was the largest book-binding house in London, and was included in George Dodd's examination of London factory trades, *Days at the Factory*. It employed 200 women in folding and sewing whose weekly earnings ranged from 10s. to 18s. A small number of girls were taken on as learners each year, paid no premium the first year, and became journeywomen after two years, aged fourteen. Most houses were much smaller, employing only six or so 'learners', and perhaps a few apprentices. The apprentices in the better houses were always boys, who were taught the entire trade for a premium (£25 at Messrs Collier) over a period of seven years. The 'learners' were girls who, according to Mr Collier himself, 'come for about nine months, paying a small premium of two guineas to remunerate the forewoman, who loses a good deal of time in instructing them'. In the lesser establishments it is difficult to distinguish between the apprentices and learners, both of whom served a nine-month or two-year term, and were often girls. Mr Collier went on to describe the lesser

parties in the trade who principally or entirely carry on their business by apprentices and learners; in some cases the former are boarded and lodged, and they receive very small wages during the apprenticeship, and in many cases are imperfectly taught the business; the learners, also, are only instructed in the more common part of the work. At the end of the term it often happens that the boys and young women are dismissed, because the master, doing the work at a low price, cannot afford to pay journeymen's wages . . . (He) has very frequently had occasion to dismiss women, who have been in such places of business, on account of incompetence. Has in some cases received a premium from parties who have been with small masters, and who have had again to work for some months without pay. Has had frequent complaints of the cruel way in which, in this respect, young women have been treated.[57]

Mr Collier was describing the 'dishonourable' section of the trade. One of the journeywomen at a second-rate house, Mr Cope's in St Martin's Lane, confirmed some of his claims.

Sarah Sweetman, eighteen years old.
Can read and write. Was formerly an apprentice for two years to learn the business; paid no premium; received 1s. 6d. a week; for the last three years has worked as a journeywoman. Mr Cope only executes a part of the business which belongs to the trade. There are some branches which he does not carry on. Apprentices here cannot learn all the branches; so that if they leave at the end of the term, they must go to some other house to learn the business thoroughly. In those houses where they teach all the business a premium is generally paid of 21 [£2] or 31.3s. [£3.3s.] and sometimes 51.5s. [£5.5s.] for six months; during which time they receive no wages.

Mr Cope's establishment was a second-rate house but not part of the slop trade, since he did not dismiss all his apprentices at the end of their term; most were employed afterwards as journey-women and received 'wages according to their skill'. 'With regular work from 9 a.m. till 8 p.m. they can generally earn 12s. a week', Sarah Sweetman explained. But she had not been taught all the business, and would find it difficult to obtain another situation. She concluded that,

a girl who pays a premium for six months and has no wages, and who is thoroughly taught the business, is better off than one who is not taught the whole of the branches. Those who have been thoroughly instructed, can generally command profitable employment, which the latter cannot. If witness had known when she was bound that she should not have learned all the business, she would not have come here. A considerable part of Mr Cope's business, as far as the females are concerned, is carried on by apprentices; Several have left after they have been here a short time, some of the parents thinking the work too hard.

The average day in both large and small establishments was about eleven or twelve hours, allowing one or one and a half hours' break for lunch and tea, some returned home for meals. During the 'busy times' the work is carried on till

10 p.m., 12, 2, 3 and 4 in the morning. Has often worked all night; has done this twice in one week, but only on one occasion. The apprentices generally go home at 8 p.m., and sometimes they stay till 9, 10 and 11; on which occasions they receive extra pay.

Several other witnesses confirmed Sarah Sweetman's evidence, and the intervention of parents was often mentioned. Unlike the dressmakers and milliners whose family and friends either lived out of town, or else were too poor to influence the terms of their children's employment, the parents of book-binders' apprentices probably worked in the trade themselves and knew whether or not their children were receiving an adequate training.

Hatting

'It is a fortunate circumstance' wrote George Dodd halfway through his *Day at a Bookbinder's*, 'considering the very limited

number of employments for females in this country, that there
are several departments of book-binding within the scope of their
ability.'[58] Hatting also offered 'reputable employment for females
in the middle and humble ranks'. Dodd gave an account of
Christy's, allegedly the largest hat factory in the world, which
occupied 'two extensive ranges of buildings on opposite sides of
Bermondsey Street, Southwark'. Just under two hundred
'females' were employed there in the early 1840s, and they earned
between 10s. and 18s. a week, mostly in the manufacture of
beaver hats which were fashionable at that time. Christy's was of
particular interest since it offered 'some valuable hints' on 'how
far female labour may be available in factories where the subdivision of employment is carried out on a complete scale'.

The degree of ingenuity required varies considerably, so as to give
scope for different degrees of talent. Among the processes by which a
beaver hat is produced, women and girls are employed in the following:— plucking the beaver skins; cropping off the fur; sorting various
kinds of wool; plucking and cutting rabbit's wool; shearing the Nap
of the blocked hat (in some cases); picking out defective fibres of fur;
and trimming. Other departments of the factory, unconnected with the
manufacture of beaver hats also give numerous employments to
females.

Mr Dodd did not specify the ages, class background etc., of the
women and girls, although he described the processes in which
they were employed in some detail. He concluded that 'Where a
uniform system of supervision and of kindness on the part of the
proprietors is acted on, no unfavourable effects are to be feared
from such an employment of females in a factory'. Indeed his
descriptions of the 'trimmers' underlines this point for his readers—

We enter a large square room, full of litter and bustle, and find fifty
or sixty young females employed in 'trimming' hats, that is, putting on
the lining, the leather, the binding, etc. Some are sitting at long tables
– some standing – others seated round a fire, with their work on their
laps; but all plying the industrious needle, and earning an honourable
subsistence.

Christy's, in the early 1840s, (like Westley & Clark in book-
binding) was exceptional among hatteries. It coexisted alongside

the workshops described by Mayhew in 1849 that were 'almost entirely confined to the Surrey side of the Thames, and until the last twenty years or thereabouts, was carried on chiefly in Bermondsey'. The 'tradesmen who supply the hatters with the materials of manufacture are still more thickly congregated in Bermondsey than elsewhere', and their numbers and variety imply that they were still in those years occupied in small separate workshop production, not combined under one roof as at Christy's. Women worked as hat binders, liners and trimmers; the subsidiary trades included hat lining makers, hat-trimming and buckle makers, as well as wool-staplers, hat-furriers, hat-curriers, hat block-makers, hat-druggists, hat-dyers, hat-bowstring makers, hat calico makers, hat box makers, hat-silk shag makers, and hat-brush makers. But Mayhew gives no account of women's work except in silk and velvet hats, which he claimed were 'now (1849) the great staple of the trade'.[59] No man was admitted to the 'fair' sector of hatting until he had served a seven-year apprenticeship, 'and no master, employing society men, can have whom he may choose "to put to the trade", and they must be regularly bound'. The number of apprentices was limited to two, whether the master had two or one hundred journeymen under his employ. Daughters of hatters were not formally 'bound' in this period; they probably received a similar form of training to the girls in book-binding. Hatters were generally married, Mayhew was told, and lived in the neighbourhood of the workshops. 'Some of the wives (of workmen in the "fair" sector) are employed as hat-binders and liners, but none,' Mayhew continues, 'work at slop work.'

Factory work

The division of labour between the sexes was successfully maintained when book-binding first entered the factory. But it was only much later in the century that the entire 'printing profession' was broken up into a score of different trades, and the subdivision of those trades into each of its detail processes, permitted the replacement of the skilled craftsman by the machine and/or 'cheap' labour. Then women and children moved into

work which previously had been monopolized by men, but only
into carefully demarcated work, modified by the male trade
societies.[60]

Hatting has a similar history. Christy's hat factory, like
Westley and Clark's book-bindery, combined under one roof
many processes in the manufacture of an article.

It may excite surprise, [George Dodd warned his readers] to hear
of saw-mills, and blacksmiths', turners', and carpenters' shops on the
premises of a hat maker; but this is only one among many instances
which might be adduced, in the economy of English manufactures, of
centralisation, combined with division of labour, within the walls of
one factory.[61]

But traditional skill differentials were maintained because the
labour process itself had not yet been transformed by the introduction of machinery. Fur-pulling for example, remained
women's work whether carried on at Christy's, or in the small
workshops described by Mayhew.

Factories like Westley and Clark's or Christy's, for all the
modernity which so impressed Dodd, were sophistications of the
division of labour characteristic of manufacture rather than of
modern industry. Every process in the manufacture of a hat was
centralized under one roof. But the replacement of skilled workmen by machinery was rare.

One such change may be detected from Dodd's account of
Christy's: women were in charge of the cutting and cropping
machines. Mayhew did not mention women in this work in his
account of small workshop production, so we may assume that
the innovation was the result of a mechanization of the work
process. Another isolated and striking example occurs in Dodd's
description of a rope and sailcloth factory in Limehouse.

Dodd first of all describes 'all which precedes the actual
weaving', which was 'effected in one large apartment; and a
remarkable apartment this is, both in reference to its general
appearance, and to the nature of the processes carried on therein'.
Here, women were employed on the quilling machines, work in
which they and children had always been employed even before it
was mechanized.

The quill-machines, . . . each of which is attended by one woman have a considerable number of quills arranged in a row, and made to rotate rapidly. In the act of rotation the quills draw off yarn gradually from reels on which it had previously been wound; and the women renew the quills and the reels as fast as the one are filled and the other emptied . . . The little quills in the quill-machine, rapidly revolving and feeding themselves with yarn, require but little care from the attendant, who can manage a whole machine full of them at one time.

The much more complicated process of preparing the yarns for the 'warp' of the weaver elicited the utmost admiration from Mr Dodd, but he does not specify whether the work was performed by women or not. Most significant, however, was the employment of women on the power-looms. Hand-loom weaving traditionally was men's work, but in every branch of the textile industry, women were replacing men, as machines were introduced and dispensed with the need for strength and skill. In Limehouse, for instance:

Forty of these, [power-looms] . . . are at work in the weaving room of the factory, and may from the noise they create, give a foretaste of the giant establishments at Manchester. The machine throws its own shuttle, moves its own assemblage of warp-threads, drives up the weft-threads as fast as they are thrown, and winds the woven canvas on a roller. One woman is able to manage two power-looms, to supply warp and weft, mend broken threads, and remove the finished material.

But even in sailcloth manufacture, industrialization was not complete. In this factory some men still operated hand-looms, and Dodd's account of that process contrasts strongly with the relative simplicity of the operation of the power-loom. Dodd marvelled at the

patience with which a man can sit for hours at a time throwing a shuttle alternately with his right hand and his left, moving a suspended bar alternately to and from him, and treading alternately on a lever with one or the other foot; and many have perhaps pondered how many movements of hand, arm, and foot must be made before a shilling can be earned.

Girls in the quilling factories in Spitalfields were among the highest-paid workers in the silk industry in the 1840s, where depression had reduced the hand-loom weaver's wage to 5s. 6d. in 1849. Their relative affluence was displayed in the 'bonnets with showy ribbons, the ear-drops, the red coral necklaces of four or five strings, the bracelets and other finery in which (they) appeared on Easter Monday at Greenwich Fair'.[62]

Lint scraping was also mechanized and operated by young girls who often came from the parish, and were paid 11s. to 14s. a week after apprenticeship for a twelve-hour day and one and a half hours for meals.

The attention of the Children's Commission was drawn to the trade by an 'opinion prevailing' that the children lost the use of their fingers and contracted consumption from the occupation. The witnesses were reluctant to offer such information, however.

An article in *Household Words* tells us that fifteen girls, fifty boys and eleven men were at work in the Lucifer manufactory in Finsbury in 1851. There is no account of the girls' work in the Finsbury factory, but at the lofty and spacious one in Bow, 'Swift-fingered maidens – aged from about twelve to twenty – can earn nine shillings a week, or even more; the slowest fingers earning about six', distributing the untipped tapers into frames.[63]

Topping and button-hole making in slop-work was generally done in the factory, but only because the employers feared their low wages would induce women to pawn the clothing if they were permitted to take them home. 'There is a large workshop called the factory, connected with each slop-shop emporium, and in some of them there are over two hundred hands at work' the author of 'Transfer Your Custom'[64] tells us.

Perhaps further examples of women's factory work tucked away in odd corners of the labour market would emerge in the course of research. But it is unlikely if the diligent Children's Commissioners didn't uncover them. The most important invention to affect women's work in London during the nineteenth century was the sewing machine. But it did not necessarily involve the transference of the clothing industries into factories, usually, on the contrary, it revolutionized the productivity of female waged work within the home. Indeed the effects of modern industry on the London trades in the nineteenth century were neither so uniform nor so *revolutionary* in terms of the sexual division of labour as many contemporaries, including Marx and Engels, had anticipated. Machinery and other changes in the production process were introduced piecemeal and distributed unevenly, and innovation was related as much to the supply flexibility and available skills of the labour market as to the technical requirements and possibilities within each trade.

Women's Unskilled and Casual Work

The problems of uncovering women's skilled work dwindle into insignificance once we move outside those carefully delineated domains into the vast uncharted world of unskilled and casual employment. Most women were casual workers in the sense that their employment was irregular, or seasonal, or both, and the boundaries between trades were indeterminate as women moved in and out of work according to their changing circumstances. Whether she lived alone, with a man, or with her family, whether she was widowed or abandoned, whether her husband drank, the number of children she bore, her age, all these things directly altered or interrupted a woman's working life to a much larger extent than they did a man's. This meant that there were few occupations a woman could enter and be sure of earning her living at it throughout her working life. It also meant that so much women's work tended to be the sort that was easy to pick up or put down – washing or mangling for instance, cleaning, folding, packing, stitching and sewing. It was for similar reasons that married women sought employment near their husband's work. The location of the man's trade determined the family home.[65]

A girl's working life might start very young – at five or six – helping her mother, minding a child, cleaning or sewing. An eight-year-old watercress seller had minded her aunt's baby when she was six. 'Before I had the baby,' she told Mayhew, 'I used to help mother, who was in the fur trade; and, if there was any slits in the fur, I'd sew them up. My mother learned me to needlework and knit when I was about five.'[66] Women continued working until illness or exhaustion prevented them.

Few London girls escaped a spell in domestic service. The

hierarchy of domestic servants from kitchen to ladies' maid in wealthy houses were often drawn from country estates, (like Rosa, Lady Dedlock's favourite in *Bleak House*). But servants of the tradesman and artisan classes came from among the London poor. Most working-class homes it seems, employed a young maid of all work, or a nursemaid, when both man and wife went *out* earning. The majority of children at Bethnal Green Market (held every Monday and Tuesday from 7 a.m. to 9 a.m.) were girls of seven and upwards who were hired by the week as nurses and servants mostly to weaver's families. Parish apprentices were similarly launched into 'industrial work'. Mr Fitch, vestry clerk in Southwark, informs us, for instance, that while the boys are apprenticed, 'principally to shoemakers and tailors, some to carvers and gilders, coachmakers, paper-makers, etc.' the girls 'go principally as servants, some as tambourers, straw-bonnet makers, etc; but in many of these cases they are principally occupied in household work'.[67] Other masters of workhouses or overseers gave similar accounts.

Going into service offered a girl food and shelter, as well as, if she was fortunate, the possibility of saving some money, which might later be used to set her sweetheart up in a trade. Loss of character, ill-health, inadequate clothing or marriage could all lose a girl her place. But washing, mangling, cleaning or scrubbing (floors, or pots and pans) was often taken up when necessary and available later on. The 1851 Census shows that the majority of general domestic servants were girls between fifteen and twenty-five, whereas the majority of charwomen, washerwomen, manglers and laundry keepers were middle aged and older. A woman who had worked as a mason in Ireland, for instance, 'cleaned and worked for a greengrocer, as they called him – he sold coals more than anything' when she came to England. But her daughter went into service till the fever forced her to pawn everything and left her too 'shabby' to find a place.[68]

The infinite gradations within domestic work were inform-ally measured by skill and respectability as well as income. A woman could earn 1/3d. to 2s. a day washing and charring. But as with most women's trades work was seldom regular, especi-ally in years of economic depression. A sixteen-year-old coster boy, brought up by his mother, told Mayhew that 'Mother used to be up and out very early washing in families – anything for a living. She was a good mother to us. We was left at home with the key of the room and some bread and butter for dinner,' but he went on – 'Afore she got into work – and it was a goodish long time – we was shocking hard up, and she pawned nigh everything.'[69] Washing and charring were both very hard physical work. Everything had to be done by hand and the working day was very long, from dawn till ten or eleven at night sometimes. The mother of an orphan street-seller 'took a cold at the washing and it went to her chest'; similarly, the widow of a sawyer told Mayhew that she took to washing and charring until 'My health broke six years ago, and I couldn't do hard work in washing, and I took to trotter-selling because one of my neighbours was that way, and told me how to go about it.' Laundresses and washerwomen were continually reprimanded, (as were shoe-makers), by conscientious city missionaries for Sabbath-breaking. But then a superintendent conceded that it was an occupation 'of so laborious a character, that the Sabbath is, in common with other days generally devoted to that kind of labour'.[70] Quite often a washerwoman's husband helped her with the mangling. The wife of a dock labourer, for instance, 'has a place she goes to work at. She has 3s. a week for washing, for charring, and for mangling: the party my wife works for has a mangle, and I go sometimes to help; for if she has got 6d. worth of washing to do at home then I go to turn the mangle for an hour instead of her – she's not strong enough.'[71] The income was much higher if the mangle belonged to the woman. An old watercress seller's wife earned 3s. a day taking 'in a little washing, and (keeping) a mangle. When I'm at home I turn the mangle for her', he told Mayhew.

A small laundry could be quite lucrative, and often employed several washing women. One street-seller was leaving the streets, she told Mayhew, because

I have an aunt, a laundress, because she was mother's sister, and I always helped her, and she taught me laundressing. I work for her three and sometimes four days a week now, because she's lost her daughter Ann, and I'm known as a good ironer. Another laundress will employ me next week, so I'm dropping the streets, as I can do far better.[72]

A 'respectable' laundress was paid 'about four shillings per dozen shirts, and one shilling per dozen small articles'. She pays her washing women 'from two shillings to two shillings and sixpence per day and her cronies from two shillings and sixpence to three shillings per day'.[73] Ironing, which was very skilled work, requiring careful handling of delicate materials and intricate fashions, was usually the highest paid in laundry work, receiving perhaps 15s. per week in these years.

The shopkeeping classes were as miscellaneous as those employed in domestic labour. Shopkeeping had always been women's work. The wives of small craftsmen or tradesmen traditionally handled the retail and financial side of the workshop. The Census lists women greengrocers, bakers, confectioners, dealers in vegetable foods, licensed victuallers, as well as a few grocers, tobacconists, drapers and stationers. There were also women dealers in timber, carriage building, etc., probably widows and relatively well off. A small general shop, like laundry work, was perfectly acceptable employment for the wife of a skilled workman. The most typical was the general, or chandler's store similar to the one patronized by a street sweeping gang in the Strand, which dealt in 'what we wants – tea and butter, or sugar, or broom – anythink we wants'.[74]

Street-selling was distinguished from shopkeeping by the fact that the goods were taken to the people, rather than the people seeking out the goods. It was an occupation that many women avoided unless they were born to it, because it was a hard life, and had the taint of poverty. Street-sellers eked out a precarious living, dependent on the spending power of the working classes. Work started with the early morning markets, and the street-seller sat at her pitch or walked the streets all day in all weathers.

Mayhew divides street-sellers into Irish women and English women. The latter he subdivided into four groups: firstly, the wives of street-sellers; secondly, mechanics' or labourers' wives who go out (while their husbands are at work) as a means of helping the family income; thirdly, widows of former street-sellers; and fourthly, single women. There was a sexual division of labour in street-selling too – women were principally engaged in selling fish (especially shrimps, sprats and oysters), fruit, vegetables (mainly sold by widows), and firescreens, ornaments, laces, millinery, artificial flowers, but-flowers, boots and stay-laces, or small wares: wash-leathers, towels, burnt linen, combs, bonnets, pin cushions, tea, coffee, rice-milk, curds and whey; also dolls, nuts, mats, twigs, anything cheap and small.[75] Stock was either bought from markets, swag-shops or other street-sellers, or the women made it at home. There were women street-sellers of crockery and glassware, too. They were called 'bart-erers' and usually worked in partnership with their husbands. The serviceableness of a woman helpmate in 'swopping', or bartering was great, according to one of the men of that trade.

The costermongers formed a distinct and irreligious commun-ity within London life, entertaining as they did 'the most im-perfect idea of the sanctity of marriage', and allowing their children to grow up with 'their only notions of wrong . . . formed by what the policeman will permit them to do'. Mayhew tells us that at about seven years of age the girls first go into the streets to sell.

A shallow basket is given to them, with about two shillings for stock money, and they hawk, according to the time of year, either oranges, apples, or violets; some begin their street education with the sale of water-cresses. The money earned by this means is strictly given to the parents . . .

Between four and five in the morning they have to leave home for the markets, and sell in the streets until about nine . . . they generally remain in the streets until about ten o'clock at night; many having done nothing during all that time but one meal of bread and butter and coffee, to enable them to support the fatigue of walking from street to street with the heavy basket on their heads. In the course of a day, some girls eat as much as a pound of bread, and very seldom get any meat, unless it be on a Sunday.

A coster-girl's courtship was usually short because 'the life is such a hard one', a girl explained to Mayhew, 'a girl is ready to get rid of a *little* of the labour at any price'.

They court for a time, going to raffles and 'gaffs' together, and then the affair is arranged. The girl tells her parents 'she's going to keep company with so-and-so', packs up what things she has, and goes at once without a word of remonstrance from either father or mother. A furnished room at about 4s. a week is taken, and the young couple begin life. The lad goes out as usual with his barrow, and the girl goes out with her basket often working harder for her lover than she had done for her parents.[76]

Costermongering proper was mainly a hereditary trade, but the wives of labourers went out selling, so did the children of the poor. The children sold oranges and water-cress – anything needing only a few pennies outlay. Old women resorted to street-selling to avoid the workhouse. Parishes often provided them with money or a small stock (for example bootlaces from the haberdashery swag-shops) to enable them to scrape a livelihood, relatives and friends donated the same. An old lady in the East End who had broken her hip when washing and walking in her pattens (clogs) had a basket of 'tapes, cottons, combs, braces, nutmeg-graters, and shaving glasses, with which she strove to keep her old dying husband from the workhouse'. Her husband was very sick now, but he 'used to go on errands' she told Mayhew, 'and buy my little things for me, on account of my being lame. We assisted one another you see'.[77]

Apart from domestic service, household work and the retail trades, women worked in manufacture. Mayhew's sensitive inquiries into 'poverty, low wages, and casual labour, its causes and consequences' in the 1840s uncovered the hitherto unrecognized extent of this work. He showed that the expansion of slop-work probably increased women's participation in the actual work-process of some trades – notably shoemaking, cabinet-making and tailoring – especially with the increasing phenomenon of the small master.[78] The home of a woodworker, tailor, or shoemaker was transformed into a workshop and the entire family was employed in the production of the article. Woodworkers sold on spec to slaughter-houses, upholsterers, linen-drapers, or warehouses; tailors, other clothing workers, and shoemakers worked on order from the shops and showrooms in City and East End. Family work in these circumstances often became the last ditch stand of the worker pitched from the 'honourable' sector of his trade onto the casual labour market. The elderly Spitalfields garret master who made the tea caddies which he hawked to the slaughter-houses told Mayhew, 'My wife and family help me or I couldn't live. I have only one daughter now at home, and she and my wife line the work-boxes as you see.'[79] Tailors' wives fetched and carried the goods to and from the slop-seller; the wives of woodworkers went hawking. Sometimes the small master employed other workers besides his family:

In a small back room, about eight feet square, we found no fewer than seven workmen, with their coats and shoes off, seated cross-legged on the floor, busy stitching the different parts of different garments. The floor was strewn with sleeve-boards, irons, and snips of various coloured cloths. In one corner of the room was a turn-up bedstead, with the washed out chintz curtains drawn partly in front of it. Across a line which ran from one side of the apartment to the other were thrown coats, jackets, and cravats of the workmen. Inside the rusty grate was a hat, and on one of the hobs rested a pair of cloth boots; while leaning against the bars in front there stood a sack full of cuttings. Beside the workmen on the floor sat two good-looking girls – one cross-legged like the men – engaged in tailoring.[80]

The multiplication of small masters was a response to the opening up of cheap mass markets, and to economic hardship caused by the perilous fluctuations of the trade cycle. Both phenomena were integral to the Industrial Revolution. But family work, or small workshop production was not always the grinding struggle that it became in the worst years of economic recession. Piece-rates and work conditions varied to some extent with the skill and quality of the workmanship, and these were not entirely exclusive to the 'honourable' trades, in spite of the better bargaining position of workers in those sectors. Sometimes, the distinction between 'honourable' and 'dishonourable' simply described the division between the fashionable West End trade, and the city or East End warehouses. In toy-making for instance, the principal division was between those who made for the rich and those who made for the poor. And although the Spitalfields silk industry was suffering severely, as it always had done, from

economic fluctuations in these years, pockets of family workers
remained relatively securely employed.

When we speak of families [William Bresson told Commissioner
Hickson in 1840], we must remember that in a family, when the trade
is in a good state, there is invariably more than one loom employed.
One man at a loom earns, perhaps, but 10s. in a week, but when able
to employ the labour of his wife, children, or apprentices, perhaps
three looms, and often four, are kept going, so that I cannot say. I
know many families who, when in full work, earn, or might earn,
20s. per week. My son-in-law, for instance, lives with me in the house,
and earns about 18s. This would be a poor sum for his family to live
upon; but then his wife, my daughter, is very quick at the loom, and
earns as much, or rather more, than he does himself.[81]

In spite of its decline in this period there were few trades, as
William Bresson explained, 'in which a woman is able to earn as
much as my daughter gets by working at the loom; although I
must say', he added, 'it is a sort of slavery for a woman'.

The clothing trades offered most employment to women.
Women worked in every branch of tailoring (outside the honourable sector) – on their own account as home-workers, or female
sweaters, or with their husbands. Coats, waistcoats, vests, trousers and juvenile suits were in turn divided into different branches
according to the section of the garment as well as to material,
style, fit and quality, and payment was by the piece. The poorest
slop-worker always had to find her own trimmings, thread,
candles and coal. An old lady when employed 'at all kinds of
work excepting the shirts' told Mayhew

I cannot earn more than 4s. 6d. to 5s. per week – let me sit from eight
in the morning till ten every night; and out of that I shall have to pay
1s. 6d. for trimmings, and 6d. candles every week; so that altogether
I earn about 3s. in the six days. But I don't earn that for there's the
firing that you must have to press the work, and that will be 9d. a week,
for you'll have to use half a hundred weight of coals. So that my clear
earnings are a little bit more than 2s., say 2s. 3d. to 2s. 6d. every week.[82]

Trousers were her best paid work, they brought in 4s. 5d. a
week clear, and shirt making was the worst, leaving only 2s. 3d.
a week clear.

There were a multitude of skills concealed in the bald categories – needlewomen, seamstresses, or dressmaker. A pamphleteer wrote in the 1850s 'There is no style of cutting and fitting with which the intelligent seamstress is not perfectly well acquainted and must use her scissors in trimming and fitting.'[83] The Census (1851) lists over 43,000 dressmakers and milliners of whom the majority were outworkers. Those who received their work direct from the West End fashionable houses ('defined as those that put out the skirts') were mostly between twenty and thirty and lived in St Martins in the Fields, the Strand or St Giles, near by the houses. 'I know of no old woman who is a day worker in the superior trade.' A young day worker told Mayhew, 'You must be quick and have good sight.'[84] Others, working for the less exalted dressmaking establishments, or for the slop-trade, lived all over London (especially in the East End); they were all ages but were not necessarily paid lower wages.

All women's needle-work was very low paid. The West End out-worker was as exploited by the fashionable houses, as the East End labourer's wife was, by the showroom or warehouse – sometimes more so. Shirtmaking for the wholesale warehouses of the Minories was perhaps the least remunerative of the sewing trades, partly because the prices were undercut by the prisons, workhouses, and schools which produced shirts at starvation prices.[85] But government contract workers, who made the clothes for the army, navy, police, railway, customs and post office servants were even worse off. We learn from a maker of soldiers' trousers ('the Foot Guards principally'), that

The general class of people who work at it are old persons who have seen better days, and have nothing left but their needle to keep them and who *won't* apply for relief – their pride won't let them – their feelings object to it – they have a dread of becoming troublesome. The other parties are wives of labourers and those who leave off shirt-making to come to this. There are many widows with young children, and they give them the seams to do, and so manage to prolong life, because they're afeared to die, and too honest to steal. The pressing part, which is half the work, is not fit for any female to do. I don't know but very few young girls – they're most of them women with families as I've seen – poor, struggling widows a many of 'em.[86]

More research might lift the clouds of almost unmitigated destitution which appears to have been the fate of practically all needlewomen in the 1830s and 1840s, indeed throughout the nineteenth century. Is it over-optimistic to imagine that some sewing performed at home, or in the small workshops scattered throughout the East and West Ends of London (as well as most of the suburbs), was less exhausting and demoralizing than the general image that the 'distressed needlewomen' evokes? Mrs Rowlandson's evidence for instance, to the Children's Employment Commission in 1841, while it exposes child labour, low pay, and long hours, reveals the different strata within the shirtmaking industry, and presents a slightly more dignified if severe aspect to some of the work.

No. 758. 19 July, 1841. Mrs Rowlandson

Executes orders for Messrs Silver and Co. Employs 50 women who make shirts, blouses, caps, collars, etc. These women work at their own houses, and many of them employ 2 or 3 hands each, some of whom are children. All the plain parts can be done by girls of 8 or 9, this is the usual age at which they begin. The regular hours are considered to be from 8 to 8; one hour and a half being allowed for dinner and tea. If an order requires it they work longer, but the children are never kept more than an hour, which is paid as overtime. Girls begin with 1s., in a week or so they have 1s. 6d., and increase to 2s. or 2s. 6d. as they improve. A good adult hand, if she has good work, can earn from 10s. to 12s. Employs at this time three sisters, who can earn as much if they have regular work, which is not always the case. For making the best shirts she pays 1s. 8d. to 1s. 10d. each, having herself 2d. to 4d. for cutting out, taking in to the warehouse, etc. Some mistresses charge as much as 6d. and 8d. for giving out the work; some of the workwomen have complained of this; it has lowered the wages very much.[87]

But Messrs Silver was one of the oldest warehouses in the City, and was conducted along marginally more reputable lines than many of the flash showrooms.

The clothing trades were the most overcrowded, but many others employed women home-workers, making boxes, brushes, brooms, envelopes, matches, mats, paper bags, silk stockings, umbrellas and sacks, engaged in fur pulling or card folding. Wages were paid by the piece, and work was irregular so that even the quickest hands were often very poor if there was no adult male wage-earner in the family.

Women with a little capital set up as small mistresses in other than needlework trades, in book-folding and binding for instance, and matchbox making. A small capital was necessary either to offer as security to the warehouse which gave out the work, or to get started on one's own. The most notorious method of raising capital was by taking on parish apprentices who paid a £5 premium.

*

I have distinguished between two principal areas of women's unskilled work – in the retail/service, and the manufacturing sectors of the London economy. But these were not strictly demarcated. Women moved easily from one to the other when their circumstances changed. There was the mother of the coster girl whose father 'used to do odd jobs with the gas pipes in the streets', who . . . 'when father's work got slack, if she had no employment charring, she'd say, "Now I'll go and buy a bushel of apples," and then she'd turn out and get a penny that way'.[88] There were the street milliners who 'have been ladies' maids, working milliners, and dressmakers, the wives of mechanics who have been driven to the streets, and who add to the means of the family by conducting a street-trade themselves, with a sprinkling from other classes'.[89] There was the ex-servant girl, married to a smith, who had once owned a house in the Commercial Road where they had let out lodgings. Misfortune reduced her to making 'a few women's plain morning-caps for servants', which she sold to a shopkeeper until that outlet dried up and she sold them herself at the New Cut.[90] There were the women who turned child minding for neighbours into a small Dame School. These received short shrift from the tidy minds of Benthamite educators. Fourteen in Bethnal Green were insultingly described by a British Schools Inspector thus:

They are in general good for nothing. A broken down mechanic's wife, fit for nothing but the wash-tub, or perhaps as a last resource to keep her from the Poor-house, sets up a dame school and gets a few children about her, who learn scarcely anything.[91]

The inherent seasonality of the London trades accentuated the casual nature of most women's employments. But irregularity was not always oppressive; many London women workers took off in the summer months, for instance, to the market gardens and hop fields of Kent and Surrey. This unfettered anarchy of the female labour market gave women's work a sort of pre-industrial character strangely at odds in a self-consciously industrial age. Even Mayhew seemed to chastize casual workers for simply being casual:

> During the summer and the fine months of the spring and autumn, there are I am assured, one third of the London street sellers – male and female – 'tramping' the country . . .
> A large proportion go off to work in market-gardens, in the gathering of peas, beans, and the several fruits; in weeding, in hay-making, in the corn-harvest (when they will endeavour to obtain leave to glean if they are unemployed more profitably), and afterwards in the hopping. The women, however, thus seeking change of employment, are the ruder street-sellers, those who merely buy oranges at 4d. to sell at 6d., and who do not meddle with any calling mixed up with the necessity of skill in selection, or address in recommending. Of this half-vagrant class, many are not street-sellers usually, but are half prostitutes and half thieves, not unfrequently drinking all their earnings, while of the habitual female street-sellers, I do not think that drunkenness is now a very prevalent vice.[92]

Many women's employments merged almost imperceptibly into the many partial and residual forms of work which were the mark of poverty or even destitution. The dividing line as far as it existed, was determined not so much by the demands of the economy as by sickness, accidents, old age or the death of a husband or lover. The most frequent visitors to the night refuge in Playhouse-yard, Cripplegate, for instance, were 'needlewomen, servants, charwomen, gardenwomen, sellers of laces in the street and occasionally a beggar woman'.[93] Into this amorphous residuum were tossed all those occupations which respectable Victorians identified with 'vagrancy' and 'vice' – slop-workers, hawkers, trampers, street-sweepers, mudlarks, the inmates of lodging houses, the pickpockets who slept in the baskets and offal around Covent Garden. 'We can take nearly a hundred of them', a Covent Garden policeman told a parliamentary committee in 1828, 'particularly at the time the oranges are about. They come there picking up the bits of oranges, both boys and girls, and there are prostitutes at eleven, twelve and thirteen years of age.'[94]

Prostitution or the workhouse were immanent and real threats to the unsupported woman without a trade in periods of economic distress, and prostitution was often the chosen, desperate alternative to the workhouse. There is no space here to sketch the multifarious wealth of ingenious and pathetic forms of clinging to a livelihood, nor to trace the twists of fortune that regularly deposited the women in these twilight regions of the labour market. Let one 'needlewoman' rescued for posterity by Henry Mayhew speak for all of them.

I am a tailoress, and I was brought to ruin by the foreman of the work, by whom I had a child. Whilst I could make an appearance I had to work, but as soon as I was unable to do so I lost it. I had an afflicted mother to support . . . I went on so for some months and we were half starved . . . I could only earn from 5s. to 6s. a week to support three of us, and out of that I had 1s. 6d. to pay for rent, and the trimmings to buy which cost me 1s. a week full. I went on till I could go on no longer, and we were turned out into the street because we could not pay the rent – me and my child; but a friend took my mother . . . At last of all I met a young man, a tailor, and he offered to get me work for his own base purposes. I worked for him . . . till I was in the family way again. I worked till I was within two months of my confinement. I had 1s. a day and I took a wretched kitchen at 1s. a week, and 2s. I had to pay to have child minded when I went to work. My mother went into the house, but I took her out again, she was so wretched and she thought she could mind the child. In this condition we were all starving together . . . (my mother) died through a horror of going into the workhouse. I was without a home. I worked till I was within two months of my confinement, and then I walked the streets for six weeks, with my child in my arms.

At last I went into Wapping Union . . . [where both children died in the workhouse].

I came out again and went into a situation. I remained in that situation fourteen months, when I was offered some work by a friend, and I have been at that work ever since. I have a hard living, and I earn from 4s. 6d. to 5s. a week. My children and mother are both dead.

The tailor never did anything for me. I worked for him and had 1s. a day ... From seven in the morning till one or two o'clock I work at making waistcoats, and coats. I have 5d. a piece for double breasted waistcoats and coats, and 10d. and 11d. a piece for slop coats. I can assure you I can't get clothes or things to keep me in health. I never resorted to the streets since I had the second child.

Postscript

It seems premature to 'conclude' on the basis of research that remains preliminary. Nevertheless, this outline of women's work in London does highlight some neglected aspects of the 'industrial revolution' – in particular, the effect of that process on the sexual division of labour.

The industrial history of London in the nineteenth century demonstrates the strength of Marx's dictum that the capitalist mode of production revolutionizes the character of every manufacturing industry, whether or not modern industry is introduced. Machinery and the factory system were neither as universal nor as immediate in their application, as many had predicted in the 1830s and 1840s. Industrial transformation in London was characteristically expressed in the slop and sweated trades which resisted the factory throughout the nineteenth century, founded as they were on a minute division of labour and having at hand a plentiful supply of cheap manual labour. Women formed the basis of this labour supply. But women's position as wage workers extended beyond the manufacturing industries. Demand for female labour in the service and retail trades ebbed and flowed with the fluctuations of the trade cycle, and so – outside social production – did prostitutes, thieves and other 'fallen women'. Needlewomen and other home workers, small mistresses and their apprentices, charwomen and maids of all work, fit uneasily into the conventional image of 'the working class', but these were the expanding areas of the female labour market in nineteenth-century London; and in none of these trades and occupations were women's wages ever high enough to secure for them and their children economic independence from men.

Throughout the nineteenth and twentieth centuries, amid all the technical changes within trades as well as the industrial transformation of London as a whole, a survey of women's work reveals the tenacity of the sexual division of labour – a division sustained by ideology not biology, an ideology whose material manifestation is embodied and reproduced within the family and then transferred from the family into social production. As technical innovation toppled or abolished old skills, new ones replaced them, creating yet another male-dominated hierarchy of labour powers in trade after trade. It is the consistency of this articulation of the capitalist mode of production through a patriarchal family structure – even at the most volatile moments of industrial upheaval – which must form a central object of feminist historical research.

3

Women and Nineteenth-Century Radical Politics: A Lost Dimension

DOROTHY THOMPSON

Historians of the women's emancipation movement have observed the considerable gulf that existed between the aspirations of the middle-class emancipators and those of women lower down in the social scale in Victorian society. One of the many hypocrisies of Victorian conservative thought was its typification of woman as a frail, delicate and decorative creature, and its simultaneous tolerance of, and indeed dependence on, the exploitation of vast numbers of women in every kind of arduous and degrading work, from coal-mining to prostitution. Such women, labourers and servants, had no need to fight for the right to work – society would not have survived long had they been prevented from working. Their work was low in the scale of social recognition and of payment, and stable organizations to improve or protect their standards of pay and conditions were not organized until near the end of the nineteenth century. Such changes as were made by law in their conditions of work were the result of radical or humanitarian campaigns rather than of the organizations of the women themselves; these campaigns were concerned as much with the moral welfare of women operatives and with the stability of the working-class family as with the improvement of the status of women as workers.

The expansion of British manufactures and the rapid industrialization of the late eighteenth and early nineteenth centuries did not mean the introduction of women into manufacturing industry. They were already an essential part of the labour force in pre-mechanized industry. What did change in some key industries, however, was the location of work; the arrival of the independent factory worker, woman or child, working away from home, but returning to her home and still responsible to it and dependent on it, was new, certainly on the scale in which it existed in the textile manufacturing districts by the early 1830s. It is possible to exaggerate the reality of the 'independence' of women in economic terms – the wages they were paid were reckoned as a contribution to a family wage rather than as the support of an independent worker.[1] Nevertheless, 'public' work alongside other members of her own sex, and a regular wage, paid to her, even if legally the property of her husband, might have been expected to produce a more active awareness among working-class women of trade and political questions and of public matters generally. The purpose of this paper is to show the extent to which women did take part in the early radical movement. The period is one in which working-class radicalism combined traditional forms of action – mass demonstrations, processions, open political activities involving whole families and whole communities, together with early versions of the more sophisticated organizational forms which were to be the pattern of later nineteenth-century politics.

Chartism was the culmination of fifty years of political and industrial activity among the British working people. In those years the manufacturing districts responded to the changes brought about by the rapid alterations in the pace and patterns of work in various ways, some defensive, some active and assertive. A long series of strikes and turn-outs in the main manufacturing trades – wool and linen weaving, wool combing, tailoring, shoemaking – resulted in the defeat of the strikers and the speeding-up of mechanization. The retention of old work-patterns, customs, and methods of payment were obviously not to be achieved by action within individual trades. The working people turned therefore to political action or general unionism, seeking a more general defence of wage levels and some degree of political control over the pace of mechanization. In these years political and industrial issues can rarely be separated. Faced with new industrial techniques, the workers sought a defence against the redundancy of men skilled in the old techniques and the control of the use of women's and children's labour to replace that of men in the new factories. In the search for alternatives to the uncontrolled introduction of machinery, a number of choices were presented. For some, the arguments of Owenites and other radical and socialist thinkers suggested ways in which the new machines could be a blessing and not a threat. Other radical alternatives agreed in proposing a different organization of industry, with a more equal distribution of the new wealth which was being created, and the use of some of it for the education of children, the care of the sick and aged. They argued for a better way of life for the workers in the industries as well as for the owners and traders.

The spectrum of radical thought, by the 1830s, stretched from a generally defensive stance, in which the values of the older domestic–industry communities were upheld – the supervision by the parents of their children's upbringing and training, the status of the man as the head of the family and the main wage-earner, the value of the old unmechanized skills, through more aggressive demands for the right to organize to protect wages and working conditions, and for access to the political system by means of the suffrage, to the total rejection of private-enterprise industrial capitalism in favour of a more rational organization of industry which should eschew competition in favour of co-operation. Large-scale industrial production was still a minute sector of the total of productive industry, and the possibility of taming and controlling it was not at this stage seen by many as a total impossibility.

In 1832 the Reform Bill admitted the middle classes to the franchise. The old, rigid and irrational system of representation gave way, apparently under pressure, but without an armed uprising, to a system of representation which was uniform throughout the country, and which made a place in the political world for the non-landed property-owners. The working classes in London and the provinces had formed a part of the pressure which had brought about the reform. When it became clear that the new interests were ensuring both the finality of the reform settlement and the statutory reinforcement of the middle-class demands for the more effective disciplining of labour, exemplified in the Poor Law Amendment Act and in the series of anti-trade

union cases in the courts, the response from the working class
was one of fear of an outright attack by the authorities on working-class institutions and standards, combined with a positive
and hopeful resurgence of political activity aimed at the extension
of the franchise. Chartism, for all the strongly defensive element
which it contained, was basically an optimistic movement. The
Chartists and their followers really believed that they would
achieve the vote, and that the achievement would be followed by
a far greater attention on the part of the authorities to the needs
of the labouring people; they believed in the possibility of major
changes in the structure of power and authority in British society
which would result in a more egalitarian and humane system. In
that alternative system, women would play a more equal part than
they played in contemporary society.

That this optimism existed can be amply demonstrated, and
the story of women's part in Chartism needs to be told to emphasize this. What is more difficult to understand, however, is why
this element disappeared from radical thought and action some
time in the 1840s. Working-class women seem to have retreated
into the home at some time around, or a little before the middle
of the century. Up until that time there is evidence of their active
participation in the politics of the working communities.

The Reform agitation which was renewed after the end of the
Napoleonic Wars took on a mass character in some of the manufacturing districts, in particular among the cotton workers of
Lancashire. In his autobiography Samuel Bamford has left a
vivid description of the experience of one local leader in these
years. He claims personal responsibility for the formal admission
of women into the councils of the reformers.

At one of these meetings which took place at Lydgate, in Saddle-
worth, . . . I, in the course of an address, insisted on the right, and the
propriety also, of females who were present at such assemblages,
voting by show of hands, for, or against the resolutions. This was a
new idea; and the women who attended numerously on that bleak
ridge, were mightily pleased with it, – and the men being nothing
dissentient when the resolution was put, the women held up their
hands, amid much laughter; and ever from that time women voted at
radical meetings . . .[2]

Whatever the extent of Bamford's personal responsibility for the phenomenon, there is no doubt that the reform movement included many women, and that female political unions, with their own committees and officers were formed. When the reformers from the weaving communities formed their columns and marched to Manchester to take part in the greatest demonstration yet held for Parliamentary reform, at St Peters Fields on 16 August 1819, many women took part. Bamford's Middleton contingent set off, with 'At our head a hundred or two of women, mostly young wives, and mine own was amongst them. A hundred or two of our handsomest girls – sweethearts to the lads who were with us – danced to the music or sang snatches of popular songs . . .'[3]

Bamford includes, together with his own vivid account of the events of that day, the account remembered by his wife who had been separated from him in the immense crowd. Sixty-five years later when the radicals of Failsworth organized a demonstration against the House of Lords at the time of the Third Reform Bill, they took with them on the demonstration a group of ten old radicals, all of whom had been present at the Peterloo massacre, taking with them the banner which they had carried in 1819. Four of the ten were women.[4]

The women in the manufacturing districts were new to politics, as, too, were many of the men. But, like the men, many had experience of other forms of protest. There is ample evidence of women's participation in food riots and other demonstrations in the eighteenth and early nineteenth centuries. Southey recorded the great ferocity of the Worcester glovemakers.

Three or four years ago the English ladies chose to wear long silken gloves; the demand for leathern ones immediately ceased, and the women whose business it was to make them were thrown out of employ. This was the case of many hundreds here in Worcester. In such cases, men commonly complain and submit; but women are more disposed to be mutinous; they stand less in fear of law, partly from ignorance, partly because they presume upon the privilege of their sex, and therefore in all public tumults they are foremost in violence and ferocity. Upon this occasion they carried their point within their own territories; it was dangerous to appear in silken gloves in the streets of this city; and one lady who foolishly or ignorantly ventured to walk abroad here in this forbidden fashion, is said to have been seized by the women and whipped.[5]

At about the same time 'Lady Ludd' was leading a demonstration in Nottingham against a baker who had put up the price of his flour by twopence a stone:

> Several women in Turn-calf alley [stuck] a half-penny loaf on top of a fishing rod, after having raddled it over and tied a piece of black crepe around it, to give it the appearance of bleeding famine decked in sack-cloth. With this, and by the aid of three hand-bells, two born by women and one by a boy, a considerable crowd of women, girls and boys soon collected together.[6]

At a less spontaneous level of activity, there are numerous examples of female friendly societies during the very early years of the nineteenth century. These provided sick and burial benefits, and also must have served as social organizations. Many had rules insisting on sober and decent behaviour, including in at least one case sanctions against any member having irregular sexual relations with the husband of a fellow-member. Little is known in detail about these societies, or about the extent to which they took on functions related to trade union activities in the periods of the illegality of the unions, as many men's societies seem to have done. But they were clearly organized and run by women, and not only unmarried women. There were also female lodges of many of the male friendly societies, Rechabites, Druids, Oddfellows and so on.[7]

In the early trade unions the women's part varied from trade to trade. In most trades the problems involved in the much lower pay rates accorded to women's work made their regular co-operation with the men difficult, although amongst the weavers there appears to have been equality of rates (which were of course piece-rates) and membership of the union was open to both sexes. When James Burland attended a meeting of striking Barnsley linen weavers in 1829, and wanted information about one of the speakers, he turned to his neighbour, 'a tall, raw-boned masculine-looking old woman with a pipe in her mouth' to ask about the speaker and the strike.[8] In 1832 the *Leeds Mercury* reported that

The card-setters in the neighbourhood of Scholes and Hightown, chiefly women, held a meeting to the number of 1,500, at Peep Green, at which it was determined not to set any more cards at less than a halfpenny a thousand.

together with the presumably tongue-in-cheek comment that

Alarmists may view these indications of female independence as more menacing to established institutions than the 'education of the lower orders'.[9]

When in the summer of 1834 the radical and trade union movements erupted into the short-lived Grand National Consolidated Trades Union, the women were present in the lodges of Operative Bonnet Makers, Female Tailors, and simply of Women of Great Britain and Ireland.[10]

Women, then, played an important part in the work processes and in the social and public activities of the community. As the people turned towards more political forms of action in the 1830s men and women took part together in these actions. The illegal unstamped papers of the campaign against the newspaper taxes in the early thirties were hawked around the country by women as well as men. When Brady of Sheffield was returning home after serving a term of imprisonment for selling the *Poor Man's Guardian*, he was met and escorted through Barnsley by the local radicals carrying lanterns and accompanied by a band of music. Brady was, as one account stated, 'the hero of the hour. But no less was Mrs Lingard, the heroine, for she was present with an armful of unstamped papers which she cried publicly for sale, and for which, we need hardly say, she did not lack customers.'[11] Mrs Lingard was the wife of a radical Barnsley shoemaker turned newsagent, Joseph Lingard, and the mother of Thomas, later to be a leader among the Barnsley Chartists. The Lingards are an example, of which there are many, of a radical family in which both sexes and more than one generation took part in the local leadership. In Leeds in the same period Alice Mann was a leading figure in the publication, sale and distribution of unstamped journals.[12]

During the riots, disturbances and demonstrations of the 1830s the presence of women in the crowds was remarked by all observers. In the movement against the New Poor Law of 1834, for example, which swept through the manufacturing districts of the north in 1837, women and girls were to the fore, as they were in the public demonstrations of the short-time committees.[13] Writing from Yorkshire in 1838, Lawrence Pitkeithly, a leader of the short-time and anti-Poor-Law movements, urged his fellow radical James Broyan of Nottingham:

I hope you will get your women to work and mob all the bastile blackguards who are in or who come to your Town – persevere and you must conquer, be tame and there is nothing but Bastiles for you . . .[14]

The presence of women, almost as shock troops in these violent demonstrations is certainly well established at least up to 1842, when F. H. Grundy, describing his experience of the crowd during the Plug Riots, referred to one confrontation between the tired marchers and the troops, 'all were hungry, evening was coming on; and although a few stones were thrown, chiefly *of course*, by women, when the chief magistrate came forward to read the Riot Act, the mob dispersed for that time peaceably'.[15]

By the beginning of the Chartist period, the manufacturing districts of Lancashire, Yorkshire, Nottingham, Scotland, South Wales, Newcastle, and the West Midlands had an established tradition of radical and industrial activity, more recent but perhaps more widespread than the older Jacobin traditions in the cities. By the 1830s there were in most districts radical families in which more than one generation passed on traditions, beliefs and radical folklore to the children and to political newcomers. Many Chartist reminiscences later in the century recall a childhood or youth spent in close association with this tradition. Benjamin Wilson, Halifax Chartist and later historian of the movement in his town, recalled in 1887 his upbringing in Skircoat Green 'a village that had long been noted for its radicalism'. 'The Women of this village were not far behind the men in their love of liberty, for I have heard my mother tell of their having regular meetings and lectures at the house of Thomas Washington, a shoemaker . . . and they too went into mourning [at the time of Peterloo] and marched in procession, Tommy's wife carrying a cap of liberty

on the top of a pole . . .' When Wilson moved to his uncle's house
to work as a bobbin winder and warehouse boy, it was his aunt
'a famous politician, a Chartist and a great admirer of Feargus
O'Connor' who first introduced him to politics.[16] Peterloo figures
prominently in the upbringing of the Yorkshire and Lancashire
Chartists. Wilson was in fact born in the same year, but learned
about it almost as soon as he learned to talk. Isaac Johnson, of
Stockport, when imprisoned for his Chartist activities in 1839,
impressed H.M. Inspector of Prisons as

A shrewd man – a republican I suspect upon principle; uneducated
which he explains was owing to his being turned out of school, after
gaining six prizes, in consequence of his father obliging him to go to
school in a white hat with crape and green riband at Peterloo time, for
which he was expelled and never went anywhere afterwards.[17]

W. E. Adams, later to become editor of the *Newcastle Weekly
Chronicle*, was an ardent Chartist as a young man in Cheltenham:

Few men now living, I fancy, had an earlier introduction to Chartism
than I had. My people, though there wasn't a man among them, were
all Chartists, or at least interested in the Chartist movement. If they
did not keep the 'sacred month' it was because they thought the sus-
pension of labour on the part of a few poor washerwomen would
have no effect on the policy of the country. But they did for a time ab-
stain from the use of exisable commodities.[18]

Another Chartist, William Aitken, weaver, schoolmaster and
life-long radical, recalled the women who introduced him to
politics as a very young man in Ashton-under-Lyne, one of the
most radical districts in Lancashire:

My earliest remembrances of taking part in Radicalism are the
invitations I used to receive to be at 'Owd Nancy Clayton's' in Charles-
town, on the 16th of August to denounce the Peterloo massacre and
drink in solemn silence 'to the immortal memory of Henry Hunt' . . .
This old Nancy and her husband were both at Peterloo, and, I believe,
both were wounded, at all events, the old woman was. She wore on
that memorable day a black petticoat, which she afterwards transformed
into a black flag which on the 16th of August used to be hung out and a
green cap of liberty attached thereto. In the year 1838 a new cap of

liberty was made, and hung out with the black flag on the anniversary of the Peterloo massacre. These terrible and terrifying emblems of sedition alarmed the then powers that existed and our then chief constable – no lover of democracy – was ordered by a magistrate to march a host of special constables and all the civil power he could command to forcibly seize and take possession of these vile emblems of anarchy and base revolution. Off they marched . . . but the women of that part of the borough heard of the contemplated raid that was likely to befall their cherished emblems, and the women drew them in from the window and hid them. Up this gallant and brave band of men went to the front door of poor old Nancy Clayton, and placed themselves in daring military array while the chief constable with a subordinate marched upstairs, and amongst the women there he found my old friend 'Riah Witty, who told the writer what follows. Imperiously and haughtily, as became the chief of so noble a band and in so righteous a cause, he demanded the black flag and the cap of liberty. My old friend 'Riah said

'What hast thou to do wi' cap o' liberty? Thou never supported liberty, not aught 'ut belongs thee?'

However, the chamber was searched and the poor black flag was found under the bed and taken prisoner . . . the house was searched from top to bottom for the cap of liberty, but neither the genius of the chief or his subordinate could find the missing emblem of revolution. Off this gallant band of men marched with poor old Nancy's petticoat – the black flag never more to grace a radical banquet of potatoe pies and home-brewed ale . . .

The Saturday after this grand demonstration 'Riah Witty met the chief constable, and she exclaimed

'Now, thou didna find that cap o' liberty, did tha?'

'No' he said, 'I didna 'Riah, where wur it?' She said

'I knew thou couldna find it; it were where thou duratna go for it' . . .[19]

Female radical organizations with a continuous existence throughout the twenties and thirties are rare, but the anti-Poor-Law demonstrations of 1837 saw the growth or revival of female associations in a number of centres. In the small wool-manufacturing township of Elland in the West Riding of Yorkshire, the female radicals held meetings in the pre-Chartist period, with women as speakers. After one such meeting, Elizabeth Hanson was taken to task by the *Globe* newspaper for her attack on the

New Poor Law, and for her lack of understanding of the laws of political economy. Her reply was spirited:

Sir – I am surprised that your sagacity as a politician and public instructor should not comprehend my meaning with regard to the distress that I made mention of at the female public meeting at Elland. In speaking of that subject you say – 'Could not my female quickness show me that the distress was taking place under the old poor law'. I knew that, sir, as well as you. I knew at the moment I was speaking, and every one must know that has common sense, that neither the old poor law nor the new one, had anything to do with producing the distress.

The distress, sir, is the effect of the bad arrangements of society; but then the poor law, which is a sure badge of those arrangements, is given for a corrector or a palliative . . .

. . . You say, extend our commerce. We have ransacked the whole habitable globe. If you can find out a way to the moon, we may, perhaps, with the aid of paper, carry on our competition a little longer; but if you want to better the condition of the working classes, let our government legislate so as to make machinery go hand in hand with hand labour, and act as an auxilliary or helpmate, not a competitor.[20]

Elizabeth Hanson seems to have been a member of another radical family, possibly the wife of Abraham Hanson, weaver and lay preacher, and the mother of Feargus O'Connor Hanson, born in 1837. The naming of children of both sexes after leading radicals was a common practice in these years. In 1849 the *Morning Chronicle* correspondent noted

A curious indication of the prevailing shade of radical politics in the village (Middleton, Lancs.) is afforded by the parish register, the people having a fancy for christening their children after the hero of the minute. Thus, a generation or so back, Henry Hunts were as common as blackberries – a crop of Feargus O'Connors replaced them, and latterly there have been a few green sprouts labelled Ernest Jones.[21]

The chair at the meeting at which Elizabeth Hanson spoke was taken by Mary Grassby, who was also attacked by the *Globe* for her unseemly actions. She, too, replied with a spirited defence. The Elland female radicals maintained their public activity, issuing an address in 1838 to welcome the return of the Dorchester labourers in the spring of that year. The address con-

gratulates the men on their release, but urges them to join in the
campaign to secure the pardon and release of the Glasgow
Cotton Spinners, who had been sentenced for conspiracy in
1837, and whose case was the second major Trade Union
prosecution in the immediately pre-Chartist period.[22] The
Elland women were outspoken supporters of Richard Oastler
and opponents of the New Poor Law, as were the women of
Staleybridge, Lancashire, who were reported in February 1838
to be getting up a petition against the New Poor Law to match
that of the men, which had already gathered several thousands
of signatures.[23]

In June 1838, a letter appeared in the *Northern Star* addressed
to the women of Scotland, and signed 'A Real Democrat';
it began:

Fellow Countrywomen – I address you as a plain working woman – a
weaver of Glasgow. You cannot expect me to be grammatical in my
expressions, as I did not get an education, like many other of my
fellow women that I ought to have got, and which is the right of every
human being . . . It is the right of every woman to have a vote in the
legislation of her country, and doubly more so now that we have got a
woman at the head of the government . . .[24]

This is one of the rare cases in these years in which the demand
for the vote for women is put specifically by working women. In
general their demands are more social and more general, like
those of the female radicals of Rochdale, who established their
society in the following year 'determined publicly to show the
world that they know their rights and will maintain them'.[25]

Women appeared, then, to be assuming a radical stance in the
post-Reform Bill period, either by forming their own organizations or by taking part in demonstrations and actions together
with their husbands and families. As the radical movement
gathered momentum in the years, 1837, 1838 and 1839, there
seems little doubt that the women were part of that momentum.

When Henry Vincent visited the West Riding of Yorkshire as a
missionary from the London Working Men's Association, to
encourage the formation of provincial associations, he was
almost overwhelmed by his reception. From Huddersfield – the
home of Richard Oastler and Lawrence Pitkeithly – he wrote:

Our meeting was called for four o'clock in the afternoon, we were met at the entrance by some friends who conveyed us to an inn where we partook of tea. We were then conducted through the town amidst delightful scenes of excitement. The townspeople cottagers and farmers, with their wives and daughters all came out of their little houses and flocked with us to the meeting. The meeting took place in a hollow, just at the entrance of the town, which was bounded on all sides by green hills – the men all stood in the hollow, whilst the pretty lasses and women with white aprons and caps trimmed with green, sat all around the sides of the hill. I never witnessed a more gratifying sight in my life . . .[26]

He toured England in 1837 and 1838, and was impressed by the fact that not only did many women attend all the public meetings at which he spoke, but at a number of places they obviously had their independent organizations. In Trowbridge (Wilts.) the ladies presented him with a 'handsome suit of clothes', to which the weavers of Tiverton added a 'beautiful waistcoat piece, weaved by themselves'.[27] At Birmingham the vast crowd which followed Vincent and the local speakers to Holloway Head for an outdoor meeting included women as well as men – 'as far as the eye could reach was a splendid variety of male and female beauty . . . there were full 50,000 women, all neatly and cleanly attired'.[28] At Hull the new hall was 'Crowded to suffocation – and the gallery delightfully ornamented with ladies'.[29] At Bath, in October 1838 he organized a meeting for the women alone.

I signed an address late on Saturday announcing that I had obtained Larkenhall Gardens, situate about a mile from the city and invited the ladies to attend at three o'clock . . . yesterday afternoon the whole road leading to the place of meeting was crowded by highly respectable females, some on foot and others in coaches and various vehicles wending their way to the place of meeting – the gardens which will hold at least 5,000 were crammed to suffocation – no males allowed within except Mr Kissock . . . Mr Young . . . and myself. There were hundreds outside who could not get near the place.[30]

At Blandford, in Dorset 'the country lads and lasses were seen flocking over the fields and hills in all directions' towards the place of meeting outside the town. As the speakers arrived at the hustings they received 'the usual friendly salutations, the men cheering us and the women clapping their hands and waving their handkerchiefs'.[31]

Throughout the country, in all areas with a history of open radical activity, the women seem to have come into Chartism with the men. They often set up their own organizations, usually with some help and encouragement from the men. In Newcastle-on-Tyne the first meeting of the Female Chartist Association was chaired by James Ayr, a well-known local radical. Men were admitted to the meeting with an entrance fee of twopence, women free.[32] Other places, like Bath, had their own officials from the beginning. Mrs Bolwell, at Bath, had chaired the meeting at which Vincent spoke, and had made, he said, a very good speech. But, like the women at Elland, and like Mrs Anna Pepper of Bradford, who addressed the female Chartists of that town on the political duties of women in December 1840, she was speaking to an all-woman audience. Women do not seem to have appeared in the chair or on platforms before mixed audiences, although men sometimes found themselves addressing an all-female audience.

'Hurrah for the women' began one report in the *Northern Star*:

On Wednesday last Mr Reeves of Sunderland visited this place (New Durham) to get up a meeting in support of the Charter. A room having been obtained, Mr Reeves proceeded to the spot about the time announced for the meeting, but to his surprise, instead of finding a room full of men (who had not had time to get there so early, just having left work) every part of the large room, window seats and all, was occupied by the canny women of this place. This was an agreeable surprise to Mr Reeves and, whether he would or not, there was nothing left him but to address the women, for they got him into the room, locked the door, and set him upon the chair, declaring that he should not leave until he had formed a female association. This was done, and the next morning half a dozen of these patriotic women were running about the town, with a paste-pan and bills, calling another meeting for Saturday next . . .[33]

The female radical associations, of which more than twenty are mentioned in the *Northern Star* during the first two years of Chartism's formal existence, were concerned in a variety of activities besides public meetings. In Sheffield, under the leadership of Mrs Peter Foden, they collected names of sympathetic women and enjoined them 'to instil the principles of Chartism into their children'.[34] They attended meetings and demonstrations, prepared banners and flags, decorated the halls and the speakers' waggons. They organized and took part in social events, from the radical suppers of 'potatoe pie and home-brewed ale' of Nancy Clayton to the more ambitious soirées and musical evenings organized in other areas. They took a major part in the educational efforts which some localities made, which included Chartist and Democratic chapels, Sunday Schools and even day schools. All of these required the active support of the women to succeed, as did the important form of working-class pressure, exclusive dealing. In largely working-class districts, the holders of the £10 franchise for a parliamentary vote would be mainly shopkeepers and publicans. Many of these relied on working-class custom for their livelihood, and it was possible, therefore, in the days of open voting, for considerable pressure to be brought on at least a small number of voters. Early in 1839, the Barnsley Chartists who were collecting money for the Chartist National Rent, and for the defence fund set up to provide legal aid for the arrested leader, Joseph Rayner Stephens, resolved

that the persons who have canvassed the shopkeepers of the town for contributions towards the national rent and Stephen's defence fund, be requested to draw up a list of those who complied with their solicitations, such list to be read each night by the chairman or secretary as a preface to the business of the meeting and an index to exclusive dealing.[35]

In Halifax, Ben Wilson recalled several tradesmen who prospered on the custom of their fellow-Chartists, such as James Haigh Hill, a butcher in the Shambles, and known as the Chartist butcher, who employed a comber called Boden, a leader in the movement and one of the best speakers in Halifax. 'I have seen crowds of people in front of his shop on a Saturday night, and on one occasion he had a band of music there . . .'[36] The thousands of small purchases by working households could represent a considerable financial power if it was organized. Opponents of the Chartists, or tradesmen who had given evidence against Chartist prisoners in courts found this to their cost in more than one strong centre of Chartism.[37] Working-class purchasing power could also be used to support leaders of the movement in small businesses, as well as to embark on attempts at cooperative trading. All these activities required the agreement and active cooperation of the women in the communities, and were carried on successfully in those areas in which men and women took part together.

A form of demonstration which occurred in some centres was the peaceful occupation of the parish church by a large body of Chartists on the Sabbath. They sat in pews for which they had paid no rent, and often insisted that the incumbent preach from a text of their choosing such as 'He who does not work, neither shall he eat', or 'Go now ye rich men, weep and howl for your miseries that shall come upon you' and many others of this kind. Some clergymen used the occasion to preach an anti-Chartist sermon, and one, the Rev. Francis Close, perpetual curate of Cheltenham Parish Church, published the two sermons which he addressed to the Chartist occupations, the first to the men, the second to the Female Chartists of Cheltenham.

It were bad enough [he complained] if they used their influence over their husbands, their brothers and their fathers to foment discord, to promote a spirit of sedition, and to excite instead of allaying the bad passions of those amongst whom they live: but alas in these evil days – these *foreign* days on *British* soil, not content with this, women now become politicians, they leave the distaff and the spindle to listen to the teachers of sedition; they forsake their fireside and home duties for political meetings, they neglect honest industry to read the factious newspapers! and so destitute are they of all sense of female decorum, of female modesty and diffidence, that they become themselves political agitators – female dictators – female mobs – female Chartists![38]

The politics of the early years of Chartism, although distinguished from earlier movements by their scale and extent, were nevertheless in patterns similar to traditional forms of protest and agitation. Demands, even the demand for universal suffrage, were often couched in terms which suggested the restoration of lost rights rather than the establishment of new ones. The defence of their children from the factory system, their own and their husband's jobs from increasing exploitation, of which mechanization was only one aspect, and resistance to the encroachments of a centralizing state, as exemplified by the harsh New Poor Law and the proposals for a great extension of the police, were sufficiently strong motivating forces to get the women to take an active part in Chartist politics. There were, however, some men and women who went further, and proposed fundamental changes in society; these included the Owenites, for whom the traditional institutions of marriage and the nuclear family were seen as hindrances to the development of a genuinely cooperative community. These supporters of 'the social system' mounted a regular attack on the laws relating to divorce and marriage, and delighted in producing evidence of the injustice and inhumanity of the existing arrangements – from stories of murder and violence like the case of the murder by her husband of the wife in an unhappy marriage – 'Verily the Christians may well abuse the marriage system of the Socialists for their own is without a fault!' to more light-hearted incidents like the one in which an anti-socialist lecturer, attacking the Socialists' ideas on marriage at a public meeting in Liverpool was interrupted by his own deserted wife, who had read the announcement of the meeting and had come 'to see him and hold a little discourse with him upon certain points of importance. Such is a specimen of some of the opponents of the social system.'[39]

The Owenites included women among their lecturers, and enrolled them in their community projects. B. Warden, of the East London branch, in address to the members of the Cambridgeshire Community, made a particular appeal to the women among them –

Sisters of the community! you who have all to gain and nothing to lose, – you who have been counted politically dead in law, – you whose rights have never been recognised except by the social system, remember, I say, you must get knowledge; on you mainly depends the character of our youths; on you depend mainly the peace and happiness of the community circle. Without you the superstructure would be unfinished; you, the chief cornerstone that the builders rejected, have become the bulwark of our peace and unity.[40]

Many of the Owenites were also Chartists, for the pure doctrine of Owenite Socialism did not concern itself with day to day politics, and those who accepted Owen's general critique of competitive capitalism but nevertheless also wanted to engage in contemporary politics joined in the agitation for the suffrage.

Although women undoubtedly took part in the work of the small number of Owenite communities[41] and in the even smaller Socialist groups such as the St Simonians (who advertised with each copy of *New Christianity or the Religion of St Simon* 'a coloured portrait of a St Simonian female'),[42] little evidence of such 'advanced' thought appears in the statements of the female Chartists. The women's protests are usually more or less those expressed by the Female Political Union of Newcastle-upon-Tyne in February 1839.

... We have seen that because the husband's earnings could not support his family, the wife has been compelled to leave her home neglected and, with her infant children work at a soul and body degrading toil ... For years we have struggled to maintain our homes in comfort, such as our hearts told us should greet our husbands after their fatiguing labours. Year after year has passed away, and even now our wishes have no prospect of being realised, our husbands are over wrought, our houses half furnished, our families ill-fed and our children uneducated ...[43]

In the outbreaks of violence which occurred during the summer of 1839, men and women alike took part. At Llanidloes, where the local crowd 'rescued' a group of Chartists who had been arrested by Metropolitan police brought in for the purpose, witnesses agreed on the active part taken by the women.

Some of the women who had joined the crowd kept instigating the men to attack the hotel – one old virago vowing that she would fight until she was knee deep in blood, sooner than the Cockneys should take their prisoners out of the town. She, with others of her sex, gathered large heaps of stones, which they subsequently used in defacing and injuring the building which contained the prisoners ...[44]

The Llanidloes riot was one of the few occasions during the Chartist period in which women were arrested and sentenced for their participation. In general, the policy of the authorities seems to have been to arrest a considerable number of people, but only to send for trial a small proportion of those arrested, rarely including women in that number.

In the so-called Plug Riots of the summer of 1842, perhaps the last major example of the 'old' open politics of the working communities in the industrial districts, the presence among the strikers of great numbers of women is well attested. Frank Peel, an eye-witness of the events he described, recalled the scenes as the thousands of factory workers marched into Yorkshire from across the Pennines:

. . . no inconsiderable number of the insurgents were women – and strange as it may seem, the latter were really the more violent of the body . . .

The thousands of female turn-outs were looked upon with some commiseration by the well-disposed inhabitants, as many were poorly clad and not a few marching barefoot. When the Riot Act was read, and the insurgents were ordered to disperse to their homes, a large crowd of these women, who stood in front of the magistrates and the military, loudly declared they had no homes, and dared them to kill them if they liked. They then struck up the Union Hymn –

> Our little ones shall learn to bless
>   Their fathers of the union,
> And every mother shall caress
>   Her hero of the union.
> Our plains with plenty shall be crowned,
> The sword shall till the fruitful ground,
> The spear shall prune our trees around,
>   To bless a nation's union.[45]

F. H. Grundy, another eye-witness, was impressed by the fact that the crowds in Halifax who welcomed the strikers – crowds made up of local working people who were not by any means in the same straits of economic necessity as the Lancashire strikers – contained many women. One of the most violent clashes in the whole episode occurred when the Halifax crowd attempted the rescue of a number of prisoners who were being taken away under military escort. On the morning when the rescue was to take place, Grundy wrote, the road out of Halifax was

like a road to a fair, or to the races . . . I wondered much at the multi-tude of persons collected in the neighbourhood, talking eagerly, but all busy – women as well as men – in rushing along the various lanes . . . with arms and aprons full of stones taken from the macadamized heaps of blue metals placed along the turnpike road.[46]

The stones were used to attack an ambushed group of soldiers. Grundy, and other witnesses, insisted that the ambushers were the people of the locality and not outsiders.

In the general tumult of Chartist politics, then, women took their part. They joined in protests and action against the police, the established Church, the exploitation of employers and the encroachments of the state. They articulated their grievances sometimes in general political terms, basing their case on appeals to former laws and to natural rights, sometimes in ethical or religious terms, appealing to the Bible for the legitimation of protest ('I know' moaned the Reverend Close 'that that sacred volume has been prostituted to all but treasonable purposes . . . the old quaint perversions and accommodations of scripture language so common in the days of Oliver Cromwell have been revived . . . and directed against the peaceable in the land . . .'[47]) In the course of the Chartist movement, however, new forms of political organization were emerging, and new political formulations. How far did these affect the women?

On the central question of the admission of women to the suffrage, the Chartist attitude was always ambiguous. '*I believe*', wrote Elizabeth Pease in 1842 'that the Chartists generally hold the doctrine of the equality of woman's rights – but I am not sure whether they do not consider that when she marries, she merges her political rights in those of her husband . . .'[48] R. J. Richardson, who wrote his pamphlet on *The Rights of Woman*[49] in Lancaster gaol in 1840 certainly presented this point of view, partly because, like many Chartist writers, he was concerned to argue his case within the existing legal framework. He maintained, however, that unmarried and widowed women were entitled to full political and social rights, including the vote. His case was argued from the standpoint of a north country workman, who saw the women as the educators in the family, and as workers in the industry of the locality. His support for the rights of women rests on this view. The more 'sophisticated' political arguments of some of the London Chartists seem to rest *in fact*, on a generally lower assessment of women.

William Lovett describes in his autobiography the care which he took to explain political questions to his wife:

In all these matters I sought to interest my wife, by reading and explaining to her the various subjects that came before us, as well as the political topics of the day. I sought also to convince her that, beyond the pleasure knowledge conferred on ourselves, we had a duty to perform in endeavouring to use it wisely for others . . . in looking back upon this period how often have I found cause for satisfaction that I pursued this course, as my wife's appreciation of my humble exertions has ever been the chief hope to cheer, and best aid to sustain me, under the difficulties and trials I have encountered in my political career . . . [50]

It does not appear to have occurred to Lovett, however, or to his fellow-members of the London Working Men's Association, to include women in their political councils, or even to enrol them as members of any of the organizations they sponsored. Lovett was happy to allow his wife to take over his position, at half his salary, when the First London Cooperative Trading Association could no longer afford to pay him to be storekeeper. He does not, however, seem ever to have considered that she or any other woman had anything to offer the councils of the organization. The complaint which he records, of lack of interest on the part of the members' wives in shopping at the cooperative store, might have been avoided had they taken more part in the planning and policy of the stores. Lovett records that he and some other members of the committee which drew up the original People's Charter had wished to specify women's suffrage among the main points. They were over-ruled however, because 'several members thought its adoption in the Bill might retard the suffrage of men'. [51] In most Chartist statements the matter was left vague. Undoubtedly the majority of Chartists of both sexes saw the main issue as one of class. The attainment of political power by the men of the working class would bring great benefits to the whole class, and the extension of political rights, on grounds of natural justice, to women might well be expected to follow. Moreover, as with other reforms short of the suffrage, there were disadvantages to be seen in their premature achievement. In a society basically divided between the propertied and the unpropertied classes, the granting of a vote to women in the propertied class before granting it to men of the working class could be seen only as the further strengthening of the existing holders of power. Nevertheless, the issue of the vote for women did appear from time to time in the literature. The National Association, formed by Lovett and others after his release from jail, declared in its *Gazette* that it intended to make the rights of women 'as much the object of its attention and advocacy as the rights of man'. 'In this respect at least' it declared,

working men stand convicted of adopting the same ungenerous policy towards women, which other classes adopt towards them. The middle class will not advocate universal suffrage for fear of perilling corn law abolition or a household franchise; and the working men will not advocate the admission of women into the representation lest it should delay their own . . .[52]

But what did it amount to? Some women Chartists did write in to the *Gazette*. 'As one of the sex whose rights you profess to uphold' wrote one correspondent,

you will not, I hope refuse me a corner in your paper to express my opinion upon a subject perhaps within the peculiar jurisdiction of a woman.

On Monday last I followed in the train of the grand procession which bore the National Petition to the House of Commons. And whilst I was much pleased with the general demeanour of those who composed it, yet I could not help remarking what a number of dirty men and women there were about. Surely, sir, upon such an occasion every labouring man and woman, whatever their common occupation might have made it a point of duty to come tidy and cleanly. A little soap and water must have been accessible, and though the clothing might have been ragged the face and hands need not have been grimy. I am not exaggerating when I say that I noticed hundreds who looked as though they had not performed their ablutions for a week! It made me quite uncomfortable, I assure you sir.[53]

Other female correspondents wrote in the same vein. A comparison of these women with the ragged Lancashire turn-outs of 1842, or with Mary Holberry, arrested with her husband in

Sheffield in 1840 for complicity with him in armed conspiracy, though released afterwards for want of evidence; or with Mrs Adams, wife of the secretary of the Cheltenham Chartists, arrested for displaying for sale the banned free-thinking journal the *Oracle of Reason* while her husband was serving a month's imprisonment for selling it, illustrates the great variety of political experience and attitudes contained within Chartism. The wide differences of culture and outlook were as great or greater among the women as among the men.

The ten years from 1838 to 1848, in which Chartism was the main political expression of the social and industrial aspirations of the working people, saw many changes in the movement. The foundation of the National Charter Association in 1840 and of a number of lesser associations on a national scale brought more formality into the politics, while the development in the later forties of more stable forms of trade union organizations and of cooperative ventures drew the energies of many local Chartists into new forms of continuous activity. The immediate sense of crisis which had been present in the early years lessened, and more varied and less defensive strategies for political action and social reconstruction were debated. This was the period in which Chartist leaders were taking part in discussions about European socialism, making contacts with advanced thinkers in Europe and America, taking an address of welcome to the Provisional Government in Paris in 1848. It is also the period in which, except for a few areas, the women disappear from working-class politics.

A few female sections of the NCA appear from time to time in the lists published in the early forties. But there are no nominations from them for women members to serve on local or national committees, nor any suggestion that any women ever held office once the Chartist organizations were formalized. In the General election of 1847, when exclusive dealing was again practised in areas of Chartist strength, like Nottingham and Halifax, the women's support must be assumed from its success. Indeed, in Halifax the women were prominent in the celebrations which followed Ernest Jones's victory at the hustings (and inevitable defeat at the poll). At the tea party to present a gold watch to their candidate, they were determined that the radical colour should be well represented. Ben Wilson was present at the first sitting down 'which was largely composed of women. Some had their caps beautifully decorated with green ribbons, others had green handkerchiefs, and some even had green dresses. I have been to many a tea party in my time, but never saw one to equal this.'[54] But this was a rare occasion. In the later Chartist period it was rare for the women to be much in evidence. Benjamin Deacon declared in 1856:

It has long been a matter of serious consideration with me why the Chartist body have not sought the cooperation of women more than they have done. If the priesthood can secure their services to keep the world in mental darkness, why should not we seek their aid to adorn our platforms in espousing the cause of liberty?[55]

Even Ernest Jones, who was always concerned with women's rights, and who belonged to organizations among the Manchester middle classes in his last years there which supported women's suffrage, has very little to say on the question in his Chartist journalism. This was certainly not because he was unaware of the question. In the foreword to a highly sensational serialized novel which he wrote in his *Notes to the People* in 1851–2, he declared,

. . . society counts woman as nothing in its institutions, and yet makes her bear the greatest share of sufferings inflicted by a system in which she has no voice! Brute force first imposed the law – and moral force compels her to obey it now.[56]

But almost nowhere in the journal is there any indication that Jones or any other of the Chartists at this time were seeking to involve the women of the working class in political activity to remedy their situation. The only contribution to the *Notes* which suggests that there remained any women who were interested in Chartism in an organized way, came when Jones was running a campaign against the custom of Chartist groups meeting in pubs and pot-houses. A letter was published from the corresponding secretary of the Women's Rights Association of Sheffield. Jones introduced it with a welcoming note:

. . . the voice of woman is not sufficiently heard, and not sufficiently respected, in this country. The greatest test of enlightenment and civilisation among a people is the estimation in which woman is held, and her influence in society. Woman has an important mission in this country, and our fair friends in Sheffield shew themselves worthy of the task.

The letter, signed 'on behalf of the meeting' by Abadiah Higginbotham, welcomes Jones' article on 'Raising the Charter from the Pot-House' with a vote of thanks, and urges him to continue the campaign. It continues,

. . . did our brothers but admit our rights to the enjoyment of those political privileges they are striving for, they would find an accession of advocates in the female sex, who would not only raise the Charter from those dens of infamy and vice from which so many of us have to suffer, but would, with womanly pride, strive to erase that stigma which by the folly of our brothers has been cast on Chartism, not only by exercising their influence out of doors, but by teaching their children a good sound political education. This sir, will never be done while men continue to advocate or meet in pot-houses, spending their money, and debarring us from a share in their political freedom.[57]

The final sentence may indeed be a clue to one reason for the decline in women's participation. In the early years drinking does not seem to have separated the sexes to the extent that it undoubtedly did in the later nineteenth century. When the Barnsley Chartists were in prison in 1839–40, the radicals of the town had helped their families by supporting them in small businesses, and one of the leading women Chartists, Mrs Hoey, had kept a beer-shop whilst her husband Peter was in prison. A threat by the magistrates to take away her licence if she continued to allow Radical meetings there suggests that this had become the custom. As the numbers of active Chartists declined, and fewer localities were able to maintain their own premises, the beer-shop offered an obvious meeting-place. If this trend coincided with the increasing influence over working-class women of the Temperance movement, and with the withdrawal from work outside the home, it may well have accentuated, although it could not have caused, the move of the women away from politics.

The fact of the withdrawal from public activity by the women of the working class is incontrovertible. The reason or reasons are not by any means clear. The explanation may lie partly in the 'modernization' of working-class politics. In moving forward into mature industrial capitalist society, important sections of the working class developed relatively sophisticated organizations, trade unions, political pressure groups, cooperative societies and educational institutions. These enabled them to protect their wages and working conditions, and to claim for themselves some share in the increasing wealth of the country. By the later forties the rate-paying franchise for local government in the boroughs included a significant section of the higher paid workers who were able to take part in local government, and in some cases to wage a successful campaign against local corruption. In a variety of ways they were able to find means of protecting their position within an increasingly stable system. They left behind the mass politics of the earlier part of the century, which represented more of a direct challenge to the whole system of industrial capitalism at a stage in which it was far less secure and established. In doing so, the skilled workers also left behind the unskilled workers and the women, whose way of life did not allow their participation in the more structured political forms. These forms required both regularity of working times and regularity of income for participation to be possible. This cannot be the whole answer, however, since even the wives of skilled workers took little formal part in the cooperative or educational organizations which occupied their husbands. A change seems to have occurred in women's expectations and in their idea of their place in society. In the light of the hideous stories of unskilled child-care and the over-working of women and children in the factory areas of the earlier part of the century the positive gains from the increasing tendency for married women with children to stay at home and care for their children do not need to be stressed. But in return for these gains, working-class women seem to have accepted an image of themselves which involved both home-centredness and inferiority. They could not, in the nature of their way of life, assume the decorative and useless role which wealthier classes imposed on women in this period, but they do seem to have accepted some of its implications. The Victorian sentimentalization of the home and the family, in which all important decisions were taken by its head, the father, and accepted with docility and obedience by the inferior members, became all-pervasive, and affected all classes. The gains of the Chartist period, in awareness and in self-confidence, the moves towards a more equal and cooperative kind of political activity by both men and women, were lost in the years just before the middle of the century. As happens from time to time in history, a period of openness and experiment, in which people seem prepared to accept a wide range of new ideas, was followed by a period of reaction, a narrowing down of expectations and demands. One of the losses of this process in the Victorian period was the potential contribution to politics and society generally of the women of the working-class communities.

4

Landscape with Figures:
Home and Community in
English Society

LEONORE DAVIDOFF, JEAN L'ESPERANCE
AND HOWARD NEWBY

Home

Two birds within one nest;
Two hearts within one breast;
Two souls within one fair
Firm league of love and prayer,
Together bound for aye, together blest.

An ear that waits to catch
A hand upon the latch;
A step that hastens its sweet rest to win;
A world of care without
A world of strife shut out,
A world of love shut in.

DORA GREENWELL,
Cornhill Magazine, September 1863

The house constitutes the realm and, as it were the body of
kinship. Here people live together under one protecting roof.
Here they share their possessions and their pleasures; they
feed from the same supply, they sit at the same table. The
dead are venerated here as invisible spirits, as if they were
still powerful and held a protecting hand over their family.
Thus, common fear and common honour ensure peaceful
living and cooperation with greater certainty.

FERDINAND TONNIES
Community and Society, 1887
(trans. Charles P. Loomis, 1957)

In the current renewed discussion of 'woman's place' it is of primary importance to examine how such ideas fit in with other aspects of the society. Little is gained and much is lost in analysing women as a 'problem' separate from what goes on in the economic, political and social structure. In order to make this analysis more explicit we have looked at some of the uses made of sexual differences by our society historically.

We have chosen to do this firstly, because it is marginally easier to stand back and try to see what was going on in a situation a little removed from the present by time, but also because we feel that the period from the end of the eighteenth century was crucial in setting the stage, both in structural and intellectual terms, for the present situation. Girls are still socialized into an on-going role by their female elders, which despite many superficial changes makes the young woman of the 1970s born about 1950 not basically so very different from her grandmother born in 1900 or even her great-grandmother born in 1875.

The ideal setting of women's lives in the home is a constant theme of the whole period. Analogous to it is the theme of the village community as the ideal setting for relationships in the wider society. These ideas had been present in Western thought for a very long time but during the period of which we are speaking they took on a special saliency; they were seen as an important controlling mechanism in the face of unprecedented changes in social relationships. It is our purpose in this paper to make these themes, *home* and *village community* manifest, to draw out the similar ways in which they were used to contain similar kinds of power relationships. Not only were these concepts analogous, however, they were interconnected. The very core of the ideal was home *in* a rural village community. Despite the close parallels between the two themes, however, there were two important differences in the two sets of ideal relationships. The home but not the community included legitimate sexual relations between the superordinate and one of his subordinates, i.e. husband and wife. Secondly, although the home, like the village, was ideally sheltered and separated from the public life of power – political, economic, educational, scientific – this separation was doubly enforced by the physical walls of the house, by the physical boundaries extending to hedges, fences and walls surrounding its garden setting. The intensity of privacy was, of course, related to the core sexual relationship in marriage. The home, even more than the village, represented an extreme of the privacy in which individualism could flourish. On first sight this individualism might seem the antithesis of the 'community' which our two themes represent. If we look more closely, however, we will see that the individualism refers *only* to the orientation of the master/husband; the privacy was used by him when he cared to invoke it.

To understand the way in which these themes were drawn, the uses to which they were put, the effects which they had on the 'socially invisible' within their orbit, it is first necessary to discuss the ideas themselves and the social structure of which they were a part, in more abstract terms. Only then is it possible, we believe, fully to understand the impact they had on women's lives.

It was Max Weber who most thoroughly explored the structural bases of various forms of social domination. He articulated what many nineteenth-century members of the élite no doubt instinctively felt, namely that a system based *solely* on coercion, whatever the basis of this domination, was infinitely less stable, than one based upon legitimate authority. Weber also recognized that the most stable form of authority was traditional authority – 'the sanctity of the order and the attendant powers of control as they have been handed down from the past'[1] – since authority was granted both to the tradition itself and to the *person* embodying that tradition. This gave those in positions of traditional authority considerable freedom to manoeuvre in the face of external circumstances while still maintaining the legitimacy of their rule. The personal nature of the relationship is thus important, for not only is it likely that authority is most effective on the basis of face-to-face contact but it promotes a coherent and consistent set of *ideas* which interpret the exercise of power in a manner that reinforces legitimacy.

What is of central importance in the maintenance of legitimacy is the ability to elide evaluative and factual definitions – not only *does* the individual exercise power but it is believed that he or she *ought* to do so – enabling élite interpretations of the situation to be the only ones. It is not necessary that these ideas make up an 'ideology', as that word is often understood, for they usually become conscious and articulated only in times of crisis and attack. On the other hand, they do constitute an ideology at a much deeper level: a pervasive world-view that structures the taken-for-granted assumptions about social relationships and moulds, beliefs and behaviour.

The onset of industrial capitalism increasingly undermined the previous hierarchical economic and social structure as well as the deferential personal relations associated with it. The ideology of home and community persisted as an underpinning to traditional authority in the face of this threat for, as Perkin has pointed out, 'the personal face-to-face relationships of patronage, unlike the impersonal solidarities of class, could only exist in a society distributed in small units, a society of villages and small towns in which everyone knew everyone else'.[2] Because deference to traditional authority is most easily stabilized in relatively small face-to-face social structures, the corollary is an emphasis on the correspondingly small unit of territoriality within which the desired social system could be maintained. It has been overlooked by many historians just how zealous the Regency and Victorian upper and middle classes were in their attempts to recreate wherever possible conditions favourable to a stable deference to traditional authority.

Increased physical as well as social mobility made possible by the railways added to the unease of élite groups, established aristocracy and gentry, as well as newly wealthy middle class. The necessity for constant redefinition of their 'place' under these conditions made appeals to a nostalgic and seemingly more stable past of rural community even more attractive. Overseas expansion, too, made images of Home amidst the green surroundings of the English village a particularly compelling ideal.

In addition to a reaction to new economic and demographic forces, the desire for stability reflected a fear of the *doctrines* which these forces followed; on the one hand the unrestrained *laissez-faire* market determinism of commercial capitalism (both rural and urban) and, on the other, the appeals to egalitarianism and liberty of the French Revolution.

The growing middle class, who in many ways benefited directly and magnificently from the results of these doctrines were in a dilemma. It was to their distinct advantage, as families, to enter the 'great world' of politics and society as well as business. This entailed a considerable mobility; to foreign countries, to London, to the county seat. But their base of operations was the private home, their ideal location a very local leadership, their identity also a local one. By remaining 'out-of-the-world' they might miss what the world had to offer; by entering it they might become tainted by it. Far better to adhere to an ideal of privacy and local commitment while, in fact, joining the worldly scramble as energetically as possible.[3]

We are concerned in this paper with the home and community as *ideals*. The domestic and rural idyll provided a 'cognitive and moral map of the universe, as a response to the need for imposing order'[4] in an increasingly troublesome, impersonal and alienating real world. As such they contained a number of related dimensions. First, the home and the village community represented two of the small units of territoriality upon which deference to traditional authority depended; each was, so to speak, the spatial framework within which deference operated. However, the home and the village community were not merely geographical expressions, since the physical boundaries were also cognitive boundaries, limiting aspirations and ideas about what was possible and desirable. In this sense 'horizons' were both visually and socially limited.[5] The ideology of the home increased the traditional authority of the household head, emphasizing a solidarity of place while identifying the husband's personal authority over wife, children and servants. Similar ideologies of community were, consciously or unconsciously, put forward to promote integration between the various classes and status groups which made up a particular locality. In each case symbolic – and often substantive – boundaries could be maintained, within which those in the dominant positions could provide compatible definitions of subordinate roles. Within the home and within the community, subordinates 'know their place' because their self-contained situation allows them only limited access to alternative conceptions of their 'place' from outside.

One of the important 'feedback' effects of such a model was that the head of the household, just as the resident gentry in the village, felt that he had the legitimate right to make decisions which affected not only the everyday life but the total future of their subordinates, without consulting them. The resulting ignorance of the outside world was then used as a reason for not giving them responsibility, and their misuse of language and slow responses made them objects of derision. They could be ridiculed as country bumpkins, the 'little woman', or cute children. If they were young and sexually attractive, ridicule took the form of gentle teasing and amusement, or it could become coarse and brutal mockery in the case of, say, agricultural labourers. Such ridicule is particularly devastating within the authoritarian situation we have described above.

The more cut-off, the more 'total' this situation, the greater the likelihood that the definition will remain coherent and thus order and stability maintained; 'outside agitators' were not welcome in either home or village community.

Both settings were also seen as idealized 'organic' communities, hierarchical in structure, with a head, a heart and hands to maintain the life of the organism. For this reason both the home and the village community were incomplete without a full set of characters: 'The family as we understand it, is a small community formed by the union of one man with one woman, by the increase of children born to them and of domestic helpers who are associated with them.'[6] The ideal village, also, had its resident squire or aristocrat, its prosperous farmers and contented labourers. In each case the individuals fulfilling these roles were seen in stereotyped form; their basic relationship was one of deference and service on the one hand and kindly, protective patronage on the other.

This double-yoked model we have called the Beau Ideal ('that type of beauty or excellence, in which one's idea is realized, the perfect type or model', 1820, *OED*). In the domestic architecture, model villages (in both pasteboard and real bricks or stone), suburban development and new towns of the nineteenth century, the upper and middle classes briskly undertook the task of creating the necessary infrastructure to approximate the Beau Ideal, and, in a circular process, this social image in turn contributed to the physical landscape. Thus was laid the groundplan of retreat from the unwanted and threatening by-products of capitalism (and progress) – destitution, urban squalor, materialism, prostitution, crime and class conflict.

As with any successful legitimating ideology we are aware that there may be some difficulty in perceiving these phenomena *as* ideology rather than as 'reality'. This problem in part stems from its very pervasiveness. It was adopted by a wide spectrum of social groups in all parts of society, and through its physical manifestations as well as through oral and written traditions it remains very much a part of our thinking about the social and physical world.

There are attractive features in the Beau Ideal, but the reality of rural life was something more than a kind of perpetual June with grass forever green, trees in leaf, roses blooming and hot summer sun on waving fields of corn. Of course a warm house, a reasonable degree of domestic order, well-cooked food and an affectionate family are conducive to well-being. But we must be wary of the idea that home and community were 'natural'[7] social arrangements from which everyone benefited. In each case there was an ugly, exploitative underside which it was the purpose of the ideology to overlook and deny. Paternalism easily became either overbearing officiousness or even tyranny; on the other hand it could justify self-centred neglect of subordinates' welfare. Self-sufficiency became isolation, close-knit sociability lapsed into cruel gossip.

What has occurred has been the blurring of the aesthetic, particularly the physical environment, and the social – because it was assumed that the village or the home could be aesthetically pleasing, it was assumed that they contained an equally highly valued social existence. Consequently the model stimulated a particular perspective on the problems of poverty and exploitation. Firstly, where the poverty of the farm labourer (or servant) was acknowledged – and it occasionally was – its importance was over-ruled by the alleged metaphysical delights of working within such a culturally approved environment. The farm labourer, or the servant, or the wife, or child, was, therefore, not regarded as being exploited, *not* because their subordination was not, at least sometimes, acknowledged but because this subordination did not matter when set beside the domestic and rural idyll.[8]

The emphasis here is either on the aesthetically pleasing surroundings within which the relationships are set or upon the feelings of security consequent on decision-making being taken over by social superiors. To a certain degree the psychological stability that arose from 'knowing one's place' and from having no doubt as to the nature of one's 'place' was real enough, but this is not to say that those at the bottom of the social hierarchy uniformly regarded their existence as a desired one. The 'underworld' of the rural village and below the stairs, much less the darker side of the nursery or even the marriage bed, is evidence enough of this. In each case the system depended upon cheap labour, poverty and a downtrodden, and often socially invisible, working population.

Secondly, the superior's role was not only seen as rightfully his, enveloping him in the merited glow of the contrast between his worthy enjoyment of the fruits of the earth and the menial narrow lives of his subordinates, but this disparity was seen as necessary, a harmonious and indispensable part of the organic whole.

This is not to 'expose' Victorian 'hypocrisy': each age unconsciously recreates its Beau Ideal in its quest for stability and order within a hierarchical and changing society. In this respect the Beau Ideal is an attempt to manage the tensions that arise out of any social hierarchy, tensions that are still with us today.

The Rural Idyll

During the nineteenth century it was taken for granted that real communities could only be found in the English countryside. It was in rural England that the sense of community reigned and where the apparently automatic acceptance of the 'natural order' of things ensured that the norms of deference and paternalism remained at their strongest. One of us has noted elsewhere the easy assumption that community was *par excellence* a rural phenomenon,[9] where the Good Life prevailed amid the placid and the harmonious – 'a beautiful and profitable contrivance, fashioned and kept in smooth working order by that happily undoubting class to whom the way of life it made possible seemed the best the world could offer', as Best has described it.[10] As if to emphasize its rural roots, the term community was often provided with the adjective 'organic'. It was a neat conjunction of the connotations with agriculture and fertility and those with mutual and reciprocal cooperation for the good of all. The organic community was the epitome of the stable social hierarchy which the Victorian upper and middle class wished to preserve, or, where it had been disrupted by the intrusion of industrial and urban growth, recreate. This view of English rural life became such a literary convention that it is now one of our most ingrained cultural characteristics, commonly viewed as man's 'natural' abode, what Ruth Glass has summarized as 'a lengthy, thorough course of indoctrination, to which all of us, everywhere, have at some time or other been subjected'.[11] As it was succinctly summarized in 1806:

Such is the superiority of rural occupations and pleasures, that commerce, large societies or crowded cities may justly be reckoned as unnatural.[12]

This idiom has been impressed on the mind's eye through the years by vivid visual images. One such is village and great house joining harmoniously to play cricket on the village green, bathed of course in the magic golden/green light of an English summer afternoon. Another is the thatched cottage with heavily scented bowers of honeysuckle and roses climbing round its porch.

The reality, however, was that the aggrandizement of the landowning class, which had resulted from enclosure, created a rigid and arbitrarily controlled hierarchy in most rural areas of England. The cohesion of the traditional English landowning class rendered their power extensive. They were in ultimate control of all local institutions in many rural villages – economic, political, legal, educational, domiciliary, religious, etc. – and almost by definition in rural areas they held, either individually or as a class, a virtual monopoly over employment opportunities. Their power was, therefore, virtually total, tempered only by their gentlemanly ethic of obligation to their inferiors – just as the subordination of the agricultural labourer was equally extensive.

By the end of the eighteenth century enclosure had reduced large numbers of the independent rural population to this position of total subordination, a proletarianization of the rural labour force which occurred only a short space of time before industrialism wrought a similar change in relationships in the towns.

It must be emphasized, then, that the view of the village community as man's natural habitation, the repository of all that is ancient and immemorial in life, *is* a convention. The reality of rural experience was *not* laid down on paper by the vast majority of the rural population – instead, they gave their verdict on the supposedly idyllic qualities of rural life by voting with their feet and moving to the towns. Perhaps one brief counter-example will highlight the partiality of the conventional view. George Crabbe was able to write from centuries of inherited experience of the Suffolk countryside and, in *The Village*, was not above a little sarcastic humour at the expense of literary custom:

> I grant indeed that fields and flocks have charms
> For him that grazes or for him that farms;
> But when amid such pleasing scenes I trace
> The poor laborious natives of the place,
> Then shall I dare these real ills to hide
> In tinsel trappings of poetic pride?
> No...
> By such examples taught, I paint the Cot,
> As truth will paint it, and as Bards will not...
> O'ercome by labour, and bow'd down by time,
> Feel you the barren flattery of the rhyme?
> Can poets sooth you when you pine for bread,
> By winding myrtles round your ruin'd head?
> Can their light tales your weighty griefs o'empower,
> Or glad with any mirth the toilsome hour?

The originality of Crabbe lies in what he includes in his portrait of the rural world – the oppressive nature of rural society, poverty, *work*. Crabbe's rural way of life consists not of a 'natural order' but of a very real social hierarchy whose effect on those at its base was little different from the effect of industrialization on the urban working class:

> Here joyless roam a wild amphibious race,
> With sullen woe display'd in every face;

> Who far from civil arts and social fly,
> And scowl at strangers with suspicious eye.

Of course, Crabbe stood apart from the mainstream of the English literary tradition (*The Village*, written in 1783, was in fact Crabbe's counterblast to Goldsmith's *The Deserted Village*), where the rural idyll and the organic community remained an all-encompassing theme. From the middle of the eighteenth century it had become conventional to use the antithetical device of comparing the rural way of life – and its ecological derivative – with the city. It is a tribute to the endurance of this convention that even today, to many of us the adjective 'rural' has pleasant, reassuring connotations – beauty, order, simplicity, rest, grass-roots democracy, peacefulness, *Gemeinschaft*. 'Urban' spells the opposite – ugliness, disorder, confusion, fatigue, compulsion, strife, *Gesellschaft*.[13] It was summed up by Cowper writing only two years after Crabbe, in his damning verdict that

> God made the country, and man made the town,
> What wonder then, that health and virtue . . .
> . . . should most abound.
> And least be threatened in the fields and groves?

The characteristics of this literary tradition have been extensively analysed in all their ramifications by Raymond Williams in his book, *The Country and the City*. As Williams points out, the idyllic view of rural life, though possessing lengthy antecedents, became dominant during the eighteenth century, when agrarian capitalism triumphed: '. . . you might almost believe – you are often enough told – that the eighteenth-century landlord, through the agency of his hired landscapers, and with poets and painters in support, invented natural beauty'.[14] The idealization of the rural world and its associated social order was taken up by the nature poets in their use of nature as a retreat, as a principle of order and control. Life in the countryside was viewed as one of harmony and virtue, as static and settled. It consisted in Gray's words of 'peace, rusticity and happy poverty'. It was this idealized version of rural continuity and virtue that was increasingly used as a yardstick by which to measure the degradation of urban society.

In the early reaction to urbanization, however, another image overlay this: the view of the organic community as the life of the past – John Clare's 'far-fled pasture, long vanish'd scene'. The organic community, in other words, was always slipping away. This was partly due to the problem that many rural writers had of incorporating the manifest changes of rural life into an over-riding image of it which eliminated any dimension of change. Change could thus only be considered by placing it against an unchanging institution instilled with tradition and antiquity. Hence the rural community was particularly susceptible to the 'Golden Age' syndrome, the nostalgia for a half-remembered past, especially as migration was occurring *from* the countryside *to* the towns. The largest share of the responsibility for idealizing and popularizing a mythical merrie England in the countryside belongs to Cobbett. A host of nineteenth-century writers repeated Cobbett's vision of an ideal rural society, a society which consisted, in the words of his biographer, of 'a beneficent landowner, a sturdy peasantry, a village community, self-supporting and static'.[15] They were also to repeat his idealization of the Middle Ages which was to become so prevalent in nineteenth-century social criticism, and which Chandler has summarized as 'a dream of order'.[16] Cobbett in an argument with a contemporary wrote: 'You are reducing the community to two classes: *Masters* and *Slaves* . . . when *master* and *man* were the terms, everyone was in his place and all were free'.[17] Cobbett's arcadian vision of a happy peasantry and a sturdy beef-eating yeomanry was a picture repeated by Coleridge – 'a healthful, callous-handed, but high and warm-hearted tenantry'[18] – by Carlyle, Kingsley, Engels, Ruskin and many others. Indeed, to trace in detail the scope and pervasiveness of this deeply rooted cultural trait would be to construct an inventory of virtually all nineteenth-century British social thinkers as well as myriads of poets, writers, artists, intellectuals, etc. This view of countryside and village society as natural – 'the proper place for the proper Englishman to dwell in'[19] – continues in often subtle and unconscious ways to affect English literature and art, aesthetic ideas, politics, physical planning – and indeed its social science.[20]

It was, then, to the village community that the Victorian middle class looked as a haven from the industrial world. This was not simply a matter of the aesthetic qualities of green fields as opposed to city streets, but of the kind of society into which the individual fitted. The whole concept of community was invested with an emotional power which made it much more than merely locality; it had a greater sense of integration and meaningfulness, a sense of being more attuned to the realities of living, simply of 'belonging'. As one nineteenth-century American visitor pointed out, a country house meant much more than a house in the country:

> They have *houses* in London, in which they stay while Parliament sits, and occasionally at other seasons; but their *homes* are in the country. Their turretted mansions are there, pictures, tombs . . . The permanent interests and affections of the most opulent classes centre almost universally in the country.[21]

Ensconced in this pastoral world the 'opulent classes' could indulge their recreational tastes – hunting, shooting, picnics, parties, balls – secure in the knowledge that the rural working class would remain quiescent and obliging – except in the hidden – and, therefore, publicly unacknowledged – class warfare of poaching. For as long as the village community remained a largely isolated and remote social world, the influences and judgements of the traditional élite members remained paramount within it. There was no opportunity to question the justice of which rights were being exchanged for which obligations. As Lord Percy was later to point out, any landowner, great or small, 'could manage men with whom he could talk'.[22] By their ideological alchemy they were able to convert the exercise of their power into 'service' to those over whom they ruled and a rigid and arbitrarily controlled hierarchy became the 'organic community' of mutual dependency. It was not, therefore, surprising that their leadership should be widely regarded as natural.

The Domestic Idyll

As the nineteenth century progressed and England became more urbanized, the real countryside became less accessible to the urban middle class. The custom of holidays in the country which had begun in the 1840s meant that most children grew up knowing only the superficial sun-filled pleasures of the country in summer; the thatched-cottage ideal of family life was thus annually reinforced. This ideal was, of course, deeply interwoven with the same quest for harmony. The home was to a house, what community was to a locality.[23]

Although from the seventeenth century onwards there had been an emphasis within the middle class on the home as a moral force, these arguments became more widespread, closely allied to the reform in temperance and the religious revival of the late eighteenth and early nineteenth centuries. They were part, too, of the great moral transformation of that time. The intensity of concern can be traced through the spate of literature from the early part of the century – advice manuals, tracts, poems, etc.[24] In a direct comparison with events in France, a writer in 1841 said: 'Household authority is the natural source of much national peace: its decline is one of the causes of the reckless turbulence of the people.'[25]

Cobbett illustrates the fusion of the two ideals. Again acting as the radical with a nostalgia for a golden past, he sighed for the self-sufficient household, in an heroic effort to stem the intrusion of wage work into family economy. He idolized cottage life where each is busy with his allotted task, the women never so attractive as when busy in the dairy making their own butter, kneading their own bread. Nostalgia was here too for a past when servants knew their place, children obediently followed parental directions and wives were untouched by siren calls from the great world and misguided prattlings about independence.

The underlying theme of 'home' was also the quest for an organic community; small, self-sufficient and sharply differentiated from the outside world. Like the village community it was seen as a living entity, inevitably compared to the functional organs of a body, harmoniously related parts of a mutually beneficial division of labour. The male head of this natural hierarchy like the country squire, took care of and protected his dependents.

The Master: the Husband, the Father, the Head of the House, the Bread-Winner is the responsible individual whose name and power upholds the household . . . He holds the place of highest honour; he is the supporter and sustainer of the establishment. He is also legally and politically responsible for all the other members of the family . . . such are the duties of a master, a husband and a father.[26]

It was he, therefore, and he alone who could be joined to the wider society as an individual and a citizen. His dependents, in turn, responded to him with love, obedience, service and loyalty. Ideally no taint of market forces should corrupt the love–service relationships within the domestic citadel.

In keeping with the functional analogy, members of the household were to be sharply differentiated by task, sex and age. Legitimate relationships were seen as vertical only. Subordinates' whole lives were to be spent within the community thus ensuring total loyalty, privacy and trust. Wives, servants and children, the major subordinate constituents of the household, were never to leave the precincts of the 'domestic domain' except under the closest scrutiny and control.

In the construction of this 'country of the mind', the idea of domesticity as a general good was intimately tied to the powerful symbol of the home as a physical place. The house became both setting and symbol of the domestic community. In the upper-income ranges, the house's carefully guarded entrances with drives, gates and hedges, its attended portals and elaborate rituals of entrance created a sense of security as well as preserving its inmates' rank from pollution by inferiors. Throughout the middle class and in respectable working-class homes, the front privet or iron fence, whitened doorsteps, clean curtains and shining brass door furniture presented the household to 'the World'.[27] The 'temple of the hearth' became a powerfully evocative image, not only in literature but in house design, and in spending resources of servants, labour and income in the lavish use of open coal fires in a deliberately wasteful manner.

Then as the dusk of evening sets in, and you see in the squares and crescents the crimson flickering of the flames from the cosy sea-coal fires in the parlours, lighting up the windows like flashes of sheet lightning, the cold cheerless aspect of the streets without sets you thinking of the exquisite comfort of our English homes.[28]

Servants were separated behind soundproofed baize doors in the back regions of the house and children were confined to the nurseries (even if this was no more than one small upstairs room). There was also a strong tendency to segregate the sexes physically within the house. In larger houses this took the form of male study or smoking rooms for the men, a ladies' boudoir, separate staircases and water closets – and even separate bedrooms for the master and mistress.[29]

Although the idea of home had such a universal appeal, what was not usually explicitly stated was the point of view of the speaker or writer. Even when the writer was a woman, the underlying imagery is the unacknowledged master of the household looking *in*, so to speak, at the household he has 'created'. The 'domestic interior' awaits his coming, his return.[30] Little explicit information is given about where he has gone or what he does when away from home. Ideally, he remains, as a country gentleman, part of the extended rural idyll. As squire his house has a study or business room full of masculine features, where he sees his tenants, does his accounts, acts as magistrate and law giver to his dependants and retainers. This room is entered by the master from the house but has its external entrance from the backyard only. Ideally there should be no need for him to leave his estate and village to enter the sordid world of commerce or manufacture. Military exploits and service overseas might be necessary as a 'higher duty' to king and country; but his heart was always turned to home, 'the place of Peace, the shelter from all fury' (Ruskin); it was for the master's benefit that the shelter existed.[31]

In fact, of course, the mythology of home primarily appealed to the professional and bourgeois groups who did face the 'cold winds' of the market place. To the doctor coming home late in the evening:

> For home opened its wide door to him he thought and seemed to say 'come in'; here you have a right to enter, a right to be loved; whatever befalls you without, come in; forget your suspense, put away your fears for tonight. Welcome, Welcome![32]

The house mistress, ideally the wife, was the lynch pin of the static community.[33] It was she who waited at home for the return of the active, seeking man. Her special task was the creation of *order* in her household, the regular round of daily activity set in motion and kept smoothly ticking over by continued watchfulness; doing everything at the 'right' times, keeping everything and everybody in the 'right' place. The function is made explicit in one of the best known sources of this concept, Ruskin's lecture 'The Queen's Garden'.

> The woman's power is not for rule, not for battle – and her intellect is not for invention or creation, but for *sweet ordering*, *management and decision*. She sees the qualities of things, *their class*, *their places*. (our italics)[34]

In literature, from highbrow to popular, the wife–mother–house-mistress image often merged with the physical symbol of the house so that it became difficult to visualize the woman as having a separate identity from the house; in a sense she *became* the house. This symbolic elision is clear in literature. As R. Gill has said of Mrs Ramsay in *To The Lighthouse*, 'it is this quiet but intuitive woman who creates community within the house'. Of Mrs Swithin in *Between the Acts* and Mrs Wilcox in *Howard's End* he writes 'they are healers, the unifiers and within their communities they are symbolized in every case by the houses they inhabit'.[35]

If the husband (grown-up sons or brothers) looked for action, adventure, amusement away from home, then it was a fault of the domestic atmosphere, and wives (daughters, sisters) must strive to win them back by making home more attractive, warmer, better organized, more comfortable, more sprightly to counteract the weaknesses of male human nature. For the domestic organic community was the upholder of moral order in a chaotic external world. Women created this order by 'being good' themselves. There was, in fact, very little they could do actively to change their men; it was rather their general example and passive influence which ultimately alone could save men from their baser selves, through their redeeming power 'to love, to serve, to save'.

In the early part of the nineteenth century, this moral redemption was stated in religious terms, the 'sanctity' of home was described in a religious idiom. Family worship symbolized this fusion. The basic concepts of domestic peace and salvation, however, remained deeply part of a secular morality well into the twentieth century.

The essence of domesticity in the daily round, the weekly and seasonal rituals within the home, emphasized the cyclical and hence timeless quality of family life in opposition to the sharp disjunctive growth and collapse of commerce and industry. The stability and timelessness was often enhanced by nostalgic memories of one's own childhood home and the attempt to re-create it for one's children. These qualities were seen as part of the naturalness of domestic life; the family was felt to be part of nature (ideally of course, located in its rural, natural setting) in opposition to the unnaturalness of factory or counting house.

However, as we have seen within the rural idyll, it was 'natural' in selected aspects only. Mothering and nurturing in a general way were important elements in domestic symbolism. The mother–wife was the protector, guide and example of morality. Women's sexuality, on the other hand, was denied, as well as the sexuality of children and servants. This was one of the reasons for the 'no followers' rule and for trying to oversee servants and children's activities day and night. Since it was obviously an impossible task, indications of sexual activity by household subordinates had to be denied or ignored whenever possible.

Sexual passion was cast out of the domestic ideal partly because it could be used to found the basis of an alliance among subordinates which would run counter to the legitimate bonds of authority and deference within the hierarchy. In any case what was called natural was a carefully selected, trimmed, even distorted view as only a very limited form of sexual behaviour could be formally admitted. The problem was to contain sexuality for procreation only within married love. The elevation of the home to mystical levels of sanctification, the sacredness of 'the walled garden', demanded an intensification of the double standard despite marriage on the basis of personal choice and love, not on that of parental arrangements.[36] The carefully cosseted married woman (and her forerunner the even more carefully guarded pure, innocent, unmarried daughter) living at home, never going into public places except under escort and then only on the way to another private home, surrounded by orderly rooms, orderly gardens, orderly rituals of etiquette and social precedent was in stark contrast to the woman of the streets, the outcast, the one who had 'fallen' out of the respectable society which could only be based on a community of homes, to the *ultima Thule* of prostitution.

As the patriarchical family had been held up as the ideal base unit of both State and Church since the rise of Protestantism, those people who had no place within it constituted a threat to social order. Despite the strong drive to envelop everyone within the domestic framework, Victorians even more than their predecessors, had to come to terms with the existence of un-attached adults. (Single women, of course, were particularly threatening, especially as the sex ratio became more unbalanced in marriageable age groups through the emigration of young men and a rise in the age of marriage.)

The cult of domesticity rested firmly upon the double standard of sexual conduct. One rule for men and another for women demanded that the latter, of course, be divided into two groups: the 'pure' and the 'fallen'. The two groups must never encoun-ter each other, and the pure must pretend not to know of the existence of the others. The home was the habitat of the pure; the city streets the haunt of the fallen. The separation of women into two classes was well established by 1750 and was based on a combination of economic and ideological changes. The single or unattached woman first began to be perceived as a social danger late in the seventeenth century. The word 'spinster' was then used in an approbrious sense for the first time[37] and that of 'old maid' was invented. Daniel Defoe spoke of the 'set of despicable creatures, called Old Maids' and there are innumerable literary caricatures of the type in eighteenth-century literature.

Part of the problem was of course due to the growing em-phasis on the degrading effects of work on women with any pretentions to gentility:

There are many methods for young men . . . to acquire a genteel maintenance; but for a girl I know not one way of support that does not by the esteem of the world, throw her beneath the rank of a gentle-woman.[38]

The publication of Richardson's *Pamela* in 1740 finally crystallized a new stereotype of femininity. The model heroine is very
young, very inexperienced and so delicate that she faints at any
sexual advance; essentially passive, she is devoid of any feelings
towards her admirer until the marriage knot is tied. This view of
women's sexual nature, of course, ran counter to the commonly
accepted idea in previous centuries that women's desires were
much stronger than men's and that married men should beware
of unduly arousing their wives lest they become insatiable.[39]

If purity was the prime female virtue it was particularly en-
dangered by the promiscuous life of the city. The multifarious
pleasures of eighteenth-century London could only represent the
road to damnation for the virtuous woman; it is significant that
Richardson's Clarissa finally 'falls' because of her unfamiliarity
with wicked city ways. The life of the streets, of inns and public
gardens once commonly enjoyed by men and women of all
classes, became more and more restricted to poor women, or to
the appropriately named 'women of the town' who could no
longer have any pretence to respectability or decency.[40] By about
1820 prostitution had become '*the* sin of the great cities' and the
opposition of pure country girls and abandoned town women
was well established. The city streets were the downfall of many
virtuous men who 'would have escaped the sin altogether, had
they not been exposed to the incessant temptations thrown in
their way by the women who infest the streets'.[41]

To the nineteenth-century thinker man's sexual needs were so
overwhelming there could be little hope of changing masculine
behaviour; control of the women was the way to ensure that
young men escaped the supposedly debilitating effects of fornica-
tion. Medical opinion especially campaigned vigorously from the
1840s for police control and medical inspection of the 'women of
the town', ostensibly in the interest of public health, but revealing in their language, a close approximation in the minds of the
writers between the refuse of the streets and the women.[42]
'We object *in toto* to Ladies Committees,' wrote the *Quarterly
Review* in 1848 in an article on Penitentiaries. 'We cannot think
a board of ladies well suited to deal with this class of objects . . .
we may express a doubt whether it is advisable for pure-minded

women to put themselves in the way of such a knowledge of evil as must be learnt in dealing with the fallen members of their sex.' But during the next twenty years women themselves protested against their isolation from their sisters and contested with the many middle-class men, who, like Charles Dickens, had become passionately involved in rescue work, their suitability for this task. 'It's a woman's mission,' wrote Mrs Sheppard who ran a home for the fallen in Frome, 'a woman's hand in its gentle tenderness can alone reach those whom *men* have taught to distrust them'.[43]

Rescue work became an acceptable part of the multiplicity of philanthropic activities in which middle-class women now involved themselves and for which their essentially domestic nature was supposed especially to suit them. Within the village, charity and cottage visiting was part of the duty of the mistress of the house; given her special moral qualities she forged the link in the hierarchical chain; made palatable the subordination through her gracious loving kindness. 'For it is this human friendship, trust and affection, which is the very thing you have to employ towards the poor (of the country parish) and to call up in them ... Visit whom, when and where you will; but let your visits be those of woman to woman.'[44] All married women had, at least, tasted the fruits of knowledge. Single women in their purity, on the other hand, were particularly suitable (and conveniently available) for such good works.

But within the city there were no such bonds:

The rich, the refined, the educated and the religious are leaving the centre of London (the poorer parts of London) and going, through the medium of railways and steamers, to the beautiful suburbs, to live in the midst of green fields and under the shade of charming trees, there they can breathe the perfume of flowers, where there is no profligacy, drunkenness or crime. They are leaving the poor, and the working class to fester together in filth, ignorance, misery and crime.[45]

The organized charity of the latter part of the nineteenth century was an attempt somehow to reproduce the organic community (and its controls) within the impersonal city to bridge the terrible gap and reaffirm the bonds of deference.[46] For this alone women might leave their homes, their place.

The Beau Ideal

We have seen that the rural and domestic idylls had many features in common. Territorially, these two areas merged together in the symbolism of the garden where nature could be enjoyed but was also tamed and controlled. About 1800 there was a move to unite the great house with its surroundings. Terraces were re-introduced, often balustraded with urns and other 'garden-furniture' which helped link the house with the garden which became another bounded space for social interaction.[47]

Throughout the nineteenth century the art of landscape gardening expanded rapidly. In 1851, these were 4,540 domestic gardeners; by 1911 they had increased to 118,739. While women were urged to take their share in this interest, there was still a basic division between indoor and outdoor activity being appropriate to females and males respectively. As an instrument of education, however, the garden was considered ideal for both sexes, and, indeed, the metaphorical equation of gardens, growth, fruition through tender care was a strong one in literature about children of this period; childhood as part of the organic community.

It was in the 1820s, 1830s and 1840s too, that the Scottish *émigré* landscape gardener, John Claudius Loudon edited his very successful *Gardener's Magazine and Register of Rural and Domestic Improvements*. His primary audience was the newly wealthy middle class who were investing in large suburban villas with gardens rather than grand parks as his own model semi-detached house and garden in Bayswater indicated. This emulation went down the social scale:

that this was a matter of class is very clear from one rather curious phenomenon: the man who, although he lived in the country, say upon the outskirts of a county town, but felt himself to be, in income and social habits, a member of the urban small burgers class, had not a cottage garden but a garden which in style and plant material was a suburban garden.[48]

Loudon's goals for the middle-class house and garden were suffused with the longing to approximate the orderliness and functions of the great country house. Robert Kerr, another very influential ex-Scotsman and architect, succinctly summarized this aspiration in his well-known book *The Gentleman's House* (1864) in which he set out the fundamentals of England's 'peculiar model of domestic plan, the *Country-Seat*'. 'Let it be again remarked that the character of a gentleman – like Residence is not a matter of magnitude or of costliness, but of design – and chiefly of plan; and that, a very modest establishment may possess this character without a fault.'[49]

In 1883, Loudon published what was, in effect, a Utopian fantasy which the anonymous author – an architect – admitted was no longer really feasible in times when great disparity of wealth was no longer so acceptable (sic) yet he calls it 'The Beau Ideal' of an English villa, a picture of a modern English villa as it ought to be, and follows this with a thirty-page description of an imaginary country house, its gardens, its farm, its village.[50] This was to be in fact, 'the true home epitomizing social, histori- cal and cosmic community'.[51] Twenty-five years later, in the heyday of country-house building, architects were no longer so reticent.

Providence has ordained the different orders and gradations into which the human family is divided, and it is right and necessary that it should be maintained . . . The position of a landed proprietor, be he squire or nobleman, is one of dignity. Wealth must always bring its responsibilities, but a landed proprietor is especially in a responsible position. He is the natural head of his parish or district – in which he should be looked up to as the bond of union between the classes. To him the poor man should look up for protection; those in doubt or difficulty for advice; the ill disposed for reproof or punishment; the deserving, of all classes, for consideration and hospitality; and *all* for a dignified, honourable and Christian example. He has been blessed with wealth, and he need not shirk from using it in its proper degree. He has been placed by Providence in a position of authority and dignity, and no false modesty should deter him from expressing this, quietly and gravely, in the character of his house.[52]

The English country house, seen in this way was 'the great good place' and embodied in its social relationships to its attendant village, its setting in gracious gardens, the 'unity of past, present and future; unity with nature . . .' In an era of travellers, wanderers and seekers the country house remains a 'still point' in an ever turning world, 'the sense of home, of place'.[53]

The large-scale English country house of the Beau Ideal could, in fact, only be achieved by a small minority. A true estate employed everyone in the area as labourers and ideally recruited all servants, both indoor and outdoor, from the children of estate workers. But even in the early part of the nineteenth century middle-class bankers, professional men and merchants, divorcing their source of income from their personal living started developing suburbs in imitation of this ideal.

This is born out in the detailed study of the development of Hampstead.

The prime object of this exercise was to create a series of residential estates, each house set in its few acres of park-like grounds and surrounded by its own paddock and meadows to give a perfect impression of a country estate in miniature; a rural-illusion which was yet, in the early nineteenth century, more than a half-truth, and one which was within reach of the successful business or professional man whose affairs did not demand an excessively punctilious attendance at the office.[54]

As time went on, the scale of these suburban villas decreased as land near city centres became scarce and the meadows and paddocks disappeared, but the illusion of rural community remained as the basis of all suburban development.

In fact, this development has always been a commercial venture based on the market value of land and houses, but the shape and lay-out of the houses and gardens, the favoured gabled or mock-tudor style, reflects the yearning for the rural community. When the widened gulf between the classes was becoming painfully clear in London in the 1880s one proposed solution, the 'true answer to the bitter cry of outcast London' was to revitalize the declining village with the transfer, and thus the regeneration, of the urban population; the creation of industrial villages. Although this idea never became a serious commercial venture, it did have an effect on the garden city movement.

Suburban life is the ultimate experience in the *separation* of classes. From the time of its origins in the eighteenth century the very rich and the very poor were excluded, and the middle-class pattern could develop unmolested, safe both from the glittering immorality of the fashionable world and from the equally affronting misery and shiftlessness of the poor.

The growth of professional landscape gardening and the increasing popularity of suburban homes were the enduring physical expressions of the Beau Ideal. The harmonious community of village and home, however, appeared in every guise. It was the unmistakable message of sermons, hymns, poems, popular songs, wall texts, household manuals, annuals, tracts, magazines and novels. The written word, an important new medium for a mass audience, was supplemented by illustrations in periodicals, advertisements and calendars. (This has continued to the present day in colour photographs and posters such as the 'Come to Britain' campaign of the British Tourist Board.) And the whole genre of nineteenth-century children's literature is full of paeans to family and village life.[55]

The Beau Ideal in Action

As with the rural idyll, discussions of conflict or constraint were avoided in descriptions of domestic community. In fact, of course, the household could be not only an 'earthly paradise' but its opposite, a 'hell on earth', a prison.

The fact that no other external relationships were sanctioned for its inmates, at least below the rank of master, could make men tyrants over their wives, mothers over their daughters and both over their younger children and servants. The home could be not only a walled garden but also a stifling menagerie of evil forces unchecked by interference from any higher authority.[56] Even if such depths were not reached, middle-class homes not 'in' the fascinating social game of upper-middle or upper-class Society, could be the incarnation of routinized boredom. Men and boys had alternative living places in, first, boarding schools, then college halls, barracks, clubs and chambers where they could be 'serviced' and find companionship. They might, indeed, feel guilty about such escapes but nevertheless they could legitimately flee to them. Without nunneries and with the suspicions cast on sisterhoods of any kind, the lack of openings overseas, girls and women had *no* alternative unless it be the homes of other relatives or friends.

Because one of the goals of family life was in keeping up a front, if not to rise in the ranks of society, at least to keep up respectability, the impetus always was to aim at the highest standard of living possible. This meant a constant urge to live beyond the means of the household and to make up the difference by exploiting the labour of the most subordinate members, i.e. young servants, children, unmarried daughters and in lesser households, wives. The cash worth of such labour was played down, the ideal was the old family retainer, whose love and loyalty to the family was reward enough, no matter how hard the work. The spiritualized dwelling-place often bore little resemblance to the realities of half-cooked mutton, egg-stained table cloths, recalcitrant boilers and wailing, puking babies of real life. But the fact that the ideal, if it was even attempted, depended on hard, unremitting drudgery performed by often lonely, tired out, young maid servants secreted away in underground basements, sleeping in freezing attics, carrying hods of coal and heavy toddlers from early morning to late at night was not allowed to intrude on the dream; no one ever asked subordinates how they viewed the household. Joyce Cary described his childhood home in London in typical imagery:

It was hierarchic . . . everyone had his place in it . . . There were enormous pressures, as in every human society, but in Cromwell House at that time they were in balance. And the result was a society highly satisfactory to everyone's (sic) needs of body and soul – imagination, affection, humour and pride – a house unforgettable to those who knew it.[57]

The power relationships which included controlling the definition of the situation permitted overtly sexual exploitation within the household without admitting it as such. It is clearly very difficult to find direct evidence on this subject, to sort out what was a voluntary response by girls and what was part of their confined and powerless position within the household. Virginia Woolf's much older stepbrother's visits to her bedroom when she and her sister were in their early teens seems to have been such a case.

The shame and secrecy surrounding sexual matters was a useful screen which the superior could usually count on to protect him from the consequences. A young servant girl dare not tell her own family of the master's advances for fear *she* would be punished.[58]

Family life was even more deeply wracked, however, by the contradiction in the whole basis of the domestic idyll, for the standard of living of the household depended ultimately on income. The reality of middle-class life was not centred on a country gentleman's estate but on the product of mainly urban livelihoods from investments, commerce, the professions and manufacture. Especially in the early years of the nineteenth century, this income was insecure, liable to sudden shifts and drops. Home as stability and a haven unsullied by change was in reality exceptionally vulnerable to bailiff's men and forced removal to living in lodgings, which represented the symbolic breaking up of home because it was particularly degrading to share a house with others on a commercial basis.

The harmonious ideal of home not only obstructed a more realistic view of its economic base but also had far-reaching secondary effects on all members of the household; effects particularly momentous for the female and the young. Inculcation into appropriate attitudes and behaviour started in early childhood. The middle-class girl was seen as responsible for setting an example to younger brothers and sisters when she was hardly out of infancy herself, for keeping them quiet and orderly by demonstrating ladylike behaviour.

The little girl in the nursery is quite ready to set herself up as guide and monitress to brothers two or three years older than herself; girls became mentors at a very early age and how many husbands are kept in good order by the love of training that is in the nature of their wives![59]

Little boys, on the other hand, were to be manly, to observe the etiquette of doffing caps, opening doors, offering chairs to ladies, to protect their sisters from insult and physical harm. In fact, of course, there was bullying and teasing, hero worship and snubbing cutting across sex lines. The framework of expectations, nevertheless, did put severe restraints on girls, from the physical immobility because of their clothes to the imaginative restrictions resulting from the strictures of genteel etiquette. It was girls, after all, who grew up with a special and personal obligation of filial obedience and deference.

Although the conventional picture was of man, wife and children, the tensions of sexuality in such households meant that many of the idealized households in fiction were of brother and sister, father and daughter, uncle and niece, where obedience, moral purity and gentle influence could be brought to perfection, without the disturbance of physical sex.

In any case, girls and women actually spent a good deal of their time only with other women. They were very often educated at home, or if at school only with other girls, and afternoon calls were almost entirely female affairs in the middle class. House parties, balls and dinners where the sexes mixed were highly ritualized. Just as many of men's closest and most meaningful relationships were with boys and men at school, in college, in the army or in the all-male office or club, so much of women's emotional life was centred on other women; kin, friends or even servants.

In terms of economic support, however, the effect of the domestic idyll on the livelihood of middle-class girls and single women was pernicious indeed. The vast reorganization of work patterns which took place from the 1750s onwards meant that more single young women came to the city in search of work than ever before. Daughters and single women in pre-industrial society had worked on farms, in domestic industry and in the shops of craftsmen alongside other family members. But the cult of gentility meant that by the third quarter of the eighteenth century the increasing pressure for girls to give up any economic activity and become accomplished young ladies living at home had had an effect. This development long *antedates* Victoria's reign and is a concomitant of the acceptance and the ideal of female purity. By the 1840s the plight of the unsupported middle-class single woman forced into underpaid governessing, became one of the best documented problems of mid-Victorian society. Governessing, or being a 'companion' was the only respectable occupation for middle-class women because it was located in a private home and could be regarded as a pseudo-familiar position with either very little or even no cash reward to degrade her femininity.

Such a solution, however, was always seen as second best. Within the ideal a woman should always remain in the home of a male relative yet the single, dependent woman was in a particularly deprived state within that home. Although her help could be used within the home to aid the wife and mother in her multifarious responsibilities, her presence there always held a threat. The controversy over the Deceased Wife's Sister's Bill shows the fears which could prey upon the family over the sexual and authority position of the wife and single woman.

With the growth of industrial towns, however, many working-class girls became factory workers or came to residential towns as servants. These hordes of unattached women were seen as a more threatening problem than young men, for one fallen woman could ruin so many men.[60] The battle to bring girls within the domestic sphere lies behind a great deal of the charitable efforts throughout the nineteenth century; for example, Dr Barnardo on factory employment:

The East End of London is a hive of factory life and *factory* means that which is inimical to *home* . . . they [the factory girls] are easily thrown upon the world to 'fight for their own hand'; there is bred in them a spirit of precocious independence which weakens family ties and is highly unfavourable to the growth of domestic virtues.[61]

In the late 1850s many organizations were founded to provide a home for milliners, seamstresses, shop-assistants and flower-sellers who were felt to be at risk in the city.

In every district of London, and of every other large town or populous neighbourhood indeed, wherever there are young females who are neither employed in domestic service, nor under the tender guardianship of a mother or other relatives – provision should be made to supply them with home society, love and care.[62]

Such arrangements were considered makeshift substitutes for the home. On the other hand, it was recognized that working-class girls in reality had to be self supporting, and thus domestic service within a private home where the servant could be enfolded once again within the bonds of community was felt to be the ideal occupation for

they [domestic servants] do not follow an obligatorily independent, and therefore, for their sex an unnatural career: – on the contrary, they are attached to others and are connected with other existences which they embellish, facilitate, and serve. In a word, they fulfil both essentials of woman's being: *they are supported by and they administer to men.* (author's italics)[63]

Yet servants out of place were also without a home. Although charitable efforts were made to provide a place for them to go, such as the Female Servants Home Society, the impetus was a fear of unattached young women. Thus it is no accident that the Secretary of the FSHS was David Cooper also secretary of one of the leading organizations for the reclamation of fallen women, The Rescue Society. Domestic servants were in fact one of the major sources of prostitution but this was due to economic and social forces at least partially produced *by* the domestic ideal. In towns such as Dundee which was a major centre of women's employment in the jute industry, prostitution was almost unknown.

From the founding of the first penitentiaries domestic service had been seen as the future of the repentent fallen. The Rescue Society even offered training in housework and laundering as part of its programme of reclamation and most of its 'graduates' did indeed go into service, yet of 450 girls in their Homes in 1870–71, 412 *had been* domestic servants. That the loneliness and privations of the life of a woman in a small household might make even prostitution look attractive was never considered. Even the organizations specifically created for the social and organizational needs of working-class girls were both structurally and ideologically based on family imagery often reinforced by constant references to the Royal family.

The structure of such a society emphasized personal relations between the working-class girl 'member' and upper-class 'associate' operating as a family relationship (although significantly, as Harrison points out, a family without fathers or brothers). Thus any potential political activity for working-class girls and women was snuffed out at its source under the pervasive familistic model.[64]

It is still very unclear how far working-class men or women accepted the domestic idyll for married women, even in a watered-down version, as part of their own life-style. Clearly it varied widely from place to place and within occupations and over time. It does seem to be at least in its negative form, i.e. the wife not working and 'keeping house' full time, a strand in the definition of the desired working-class respectability.[65]

For example, Martha Vicinus has noted how even working-class writers who had personally experienced the process of urbanization, even in the latter half of the century, were unable to come to terms with it except by reinvoking a half-remembered idyllic rural past, a garden metaphor, and translating this by 'taking nature into the home, behind the red bricks, so that a metaphoric refuge has been created'.[66]

Ben Brierley's solution to the 'Bedlam' of Victorian Manchester was as follows:

Bedlam, however, was not a social desert without its oasis. Stiffy's home glimmered out in the cloudy void like a green spot upon which a streak of refreshing sunlight had settled. It was a home that you would think ought to have had more genial companionship than could be found among squalid dens, where vice and unkindly feelings gendered and grew in festering loathsomeness. It was a home that ought to have had such associations as green meadows, blossoming hedgerows, gardens, the song of the wild bird, and the breath of the sweet moorland breeze. But had it been placed among the wigwams of some savage tribe it would have been just the same, for 'woman' had made it what it was; and she has the power to make such a place a Paradise or Pandemonium, whichever she wills.[67]

Middle-class commentators, however, were more explicit; by insisting that wives both could and should be supported at home, they defined this problem out of existence. As a result, working-class married women formed the army of casual workers: chars, washerwomen, harvesters and fruit-pickers, outworkers, the most exploited section of the whole economy.

Work for girls and single women became one of the rallying points of the nineteenth-century feminists, yet it was seldom clearly seen as related to the question of work for married women – and widows. Two overwhelmingly important results of the application of domestic ideology were often admitted as regrettable but inevitable. Firstly the overcrowding of girls and women into a narrow sector of wage work and secondly low wages:

Women's earnings are, rightly or wrongly regarded for the most part by both employers and employed as merely supplementary to those of the head of the family and the rate of wages is fixed on this assumption.[68]

Into the Twentieth Century

The direct continuity between the nineteenth-century Beau Ideal of the rural organic community and the twentieth-century approach to town and country planning has been traced in detail by Peterson, Thorns and many others.[69] The desire for an ordered social world which prompted the construction of model villages and towns like New Lanark, Saltaire, Port Sunlight and Bournville also stimulated Ebenezer Howard's 'Garden City' movement in the first decade of the twentieth century. The Garden Cities – a wonderfully felicitous Edwardian phrase which captured exactly the desired balance of rusticity and propinquity – were planned experiments in Utopian living outside London, at Letchworth and Welwyn. They were the precursors of the British New Towns, which were to be similarly inspired by a utopian zeal. The Garden Cities conveyed a uniformly suburban appearance which has since spread to estate design both in Britain and the United States.

Suburbia became the last refuge of the Beau Ideal for architects and planners. Here they attempted to create the conditions for an arcadian existence – 'city homes in country lanes' – what one critic has summarized as lying 'somewhere on the urban fringe, easily accessible and mildly wild, the goal of a "nature movement" led by teachers and preachers, bird-watchers, socialites, scout-leaders, city-planners and inarticulate commuters'.[70] To many dwellers (but not as often their isolated wives) suburbia meant the sylvan, the natural, the romantic, the lofty and the serene, the distant but not withdrawn, neither in nor of the city, or the countryside, but at its border. 'Living in the country' as one commuter announced to *Harper's Weekly* in 1911, meant 'allowing the charms of nature to gratify and illumine, but not to disturb one's cosmopolitan sense'.[71] Here one was offered 'the cream of the country and the cream of the city, leaving the skim-milk for those who like that sort of thing'.[72] The Garden City Movement became a focus for such sentiments in Edwardian England. Here, in Howard's own words:

The town is the symbol of society – of mutual help and friendly cooperation, of . . . wide relations between man and man . . . The country is the symbol of God's love and care for man. All that we are and all that we have comes from it . . . It is the source of all health, all wealth, all knowledge. But its fulness of joy and wisdom has not revealed itself to man. Nor can it ever, so long as this unholy, unnatural separation of society and nature endures. Town and country *must be married*, and out of this joyous union will spring a new hope, a new life, a new civilisation . . . [73]

After the First World War, the basis of middle-class housing shifted to ownership rather than rental in the new outer-suburban developments. For the first time, too, there was a chance for the expanding white-collar sector and even upper-working-class families to own the by now ubiquitous semi-detached house with the possibility of having a 'tradesman's' entrance at the back, the illusion of privacy, gardens to give an air of rural surroundings.

Many of the Londoners dreaming of a new house in the suburbs were seeking to renew contact with the rural environment . . . they looked for at least a suggestion of the country cottage in their new suburban home . . . assiduously, often clumsily they strove to evoke at least a suggestion of that rural-romantic make-believe which was the very spirit of suburbia.[74]

They were seeking very much the same qualities that their grand-fathers had sought, 'the subtly mixed aromas of Pears soap, Mansion Polish and toast . . . The ambience of peace and stability'.[75]

At the heart of the suburban dream was the housewife. The immediate post-war unease, the signs of many women wanting to pursue a new social consciousness and a reluctance to return to the old domestic confines were stifled and forgotten. In terms of one of the most powerful cultural reflections of women's position, 'the new periodicals [for women] dedicated themselves almost without exception to upholding the traditional sphere of feminine interests and were united in recommending a purely domestic role for women'.[76] The celebration of domesticity had obvious connections with the need to sell consumer durables, connections made evident in the model mock-ups of homes in the annual *Daily Mail* Ideal Home Exhibitions which began in the 1920s. Ironically, one of the greatest pressures to renew the domestic idyll at this time was the increased work load on middle-class wives because of the exodus of domestic servants from middle as well as lower-middle-class homes after the First World War. Servants had few illusions about the domestic idyll as we have seen and few hesitated to leave when alternative work was available.

The depression atmosphere of the 1930s also favoured the saving and protecting aspects of home life. The rhetoric of home continued to be a powerful rallying point throughout the Second World War, despite the mobility of all family members and especially the wider opportunities war offered to women.

I believe the value of a comfortably run home and family to be of immense moral and civic importance . . . that Woman not only has, but should confidently wield a special influence over Man. The feminine spiritual vision sees, or rather senses, further than man's.[77]

This was written in nineteen, not eighteen, forty-five.

In the course of the twentieth century, however, middle-class girls, as opposed to older women, were increasingly able to shun some of the demands of home discipline and obligation. They gained a degree of economic independence through the growth of the clerical sector for jobs and even social independence in bed-sitters and flats. As the 'daughter-at-home' expectation waned, the married woman and mother became more than ever the identifiable constituent of the home. Increased educational opportunities for girls widened this generation gap.

The more that the wider society grows in centralized corporate and state power, in size of institutions and in alienating work environment, the more that the home becomes fantasized as a countering haven.[78] Home-baked bread, French farmhouse cookery, wine making, organic gardening – the whole gamut of 'creative homemaking' have become the suburban substitutes for the fully fledged return to the self-sufficient small holding, only made real by a tiny minority.

When the rosy spectacles are laid aside, however, it is clear that what to the husband and children can be a refreshing hobby – after all they are more often than not the consumers, not the producers, of the home-made jam – to the wife can be another variant of the natural mother image and in everyday terms can mean longer than ever hours at the chopping board. Moral and nutritional reactions to packaged foods in the 1970s are as inextricably confused as the same reactions to tinned foods three generations ago.

The point has been made that the Beau Ideal was a model, a way of composing reality that helped to create that reality in a very concrete way, often embalmed in the bricks and mortar of houses, the lay-out of roads and services with which we are still living. Both the village and home sectors of this ideal represented a defence against various attacks on the social structure which made, particularly members of the middle class, fearful of disorder in every sphere of social life. The model was seen to stress consensus and affective ties. It thus shifted attention away from exploitation of groups and emphasized individual relationships.[79] It denied the reality of, and thus made less viable, the existence of households with other structures namely without male heads, with working wives and mothers.

Ideal communities are supposed to be both self-sufficient and self-regulating, therefore, there is no need to protect the weaker members because protection is inherent in the relationship. The concern with harmony and control meant that there was a tendency to see the social/spatial world as a theatre, the unfolding of carefully selected roles. This theatre was complete with a front and back stage so that disrupting elements could be kept out of sight, and hopefully out of mind.

But the ultimate end of perfect order is sterility, even death. Despite the organic imagery, the leafy bowers and garden setting, this strain towards absolute harmony was full of tension. The anonymous creator of the 'Beau Ideal of the English Villa' sensed this dilemma. He recognized that the gentleman's residence should be within sight of, but well screened from, the village; that living creatures, i.e. cattle and labourers must be present as a generative force, although carefully regulated and kept in the background.

As the most beautiful landscape is incomplete without figures, so the general effect of a park is always lonely, unless it have a footpath frequented by the picturesque figures of the labouring classes and giving life and interest to the scene.[80]

Similarly within the house, after giving an extremely detailed catalogue of furniture and decoration, he notes that in the drawing room, 'most of the tables must also have something upon them, to make them appear of use'.[81]

A stage set, after all, is only a pretence of life, it produces nothing. It has no base of transforming energy, either human or mechanical. Yet the effects of uncontrolled energy were the very elements that were feared; the novel and mighty energy of steam which could multiply goods a hundred fold, on the basis of which wealth could be created overnight, which left havoc and waste on the physical landscape and bitter rebellious poverty among the working class of wage labourers. Within the home, it was social and sexual energy, the thrust of the *parvenus* (at all social levels) and their offspring, which was so threatening to established ideas of hierarchy, to the 'debased pastoral' of the middle classes.[82]

Such tension between order and change has always been one of the main themes of political and social debate in English society. In the nineteenth century the struggles for greater participation in the responsibilities and rewards of society took place on many fronts. In the public debate, the desire for order was experienced in increasingly controlling legislation in the interests of public health, in the classification of prisons and workhouses and of all those who were deemed not to belong in the mainstream of national life. The Beau Ideal, however, separated women and family from public concerns and gave them their own sphere of social influence in the home.

We have lived for so many generations with this separation, which *in itself* has become such a forceful method of control, that it comes as a surprise 'that such personal and elemental feelings as those about love and women would have been so strongly influenced by the hard competitive world of business or by the pressure of intellection and doubt'.[83] The realization that this division is not a given of the universe, not a timeless and natural phenomenon, lies behind the discovery of what has been called 'sexual politics' as well as contributing to the recent interest in family history.

Much of the idiom of the model we have been discussing has been at a subliminal level in the form of visual images, and a social map where sex and class divisions are confined to certain specified physical areas. This means that it takes a special effort to see the model from the outside. It also has made the rebellion against the barren segregating categories of the hierarchy, against the ritualized narrow and stereotyped behaviour demanded by the model, a particularly disturbing one aimed primarily at an equally idealized search for life-giving self-fulfilment through unfettered sexuality.[84]

At the same time, women, especially married women, have been still left with the task of defending the remnants of the Beau Ideal, at least in its bare essentials of socializing young children into civilized behaviour and in nurturing and watching over their men.[85] In their suburban homes, wives are still expected to create a miniature version of the domestic idyll, set in subtopian pseudo-rural estate surroundings while their male counterparts swarm into central city offices and factories. Wives remain protectors of the true community, the 'still point'; a basic moral force to which the workers, travellers and seekers can return. In the archetypal portrayal of everyday life they still wait, albeit with less resignation as well as less hope, for the hand upon the latch.

5

Femininity in the Classroom:
An Account of Changing
Attitudes

PAULINE MARKS*

In *Purity and Danger* Mary Douglas wrote that '. . . it is only by exaggerating the difference between within and without, above and below, male and female, with and against, that a semblance of order is created'. (p. 4) There may be those who would reject her reasoning, but there are few who would deny that the practice exists. Teachers and others involved in education are no exception. They will exaggerate concepts of femininity in the light of which they will decide what they should teach to whom, and how the behaviour and treatment of boys and girls should differ. Unlike, for example, the distinction between 'able' and 'educationally subnormal' children, this sexual division is rarely clearly expressed in educational ideology despite marked differences in the treatment, performance and expectations of boys and girls at school.

The differences in treatment vary. They were easy to see in the early nineteenth century when what was provided for middle- and upper-class girls was very much more limited in scope than the educational provision for their brothers. Now we have to look a little closer. In a modern, sexually mixed, comprehensive school which offers a wide range of subjects to everyone, girls and boys still choose to follow those which are traditionally expected of them. This is hardly surprising – because girls are expected

*Pauline Marks was tragically killed in a traffic accident before she could finally revise this paper, which has been revised for this volume by her research supervisor, Susan Budd. The paper was part of a larger piece of research on the process of sex-typing in girls' education.

to behave thus and so, because teachers' responses will be based on that general expectation, then, of course, girls will conform to the roles they are assigned.

These sex differences in education have been accompanied by a relative unawareness on the part of educational planners and writers about education. This discrepancy poses a problem. In the early nineteenth century, few people doubted the correctness of the division, so that educational writers, when they dealt with the matter at all, produced straightforward sexist accounts of the theory behind it. Nowadays, just as the practice is relatively hidden, little or nothing is said about it by educational writers. Girls, like the working classes, are tacitly excluded from most discussions on education. The differences in treatment and the problems they cause exist – but in the official collective consciousness they do not. Thus, when educational theorists talk of the education of children or pupils, usually they are effectively talking of the education of boys (and middle-class boys at that).

When people do think about the discernible differences in educational practice, they customarily rely on two well-worn accounts with which to explain them. The first is that girls and boys differ physiologically and that the differing levels of achievement and the differing styles of education provided for them derive from this. This view varies from seeing biological factors as absolutely determining the way women should be educated, to seeing them simply as constraints. It is worth noting that even the most liberal proponents of this view never see boys as the more physiologically limited group. Those who give the second account see it as important to educate girls differently from boys because they will be treated differently in later life. So long as we know how girls will be treated during their adult lives, we are able to provide them with the education they will need to cope with this. This account leaves aside the question as to why people define femininity in the way they do.

It is easier to understand how ideas about the education of girls vary, or have varied, as soon as we see that femininity is itself a problematic notion. What is meant by it changes both over time and within different social groups. These changes in the understanding and use of the notion are reflected, of course, in the work of educational theorists. How they use it or are influenced by it will depend on when they were working and on their social background. The Bishop of Oxford made the point well in 1923 when he wrote: '[the question of girls' education] is determined by the current opinion of the status of women in the society of the time'.[1]

In order to trace, however sketchily, the relationship between ideology and social experience, a historical perspective is necessary. The research for this perspective is difficult because of the paucity of information about actual practice. Educational ideology and philosophy can be studied through the work of influential writers like Thomas Arnold or Jean-Jacques Rousseau or in the pages of government reports. The latter are important because they reveal the ideological basis on which educational legislation is made. In them we can see why institutions, the selection of pupils, curricula, etc. are as they are. But while the well-known writers and the government reports will tell us about belief and practice, and will incorporate a view of 'human nature', they will not tell us much about what actually happened in the classroom. For this information we have to turn to contemporary letters, pamphlets, autobiographies, newspaper articles and so on; the reliability of these sources is sometimes difficult to gauge. However, I will try to examine the relationship between the various definitions of femininity underlying, or incorporated into, educational philosophies, ideologies and models and the educational 'solutions' which were thought of as appropriate to the 'needs' of girls.

There are three major ways in which educators have approached the teaching of girls, and each of them has depended on differing accounts of femininity. The first way we might call 'assimilation', and it depends either on the educator seeing no difference between boys and girls, or on the decision that any such difference is irrelevant in education. The second approach sees girls either as handicapped when compared with boys, or sees them as somewhat deficient boys. Either boys are placed in a higher cultural order than girls or girls are thought to need special help to 'catch up' with boys – because of deficiencies in their biology, socialization or environment. The first form of the distinction is likely to lead to an educational solution of plural-ism. Different answers will be given to the question of the aims of educating each sex, and the content and structure of educational institutions and curricula will be different for the two sexes. If girls are thought to need special help to catch up with boys, then they will be given 'compensatory' education. Proponents of this view may say that sex differences are ultimately irrelevant in the context of education and compensatory education for girls is only needed as a short-term measure. The third approach depends on seeing boys and girls as completely different and in need of com-pletely different kinds of education with a concentration on very different subjects. This results, once again, in a pluralist solution.

It is easy to see that not only can femininity be defined in relation to the ruling standard in this way, but so too can the working class or the racially or culturally underprivileged. As the Authoritarian Personality studies suggested, a society that organ-izes its thinking in terms of a hierarchy for the sexes will probably do so for class and ethnicity as well.

Another difficulty is created by the fact that different people think differently about the objects of education. Some see it as necessarily geared to the 'needs' of the pupils, as something which is to prepare them for their future roles in society. In this case definitions of femininity or masculinity will loom large. Others may believe that education should not be specifically vocational, or should not be designed to produce particular kinds of people, but should be seen as a 'good-in-itself' with universally applicable objectives.[2] People who think thus are less likely to stress views about intellectual differences between the sexes, although they may feel that girls need help to catch up with boys. Yet others believe that education should be vocational, but they may differ among themselves about how far vocations, and thus education, should be sex-specific. They may see both sexes as having a heterogenous set of possible vocations, some more or less exclusively for boys (e.g. engineering) and some for girls (e.g. nursing) and some as open to both (e.g. teaching). It is quite common, of course, for such mixed, or open, vocations to be seen as available for the less successful boys and for the more successful girls. Those who think more or less exclusively of education as vocational are quite likely to think of boys as having a number of choices while girls are really only faced with one, i.e., marriage and motherhood.

Schoolchildren are divided up not only by their sex; their 'intelligence', social class or race may also be seen as limiting them to certain sorts of education. The judgements made about what a girl is able to learn, or about what she ought to learn, are qualified, to some extent, by how intelligent she is thought to be or by the social standing of her parents. For example, it has been very widely assumed in Britain that the able child of either sex can benefit from an education which is 'good-in-itself', whereas the 'less able' can only benefit from an education which is largely vocational.

At one time it was thought that the children of the gentry would benefit from a 'good-in-itself' education, regardless of intelligence, while the children of the poor should be taught a trade. The history of educational reform in Britain can be charted in terms of the transition between different approaches. First of all, intelligence was thought irrelevant to the kind of education provided; then education was regarded as a reward for intelligence, a ladder for the able poor to climb. Next came the view that types of education should be distributed according to ability, and the final approach has been one that attempts to abandon hierarchy altogether. Girls have been slotted into these systems in different ways and at different points, but it is fascinating to discover that their 'femininity', that supposedly biological and absolute characteristic, is dependent on the viewpoint of the observer; different social origins and intellectual abilities alter the meaning of 'femininity' which is thus not a fixed concept in educational thinking.

An educational model is a complex thing whose parts may be inconsistent with one another. For example, femininity may be used at one point in the model to explain why the daughters of gentlemen cannot be educated with their brothers; but that same femininity may be ignored when it comes to the question of the daughters of artisans. Educational provision for girls during the first half of the nineteenth century was justified in terms of an ideology of pluralism – girls and boys were thought to need different kinds of education. But this applied to upper- and middle-class girls only, and working-class girls were provided with an education similar to that for working-class boys. As always, most discussion and thought was devoted to the education of the rich, especially their sons. 'Femininity' was and is a problematic category in the field of education in a way that 'masculinity' is not, and the 'needs' of girls, though explained in terms of their sex, have varied subtly according to their social background.

The way in which 'femininity' varies according to its social context raises an important question which is difficult to answer. Did the prevailing notion of femininity in the nineteenth century control educational patterns available to girls, or were these rather an outcome and reflection of economic and organizational factors already deeply embedded in all levels of society? It may well be that educational ideology and practice for girls simply reflected the existing social and economic situation, rather than educational theory expressing an *a priori* argument about the way in which girls should be educated. A legitimizing, as opposed to *a priori*, argument has, of course, no role to play in bringing about educational change.

I want now to consider the educational provision for girls from the beginning of the nineteenth century. To some extent the choice of date is arbitrary, but not altogether, for the theoretical foundations on which twentieth-century education is built were laid during this period.

Young upper-class girls and the girls of socially aspiring families were generally taught at home by their parents (usually by their mothers) and by governesses or, less frequently, by private tutors. At some time between the ages of twelve and fifteen, they might be sent to school. The majority attended private schools, although exactly how many did so is difficult if not impossible to establish, for adequate statistics are not available.[3] The few such schools prior to 1850 which were not run for profit can be divided into three classes: the denominational schools like those run by the Quakers; those established for particular sections of society like the schools for the children of clergymen, or military or naval officers; and a small number of charitable foundations like

Christ's Hospital. The use of charitable funds for education, as in the case of Christ's Hospital, demonstrates very well the bias towards the education of boys. Whereas the founder of Christ's Hospital School mentioned both boys and girls in the original document, in practice most of the resources were made available to boys. In 1865 there were 1,192 pupils in the boys' school, with twenty-seven masters, and there were eighteen girls in part of the junior boys' building with one mistress.

The conditions of the private, profit-making girls' boarding schools have been well documented.[4] The school would normally be run by a lady principal with one or two governesses to help her, but it was rare for any of them to be trained professionally, particularly as girls were excluded from the universities of the time. There were many more fashionable schools for girls than for boys, but they were much smaller – the average number attending such an establishment was in the region of twenty-five. R. L. Archer has described the aims of these schools in terms of their inculcation of femininity.

> ... to produce a robust physique is thought undesirable, rude health and abundant vigour are considered somewhat plebian . . . a certain delicacy, a strength not competent to walk more than a mile, an appetite fastidious and easily satisfied joined with that timidity which commonly accompanies feebleness .. all are held more ladylike.[5]

Girls were expected to be obsessed with fashion, to develop delicate complexions aided by starvation diets, to improve their posture with aids like straight laces, back boards, iron collars, and wooden stocks, and to keep their feet firmly in position while repeating information learned by rote. Rote-learning was the norm and the greatest emphasis was laid on gaining the 'accomplishments' – painting, singing, dancing, playing the piano, how best to enter a drawing room and so on. Visiting masters were often employed by the schools to teach these 'accomplishments'. J. Fitch, reporting to the Taunton Commission in 1864 after visiting many such schools, said that

> ... above the age of twelve the difference [between education provided for boys and girls] is most striking. Girls are told that Latin is not a feminine requirement, mathematics is only fit for boys and she must

devote herself to ladylike accomplishments . . . nothing is more common than to hear the difference in the future destiny of boys and girls assigned as a reason for a difference in the character and extent of their education, but I cannot find that any part of the training given in ladies' schools educates them for a domestic life or prepares them for duties which are supposed to be especially womanly. The reason why modern languages which are especially useful in business, should be considered particularly appropriate for women, who spend most of their time in the home, is still one of the unsolved mysteries of the English educational system.[6]

The educational experiences of middle- and upper-class girls were qualitatively different from those of boys. Secondary schools for the latter were usually very much larger, staffed by professionally trained masters, and they had curricula which were dominated by the classics. Because middle-class parents were primarily concerned with their daughters' eligibility for marriage, they educated them to this end. The classical-liberal education received by their sons approximated much more closely to the idea of an education which was 'good-in-itself'. One of the most interesting implications of this division is the idea that femininity had to be achieved, cultivated and preserved, while masculinity could be left to look after itself. Some 'masculine' traits, e.g. bravery and vigour might be in need of encouragement, but the learning of masculinity, unlike femininity, was not thought of as the central task of the school.

This situation, in which the learning of femininity was stressed, reflected the obsessive concern of many Victorian thinkers and moralists with the 'home'. The rapid growth of industrialism, the increase in the size of cities and of business concerns, had led to a separation of the home and the place of work among the middle classes as well as among the poor. Capitalism demanded assertive and competitive behaviour from men at work, so increasingly the middle-class home became a refuge, a retreat which had to be preserved.[7] Women thus had a special importance: they were dependent on their ascribed status, that is on being female, and the most important goal for that status, towards which education was directed, was marriage. However, this was denied to a substantial number of women for a variety of demographic and social reasons. Among these were differing rates of infant mortality – infant girls were more likely to survive than boys – the high cost of marriage and male migration.[8] These middle- and lower-middle-class spinsters were in a socially anomalous position and could, if their fathers did not support them, be in severe financial difficulties. Their only chance of socially acceptable paid employment was teaching, which did not need specialized knowledge or experience. It involved either becoming a governess and living with a family, or working in a girls' school and teaching a restricted range of subjects.[9]

Middle-class women were excluded from the educational opportunities made available to their brothers because their future roles were set out for them and they were thought to need preparation for those roles. Girls would become wives and mothers; only the deficient woman, the spinster, had to seek a career. Hence proposals that education for girls should be extended were rejected by conservatives because they thought that such proposals, if put into practice, would rob girls of their femininity, make them more masculine, reduce their chances of marriage and thus make them deficient as women.

The situation for working-class girls was very different. There were few schools for either working-class girls or boys and those which did exist were elementary. Their curricula were designed without reference to needs and abilities thought to belong to either sex.[10] Girls may well have been taught needlework, but that apart, their experience would have been much the same as that of the boys. In the early part of the nineteenth century there was no specific ideology of education for the poor which could counteract the model of 'minimal' education provided for them by the upper class. The poor had to be civilized; in the words of Gladstone, what this meant was '. . . sound religious instruction, correct moral training, and a sufficient extent of secular knowledge suited to their station in life . . .'[11] Even so, those who reported to the Select Committee on the Education of the Poorer Classes in 1838, concluded that the kind of education given to children of the working class was 'lamentably deficient' and only extended to a small proportion of those who ought to receive it.

During the second half of the nineteenth century various groups challenged the structure and content of the education given to middle-class girls. In doing so, they called into question the class-specific notions of femininity which underlay the existing educational model. The majority of the active members of these groups were middle class, and either had been, were related to, or had narrowly avoided becoming governesses. They can be divided into three groups in terms of the assumptions they made about 'femininity' and the educational solutions that they saw as appropriate for the needs of girls.

1. *The Instrumentalists* were committed to the position that whatever the biological and social differences between the sexes, in the context of decisions about educational provision these were of very limited importance. They advocated educational assimilation as the solution to the inadequacy of middle-class girls' education. Both sexes ideally should have equal educational employment opportunities. This group included Frances Buss and Emily Davies.[12]

2. *The Liberal Humanists* were concerned to offer girls an education which would result in their becoming 'better' wives, mothers and companions than the educational opportunities of the first half of the nineteenth century allowed. They were not redefining current notions of *femininity*, but rather opting for a 'solution' which would widen the intellectual interests of girls and women generally and prepare them more adequately for their traditional role. This group included Anne Clough and F. D. Maurice.[13]

3. *The Moralists* were concerned with the duties of women as Christians. The education received by girls in the private boarding schools was, of course, the antithesis of an education aimed at producing dutiful and piously religious women. Dorothea Beale, a significant member of this group, sought a 'solution' in the form of a 'demanding curriculum' including subjects such as mathematics, logic and classics interspersed with the teaching of religion – this she believed would be conducive to the notion of dutiful womanhood.[14]

The instrumentalists questioned most of the underlying assumptions of the educational models and philosophies in the first half of the century, whereas the other two groups took the current definition of femininity for granted and believed that the future roles of boys and girls would be quite different. The second half of the nineteenth century saw educational changes which pleased members of all three groups, and which resulted in a new dominant ideology justifying an assimilation of the educational experiences of girls to those of boys. Obviously the education received by boys in the public schools and universities had not remained static throughout this period. Many reforms were achieved – for example, the content of the curriculum was widened to include subjects such as physics and history, and the idea for an education oriented towards a vocation (that is, a profession) began to dominate the educational model for middle-class boys.[15]

Part of the explanation for the changes in girls' education was due to unease about some aspects of the social position of middle-class women in the mid nineteenth century. It was in response to the financial plight of governesses and as an attempt to improve their social status that the Governesses Benevolent Institution was set up in 1843, followed five years later by Queen's College in Harley Street, which became a school for girls and women offering an academic 'compensatory education'. The opening of the GBI seemed to mark the opening of the flood-gates: letters, articles, protest meetings, theories, committees and so on began to debate about the state of middle-class girls' education. A Royal Commission on Education, the Taunton Commission of 1864, devoted one section of its findings to the education of girls, the first occasion on which a government report explicitly distinguished between boys' and girls' education. The commissioners sent inspectors to girls' private secondary schools, and received evidence about conditions in them.

Dorothea Beale, summarizing the evidence, argued that 'nothing can well be more extravagant than the waste of money and educational resources in these schools'. There was ample evidence in the Commission's report to support her views. The inspectors found that few teachers and governesses had been professionally trained, and in some cases were barely educated themselves. The girls were reported to be absorbed in the minutiae of dance steps and etiquette. In one school, an inspector reported, he had questioned an eighteen-year-old girl as to what she remembered of a recent visit to Paris, and she answered that she recalled two things – that she had seen the Empress and she had been very plainly dressed; and that she had seen some priests in a church, and they had been magnificently dressed.

The substantive changes in girls' secondary schools during the latter part of the century meant that the new ideology advocating educational 'assimilation' became more acceptable. Girls' schools were founded with curricula approximating to those in equivalent boys' schools; girls were successful in external examinations which had previously been restricted to boys, and a very small number of women students were admitted to university in the 1870s. Although girls were admitted to the Cambridge Local Examinations in 1865, and Oxford's in 1870, unlike boys they were not placed in order of merit but were given a *pass* or a *fail*. It was argued that girls were unable to deal with competition and would be likely to respond badly to it. London University opened its examinations to women students in 1878, apart from the medical schools which remained barred to females. Colleges for women were opened at Cambridge in 1870 (Girton), and 1871 (Newnham). Girls were not given the class of their degree but were officially informed that they had either passed or failed. At Girton, where Emily Davies was Principal, women were encouraged to compete with men on an equal basis; a position which was consistent with her membership of the instrumentalist group. At Newnham however, it was originally intended that *if* the girls wanted to take examinations, these should be different from those taken by men students so as to avoid the 'unpleasantness' of outright competition; Anne Clough's sympathies were with both the liberal humanists and the moralists. Newnham, however, eventually followed Girton's lead.

The reaction to these innovations was fierce. The fears which were expressed as to the effects of education on women and the way in which this would reverberate through society demonstrated the relationship between 'femininity' and key social institutions such as the home, female chastity, and the separation of women from any active role in the social domain. The main fear was that educating women would lead to a decline in the importance of the home, and hence to a decline in morality generally. Just as the Victorians maintained a double standard of morality between the sexes, so did they maintain a double standard of morality between the private and public domains. Trollope, Dickens and other Victorian novelists often depicted the contrast between the ruthless entrepreneur or financier at work, and his sentimental but authoritarian attitude to his family. The importance of the idealized 'home' as refuge and safety-valve was very great, apart from the Veblenesque desire to demonstrate financial prosperity by maintaining one's women in conspicuous and decorative idleness.

The tension and antagonism produced by changes in girls' education is hard to understand unless we see that an elaborate system of symbolic boundaries was being broken down. Male fears of competition from women in jobs, examinations and so on were all the greater in that symbolically women were stepping from a different and non-competitive world, and thus were polluting the values of both the world they left – 'the home' – and the world that they entered. The reluctance to allow them to compete, the fear that this experience might irrevocably contaminate them, demonstrated the importance of the symbolic separation between mens' and womens' worlds.

> . . . boys are sent out into the world to buffet with its temptations, to mingle with bad and good, to govern and direct . . . girls are to dwell in quiet homes, amongst a few friends, to exercise a noiseless influence, to be submissive and retiring . . . to educate girls in crowds is wrong.[16]

Other anxieties and rationalizations about 'femininity' were also aroused. The educated woman, the bluestocking, then as now, was thought to be at once over-sexed and not sensual enough, both masculine and neuter. The general concern with eugenics and the breeding capacities of the race which had resulted from the Darwinian revolution extended to the effects of educating girls

> . . . in regard to the possible effect on health and physical vigour of women students. It was feared that the opening of new facilities for study and intellectual improvement would result in the creation of a

new race of puny, sedentary and unfeminine students, and would destroy the grace and charm of social life, and would disqualify women for their true vocation, the nurture of the coming race and the govern-ance of well-ordered, healthy and happy homes.[17]

Evidence from the medical profession was brought forward by those who subscribed to the ideology of educational pluralism: the development of nervous troubles and the harming of the reproductive organs were said to be likely consequences of a 'boy's education'. Medical men repeatedly argued that it was of the utmost necessity to rest during menstruation. Dr Matthew Duncan claimed that a boy's education would result in women's reproductive organs being harmed. He suggested to the BMA that such an education would produce amenorrhoea and chlor-osis, and destroy sensuality 'of a proper and commendable kind'. H. Spencer thought that flat-chested girls, after a period of higher education, would be unable to suckle infants.[18] It is a striking demonstration of the class-related nature of the debate that no one appeared to derive from these beliefs any concern about the working conditions of girls and women who were servants or factory-hands.

In spite of the substantive changes which took place in educa-tion for some girls, the pluralist ideology remained dominant. It has been said[19] that of all girls receiving secondary education in England in 1898, 70 per cent were being educated in private boarding schools, often in towns where grammar and high schools had empty places. The chief advantage of boarding schools was that they were socially homogeneous: eligibility for marriage and not the content of their daughter's education remained the dominant concern of middle-class parents. However, the ideology advocating 'assimilation' seems to have had some impact on these private schools; hence the following advertisement for,

Ellerslie High School and College, Blackheath
Boarding School – but otherwise conducted similarly to the high *day* schools . . . but without the indiscriminate mixture of all grades as the Public High Day Schools.[20]

During the latter half of the nineteenth century working-class girls benefited together with boys from the improvements introduced by the 1870 Education Act, when for the first time children were legally entitled to public primary education (although attendance was still voluntary).[21] Those advocating improvement in the quality of 'mass' education tended to be members of the middle classes, who ironically were arguing the need for increased differentiation in the content of the education offered to working-class boys and girls, no doubt prompted partly by their dependence on the domestic services of working-class girls. It was argued that the type of educational provision made for the poor should be determined by their need for vocational training – for instance, as domestic servants.

James Booth, writing about the education of the working-class girl in 1835, asked '... why should she not be taught to light a fire, sweep a room, wash crockery and glass without breaking them, wash clothes and bake bread?'[22] The philanthropic members of the middle classes also believed that if working-class women could be educated to run their homes 'well', they would re-create the sacred middle-class resting place, and would thus discourage men from visiting public houses, and thus drunkenness, poverty and wife-beating would be stamped out. As a result, there were many schemes to include the domestic arts in the curricula of elementary schools. Those who provided a vocational education for working-class girls worked on the assumption that girls would become first servants and then housewives. Much of the treatment of domestic servants was equally based on the supposition that they would eventually become housewives.

In the twentieth century, the recipients of the vocational education were redefined as the 'less able'. The able daughter of poor parents who climbed the ladder of educational opportunity was rewarded with an academic education on the 'assimilation' model. Her brothers and sisters who remained to receive a vocational education in the junior technical schools, which were started in the first decade of the twentieth century, found that vocations were defined in a sex-specific way, and that notions of 'femininity' were here mediated less by psychological assumptions than by the nature of the women's employment market.

During the twentieth century we have seen a growing commitment to the educational ideology of equality of opportunity for all children, a commitment which has included assimilating the educational experiences of girls to boys. This commitment was neither immediate in its appearance nor uniform in its manner amongst those involved in the process of education. For example, many educationalists in the Conservative Party remain committed to the continuing existence of a private sector in education. The commitment to the ideology of equality of opportunity derives partially from the necessity for the 'ruling class' to choose more 'universal' grounds for selection and privilege in education. With the founding of the mass party and a universal franchise, combined with the trade union movement's commitment to a universal system of secondary education from the 1890s on, those in power were obliged to think in terms of the expansion and improvement of educational facilities for the whole population. In reality, as has often been shown, a very great gulf has existed between this ideology and actual practice.

With the 1902 Education Act, the government officially recognized that secondary education was a fit object for public expenditure and should eventually be extended to all children. The majority of the working class were using the elementary schools for their formal education, in which little differentiation was made between boys and girls in terms of the selection of the content of curricula, etc. This was so in spite of protests from middle-class people worried about the 'servant problem'. For instance, in 1916 Edith Sellers asked over 1,000 working-class girls about their career aspirations. Finding that most answered in terms of factory work or typing, and that only fifty wanted to become servants, she wrote, '. . . surely their choice of calling in life is proof that there is something wrong somewhere in our system of elementary education?'[23] The history of girls' education in the twentieth century reveals significant class differences; as I have implied, these differences are often officially legitimated in terms of the 'needs' of the 'less able' and the 'academically able' child. These labels can often be taken as euphemisms for 'lower-working' and 'lower middle to middle-class' respectively; the upper classes escape such labelling by being educated in the private sector.

Many upper- and upper-middle-class girls during the first few decades of the twentieth century continued to experience the type of education which had been deemed appropriate for 'young ladies' in the nineteenth century. But middle-class girls were much more likely to receive an education which would offer them many of the same opportunities as their brothers, i.e. a public day school with an academic curriculum; possibly followed by university. However, this did not lead to the position held by the nineteenth-century instrumentalists. Instead, the experience gained in the education of girls was increasingly used to differentiate between the supposed intellectual capacities of the sexes, and thus to rationalize the different choice of subjects. In a series of papers written by members of the Association of Headmistresses (voicing the opinion of the most influential group of middle-class female educators) we find that the majority of contributors emphasized those differences between the sexes which pointed to the necessity of differential treatment within the same general kind of education. Girls were said to 'lack reasoning power, were unable to give a lucid direction, an accurate description or a clear and logical explanation'.[24]

The conclusion drawn from these assumptions was that girls were innately predisposed towards certain subjects. It was believed that girls found mathematics and science difficult to grasp and that few would want to specialize in them. It was argued regularly that it would be conducive to the cultivation of 'good health' and prevention of 'overstrain' if science (particularly physics and chemistry) and mathematics (not arithmetic) were eliminated from the curriculum of girls' secondary schools, or at the very least these subjects should be given a subordinate place. The assumption that girls dislike and are bad at science and mathematics has been consistently held throughout the twentieth century. It is interesting to speculate how this notion was originally conceived, as its influence on the shape of girls' secondary education has been considerable. Girls' schools found great difficulty right from the beginning in obtaining qualified science teachers, reasonable laboratory space and resources, etc.[25] In many ways, therefore, middle-class girls' education tended to be a compromise between the 'solutions' of *assimilation* and *pluralism*.

The majority of working-class girls did not have access to

secondary education as free scholarship places were scarce. Some were able to afford a two- or three-year course at the Junior Technical Schools, which provided vocational training of a sex-specific nature. Others, whose parents could not afford further education beyond the age of thirteen, could attend 'continuance' classes. Their aim, according to the Board of Education, was to ' . . . train girls to become efficient workers and the mothers of healthy children', though they found that the long hours worked by girls meant that few attended.

By the first decades of the twentieth century, a pattern was seen to be emerging in a girl's education similar to that for boys; a small, highly able élite was identified and given an academic education which led on to university. The number of girls so identified, however, was always very much smaller, and many observers considered that, unlike boys, by becoming highly educated they were forfeiting their chances of gaining the goals natural to their sex. Several 'emancipated' women appeared to be regretting it: Alice Ikin, for example, an ex-Newnham scholar, thought that 'the next stage of woman's emancipation must allow of the combination of intellectual development and motherhood', and an old pupil of Francis Buss, from the North London Collegiate felt that

. . . instead of facing squarely the real needs of future wives and mothers, as the vast majority of girls were to be, Miss Buss seized the tempting instrument at her hand . . . the stimulus to mental ambition afforded by outside exams.[26]

These views no doubt reflected the social position of the few highly educated women of the period. Until the First World War, women's employment opportunities were severely restricted and they were often required to relinquish their jobs on marriage. The view that they would have to choose between a career (usually teaching) and marriage was thus socially created but perfectly real; graduate women at this period in fact were less likely to marry than their non-graduate sisters. Various biological bogies continued to be raised. Havelock Ellis thought that the active and athletic life of some contemporary women made their confinements so difficult as to endanger their babies;

another commentator feared that the present-day methods of educating girls had made them less capable of bearing and nursing their children. Things had got even worse in America, apparently – one doctor could only find 4 per cent of his countrywomen physiologically fitted to become wives and mothers.[27]

The impression that one is left with after reading educationalists and doctors of the period discussing topics such as the impact of education on childbirth or menstruation is that women and girls have a fixed store of energy, a little bit of which is used up every month. If 'education' or physical exercise uses up too much of this irreplaceable store, then girls' health will be damaged with unpleasant consequences for future generations. It is fascinating to note that the best way to prevent 'overstrain' was to eliminate science from the curriculum of girls' secondary schools, or at least considerably to reduce its importance.[28]

In 1922, these problems were confronted directly by the Hadow Report on the differences of curriculum appropriate to the 'needs' of boys and girls. For the first time, 'male' and 'female' were treated as problematic categories in educational research commissioned by a government body. Academic experts – principally Cyril Burt and R. L. Thorndike – were asked to provide evidence concerning the innate differences between the sexes in mental capacity and educability. They concluded that the most important characteristic of such differences was their small amount. But the teachers who gave evidence to the Committee accepted the current notions of femininity and masculinity and reported that they found boys more original, constructive and self-assertive; girls on the other hand were seen to be persevering, industrious, passive, imitative, emotional and intuitive. Girls were reported to be more lethargic in secondary school, and naturally more prone to opt for arts subjects.

The committee seemed on the whole to accept the non-expert evidence, and thought that since girls were less capable of prolonged mental effort and more prone to neurotic disturbance than boys, it would on the whole be desirable to educate them differently. But they were not prepared to suggest an alternative model for their education, and felt that the solution should be found by teachers themselves. We can only speculate as to the extent to which women teachers in the twenties and thirties were able to transcend the boundaries of their own experience and of the conventional wisdom. Overall, the assumptions about 'femininity' and the effect that they had on the provision of educational facilities for girls of different social classes changed very little between the latter part of the nineteenth century and the first few decades of the twentieth century, despite the general improvement in both the quality and quantity of education available.

The publication of the Norwood Report in 1943 and the subsequent 1944 Education Act heralded a new era in secondary education. For the first time LEAs were required to provide secondary education for all children up to the minimum age of fifteen. Fees were abolished in maintained secondary schools from 1945. The marked gulf between the ideology of equality of educational opportunity for all children of both sexes and actual educational practice promised to be diminished as a result of this Act – at least in the public sector of the educational system. However, educational selection as a principle continued to operate – although the criterion for selection became 'innate ability' (measured IQ) rather than 'social class' (as in the Taunton Commission, for instance). As I have suggested this resulted in general use being made of the labels 'academically able' as referring to those children who were believed capable of benefiting from a grammar school education which was defined as 'good-in-itself', and a large residual category of 'less able' who were believed to be suited to a more practical and 'relevant' education defined as being oriented towards a *vocation*. Together with the belief in the different 'innate abilities' of children went an assumption of their 'natural interests', which the Norwood Committee considered varied between the sexes. For girls these were still defined as marriage and motherhood, and for boys, a concern with a job or career. This assumption represented the official legitimation of actual differences in the content of the curriculum for boys and girls, particularly in the case of the 'less able'. Like the Hadow Committee, the Norwood Committee subscribed to the belief that there were innate differences between the sexes, but did not recommend the construction of alternative sex-based models of education. Flexibility of curricula and autonomy for teachers were again thought to be adequate solutions. Teacher autonomy would be necessarily somewhat curtailed in those schools catering for the 'able' child, i.e. in grammar, direct-grant and private-sector secondary schools, where the structure of curricula and subject choice was constrained by the external demands made by examining bodies and universities.

In spite of the existence of universal secondary education offering equal opportunities for those of equal measured ability, within each category of ability marked differences in the performance, aspirations and expectations of the sexes have continued to exist. These differences have not been defined as a problem either by official Government bodies, by whom they have been generally taken for granted, or by researchers. In those schools catering for middle-class and/or 'able' children these differences manifest themselves in terms of subject choice, numbers of public examinations taken and passed, age of leaving school, destination after leaving, career aspirations, and so on. Documentation describing the differences between the sexes is available in the annual volumes of the *Statistics of Education*. In schools catering for the 'less able' or working-class child, differences of the same sort are found, and in addition there is even more marked sex-differentiation in the provision of 'vocational' courses such as engineering or typing, metalwork or needlework, which are usually only available for those of the appropriate sex.

The Crowther Report, 1959, noted that the less able the girl, the more sex-based her school curriculum was likely to be. It is stated that, of the 'far more able' girls,

there is not much scope in school hours for giving them any education which is specifically related to their special needs as women.

With the less-able girls, however, we think schools can and should make adjustments to the fact that marriage now looms much larger and nearer in the pupils' eyes than ever before.[29]

It is difficult to see why, if interest in marriage and one's personal appearance is seen as 'natural' and a dominating interest for all girls, it is necessary for this interest to be incorporated into the educational experience of the 'less able' girls only.

Currently, many educationalists are committed to an educational 'solution' of assimilation – at least in theory – for the 25 per cent of 'able' girls in the public sector of education, and to educational pluralism for the 'less able' remainder. Substantive differences between the sexes still exist at both levels, however much they have been reduced.

Several possible explanations exist for the differences in subject-choice, etc., between boys and girls. Part of the difference may be due to the differential allocation of resources to boys' and girls' schools. Girls' schools have found it more difficult to employ qualified science and mathematics teachers, and have in the past been allocated less laboratory space. The introduction of comprehensive coeducational schools should remove this sort of difficulty. In addition, different opportunities after school may affect the choices made by boys and girls. The quotas and barriers which limit the number of girls at medical schools, at Oxbridge, in some of the professions and apprenticeship schemes have not always been abolished and often continue to exist informally. Above all, teachers, parents and pupils themselves have notions of 'femininity' which affect the treatment and expectations of girl pupils.

Conclusion

Throughout this essay, it has been necessary largely to ignore the variations between schools in terms of their size, source of finance, traditions and whether they are single-sex or coeducational. These are important considerations, but for the purposes of this essay I wanted to make very general preliminary statements about the relationships between ideology and practice in the history of girls' education.

In my opening paragraphs I suggested that 'male' and 'female' have not been prominent explanatory categories in educational models and philosophies in the way that the categories 'able' and 'less able' have been. I have tried to show that notions concerning 'femininity' have been shown to vary both historically and between the social classes; and to be dialectically related to the changing roles of women in society. Many questions remain unanswered which seem to be important and interesting. For example: why have science and mathematics been defined as subjects which girls were predisposed to find difficult? Why have differences in performance between girls and boys been seen as unproblematic? How do teachers in schools define 'femininity' today, and does this affect the treatment and expectations of female pupils *vis-à-vis* male pupils?

This essay is a first step towards raising some of the problems associated with sex-typing in schools – I hope that there will be others.

6

The Education of Girls Today

TESSA BLACKSTONE

There are many false claims expressed about the performance and participation of girls in the educational system. These range from the frequently heard view that a higher percentage of girls than boys leave school at the earliest age possible, to the belief that fewer girls go into full-time higher or further education. It is hardly surprising that such myths should survive in the absence of any serious work by social scientists on this issue. Until very recently academic sociology has neglected gender as a source of social differentiation. There has been even less study of gender differentiation in formal educational systems than in some other social institutions such as the family or economic and occupational spheres. In societies where more and more importance is placed on achievement rather than on roles assigned to the individual at birth, roles ascribed to males and females have only recently come to be questioned. One reason for this is that traditional ideology about women sees their roles as innate rather than cultural. This whole topic surely calls for more attention from social scientists and those concerned with educational policy. For this reason this chapter will devote some attention to the need for research in this area.

I must begin by making my own values explicit. My own view is that current forms of gender differentiation pose a social problem. More and more women appear to be dissatisfied with the role of women as an industrial reserve army, either as unpaid housekeepers or as an underpaid work force in the labour market. This is reflected in the re-emergence of feminist movements and legislation for equal pay for equal jobs and the demand for anti-discrimination legislation. This dissatisfaction is associated with wider changes in values which conflict with the value of role-ascription on the basis of gender. Some people claim that gender differentiation is diminishing. There are, for example, fewer formal barriers to women's participation in many areas of social life. However the removal of formal barriers does not mean that barriers no longer exist. The transition has been from manifest gender differentiation, which characterizes traditional societies, to latent gender differentiation. Thus overt discrimination towards women in education or employment may be declining but this does not mean to say that discrimination does not continue to exist in a variety of hidden and subtle ways.

That unequal treatment of boys and girls in the educational system is undesirable is easy to see. Its main result is that control over one's destiny, and one's access to power and prestige will vary according to whether one is male or female. In general, the fostering of 'feminine' qualities among women is not conducive to the attainment of power or status. Gender differentiation is also likely to reduce opportunities for individual members of either sex, because limiting people to socially ascribed roles reduces the choices available to them. A further result, so far as women are concerned, of this closing of the avenues to power and status is that it encourages women in general to undervalue themselves. In a society where money and prestige through work are an important source of self-respect, this psychological undervaluing is represented structurally by the low wages paid for women's work.[1] Higher pay for women is one way to improve their confidence and their image of themselves. Another is through education: better educated women are more likely to be politically active, to be employed, to believe in sex equality and to be less likely to avoid situations of conflict. Inactive and unemployed women whose children have grown up are more likely than others to suffer from psychosomatic and other pathological symptoms.[2] Finally, just as the failure to educate working-class children is rightly seen as undesirable, so, too, is the failure to educate women. Women will remain a disadvantaged group so long as decisions about their education are taken in the light of restrictive social definitions about their future role in society.

Two further points must be stressed before looking at current educational opportunities for girls. First, the degree to which

educational change, unaccompanied by other social changes, can
alter the position of women in the wider society is limited.
Second, although I make the case for the abolition of differentiation between boys and girls in their educational experiences, I do
so on the assumption that the existing educational framework
and its ideologies will remain largely unchanged. Thus children
will still be selected by formal examinations for higher education
and the élite jobs to which this leads. I assume reluctantly, but
realistically, that inequalities in the occupational structure will
remain, but that access to privileged jobs can and should become
more open, thereby increasing women's chances of obtaining
them. Finally I assume that a redefinition of our values, so that
qualities traditionally defined as feminine are raised in status and
those traditionally defined as masculine are lowered, would be
desirable, but that this is unlikely to be achieved in the short
term. We need a fundamental revision of social values. The status
of traditional feminine jobs, such as nursing or teaching for
example, will only rise if society attaches greater importance to
nurturing roles generally than it does at present.

As recently as 1964 a much respected English educationalist
wrote an article which argued that there should be fundamental
changes in the education of girls of a kind which would allow
much more attention to be given to preparing them to be housewives and mothers.[3] The article reiterated proposals made
fifteen years earlier in a book in which the author claimed that
'the future of women's education lies not in attempting to iron
out their differences from men, to reduce them to neuters, but to
teach girls how to grow into women and to relearn the graces
which so many have forgotten in the past thirty years'.[4] Although
the article provoked a lively debate in the letter columns, with
plenty of correspondents supporting Newsom, his suggestions
for the reform of girls' education have not been taken seriously by
many educationalists, but they have clearly had some influence.
To implement his proposals would be to repudiate the work of
those who fought to obtain an education for girls which would not
be inferior to that for boys.[5] A curriculum consisting of extensive
time spent on housecraft, cooking, needlework and mothercraft,
a bias towards the imparting of social graces[6] and giving little

attention to mathematics and the natural sciences, is inferior in two important ways: it is likely to limit choices available to girls at the post-secondary stage, and it concentrates on activities related to domestic roles, which have diminishing status and little or no material rewards in cash terms.

Yet despite Newsom, it seems likely that the education of girls will develop along quite different lines. The increasing demand for women in the labour force and the declining birth rate are typical of the economic and social factors compelling change, and these combine with an ideological climate which looks for an extension of opportunities for women outside the home. Such changes would be conducive to greater social and economic equality between men and women. However, a review of current educational opportunities for girls will reveal that there is still some way to go before this is achieved.

Government reports and policy statements reflect official ideology and provide a good starting point for such a review. They state that girls should have equal access to, and opportunity in, higher education, and that there should be an equal distribution of resources between boys and girls in secondary and primary schools. Any discrimination against girls is officially frowned upon. But any accusation that it exists would probably be officially discounted too.[7] There is, in fact, little formal differentiation in the education of boys and girls, apart from some fairly obvious differences. For example, in many schools boys play football and girls play netball. In secondary schools it is common for girls to be taught to cook, sew or type while boys are taught woodwork, metalwork or technical drawing. But in a growing number of schools rigid overt distinctions of this kind are breaking down. Increasingly, the last remaining distinction is in the use of corporal punishment as a means of social control – some boys are caned, girls on the whole are not.[8]

Because the formally institutionalized distinctions are breaking down, it does not follow that more subtle forms of discrimination are on the decline as well. There have been studies of the attitudes of primary school teachers[9] which suggest that they expect boys and girls to behave differently and to be motivated differently. Because of these different expectations teachers will give different kinds of encouragement which, of course, will further affect the way children of either sex behave. For example, it is now well established that girls of seven to eight and at eleven will score better than boys in tests of verbal ability – in other words, they can read and express themselves better than boys. The studies in this area suggest that girls are, on average, three to six months ahead of boys. On the other hand, boys seem to do as well, or better, than girls in tests of numerical ability, although the findings here are less consistent; Douglas[10] found that eleven-year-old girls were slightly ahead in arithmetical skills as well as in other forms of non-verbal intelligence. Between the ages of eleven and sixteen there is relatively little British evidence about differences in the performance of boys and girls, but a study using data from Canada and New Zealand found that girls' attainment declined between ten and fourteen whereas that of boys remained constant.[11] One of the few British studies which investigates this comes to the same conclusion.[12] Although at the age of eleven girls were ahead of boys in intelligence (verbal and non-verbal), reading and arithmetic, and were behind them only on tests of vocabulary, by the age of fifteen the situation had been reversed; girls were slightly behind boys in non-verbal intelligence, reading and arithmetic and ahead of them only in verbal intelligence. Pidgeon[13] also found that girls' performance in achievement tests in mathematics dropped between the ages of eleven and fourteen.

How much of all this (assuming that it is environmentally determined and not innate) is due to teachers, and how much to parents' and peer-group influence and encouragement, is not clear. Nevertheless, it is clear that in Britain there has been practically no difference during the last decade or so in the proportion of boys and girls leaving school at the minimum leaving age.[14] However after the age of sixteen girls leave earlier than boys. This is shown in Table 1 (p. 204): whereas 6 per cent of girls left school at eighteen, 8 per cent of boys did so.[15] This is reflected in the smaller proportion of girls entering for the Advanced Level of the General Certificate of Education.

Before considering 'A' Level entry and performance it is necessary to consider Ordinary Level statistics. The 'O' Level per-

Table 1 Age of Leaving School as a
Percentage of All Leavers*

Age	1950–51		1970–71	
---	Boys	Girls	Boys	Girls
14			28 ⎫ 65	29 ⎫ 66
15	79	80	37 ⎭	36 ⎭
16	13	13	16	16
17	3	4	12	14
18+	4	4	8	6
Total	100%	100%	100%	100%

*Excluding Independent Schools
  Source: Department of Education and
Science, *Statistics of Education 1970*, vol. 2,
HMSO, 1973.

formance of girls in 1969–70 was in fact similar to that of boys
(see Table 2 p. 205). However further analysis shows that
although the numbers of boys and girls entering for 'O' Level
exams was identical, there are some differences in performance
which do not show up in the figures presented in Table 2. The
number of subjects for which boys entered was greater, but their
pass rate was somewhat lower than for girls. A slightly higher
proportion of those entering for seven or eight subjects passed
them all among the girls, and at the other extreme a slightly
smaller proportion of girls failed to pass any subjects. The somewhat lower success of the boys could be the result of attempting
more. However, what is clear is that if performance in public
examinations is used as the criterion of achievement, on most
measures girls of sixteen in Britain were in 1969–70 doing no
worse than boys of the same age.

It is at the next stage, as Table 2 shows, that there seems to
have been a clear difference between the sexes. Whereas 9 per
cent of boys obtained three or more 'A' Levels, only 6 per cent
of girls did so, and a smaller proportion of girls than boys
obtained two passes. This was due not to a higher failure rate
among the girls – on the contrary their pass rate was better than

Table 2 Boys' and Girls' Performance in the
General Certificate of Education (1969–70)

*Percentage of all leavers gaining GCE
passes.*

	Boys	Girls
3 or more 'O' Level passes	28	29
5 or more 'O' Level passes	21	22
2 or more 'A' Level passes	13	9
3 or more 'A' Level passes	9	6

Source: Department of Education and Science,
Statistics of Education 1970, vol. 2, H M S O, 1973.

the boys' – but to entering for fewer subjects. Girls have been choosing to enter for fewer 'A' Levels than boys, or their schools have been deciding to enter them for fewer subjects. Clearly the explanation has nothing to do with their 'O' Level performance. It should be mentioned, however, that the increase in 'A' Level entries over the last decade has been much greater for girls than for boys, which suggests that this particular gap between boys and girls may soon disappear.

The second important difference to have emerged is in the subjects boys and girls choose to study at Ordinary and Advanced Level. It is a well known fact that boys tend to specialize in science subjects and girls in arts subjects. But it seems likely that many people are unaware of the extent to which this is true. In the mid sixties, only 25 per cent of the girls who passed two or more 'A' levels did so in science subjects alone, compared with the 66 per cent who obtained passes only in arts subjects. On the other hand, 57 per cent of the boys who passed two or more 'A' levels did so in science subjects alone, compared with the 38 per cent who restricted themselves to the arts.[16] In 1970 more than four times as many boys than girls took 'O' level physics, nearly three times as many boys took chemistry, and of all those taking 'O' level maths, 40 per cent were girls and 60 per cent boys. These last figures are especially significant because of the fact that it is considerably easier to get a university place in pure or applied science than in arts or social sciences. Therefore subject specialism in the last years of secondary school must have an effect on the destination of school leavers aiming for higher education.

In 1969–70 19 per cent of boys and 23 per cent of girls leaving school went on to full-time further or higher education. Thus the overall proportion of female school-leavers at present benefiting from the opportunity of full-time education after leaving school is higher than that of boys. However, the kind of post-secondary education that boys and girls obtain does differ considerably, and has done since the early fifties. More than half the girls are at colleges of further education, many of them taking short, relatively low-level courses in subjects such as shorthand and typing. And within higher education nearly half the girls are at colleges of education, whereas only one in six of the boys are. In other words, the girls are more likely to be found following what are widely considered to be lower status courses in lower status institutions.

An examination of the proportions of young men and women in part-time further education also shows interesting differences. Young men are much more likely than girls to get time off from employment for education or training, whether to follow day release or sandwich courses. For example 20 per cent of boys aged between fifteen and seventeen, compared with 6 per cent of girls, obtained day release in 1970 for part-time study. The differences were even greater for the eighteen to twenty year olds, among whom most of the girls relied on evening courses to further their education. And if we exclude that part of the fifteen to seventeen-year-old population in full-time education, the differences become if anything starker: 38 per cent of the boys attended part-time day courses and only 12 per cent of the girls. In some ways this difference is more important than the differences described in higher education, because the numbers involved are so much larger.

Lastly let us examine the position of women in the universities. Although only a small proportion of young people go to them, what happens at the top of the system is of more than numerical importance. Few women at the top of the educational system means few models of educational success for those lower down, and may result in lower aspirations among sixth-form girls in secondary schools. Table 3 shows that in 1970 30 per cent of undergraduates were women. This represents an increase of about 5 per cent over a decade, since only a quarter of undergraduates were women at the time of the surveys for the Robbins Report. The lower proportion of girls must partly be a result of the smaller numbers taking two or more 'A' Levels. It must also be a result of fewer girls than boys with the requisite 'A' Level qualifications applying for places. It is not caused by smaller proportions of female than male applicants being offered places; on the contrary, statistics from the Universities Central Council for Admissions indicate that a higher proportion of the girls who apply than of the boys are accepted. However, this is to be expected, since in general, the girls who apply have better 'A' Level grades.

The proportion of postgraduates who are women falls to only 16 per cent, and the proportion of university teachers who are women drops again, to 9 per cent. There is thus a high level of drop-out among women at the different stages of transition in university education. Moreover, women academics tend to be concentrated in the lower grades, so that although 9 per cent of university teachers are women, only 1 per cent of professors are women. Attempts to describe this in greater detail, and to understand why it occurs, have been made elsewhere.[17] The lower proportion of women among postgraduate students also requires explanation, particularly as the proportion of women with the qualification required, a first-class or upper-second-class honours degree (29 per cent), is almost the same as for men (30 per cent). Women do obtain fewer firsts (4 per cent) than men (8 per cent), but part of the difference can be explained by the fact that far fewer firsts are awarded in the humanities and social sciences, where women are concentrated, than in the pure and applied sciences. Women are also less likely to obtain thirds – approximately 9 per cent compared with 13 per cent of men. Table 3 (p. 208) also shows marked differences in the proportions of women in the different faculties. In the humanities just over half the undergraduates in 1970–71 were women, but in the social

Table 3 Proportion of Women by Subject: Academic Staff
(1968–9), Postgraduate Students and Undergraduate
Students (1970–71) (Percentage)

% Women	Applied Science	Medicine	Pure Science	Social Science	Humanities	All
Staff	2	9	8	10	14	9
Postgraduates*	5	24	12	19	22	16
Undergraduates	5	29	26	33	54	30

*Excludes postgraduates not studying for higher *degrees*, i.e. certificate and diploma students.

Sources: Staff: Gareth Williams, Tessa Blackstone and David Metcalf, *The Academic Labour Market: Essays on Economic and Social Aspects of a Profession*, Elsevier, The Hague, 1974.

Students: *Statistics of Education 1970*, vol. 6, Tables 1, 4, 20, HMSO, 1973.

sciences the proportion was a third, in medicine between a quarter and a third, in pure sciences a quarter, and in applied sciences only one in twenty. These differences were slightly less among staff as a result of a higher level of 'drop out' in the humanities, but they were still marked, and presumably reflect the subject specialisms of children in secondary schools.

What conclusions can be drawn from this brief survey of the educational performance and educational experience of girls in British education? The first is that at face value there is little difference in either the educational experiences or indeed the average performances of boys and girls until they reach the age of sixteen. In primary schools boys and girls are educated together and follow the same curriculum. In secondary schools about 60 per cent of them are educated together and with a few exceptions the same curriculum is offered to both sexes. Some differences in the performance of boys and girls are apparent in primary and secondary schools, but analysis of the results of school-leaving examinations show only small differences apart from subject specialization. However, differences are very apparent in decisions made by boys and girls about what kind of schooling or post-secondary education to undertake after the age of sixteen. Perhaps girls do not link educational success with occupational success to the same degree as boys. Thus, although they achieve what the educational system expects of them, they do not make the same use of achievements as boys, because of lower expectations about their *occupational* roles.

For whatever reason, the aspirations of girls appear to be lower than those of their male peers. Is this due to institutional practices and attitudes on the part of schools and other educational organizations, or is it due to different expectations among girls about their adult lives and occupational futures, or to innate predispositions and personality characteristics which differentiate them from boys? It seems probable that biological differences, social and cultural influences, and educational practice all interact. What we need to understand better is the degree of strength of each, and which of them can be changed. I have already pointed out that girls do better than boys in primary schools, particularly in areas involving verbal skills, but that this is no longer true by the time they are fifteen.[18] Further, girls choose different subjects from boys when they get to secondary schools, fewer of them enter for 'O' levels and very many fewer for 'A' levels. After leaving school more boys than girls attend part-time further education and, in the case of those of both sexes who go on to full-time further education, girls are more often to be found in colleges of education or further education than in universities or polytechnics. Finally, fewer women go on to postgraduate studies.

The question we have to ask is what contribution if any does the educational process in itself make to this pattern? Unfortunately, very little work has been done on the questions involved and we can therefore only speculate. There are three principal areas concerned: the curriculum; teachers' attitudes; and structural aspects. So far as the curriculum is concerned, it has become increasingly clear that many of the books children use in schools strongly reinforce traditional stereotypes of male and female behaviour.[19] In various series of books from which children learn to read girls and women are portrayed as subordinate to men in a variety of ways. They are shown as less active, having less initiative, having less resilience in crises and taking fewer decisions. Women are usually portrayed as mothers and wives with no role in the community outside the home. Their lives appear to revolve round domestic chores and the care of children. While this may be true for *some* women, the proportion of women in employment, including married women with children, is rising rapidly. In 1951 22 per cent of married women were in the labour force; by 1961 this had risen to 29 per cent, and by 1971 it had leapt to 43 per cent.[20] To portray women as nothing but wives and mothers not only reinforces traditional stereotypes, and limits the educational and occupational aspirations of girls, but it also gives a false impression of what their future lives will be. This is just one example of the way in which the content of children's education may have an effect on their perceptions of their future lives and the value of education to them. There are many other areas of the curriculum, such as history or the study of literature, where the presentation of gender differences can lower girls' aspirations. Further study of curricula and their impact is required before we can be fully aware of how significant they are in affecting the expectations of boys and girls. But if girls are usually expected to identify with mothers, and mothers are typified in conventional housewife roles and females are portrayed waiting on husbands or brothers in such influential reading material as infant-school primers, it does seem likely that the self-image of girls generally will be limited. Much of the literature that children read outside school, particularly comics, tends to reinforce further the conventional stereotypes. It would be good to see what would happen if new materials were incorporated into school-books, so that mothers were depicted working outside the home, and fathers were shown in expressive roles. Neither of these are, after all, uncommon experiences.

It is also important to examine the attitudes of teachers and other adults who influence boys and girls at crucial periods in their educational development: people such as careers' advisers, youth employment officers, and even employers. I have suggested that the differences in boys' and girls' performance in primary schools can be at least partly explained by differences in teachers' expectations.[21] Teachers find boys difficult and unresponsive, and are much more likely to categorize them as lazy or poor workers, lacking in concentration or discipline or both. By contrast teachers expect girls to be more docile, attentive, diligent and less adventurous. Studies have been carried out in Britain and the USA which show that children tend to behave as teachers expect them to behave.[22] This may well explain why girls do better than boys in primary schools, where the basic skills like reading and writing are taught, areas in which conformity and diligence are likely to pay off.

We know very little about how secondary-school teachers see the differences between boys and girls or how their attitudes affect pupil behaviour; the academic studies have simply not been done. But if diligence and conformity are expected from girls, then they could well be at a disadvantage at the top end of the educational system where critical faculties must be exercised and where imagination is required. Here it is likely to be the girls who suffer from a negative image, although of a different kind from the one held by primary-school teachers about boys; an image which may impose unnecessarily narrow boundaries on their intellectual and occupational potential, and label them as suitable only for certain kinds of jobs, as unambitious and lacking in drive or initiative. This discouraging image may well account for the fact that girls take fewer 'A' levels than boys and are less likely to apply for admission to the universities. Equally, girls may choose the humanities rather than the sciences because teachers feel that these are more appropriate subjects.

It is unclear at present how far children are able to make genuine choices based on their own interests, and how far they are channelled into certain subjects which teachers consider appropriate to their sex. An examination of social processes in the school situation would help us to understand better the way in which values are transmitted and the way latent gender differentiation takes place. For this kind of research a combination of research methods would be best, including conventional questionnaires, intensive depth interviewing, and participant observation in the classroom. The difficulty at getting at the truth about all this is of course compounded because what the teachers are conveying to the pupils may well be unconscious. It is perfectly possible that teachers are unaware that they are passing onto children the values and norms derived from their own socialization. For example, it is unlikely that it would ever occur to most teachers to prepare a girl for the dual roles of worker and wife-and-mother. They are much more likely to think of these roles sequentially, so that work is something done before and after motherhood, never simultaneously.

Nor do we know enough about the effect of being taught by someone of the same sex or the opposite sex. Most primary-school teachers are women and it may well be that girls do better than boys in these schools because they can identify more easily with their teachers. In secondary schools there are three male teachers for every two female teachers, yet this disproportion does not seem great enough to allow the argument that it is much easier for boys to identify with their teachers at that stage, because cross-sex identity problems prevent the girls doing so. But as subjects tend very much to be divided up among men and women, with women concentrating on the humanities and men on the sciences, then it is easy to see how the problem could continue, and lead to fewer girls studying the sciences. We do not know whether the academic achievement of girls is higher in single-sex than in coeducational schools. Many people feel that single-sex schools should be abolished because they discriminate against girls in the area of science and mathematics; the facilities and the standards of teaching in these subjects are often inferior in girls' schools. This argument is opposed on the ground that worse problems arise if girls are put into a learning situation where they are in direct competition with boys. In a mixed-sex environment, the argument runs, there appears to be a stronger need to differentiate between the sexes. Girls find it more difficult to compete for academic success with boys than with other girls because they fear, perhaps unconsciously, that this may be threatening to the boys, who will consequently reject them as potential sexual partners.[23]

There is of course no reason why both these arguments should not be correct. In single-sex schools girls may benefit academically from the absence of boys, but suffer from poor science teaching. In coeducational schools they may benefit from better science teaching, but their academic performance may suffer from the presence of boys. After all, in both types of school fewer girls than boys are at present going on to university. More evidence about all this would be helpful.

Of all the educational differences between boys and girls, the most important in terms of its size and the numbers of young people affected is the availability of day release for boys and girls. There are probably several interrelated reasons for it. First, a substantial proportion of girls who leave school at the earliest possible moment are probably uninterested in any further education. Second, employers often do not consider it worth their while to offer girls day release, let alone to encourage or insist on it. Third, many of the semi- and unskilled jobs undertaken by girls offer little scope for further training.[24] The relative values ascribed by society to different kinds of work are important in this respect. Women and girls are not given the chance to benefit from continued education because of the low status of predominantly female jobs. The economic benefits of further education for women are almost certainly underestimated by employers.

In the face of all this there are some fairly obvious things to be done to reduce the loss of educational potential among girls. First, the ways in which the roles of men and women are presented to children could be changed, and the traditional and often false stereotypes dropped. Some care must be taken to stop rewarding children for specifically masculine and feminine behaviour; such rewards simply underline the norms instilled very early in children's lives. At the other end of the educational system courses for adults must be constructed with the specific goal of attracting women, and offering recognized qualifications. At present, the opportunities are limited to three areas. Degree level or equivalent courses in higher education rule out most adults; job training or retraining, because it assumes employment experience, rules out many women; adult education, which does not assume school-leaving qualifications or employment experience, does not lead to any qualifications either. Courses for adult women which avoid these shortcomings must be well publicized and must carry generous grants in order to remove the financial obstacles to taking them.

I have already said that there is little research into what goes on in secondary education, but there is also very little research into what happens in families and in the wider society in the socialization process. It would be interesting to carry out a long-term study of a particular group of boys and girls to see how and where gender differences are introduced. High-achievement girls could be studied in depth in order to understand more about the ways in which they differ from their less successful peers. It would be possible also to study changing attitudes among young people as they grow older, and the interaction between family and school factors over time. So far, however, long-term and continual studies of young people have given relatively little attention to the explanation of gender differences.

I began by claiming that the blueprint for girls' education envisaged by Newsom has not had much impact, because it is out of tune with important contemporary developments which affect the lives of women. It has also had relatively little impact because it is inconsistent with fundamental changes in values associated with industrialization and urbanization, 'Secularization and universalism provide new standards for comparison between men and women: equality, scientific rationalism and "criticism as a duty" have strengthened these ideas'.[25] The ascription of gender roles is becoming increasingly unacceptable in advanced industrial societies. The ideological pressure is towards equal and undifferentiated educational opportunities for both men and women. Social and economic developments are likely to reinforce this pressure. The expansion of tertiary employment and the decline of heavy manual work in manufacturing is increasing employment opportunities for women. Family planning made possible by easily administered, safe and reliable contraceptives can reduce the commitments involved in motherhood, above all by shortening the time women are responsible for young children. The practice of continued full-time employment by most women after marriage until the first child is born means that men and women can share the household chores. In this way the significance and importance attached to 'running a home' could be reduced. At the same time the expansion of tertiary employment and the decline of heavy manual work in manufacturing could increase the employment opportunities for women.

The Newsom approach to the education of girls is not the only ideological problem. Much contemporary educational writing stresses the importance of providing an education that is relevant to the interests of the children concerned. This idea has been developed for the children of semi- and unskilled workers in inner city areas (see for example Midwinter,[26] who is concerned to reduce the number of such children who are apparently completely alienated from their schools, and to cultivate self-respect and pride in their community among them). The argument, as applied to girls, runs as follows: if girls show greater interest in English and modern languages than in science and mathematics, that interest should be fostered and developed; if the study of home economics and mothercare appears relevant and useful to them, then opportunities for them to spend time on these areas should be increased.[27] However, to accept this argument in full is to accept an inherently conservative position for the schools. It suggests that they should reinforce the stereotyped self-images that many girls have, rather than play a positive role in breaking these down and in widening perspectives in the interests of more equal opportunities for girls in higher education and employment. Nevertheless, it would be unrealistic to expect the average teacher entirely to get rid of his or her entrenched values connected with gender differences. Even those who are committed to change in this respect are likely to suffer some feelings of ambivalence or conflicts of role identity. This may lead to subtle, unconscious gender differentiations rather than the obvious forms of differentiation shown in traditional societies.[28] It is clear that changes in the wider society are necessary before complete equality of treatment in the schools is possible, including changes in the structure of the family, in role playing within it, and especially in the arrangements made for the socialization of children. Further opening up of jobs traditionally monopolized by men is necessary too.

In conclusion, what I have tried to do is to identify some of the important differences in educational outcomes for boys and girls. In doing this it is clear that unequal treatment of the sexes – in so far as it exists – does not affect all achievement patterns. There is a great deal of similarity in the educational performance of males and females. Having focused on where the main differences lie, it should be easier both to study the causes of sex differences in education and also to develop effective policies to remove many of the present discrepancies. The success of such policies will depend on how far they are able to effect complex changes in attitudes among young people themselves as well as among their teachers. For example it may be possible to persuade teachers to see boys and girls in the same way so far as their academic potential is concerned, but more difficult to change their attitudes about assertiveness, ambition, competitiveness, which may be discouraged among girls with the result that achievement becomes more difficult for them. Lastly it must be stressed that it is as important to educate boys to be fathers and husbands as well as workers, as it is to educate girls to be workers as well as wives and mothers. Thus an educational process which endeavours to encourage tenderness among boys is as important as one which encourages ambition among girls. Only when men can escape from traditional stereotypes about appropriate masculine behaviour will more flexible and less segregated role playing occur within the family. When this happens it should encourage girls to seek higher and further education which reflects their ability, and, later, jobs appropriate to their qualifications.*

*I should like to thank the following people for helpful comments on a draft of this paper: Jack Barnes, Oliver Fulton, Earl Hopper, Sandy Isserlis, and the editors of this book. — TESSA BLACKSTONE

7

Woman and the Literary Text

JOHN GOODE

I want to ask whether literary analysis can be valuable to women's studies. This is very different from asking whether 'literature' can be valuable. Obviously social historians can read plays, novels and poems as well as anybody else, and there is no reason why they should not use them as documents that 'reflect' a reality – indeed, given the particular importance of the novel in the emergence of a distinct literature aimed at a female audience, that genre at least forms an unavoidable body of evidence. But they will be aware that what a novel reflects is mediated by its fictional nature, by the determination of its characteristics, by the history of forms, and by the highly specialized productive situation of the writer. And they will be aware of them as *caveats*. Literary analysis, on the contrary, has these very mediations as its object of study, for they constitute the 'literariness' of the literary text.[1] It is a question of whether such a study has anything to offer a programme of women's studies, and it is a question to which I do not have a confident answer. What I propose to do is to suggest a model of the way in which such analysis could be applied. If this has an arrogant, take-it-or-leave-it air about it, I should add at once that the context of women's studies itself seems to me to demand a radical revision of the procedures of literary analysis, and that what will be offered should not look like the literary criticism currently practised in the academies.

My starting point must be an apparently paradoxical one: that strictly a text illustrates nothing but what it is. To see it simply as a reflection of actuality (even allowing for distortions) or as a *response* to social realities postulates an interior, a removable essence which it does not have. If we can *interpret* a text, as Freud interpreted dreams, then we are either failing to represent its articulation (for texts are not dreams but the products of intentional work) or we are implying that the text has failed to transform its material, has failed to be irreducible. At the same time, the articulation itself is not independent of economic and ideological determinants, for it is made in a specific mode of production and the material it makes up (in both senses of the word) is a representation of 'reality', and a representation which is undoubtedly ideological in, at least, the largest sense of the term, in which it is axiomatic that all people, to live within society at all, must live in some relationship to whatever is the dominant ideology. In most cases a literary text will have a very particular relationship to ideology in general. What we have then is not a single relationship with ideology (illustration, reflection, response, or whatever) but a sequence of relations. First a text is a *project* which may be ideological (that is attempting to serve an ideology or oppose it from within it). Secondly, it is a project realized within determined circumstances which limit the questions it can ask, give it *margins* which rule it off from that about which it is compelled to be silent. Finally, it is an *object of production* which realizes the project, as a fiction whose specific effectivity is in making it *visible*, and in making it visible exposes it, in effect makes it *strange*, something new and unfamiliar in which the reader then rerecognizes the 'old and familiar' in new, surprising ways. Insofar as we become conscious not of an ideology trapped secretly 'inside' the text, but of the sense of ideology itself, motivating and shaping the representation, we are in the presence of a *fictional* coherence. On the other hand, insofar as the representation remains untransformed, unexposed, familiarized, we are in the presence of an *ideological* coherence. The decisive criterion is not what we are shown, but what we are allowed to see, which includes what we are not shown too.

The only formal device to be given extensive attention in English language criticism is that of the narrator. Although we should be aware of other structuring devices, it is useful to begin with this because it is precisely what articulates the relationship of the text to ideology itself (as opposed to a particular ideology). For ideology, in the phrase of the French Marxist philosopher

Louis Althusser, 'interpellates' the subject: that is to say that it calls upon the free subject to subject itself freely to that to which it is subject. The use of the narrator in fiction constitutes that interpellation because it subjects the reader to a defined subjectivity, and thus, if it is successful, makes it visible. Now, as Kate Millet in her book *Sexual Politics* (1971) has shown, the ideological transformations within sexual politics in the nineteenth century raised to a high level of consciousness the relation of 'female' and 'feminine' and its manifestation on the levels of role, status and temperament. I have chosen for analysis texts which have the questions raised in these transformations as their project, and I have sought to analyse them at the point at which the narrative mode articulates, makes into fiction, that project. My model is an attempt to structure that analysis in terms of the structure of ideology itself.

There are two primary distinctions to be made. The first is between the project (the nature of woman) realized as the *object* of male subjectivity, and the same project realized as the *subject* of woman's own experience. Secondly, within each category of subject (male/female) there is a distinction between hegemonic and estranged subjectivity. That is to say that in the first category (woman-object) the object may be situated in a structure that affirms it, and is thus an *object of consumption*, or it may be a destructuring force, an *object in the way* of a quest for assimilation, an ordeal. In the second category (woman-subject) we can distinguish between the '*free*' *subject* (woman as subject of experience licensed at least partially by ideology to oppose it), and the *subjected subject* (woman as subject of and to her experience). Beyond this, there is a further distinction to be made (as I have already implied) between texts which articulate the projects fictionally, making visible the ideology which motivates both the project and its realization, and texts which remain fictionally incoherent because the particular ideological commitment to the material is too strong to make a full transformation possible.

We shall not find that there is any mechanical connection between these different sitings within ideology and distinctions of narrative mode, but we shall find that they are given their fictional status by the narrative mode as it is deployed at crucial moments in the novel. Above all this is determined by the *axis of distance* between the woman who is the novel's centre and the narrator (who is in each case identical with the woman, but at crucial moments someone else) and the derivative *axis of distance* between the narrator and the reader. The distance may be one of sympathy or cognition or both, and it is thus difficult to state precisely how one measures it, in the abstract, but it is generated both by the events of the novel as they unfold, and by particular linguistic strategies, and in practice it is very precisely controlled. Thus a synthesis of ideological and rhetorical analysis should enable us to avoid reductionism.

Nevertheless it is only a model that I am offering. I do not claim to give a complete account of the texts that I am discussing, nor am I pretending that the model would need no modification confronted with a different range of texts. What I hope is that it will offer a way of going on.

The Girl of the Period

The first stage of the model in which woman is realized as the object of male consumption will obviously include, as its most representative examples, those texts which mythologize the conservative position in the debate about women. But we should be careful not to underestimate this position by seeing it as a merely sentimental idealization. In the late nineteenth century especially, we witness the emergence of a literature which is able to affirm the inferior status of women within a new awareness of the injustice of that status. It can do this because the traditional pieties are underwritten by a hard factual sense of the commodity situation of women. The crucial concept is 'womanliness' which is defined by its opposition to the epicene nature of the modern girl. Thus, for example, Mrs Lynn Linton:[2]

Possessed by a restless discontent with their appointed work, and fired with a mad desire to dabble in all things unseemly, which they call ambition; blasphemous to the sweetest virtues of their sex, which until now have been accounted both their own pride and the safeguard of society; holding it no honour to be reticent, unselfish, patient, obedient but swaggering to the front, ready to try conclusions in aggression, in selfishness, in insolent disregard of duty, in cynical abasement of modesty, with the hardest and least estimable of the men they emulate; *these women of the doubtful gender* have managed to drop all their own special graces while unable to gather up any of the more valuable virtues of men.

('The Epicene Sex', II.236. My italics)

What is interesting here is not the ideas in themselves (except insofar as they neatly represent the commonest clichés) but the attachment of the moral virtues of 'the womanly woman' (II.118) to sexual attractiveness. Mrs Linton is fully aware of the degradation of male idealization. In an essay called 'Affronted Womanhood' she writes that 'the idea of the sacredness of womanhood condemns woman to a "moral harem".' (I.87) and she condemns in 'Feminine Affectations', as 'the real tyrant among women' not the feminist but 'this soft-mannered, large-eyed, *intensely womanly* person who says that . . . the whole duty of woman lies in unquestioning obedience to man' (I.92–92 my italics). Nevertheless, even this condemnation makes it clear that the actual power of woman is confined to the one commodity she has – her womanliness. And throughout the book the assault on feminism is related to the economics of sexuality:

To most men, indeed, the feminine strong-mindedness that can discuss immoral problems without blushing is a quality as unwomanly as well developed biceps or a 'shoulder-of-mutton' fist. (I.132)

The girl of the period is a poor imitation of the mondaine – 'Men are afraid of her and with reason. They may amuse themselves with her for an evening, but they do not readily take her for life' (I.7). It is not merely an offence against the ideology for a woman to be unwomanly, but bad market research: 'she is acting *against nature* and her *own interests* when she disregards their (men's) advice and offends their taste' (I.9). And when she moves from the level of temperament to that of role, the economic system is more clearly invoked. Arguing that it is for man to provide and for woman to dispense, she writes:

Any system which ignores this division of labour, and confounds these separate functions, is of necessity imperfect and wrong. (I.38)

The moral argument which persistently has a theological rhetoric ('her consecration as a helpmeet for man' – II.118) is always carried by a definition of what is sexually attractive, womanliness, and that in turn is made important because it is woman's only marketable commodity in a world where her only mode of production is marriage.

The potency of these connections can be illustrated by a radical and intelligent letter in Harry Quilter's collection *Is Marriage A Failure?* (1887)[3], signed 'Glorified Spinster, Reading'. It argues strongly that 'As a class women are oppressed and men the oppressors' and even that 'marriage is not essential to a woman's life'. Nevertheless, the declared aim of the letter is to protest against the desecration of 'the venerable sanctuary of wedlock'. 'I do not believe,' she goes on, 'that any woman with a spark of *womanliness* in her could honestly uphold such a doctrine'. And the reason is that it would only mean more 'degradation and oppression of the weaker sex' in 'the race of life'. Again it is notable how we pass from the quasi-religious rhetoric, 'venerable sanctuary' to 'womanliness' and from there to a metaphoric reference to the market economy, 'the race of life'. Most of the letter is a defence of the independent woman, but it is very much in terms of her 'compensations' and marriage is upheld because it offers some contract in a world in which '"might has been right" for long ages'. Quilter's own preface more blatantly stresses the hard economic reality that supports the traditional pieties:

> The purpose of happiness is really no part of the purpose of marriage ... marriage is what it is through the necessities of society; and that so long as society has the same necessities, and finds them fulfilled by marriage, the institution must be considered to be a success, though every married man and woman in the world were unhappy.

The proper study of the ideology of this period would need to analyse the complex turns of language in such texts as these, but I think I have quoted enough to show how the ideology sharpens itself into a religious rhetoric to mediate a hardening economism, and that 'womanliness' becomes the major commodity for women as a class, equivalent to labour in the working class, and thus the most vulnerable, most mythic part of the object. 'Grant that women are the salt of the earth, and the great antiseptic element in society' (I.107) as Mrs Linton asks us to, and we shall expect to find in the fiction of the period not chivalry or piety as the major motive, but exchange value.

The texts that belong to this category do not, therefore, relate to ideology as a set of hidden values, but as an affirmative structure confronted with a specific resistance: the awareness of the injustice of the *status* of women. That which tends to meet and overcome the resistance is a realized dogma of *temperament* – the nature of woman or womanliness – underwritten by economically determined prescriptions of *role*. The narrative mode, in order to dramatize the resisting awareness, must clearly summon the woman as subject, but must equally transform this subject through a strategic manipulation of the axes of distance, into an object of male epistemology so that it may appear as a valuable commodity. The male epistemology may realize itself in the text in a number of ways: as a dramatized male spectator in the text, or as implied male author/reader,[4] or, as in the case of many novels written ostensibly by and for women, as a reflected induction in the mediation of the novel by the implied female author, as though there were a shadowy overseeing audience beyond the immediate reader. We shall see all these means operating in the texts I have chosen to use as examples.

Mrs Oliphant's *Madam*[5] is a novel with a familiar motif: renunciation. The title itself alerts us both to the status and the temperament of the heroine, whose name, in case we miss the point, is Grace. The project of the novel is the continuance of the temperament through suffering and self-denial once the status has been denied. Madam is the second wife of a hysterical invalid squire who, besides being neurotically punctilious about time and dress, has imposed on her a cruel marital condition: she is to be so totally the wife and mother in his house that she is never to see the son she has had before their marriage. Compliant in everything, she only breaks this condition when the son gets into trouble, meeting him in secret in the park of the great house just before dinner. Not only is she late, she betrays her offence by a bramble which is caught in the train of her skirt. It is too much for the squire who is sent into a mortal paroxysm of rage. He lives long enough only to summon his lawyer to attach a codicil to his will disinheriting the children of their marriage if Madam ever sees them again. Forced to renounce her maternal role for a second time, she goes to live abroad with the reprobate son, suffers calumny and the bewildered disgust of her family, and lives out a fruitless devotion. She sees the other children only on her deathbed, the will is bypassed and they are safe from dispossession.

As this summary will suggest, it is a thin and sentimental novel, but what is interesting about it is that the renunciation is motivated by an acceptance of rules that are openly seen to be capricious and cruel. This is not just a matter of romantic indignation: the home, which is the theatre of womanliness, is realized as a self-denying facade. Thus, Rosalind, Madam's stepdaughter, has to learn how to be a woman early in the novel by obliterating her own distress:

She flew like an arrow through the hall, and burst into the sanctuary of domestic warmth and tranquillity as if she had been a hunted creature escaping from a fatal pursuit with her enemies at her heels. Her hands were like ice, her slight figure shivering with cold, yet her heart beating so that she could scarcely draw her breath. All this must disappear before the gentlemen came in. It was Rosalind's first experience in *that strange art that comes naturally to a woman of obliterating herself and her own sensations;* but how was she to still her pulse, to restore her colour, to bring warmth to her chilled heart? She felt sure that her misery, her anguish of suspense, her appalling doubts and terrors, must be written in her face; but it was not so. The emergency brought back a rush of the warm blood tingling to her fingers' ends. Oh, never, never, through her, must the mother she loved be betrayed! That brave impulse brought colour to her cheek and strength to her heart. She made one or two of those minute changes in the room *which a woman always finds occasion for* . . . Then Rosalind took up the delicate work that lay on the table, and when the gentlemen entered, was seated *on a low seat within the circle of the shaded lamp*, warm in the glow of the genial fireside, her pretty head bent a little over her *pretty industry*, her hands busy. She who had been the image of anxiety and unrest a moment before, was now the culminating point of all the soft domestic tranquillity, luxury, boundless content and peace, of which this silent room was the home. (I. My italics)

Given that this is a house dominated by a shrieking little father supported by a scheming and spying housekeeper, the last sentence might seem to be heavily ironic. But it is not, because the woman somehow contrives to make it what it is, and Mrs Oliphant makes it clear that it is by her own self-obliteration: to be a woman is to be the culminating point of a silent room. That the 'art' should come 'naturally' is vitally important: it is an art that involves being what one is not, but, of course, within the ideology, the nature of woman is defined precisely in terms of being something *for others*. It is Rosalind's 'brave impulse' that provides the basis of the art, and it is her training as a woman, 'pretty industry' that makes it reliable.

So right from the start, we are aware that the situation of woman would be impossible if it were not for the 'nature' of woman which is an ideological concept. This is, to some extent, demystified by the harsh social realities. Madam's slight failure in the natural art of woman means that she loses her Madamish status which is her whole identity: 'She was pulled rudely down from the pedestal she had occupied for so long . . . Though she had been supposed so self-sustained and strong in character, she was *too natural a woman* not to be deeply dependent upon sympathy' (XXXIX). The ideology is clearly operative again in the second sentence, but the word 'pedestal' should alert us to Mrs Oliphant's sense that it is woman's 'nature' to practice an *art* which is self preserving because it creates fictions. It is not woman's nature to be the culmination of a room, but to create the *illusion* that it is because she is nothing without it. Thus as well as an ideological programme (the self-obliterating nature of woman), there is an interrogative voice not letting us forget its fictionality. When one of Rosalind's suitors echoes Ruskin ('The kind of girl I like doesn't hunt, though she goes like a bird when it strikes her fancy. She is the queen at home, she *makes a room* like this into heaven'), she retorts that it is 'A dreadful piece of *perfection*' (XXIX. My italics). And when Madam is going away, she finds sanctuary in the very opposite of the stable, lighted, sociable drawing-room – a railway carriage – 'the protection which is afforded by the roar and sweep of hot haste which holds us as in a sanctuary of darkness, peace and solitude'

(XXXVII). But the total movement of the novel leaves such challenges unconfronted and untransformed. The only coherent opposition to the self-obliteration myth is given to a ridiculous aunt and a strident younger daughter, and the novel is really nailed down by a benevolent uncle's wan comment: 'If this were a time to philosophize, I might say that's why women in general have such hard lives, for we always expect the girls to keep the boys out of mischief, without asking how they are to do it' (XVI). Rosalind ends by marrying her Ruskinian suitor without changing his views, and Madam preserves the drawing-room, remains its culminating point by an act of self-obliteration so complete that she is absent from what she makes.

An ideological coherence is then preserved despite the novel's subversive moments, and this is achieved by the manipulation of the point of view. From what has been said already, it can be seen that the cognition (the *awareness* of the art of woman's nature) is shared between Rosalind and Madam, so that the suffering that it brings is never sharply focused. The moment in the railway carriage is more a moment of collapse than of self-appraisal and the use of 'pedestal' is Mrs Oliphant's rather than Madam's. In fact we see very little of what Madam goes through: to see that would be to separate her (as subject) from her role and the novel maintains a religious integrity between them. When, near the end, after a long absence from the narrative, we see into her mind, it is only to see how she reflects on what has already happened, what she must accept: 'She had always known that sometime or other, these men would look at her so, and say just those words to her, and that she would stand and bear it all, a victim appointed from the beginning' (XXXVI). 'Always' and 'appointed' are words that bypass the actual experience of suffering and hold her subjectivity at a safe distance. It is Rosalind who undergoes the awareness of incongruity before it hardens into a given pattern, and she suffers only vicariously as the helpless and baffled spectator of her stepmother's action: and in terms of the events of the narrative, she is one of its beneficiaries. In spite of a number of authorial comments distinguishing between what happens in novels and what happens in 'real' life (which is of course claimed as the province of this novel), Madam is finally presented to us as explicitly a tragic figure: 'They are all gathered together again,' the dying Madam says, 'for the end of the tragedy' (XLIX). There could have been a bitter irony in this, but because Madam is kept by the narrative mode at a fictive remove, the fiction of her 'nature' is never made visible: she remains, to the end, Madam, admirable, culminating point of the domestic room, an object for our peace and comfort.

I want to contrast this text with Henry James's novel *The Portrait of A Lady*.[6] *The Portrait of A Lady* is the story of Isabel Archer, a young, faintly emancipated American girl brought to Europe by her aunt, the wife of a wealthy banker spending his retirement in England. The banker's heir, Ralph Touchett, a hypochondriacal aesthete, persuades his father to leave Isabel the bulk of his fortune so that she can be liberated completely from economic circumstances. After boldly rejecting the offers of a prosperous American businessman who pursues her through Europe (Caspar Goodwood) and an English lord, Isabel seems set for an exciting career. But she falls prey to the scheming of two more American exiles, Madame Merle and Gilbert Osmond who have a daughter Pansy, passed off implicitly as the child of 'widower' Osmond's first marriage. Conned by Osmond's aura of melancholy and aristocratic pride, Isabel marries him and quickly learns that she has married an empty and conventional tyrant. She defies him once by returning to England to see the dying Ralph but when Caspar Goodwood offers to take her away from her marriage, she refuses. Osmond is busy scheming for his daughter's prosperous unhappiness, and partly to protect the child, and partly to accept her fate, she goes back to Rome where her husband lives. James's novel offers a comparable programme to that propounded in *Madam:* the nature of woman as object of appreciation, realized as the story of the acceptance of a limiting and incongruous role, but realized, as I shall argue, with a coherence which makes visible the ideological shaping of the story. The programme is explicitly stated near the beginning of chapter XXXVII when Edmund Rosier, an ineffectual American connoisseur living in Europe, comes to Rome to see the heroine for the first time after her disastrous marriage to another American aesthete:

The years had touched her only to enrich her; the flower of her youth had not faded, it only hung more quietly on its stem. She had lost something of that quick eagerness to which her husband had privately taken exception – she had more the air of being able to wait. Now, at all events, framed in the gilded doorway, she struck our young man as the picture of a gracious lady.

The image is fittingly pictorial not only because our young man is a collector, but also because Isabel has become what she is because of the connoisseur who liberated her with his father's money because he wanted to see what she would do with it, and the husband who plucked her as the prize of his collection. The ironies of the image are clear – the gilded doorway both embellishes her image and fixes her in it. We know that Rosier's appreciation is superficial, and five chapters later, in the rightly celebrated chapter XLII, we are to see direct into Isabel's mind and understand the suffering that underlies the image. Nevertheless the novel remains truly a portrait, and if the primary function of the portrait as a genre is to 'confirm one's position', in the phrase of the art critic, John Berger (*Selected Essays & Articles: The Look of Things*, Penguin, 1972), James's own criticism makes it clear that he sees portraiture as an image that invokes interpretation, a guessing of the unseen from the seen in the manner of Walter Pater's famous passage on the Mona Lisa in *Studies in the Renaissance*. What such interpretation does is not to contest the image but to use it so that a 'gracious lady' summarizes not merely an appearance, a status and a role, but also the expression of a nature brought to fixity by experience. And chapter XLII has exactly the same sense of completeness that we have noted in the presentation of Madam's consciousness: 'There was an *everlasting* weight on her heart – there was a livid light on *everything*' (my italics). The absolutes create the distance – that is where she is. We are witnessing a reflective awareness that comes too late for Isabel, though not for our appreciation. For this highly introspective chapter resolves itself into yet another picture, subject becoming object: 'she stopped again in the middle of the room and stood there gazing at a remembered vision'.

To see the novel in this way is to run counter to the accepted view of the way it works. James himself described its conception as that of 'a young woman affronting her destiny', and its method as that of 'placing the centre of the subject in the young woman's own consciousness'.[7] But the novel does not really work in this way. In the first place, Isabel's consciousness works only in relation to the spectatorial and male consciousnesses around her – especially Ralph's – and it is Ralph who sets her up to meet 'the requirements of his imagination' (VXIII), which puts him in the position of the reader. Secondly, James only gives us Isabel's consciousness with a highly controlled authorial distance: 'The girl had a certain nobleness of imagination, which rendered her a good many services and played her a great many tricks' (VI). Increasingly, it is the tricks of her imagination that we are to watch marking out her destiny. And they are tricks because the author crucially maintains an air of bemusement which keeps Isabel's subjectivity slightly out of reach: 'The working of this young lady's spirit was strange, and I can only give it you as I see it, not hoping to make it seem altogether natural' (XXIX). The crucial transition from her rejection of her former suitors on the grounds that they will limit her freedom, to her decision to marry what she admits is a nonentity is riddled with gaps during which she is travelling and emerging 'in her own eyes, a very different person' (XXXI). And the first three years of her marriage during which she learns of her mistake, is totally omitted. Rather than being a flaw in the novel this seems to be a deliberate repression in order to prepare the reader to accept the inexplicable (the fatal trick of her imagination) as the inexorable (the inescapable suffering reflected in chapter XLII). It enables James to limit her freedom to the level of awareness, so that the coda of the novel, when she is confronted with Goodwood's offer to help her escape her fate, represents no real free choice. His kiss 'like white lightening' is an image of death, and proffers only another 'act of possession'. She has only to choose between her identity (linked to the lights of the house from which she has come to meet Goodwood in the dark), which means too the 'very straight path' back to Osmond and her gilded frame, or obliteration in Goodwood's 'hard manhood'. What is important is not the choice she makes, but the energy she summons up to make it: 'She never looked about her but only darted from the spot' (LV). The narrative mode traces not so much a development from Isabel's innocence to experience, but from our bewilderment to our admiration. She meets the requirements of Ralph's imagination not by what she does, but by what she endures and represents, a higher graciousness than Rosier sees: "And remember this," [Ralph] continued, "that if you've been hated you've also been loved. Ah, but Isabel – *adored*."' (LIV).

The point of view is thus manipulated to keep the programme intact. But this already makes it a different kind of text from *Madam*. For there, as we have seen, awareness and suffering are kept glaringly apart because Mrs Oliphant has no way of transforming the subversive insights except by trying to keep them marginal. And this is not true of James's novel. For our very awareness of the limitations and interactions of the different axes of distance in the novel brings to the surface the unasked questions of its ideological commitment. Outside the circle of fine consciences, other commentaries question its assumptions – one thinks of the comic but never repressed American journalist, Henrietta Stackpole, who has the novel's last word, and Daniel Touchett, another pristine American who is appalled by his son's idle fastidiousness, or even of the 'children of a neighbouring slum' who peer through the railings of a deserted West End square in the non-season, attracted by the animated conversation of Isabel and Ralph. These create other perspectives that alert us to the gilt on the frame of Isabel's portrait. So that when Isabel is allowed to reach a fully critical intelligence of Osmond's egoism we are compelled to see how she has been used by others, and has used them, as pictorial objects. In the end, it is the difference between 'tragedy' in Mrs Oliphant's debased ideological sense, and portraiture, because we can see the frame of the portrait. The novel is not merely the conservative response to womanhood, not the realization of a gracious lady, but a realization of her picture. What we see in the frame alerts us to the excluded space outside it. The adorable object is not 'nature' but a specific product within a specific system.

Most Dangerous of Playthings

Engels makes the point that monogamy does not exist on its own – it is always underwritten by 'hetaerism' or various forms of the sexual prostitution of women. One of the charges Mrs Linton brings against the girl of the period is that besides being sexless, she is a bad imitation of the mondaine:

> Men are afraid of her and with reason. They may amuse themselves with her for an evening, but they do not readily take her for life. Besides, after all her efforts, she is only a poor copy of the real thing; and the real thing is far more amusing than the copy, because it is real. Men can get that whenever they like; and whenever they go into their mothers' drawing-rooms, with their sisters' friends, they want something of quite a different flavour. *Toujours perdrix* is bad providing all the world over; but a continual weak imitation of *toujours perdrix* is worse.
>
> If we must have only one kind of thing, let us have it genuine, and the queens of St Johns Wood in their unblushing honesty rather than their imitators and make-believers in Bayswater and Belgravia. (p. 7)[8]

The link between feminist aggression and the idea of the other woman may seem tenuous to us, but it is common enough in the late nineteenth century, and it is what lies behind the literary convention of the *femme fatale* who is at once the object of fear and the object of fascination in the male epistemology because she represents a sexual relationship which is outside the drawing-room, a rebel not 'content to be what God and nature had made them' (Mrs Linton, p. 2). But that literary convention has to be placed in a much wider category, which would include, as well as the Gueneveres and Salomes of fantasy, such characters as Estella, in *Great Expectations*, Hedda Gabler, and Gudrun in *Women in Love*, women whose sexuality is a critical, self-realizing (and therefore within the ideology, unnatural) mode of knowledge. At the same time, it is a category in which the subjectivity of the woman becomes an object of man's ordeal, a force which disorientates the given, hegemonic world-view. In Hardy's novel, *Far from the Madding Crowd*, Bathsheba Everdene asks at one point whether she is too mannish, and her confidante replies that rather she is too 'womanish'. It is a word which usefully identifies the determinant motif of the texts in this category, as different and yet closely bound up with the determinant motif of the first category, 'womanliness'.

Although my examples are both taken from the genre of fantasy, it is important to stress that they use the resources of the novel to elicit the link I have made between the critical subjectivity of the woman and her womanishness which is the object of a male ordeal. George Macdonald's *Lilith* (1895) is a macabre romance which has gained some currency in recent years among what William Empson would call neo-Christian critics, such as C. S. Lewis, Tolkien and Auden.[9] It consists of the adventures of an orphan called Vane (the human soul whose name indicates the way the wind is blowing and the vanity of human wishes) in a dreamlike world which he enters through a mirror. His central act is to revivify the exhausted Lilith out of an impulse of naïve decency, so that she is thus released to attack the race of children (the Little Ones) whose cause he espouses. Lilith is, of course, a traditional conflation of the Hebrew demon who destroys children, and the supposed first wife of Adam, created independently from him, who quarrelled with him because she refused to have intercourse lying underneath him. From her brief appearance in Goethe's *Faust*, she becomes an archetype of the destructive woman. But whereas in, for example, a sonnet of Rossetti's, she is a static object of mystified contemplation ('And still she sits . . .') in Macdonald's story she appears as a character with a rationalized motivation. Partly this is based on a will to power, the demand for a totally submissive love, but, more importantly, it is based on an assertion of self-creation:

'I am what I am; no one can take from me myself.'
'You are not the Self you imagine.'
'So long as I feel myself what it pleases me to think myself, I care not. I am content to be myself what I would be. What I choose to seem to myself makes me what I am. My own thought makes me; my own thought of myself is me. Another shall not make me.' (XXXIX)

She is thus not simply seen as a weaver of spells, and the creator of metaphysical evil, but as the representative of an articulate human position.

In Macdonald's vision, even Lilith, the destroyer of her own daughter (and thus the rebel against parenthood) is redeemable. But the process is portrayed with a cruelty that almost reveals the theological motivation (defiance, defeat, purgation, death, redemption) for what it is – an instrument of oppression. The passage I have just quoted occurs when Lilith is confronted with Mara, a daughter of Adam and protector of the Little Ones, who tries to persuade Lilith to allow the light of the creating will to enter her so that she will cease to will against her creator. When Lilith refuses, a white-hot 'worm-thing' crawls out of the hearth and enters the body of Lilith through a dark spot in her side: 'The princess gave one writhing, contorted shudder, and I knew the worm was in her secret chamber.' Mara comments 'She is seeing herself', and significantly Vane tries to put his arms round her, but is stopped: 'Her torment is that she is what she is. Do not fear for her; she is not forsaken. No gentler way to help her was left.' Lilith now blames God for what she is, and defies him again: 'I will not be made any longer', but she cannot unmake herself, and she 'will not be remade'. So once again, she suffers a violent assault, this time, 'naked to the torture of pure interpenetrating inward light'. The horror on her face makes Vane beseech for mercy again, but Mara says 'Self loathing is not sorrow. Yet it is good for it marks a step in the *way home*, and in *the father's arms* the prodigal forgets the self he abominates.' The process of reduction continues until Lilith finally repents (that is, wishes to die), but she cannot because one of her hands is the paw of a leopard (one of the forms she appears in during the novel) and she cannot open it. This final resistance of animal nature is not overcome until she persuades Adam, the husband she has wronged, to cut it off with a sword given him by an angel at the gate of paradise which will 'divide whatever was not one and indivisible' (XLI). The hand is given to Vane who is ordered to bury it with Adam's spade in the place where the waters that Lilith, in her war on the Little Ones, had caused to disappear from the face of the earth will flow again.

Summarizing it in this way makes the book sound quite mad, but this would be too charitable a view. Auden has correctly described it as allegory, and though it is tempting to present it as material for psychoanalysis, it would be wrong to miss the element of hard calculation. The nightmare of sexual symbolism has a clear ideological coherence. Lilith has denied motherhood, asserted herself and the will to power. Her animal nature (which is identified with self assertion) has to be taken from her by a series of phallic images, and buried in the life-containing earth so that the children can be fed.

Lilith's ordeal only becomes important at the end, and the novel is mainly concerned with Vane's attempt to make sense of his vision, to which the survival of Lilith is found to be the key. Thus what she is and what she suffers is truly the object of his ordeal. That is why his interventions on her behalf are so vital, for what he has entered through the mirror is the vision of a new life which turns to nightmare because of his guilt, and the guilt comes not from his intention, which is good, but the desire to work out the right action from his own experience. He gives Lilith life, and she sucks his blood. She dashes his loved one to pieces and he tries to save her from pain. He thinks that he will save the Little Ones through knowledge, so he seeks to know Lilith. He is guilty, in short, of humanism,[10] and it is his very individuality that, however well meaning, makes him vulnerable, and is indeed related to the evil that Lilith represents. Because of this, we have no fictional coherence in the end, merely a retreat into ideology. Vane's vision is an epistemological adventure insofar as Lilith represents an obstructive obstacle in his quest for meaning and reconciliation. And yet, finally, this adventure is made marginal. Vane's sense of reality is only destroyed to make way for another, already given reality which does not challenge the moral law he takes with him, but merely sanctifies it, and the only final discovery of his spiritual education is that education is undesirable. His ordeal is over when he no longer tries to participate in the struggle between good and evil, but is content, as Mara says, 'to watch and wait'. For all its apparent complexity, the novel has very simple designs on us. And it is the reduction of Vane from quester to spectator (and finally, undertaker to the primal family) – in other words a silent modification of the point of view from autobiography to eye-witness account – that enables these designs to be accomplished. For if Vane were still trying to understand at the end, the agony Lilith goes through would be heroic, and her defeat a defeat of free will. Whereas it is the triumph of mother Eve, and father Adam manifested in imagery that is meant merely to terrify us. What happens to Lilith can happen to you too, but it will not do so if you just watch and wait.

Fantasy is, of course, always vulnerable to its ideological project in a sense in which other, supposedly 'realistic' fictions are not, because they are governed at least by an ideological practice which is reflected *within* the story (by its commitment to the contingent 'reality'). If it has to be 'like life' the actual world-view shaping that life motivates the narrative and is therefore more prone to be visible. The ideological practice of fantasy is, however, confined to the act of writing itself, so that it can be much more invisible. Although the manifestation of the nature of woman as ordeal is not confined to fantasy, as I have suggested, it is a siting of the woman which requires a much greater narrative distance than that which presents her as an object of consumption, both because she is bound to be more powerful, a super-woman, and because there is a necessary distance between the subject who experiences the ordeal and the reader for whom the ordeal is an object of consumption. But I have discussed *Lilith* in order to show that its ideological coherence is still gained at the expense of its fictional coherence: the narrative is made irrelevant by its design. And this means that the opposite is possible, that even within the realm of fantasy, fictional coherence is possible and the project visible as a question which represses other questions.

The text that will best illustrate this from within the period I am discussing is Rider-Haggard's *She*.[11] It is a novel often under-estimated even by Haggard's admirers, although it is worth noting that Freud found it full enough of 'hidden meanings' to dream about it. What gives those meanings coherence is an ordeal of male sexuality of which Ayesha (She) is the primary cause. The story is narrated by Holly, a Cambridge don who is guardian to a beautiful male called Leo Vincey. Ancient documents, a palimpsest of remembered wrongs, send them on a journey to avenge the murder by Ayesha of an ancestor of Vincey, Kallikrates (the strong and the beautiful). It is a journey which yields a sequence of metaphors of sexual struggle: a squall in which the sea heaves 'like some troubled woman's breast' (IV), difficult penetration to an amphitheatre, an attack by a lioness, a feast which is set up by the rejected lover of their man-servant to avenge her humiliation, and, climactically, a treacherous entry into a cave which contains a life-giving pillar of fire, the womb of the earth whose cleft is only crossable with the aid of the flaming sword of the sun's rays.

The struggle is dominant because the attraction of woman is treacherous and destructive. The narrator is a misogynist who seems also fairly clearly to be homosexual so that he is, initially at least, on a crusade against the female power over man, and the tribe which She rules, the Amhagger, is matrilinear with the sexual pairings decided by the women promiscuously. So that female sexuality is a threat both to the lives and the values of the Europeans. But what is important is that the revenge/crusade motif is inverted when Ayesha herself appears, for she represents not unmotivated evil, but an alternative mode of knowledge. She is presented as the fatal woman, embodiment of the very diablerie of woman, likened both to Circe and Aphrodite triumphant, but this view has to be revised. This is partly because, like Lilith, she is allowed to explain herself ('If I have sinned, let my beauty answer for it' XX), but also because Holly is compelled to change his mind: he describes her at first as 'a mysterious creature of evil tendencies' (XXI) and then later relates her wrongdoings to her wisdom:

And the fruit of her wisdom was this, that there was but one thing worth living for, and that was Love in its highest sense, and to gain that good thing she was not prepared to stop at trifles. (XXI)

She seeks the pillar of flame which will give her new life because she seeks to revolutionize the world, to conquer its laws with love. But the flame destroys her because her revolution goes against 'eternal law' – thus the ideological project, the survival of the or-deal and the conquest of its object by law is realized. The shifting perspectives of the fictional realization, have by the end, however, made this completion highly ironic. The glimpse into the 'possi-bilities of life' that Holly and Vincey have through Ayesha chan-

ges them completely so that they are estranged from the world
they have set out from and whose values they have seen triumph
as 'eternal law'.

What makes this transformation possible is the dramatization
of Holly. Ugly and rejected, in terror of woman, he comes to love
Ayesha for the beauty and knowledge she represents. The ideological object of ordeal becomes for him, because of the vision she
imparts, a supreme fiction. The journey outward becomes not a
release from the past (the revenge intention) but a journey back
to that past to reveal the puniness of male fear and its comfortable
accommodation within the eternal law, so that there can be no
return journey. The fatal woman is not here, as in *Lilith*, destroyed
to make way for the eternal mother, but to affirm the law which
becomes as a result unacceptable. Holly cannot accept that She
has finally been destroyed: the unsought vision that he has gained
compels him to challenge the eternal law as She challenges it.
Thus she is not merely allowed to speak for herself: She is brought
into relationship with the reader via Holly. Her subjectivity
modifies his and ours because it affirms the unity of knowledge
and love. *She* is a fine novel because it brings us to ask the
repressed question of its project: what does the destructive woman
destroy, ourselves, or ourselves' subjugation?

The Truth Shall Make You Free

So far we have been talking of texts that site the 'nature' of
woman in the subjectivity of man, and this means that it tends to
be something already constituted, revealed by the narrative rather
than explored and challenged by it. Even in those novels in which
we have seen the project made visible as ideology by the fictional
realization, it is not the 'nature of woman' that is called into
question so much as the nature of such a conceptualization itself
and what exclusions it makes. Once we move to texts that site
the woman as subject, the notion of woman's nature itself has to
be openly questioned, for clearly there cannot be a subject which
is not in itself problematic. Hence we turn inevitably to 'feminist'
texts. 'What is now called the nature of woman is an eminently
artificial thing', Mill writes in *The Subjection of Women* and this

is really to call into question the very process of making the woman an object in ideology. Thus we can no longer deal with projects that have as their centre a concept such as 'womanliness' or 'womanishness', since the subject woman is called upon to ask: what am I?[12]

Nevertheless, it is still possible to distinguish between the hegemonic posing of that question and the estranged posing of it. For if there can be no assumption about what a woman is, the assumption about what constitutes a *subject* can still be made. Much of the early feminist polemic is of course made within the liberal ideology. The argument is that if women are accorded the same legal rights as men, they too will be free as men are. This tends to be the case with Mill's essay, and it can be seen rather crudely emulated in Mona Caird's proposal that marriage should be treated as a contract like any other, with the terms of the agreement decided by the two parties. I do not wish to underestimate the value of liberal feminism, but it is important for my purposes to establish clearly that it questions the traditional status and role of woman from within the ideology that insists on it. It sees a contradiction in bourgeois theory and tries to rationalize it, making woman as 'free' as man (which equally entails limiting that freedom as it is limited for man, as in the free contract concept). There is no contradiction *of* bourgeois theory. Thus the ideological programme of the fictions in this category has to do with the possible freedom of woman conceived as a rational application of the social contract.

Grant Allen's *The Woman Who Did* (1894) was, in its day, a *succes de scandale*.[13] It was clearly intended to be, since its polemical programme begins outside the novel with an authorial confession: 'Written at Perugia, Spring, 1893, for the first time in my life wholly and solely to satisfy my own taste and my own conscience'. This has a direct bearing on the story since the heroine's most important attempt to gain independence is to write a novel which fails because it is too serious and sincere ('the despairing heart-cry of a soul in revolt') so that the author identifies his own liberty with that of the protagonist. Both are rebels against what Allen himself would term 'philistia'. Herminia is the daughter of an Anglican dean who decides that it would be wrong to marry the man she loves because she has seen that,

In a free society, was it not obvious that each woman would live her own life apart, would preserve her independence, and would receive the visits of the man for whom she cared – the father of her children? Then only could she be free. Any other method meant the economic and social superiority of the man, and was irreconcilable with the perfect freedom of the woman. (VI)

So she has a child without getting married or living with its father, openly and programmatically ('the truth had made her free and she was very confident of it'). But, of course, she does not live in a free society, and the truth also makes of her a sacrificial victim. We see her forced into a closer dependence on her lover and, when he dies, into a single-minded concern with the economic and emotional demands of motherhood. Even this is turned against her: the daughter grows up frivolous and conventional and when she finds out the truth about her birth, attacks Herminia with such bitterness that she leaves her no way out but suicide.

It is a superficial and sensationalist novel despite its air of apparent liberalism. The large and difficult question of woman's independence tends to be swallowed by the seemingly simpler one of illegitimacy, and Herminia's death, though it may appear from a summary to be distressing, is actually very comforting – a noble action succeeded by a noble martyrdom puts a definite end-point to the struggle. Our final attitude is foreshadowed in the dedication: 'to my dear wife to whom I have dedicated my twenty happiest years, I dedicate also this brief *memorial* of a *less fortunate* love' (my italics). Herminia's story is given, before it starts, an air of pious regret which mediates any anger or involvement it might have had. Grant Allen seems merely to be cashing in, without paying the price, on the difficult insights both into the situation of woman and the anomalies of the writer's own productive conditions that emerge from the work of Meredith, Hardy and Gissing. Allen's flirtation with radicalism and honesty is guaranteed to remain at the level of flirtation.

Nevertheless, it seems to me an instructive text. Not only is it a fairly lucid vulgarization of an aspect of female desperation which perforce found expression as one kind of feminism; it also reveals the limitations of this literary category – the way in which the ideology of the project can demolish the coherence of its fictional realization. Truth and freedom are mediated by a language that comes straight from the conventions that are challenged. What is above all stressed is Herminia's *altruism:* the nature of her love and her lover make it clear that for her, marriage would not be oppressive. She rejects it for the sake of those who are oppressed by it (she rather glibly contrasts herself with George Eliot and Mary Shelley and others who practised marital irregularities merely because that was the only way they could get what they wanted). In fact, she uses the very vocabulary of the ecclesiastical father whose mores she is challenging: '"it never occurred to me," she said gently but bravely, "to think my life could ever end in anything but martyrdom."' (III). Since martyrdom is what she consciously chooses, there can be no real development in the novel – there is nothing to be learnt from her taken freedom. And, of course, it involves a double distancing: she is distanced from her unnecessary predicament, and we are distanced from her by her purity of motive. She is not changed by what happens to her, and she changes nothing. And this is because she is not in any sense revolutionary. She merely takes the vocabulary of ideology and makes it consistent. She makes herself the free subject of her experience and chooses actions according to her own readings, but she is spared, both by her class-based confidence in a theological vocabulary, and by the abstraction of her thinking, from the irrational contiguities of economic and sexual forces – from being subjected to the life she chooses. Naturally she suffers – martyrs must suffer – but she is already armed against suffering. The point of view thus remains static. Even the discovery that she cannot make money out of writing honest novels does not sully her. We have in the end a bourgeois fable of the free subject making its way. The only difference is that the free subject is a woman, and the only difference that makes (and I do not deny that it is an important one) is that Allen cannot bring himself to falsify the reality so much that he lets her finally win. Even so what destroys her is not the conditions she has to face (she masters those with an ease that keeps the novel very short) but a relationship conditioned at an ideological level the free subject does not question – if marriage is dispensable, motherhood is not. The truth shall make you free of all but 'the truth' (ideology manifests itself as this, as well as in the form of 'convention').

Allen's novel is useful because it highlights the difficulty of a novelist attempting to write programmatically feminist literature.[14] At the same time it enables us to see by contrast the very great achievement of the writer who is closest to Mill in this period – George Meredith. Woman plays a special, and usually subversive, role throughout his fiction, and to give a full account of it would require analysis of many of the early works (notably *Rhoda Fleming* and *Vittoria*). But it is in a number of late novels that Meredith comes to focus most sharply on sexual politics: *The Egoist*, *Diana of the Crossways* and *The Amazing Marriage*. Of these, it is *Diana* that programmatically elaborates woman as the free subject encountering the social world:

> 'Oh! I have discovered that I can be a tigress!'
> Her friend pressed her hand, saying, 'The cause a good one!'
> 'Women have to fight.' (IV)

Diana, who is explicitly linked with the goddess of hunting and chastity, is an Irish wit and beauty who marries a churlish Englishman in hysterical reaction to the sexual advances of her best friend's husband. The marriage soon founders, and her husband sues her for adultery. The court vindicates her innocence, and Diana uses its verdict to justify her escape from the marriage. For much of the novel she lives as a single woman, making her living by writing novels, but she also becomes involved with a rising young politician. His sexual importunity angers her sufficiently to leak vital government information to a newspaper in order to obtain the money she desperately needs. Losing him, she is protected from further calumny by her devoted friends and admirers, the most solid of whom she marries.

Two motifs, sexual frigidity and sexual liberation, are obviously entangled, but Meredith keeps the first from providing an ideological distortion of the second[15] by the careful manipulation of point of view. Although she is realized as the free subject of her experience, it is only at crucial moments (mostly late in the novel) that we are allowed to see into her mind. Diana's wit and presence is also communicated through the diaries of 'contemporaries' (the novel is set in a past which has to be pieced together), by gossip and the anxious consciousnesses of her friends. Because of this, none of her actions can be seen as simple folly, nor even as gratuitous acts of emancipation – Diana's self is seen in a contingent world which even when it is friendly, provides a series of limiting conditions against which it is important for her to assert the motive power of her sense of freedom:

She did not accuse her marriage of being the first fatal step: her error was the step into Society without the wherewithal to support her position there. Girls of her kind, airing their wings above the sphere of their birth, are cryingly adventuresses. As adventuresses they are treated. Vain to be shrewish with the world! Rather let us turn and scold our nature for irreflectively rushing to the cream and honey! Had she subsisted on her small income in a country cottage, this task of writing would have been a holiday! . . . The simplicity of the life of labour looked beautiful. What will not look beautiful contrasted with the fly in the web? She had chosen to be one of the flies of life. (XXX)

Even in such a passage as this, when Diana is rebuking her own extravagance and regretting her own inability to conform to her 'sphere', her mind moves inevitably towards the verb 'choose'. Meredith does not give her a totally free situation, nor does he make her a paragon (as Allen makes Herminia); she is 'a heroine of reality', but he does give her the intelligence and energy to choose her entanglements out of the sphere to which she is allotted, even by the high praise of others, and the practical advice and love of her friends. Ultimately, however she may scold her 'nature', she is unable to deny it. 'Women are women, and I am a woman: but I am I, and unlike them' (XLII). We must note too that her 'nature' is not identified with an ideological concept, 'the nature of woman'. It is not a given, but a problematic question raised by the free subject. In such a context, the sexual frigidity, though it is not uncritically celebrated, as we shall see, is not a 'defect' of 'nature', but part of the armoury against the assault on her identity, a necessary stand against being reduced to the 'womanly'.[16]

There are several parallels with Allen's novel which are worth spelling out because it will make the contrast clearer. In the first place, both heroines make an explicit stand against marriage which places them very much in the liberal feminist tradition (since marriage was seen to be slavery and not a free contract). But Diana moves from theoretical rejection to bitter experience, and the transition is important. Thus, for example, before she marries, she sees a husband as a threat to freedom in a coolly abstract manner:

'I cannot tell you what a foreign animal a husband would appear in my kingdom.' Her experience had wakened a sexual aversion, of some slight kind, enough to make her feminine pride stipulate for perfect independence, that she might have the calm out of which imagination spreads wing. Imagination had become her broader life, and on such an earth, under such skies, a husband who is not the fountain of it, certainly is a foreign animal; he is a discordant note. He contracts the ethereal world, deadens radiancy. He is a gross fact, a leash, a muzzle, harness, a hood, whatever is detestable to the free limbs and senses. (IV)

Although we are not invited to ironize this, she is made to pay for the abstract and ethereal rhetoric by experiencing a grosser fact, the sexual advances of a married man. And she does marry, not to discover that this is more secure, but that a husband is more deadly than a foreign animal: 'Husband grew to mean to me stifler, lung contractor, iron mask, inquisitor, everything anti-natural' (XIV). Without collapsing her sense of freedom, Meredith makes Diana strengthen it against material existence. So the novel has no air of piety, and it does have a real suspense.

And like Herminia too, Diana is motivated by an idealism that can appear as sexual frigidity, as I have suggested. But the difference is that whereas in Allen's novel this is taken to be wholly noble, Meredith makes careful discriminations about it that foreshadow the ironies Hardy directs against Sue Bridehead in *Jude the Obscure*. That is, we are presented with it as armoury, but that in itself involves a complacency for which Diana is made to pay. Thus when her political lover, Percy Dacier, is demanding that their relationship be sexual, he says, 'I believe you were made without fire' and Diana's reply is nearly arrogant: 'Perhaps. The element is omitted with some of us: happily some

think. Now we can converse' (XXXI). What she has seen
throughout the novel is not merely that marriage is a repressive
institution but that it is one that is established by and for men,
so that women may be placed as objects in the market (the most
brilliant of the *obiter dicta* recorded by the diarists through
whom she is first presented to us is: 'men do not so much fear to
lose the hearts of thoughtful women as their strict attention to
their graces' (I)). But marriage which can be opposed with free
thought and self-containment, is not the worst kind of degradation. She pays for the idealism of her chastity when she realizes
that in the newspaper office where she sells her secret to avenge
the male oppressor and stave off the economic reality, the status
of woman drops 'from the secondary to the cancelled stage'.
It is not the regression from freedom that challenges Diana's
doing as it does Herminia's but the entry into it. This does not
merely make for greater realism, it means that the fictional
motivation of the novel is the freedom of the subject and that it is
therefore exposed and not merely ideologically asserted.

But there is a third parallel between the two novels which
demonstrates more decisively the difference between them. Both
heroines are novelists, and, just as *The Woman Who Did* postulates an aesthetic commitment which identifies the freedom of
woman with the freedom of the novelist from the pressures of
the market, so Meredith's novel, at a much deeper level, incorporates his own sense of the social limitations and contradictory
aesthetic potential of fiction. The subject woman is summoned
to declare her own power to a world that wants only statues, and
the subject novelist, very consciously the presenter of that
problematic woman, claims the freedom to substantiate a truth
that is neither 'rose-pink' nor 'dirty-drab' (Meredith's terms for
romantic and naturalistic fiction) but 'wholesome, bearable,
fructifying, finally a delight'. We have a double affirmation,
woman/fiction, making a double negation, 'domestic decoration'/
falsification. Whereas, in Allen's novel, the connection is merely,
and gratuitously polemical, in *Diana* it is absolutely vital to the
evolution of the novel. Its formal progression is from the diaries
that memorialize her, to the crises that go on in her mind – the
free subject as point of view is only won from the enigmatic

records that cannot place her as object. And this is bound up with the progressive revelation of the contradiction between the nature of the subject and what the world expects of women – a progression that moves from the crude and legally contestable possessiveness of her first husband, to the more alluring and sophisticated image of Dacier, who sees her as his 'fountain of counsel . . . the rosy gauze veiled more than cold helper and advisor' (XXXIII). In the same way that we have seen how the contradictions of the work of art (portrait) expose the contradictions of the woman-object, we see here how the problematic of the truth-telling artist exposes the problematic of the true woman subject.

The problematic for both novelist and woman is the relationship between knowing and contesting 'the dirty drab' of material existence. For the novel uses fiction to explore the limits of fiction: 'for nature will force her way, and if you try to stifle her by drowning, she comes up, not the fairest part of her uppermost' (I). When Diana frees herself from marriage, she escapes momentarily into a world of imaginative ecstasy, but this turns out to be merely a recovery of girlhood. In the material world she has to establish herself as a woman with an image, and this it is that poses for the character as for the novelist, what it means to be making something as a question. Her image is made through writing – 'metaphor was her refuge', and metaphor is explicitly linked with civilization itself, which is a curtailment of 'reality' (or so it appears in *The Egoist*). She is taken 'with a passion for reality' but she has also to be 'the actress of her part'. Caught in the shifting polarities of knowing and acting, the free subject knows its freedom only by knowing the limits of that freedom. She retains her independence from Dacier only by verbal betrayal – of the truth, but *to* the newspaper which counts her identity as nothing. And she is compelled finally to protect that identity by making it dependent, by accepting the compromise of inoffensive marriage.

The end of the novel is sometimes seen as a cop-out. Having created this free subject, the argument goes, Meredith hems her in with ironies that undermine that freedom. But the truth is that if Meredith had spared her the contiguities of her situation we

would have been left with a novel that had no fictional coherence.
Diana's freedom is legal and linguistic, but throughout the novel,
the sexual situation has been linked with other political issues.
The marriage of Diana and Warwick is likened by the diarists to
'another Union always in a Court of Law' (I) – that is England
and Ireland. And Diana herself links the situation of woman to a
recurrent topic in the novel, the growth of the railways:

> We women are the verbs passive of the alliance, we have to learn,
> and if we take to activity, with the best intentions, we conjugate a
> frightful disturbance. We are to run on lines, like steam trains, or we
> come to no station, dash to fragments. (VI)

The passage exactly pinpoints the limits I am trying to define.
Diana's first metaphor is linguistic, and it is radical (it exposes
the oppression of women by making them passive verbs). The
second is social and it is nostalgic (we are being overtaken by
industrialism). Significantly, it is Redworth she marries, an
Englishman ('They want the bridle-rein. That seems to me the
secret of the Irish character' (II)), who makes his money out of
railways. When he first seeks her at her house, the Crossways,
to restrain her from leaving the country and making her legal
position worse, he gets terribly lost because of the ambiguity
of the directions he is given. Diana is safe only in the pseudonymic
language of her independence. But outside, the larger social
forces are at work. Confronted with the brute fact of being unable
to survive without subterfuge, she is in the market for the strong
capitalist. It only makes it more telling that Redworth is such a
good man: the wedding yoke receives the sanction of grey toned
reason, just as the rose pink is avenged by the dirty drab in fiction.
'I am going into slavery to make amends for presumption',
Diana comments, and her confidante replies, 'Your business is to
accept life as we have it.' It amounts to an ideological summoning. The free subject is summoned to subject herself freely. There
is no paradox. The limits of the novel are in its language, and the
limits of the free subject in what is licensed to it. Diana pays the
price of not making a revolution: sexual politics is not apart from
industrial oppression and imperialism, but if the only connections
are linguistic, the free subject is only free within the limits of

language. Meredith's is a great novel because the summoning of the woman's nature against the social image is a programme realized within the bounds of a narrative that recognizes the webbing of the liberated consciousness in the frame that marks off the questions it asks from the questions it silences.

The Woman Pays

In this essay I have so far been considering texts which have various forms of ideological programme. I have suggested that the narrative mode, the 'point of view', within which that programme is elaborated determines whether the text realizes the programme as an ideological or fictional coherence, which in turn distinguishes between fictions that reveal by accident the limitations of the programme and fictions which expose it by its very articulation. I have not tried to suggest that there is any difference in value between the categories, rather that it resides within them. But my last category is different. Here the woman is summoned to be the subject of her experience in order that she can be revealed as subject to it; the true subject of her experience, in other words, is that of being the object of other's knowledge. This is not an ideological programme at all: it incorporates all the others but goes beyond them in calling up the questions that they repress. Chiefly it articulates the relationship between role and status in such a way that the programme itself makes the break with patriarchal ideology. I am not claiming that such texts have no ideological content but that this content remains vestigial, a residuum which is a flaw in the realization. My examples are novels by Gissing and Hardy, and it is significant that in their work there is a prior break in the consciousness of the productive relations of the author himself. Before he wrote *The Odd Women*, Gissing had written *New Grub Street* which is the first novel in English to be devoted to the portrayal of literary production in a market economy. The evolution of Hardy's fiction is from playing what he called a 'scientific game' to the open rupture that is indicated in the 'Explanatory Note to the First Edition' of *Tess of the D'Urbervilles*: 'I would ask any too genteel reader, who cannot endure to have said what everybody nowadays thinks and feels, to remember a well-worn sentence of St Jerome's: If an offence come out of the truth, better it is that the offence come than that the truth be concealed.' There is no need for Gissing and Hardy to build connections between themselves and the subjects of their novels by making the protagonists novelists, because they have already as writers made their situation as members of an alien group the very basis of their art.

The Odd Women (1893)[17] does have an explicit programme but it is not a theme exemplified by a protagonist, rather it is simply the history of a group:

> 'But do you know that there are half a million more women than men in this happy country of ours?'
> 'Half a million!'
> Her naïve alarm again excited Rhoda to laughter.
> 'Something like that they say. So many *odd* women – no making a pair with them. The pessimists call them useless, lost, futile lives. I, naturally – being one of them myself – take another view. I look upon them as a great reserve.' (IV)

Rhoda Nunn is, of course, making a theme of it, but that is her *view*, her programme as a teacher in a school to train women to a wider range of jobs than the ones they have access to. But the novel's subject is only the factual group and other characters have other responses to their oddness. Monica, her interlocutor, for example takes marriage to a crusted middle-aged male chauvinist called Widdowson as her way out. And her older sisters take refuge in brandy and the Bible. Monica's colleague at the shop where she works becomes a prostitute, 'a not unimportant type of the odd woman' (XXVIII). Gissing's particular talent as a novelist is to create a group like this while limiting the consciousness of its individual members so that their interaction is marginal or accidental: essentially each woman confronts her shared predicament, which is precisely the question of her status outside her assigned role as wife and mother, in a felt loneliness. To summarize the plot would be to give a series of banal individual stories: this is an important feature of this double articulation. What matters is the dull dawn for each of the odd women that the choices they make as the subjects of their lives are both crucial and yet prescribed to the point of meaninglessness.

This is not to say that Gissing nails the novel down with the pessimism Rhoda rejects. The work of Rhoda Nunn and Mary Barfoot, her mentor, is seen as positive and valuable and it has its successes. But its limitations are also made manifest. In the first place, it is very much a class movement. 'I must keep to my own class,' says Mary and Rhoda agrees: 'as soon as we meddle with uneducated people, all our schemes and views are unsettled. We have to learn a new language for one thing.' (VI) And, beyond this, Rhoda recognizes that it is not just a social structure she is fighting, but the biological fact the structure exploits: 'I am seriously convinced that before the female sex can be raised from its low level there will have to be a widespread revolt against sexual instinct (VI).' This is not just a matter of talk: these difficulties in the woman's movement as portrayed in the novel dominate its elaboration in one direction – though it should be added that marriage is seen as more repressive. Rhoda necessarily becomes a specific kind of egoist, a Spencerian[18] survivor whose sympathies have to have strict limits: 'human weakness is a plea that has been much abused, and generally in an interested spirit' (XIII). She has little time for Monica's depressing sisters, and cannot allow herself to be disturbed by the pupil who commits suicide. Her affair with Everard Barfoot is a battle of egoisms: he demands that they live in free union, not because he believes in it but because he wants her submission – she, for the same reason demands marriage. They drift apart because of a misunderstanding that neither will clear up. And yet this tough egoism is vindicated if anything by the more terrible story of Monica who is trapped in a brilliantly realized tyrannical marriage and destroyed by trying to escape through a romance with a treacherous sentimentalist. At least Rhoda survives to make the last comment on the dead Monica's baby: 'Poor little child!'. And maybe more than this – Rhoda's late meeting with Monica's tragedy gives her a larger sense of the group than that thematic statement I have quoted implies. Or at least we have it: for all the failure, material and emotional, in the novel, *The Odd Women* does not leave us resigned or hopeless about the women's movement. 'We flourish like the green bay-tree,' Rhoda says at the end, and because the range of consciousness is developed in the novel, we don't find this an ironic affirmation. The poor child may yet be 'a brave woman'.

Gissing can do this because he elaborates four autonomous but interdependent points of view in the novel. There is, of course, Rhoda's, which is one in which the need to make statements is increasingly brought into conflict with the recognition of motives in herself that those statements need to preclude. But this is no sentimental comedy. Rhoda goes through a series of rationalizations ('No longer an example of perfect female independence, and unable therefore to use the same language as before, she might illustrate woman's claim of equality in marriage. – If her experience prove no obstacle.' XXVI), but what remains is the resilience of her ego. By twisting the plot to create suspicion of Barfoot, Gissing might be thought to be avoiding the full confrontation with love that Rhoda seems bound to make. 'Was he in truth capable of respecting her individuality?' is a question she is never brought to answer. But the episode supplies another answer: it reveals in both the lovers a final concern with power that goes beyond the level of misunderstanding. And because Gissing equally develops Barfoot's consciousness, we know that Rhoda's decision is necessary to her survival: 'Delighting in her independence of mind, he still desired to see her in complete subjugation to him' (XXV). Through Barfoot, and through making the distance between him and Rhoda's mind always present to us, Gissing elaborates Rhoda's 'independence of mind' as an object of conquest. She is not a fatal woman but she is to him an obstacle to be overcome, and when he fails he can turn to Agnes Brissenden who is an object in the marriage market.

Rhoda's story is only given meaning by the development of Monica's consciousness. Gissing carefully establishes her as a critical intelligence which can see further than the triviality of her shop colleagues and can demand more than the pathetic capitulation to circumstances of her sisters. It is in the light of such awareness that opportunities offered by the Barfoot school merely leave her depressed and the opportunity of a 'marriage of esteem' seems like the only possible escape. But again, Gissing elaborates the story by the interaction of her consciousness with that of her husband, Widdowson, who acquires her as an object, the reward of his years of labour and self-denial. Her subjectivity thus becomes to him a painful ordeal as his image of what a wife should be becomes an intolerable repression to her. So that their relationship too becomes a struggle, not fought out on the level of ideas and trials, but through forced stratagem and detection. Rhoda and Monica never really come together though their respective ordeals would be a mutual education. Barfoot and Widdowson hardly meet though the egoism of the first is defined and challenged by the sickening alliance of moral rigidity and appropriative desire of the second. Between them they constitute the object world of woman – just as between Rhoda and Monica the subject world is articulated. And it is because the male epistemology has at its disposal the double institution of monogamy and prostitution, that the struggle of the odd women is at best a series of pyrrhic victories.

The novel's strength is that it deploys interacting but finally uncommunicating points of view, and yet, paradoxically, it is this that in the end prevents it from being a great work. For the price that Gissing pays for this double sense of the group and the isolation of its members, is that the full force of the contradiction in the woman's situation is dissipated: each of the protagonists experiences one fragment of it. It also prevents the novel from having any revolutionary potential: since the contradiction remains fragmented, it remains internal. Insofar as the struggle is turned outwards it is limited to polemic, to small pragmatic reforms (a small equalization of opportunity for middle-class girls with the right education) and to romantic subversion (which fails because it needs another man). I want to argue finally that it is precisely at the point of the limitation of Gissing's novel, that *Tess of the D'Urbervilles* begins to manifest its greatness. *Tess of the D'Urbervilles* is the story of the daughter of a poor and feckless country trader who is seduced by the scion of a *nouveau riche* family that has adopted Tess's aristocratic surname. She has a child which dies, and goes to work in a dairy where she meets and marries an agnostic intellectual, Angel Clare. On the night of their marriage Angel confesses to Tess about a former affair. Tess is encouraged to tell him about her past, but he turns against her because of it, and deserts her. After that she wanders from place to place in penury, working under appalling conditions until, to give some security to her now fatherless and evicted family, she goes to live with her first seducer as a kept woman in a near-by fashionable resort. At this point, Angel returns having learnt to regret his intolerance. In order to make herself free to go with him, Tess murders her keeper, and the pair wander off in vague flight from the police. She is arrested on Stonehenge, and the novel ends with her execution.

Hardy subtitled the novel 'A Pure Woman' and although in 1912 he said that it was added at the last moment and that the controversy it caused made him feel that it would have been better unwritten, he let it stand. And it is right, I think, because it makes clear the novel's project. But we need to be careful how we use the phrase. In the novel, he refers to her as 'an almost standard woman' which together with the fact that this discovery is made after she has ceased to be 'a maiden' makes it clear that purity is not innocence: Tess does not remain 'unsullied' by her experience, she becomes a woman by it – the first 'phase' of the novel is entitled 'Maiden' and the last 'Fulfilment'. Purity of the Christian-moral sort is demanded by Angel and his rejection of Tess is seen as a failure of sensibility. This is not an error likely to be repeated by modern critics, but another of Angel's mistakes is. He takes her as a 'visionary essence of woman', and although its etherealness is avoidable, we still have to beware of turning the project into a *theme* which pervades the novel. It is equally not a celebration of 'womanliness', that ideological absolute which is none the less ideological when it is softened with a little modern permissiveness.

'Pure woman' is a project: it is the object of a quest, not the subject of a demonstration. And that quest is Tess's who travels towards her fulfilment, and ours who see her life in 'phases'[19] (a word with many connotations, the most important of which is defined by John Stokes as 'non-teleological evolution' i.e. a structure for seeing an object of knowledge rather than the object of myth). In each phase we see a distinctive change in Tess (Maiden/Maiden No More (negation)/Rally (emergence)/ Consequence (withdrawal into illusion)/The Woman Pays etc.)

and yet the lapse of time in the novel is much greater within the phases than it is between them. Hardy thus structures an evolution and since it is an evolution towards the destruction of Tess within the phase of her fulfilment it is an evolution without end. (As notorious as the subtitle is Hardy's ironic evocation of an 'ending': 'Justice was done'.) And if it is a structure, it is a structured *movement*. The evolution of Tess is measured against a system of coordinates on a rigid body – particularly against the double polarity of Alec (*Weltlust*/fanaticism) and Angel (theoretical unconventionality/appropriative morality).

I have briefly indicated the features of the text's articulation (which needs fuller elaboration) to emphasize how experimental the novel is. Hardy mediates our relationship with Tess in many ways but it is not appropriate to see him in a simple ideological situation. He is not simply a dispassionate all-knowing sage (when he presents the valley of Talbothays as a vast expanse, giving Tess the sense of new opportunity, and then withdraws to see her as a fly on a billiard table, he ironizes her subjectivity but doesn't take us with him, or stay in that cosmic overview himself). Nor is he – as modern sentimental critics see him – a 'stricken father' who 'mourns' her. The authorial view ranges from erotic appropriation ('her flower-like mouth and large tender eyes, neither black nor blue nor gray nor violet; rather all those shades together, and a hundred others, which could be seen if one looked into their irises – shade behind shade – tint beyond tint – around pupils that had no bottom; an almost standard woman') to 'naturalistic' description ('A bit of her naked arm is visible beneath the buff leather of her gauntlet and the sleeve of her gown; and as the day wears on its feminine smoothness becomes scarified by the stubble and bleeds') to admiration ('Tess, with a curiously stealthy yet courageous movement, and with a still rising colour, unfastened her frock and began suckling her child'), to identification ('a resolution which had surprised herself . . .'). Each of these passages comes in the same chapter (XIV), and none of them are completely distinct from one another. What we are witnessing in fact is the objectification of Tess by the narrator which is acted out in the novel. At various points she is the object of consumption (for Alec and Angel, but she is also the self-

sacrificing conscience-ridden girl for us), and the object of fascination (Alec cannot leave her alone, and she is finally, literally
his *femme fatale*: but we have seen what Hardy does with her
eyes, for us) and she is even an emancipated woman (she makes
more of Angel's liberal education than he does, and the novel is
partly structured around a sequence of gestures of liberation
against Alec, and self-asserting statements to Angel). These
mediations give substance to the subject experience of Tess herself, by making us the subject of her, and thus guilty of the object
images whose contradictions she is subject to.

The realization of the project is thus the evolution of a subject
(Tess) towards an object (which is also a contradiction-fulfilment/
death). At the beginning of the novel, it is accurate to see Tess's
consciousness as 'alienated': subject, that is, to an 'inner contradiction' between 'conscience' and 'reverie' which responds to,
but does not correspond with, an external contradiction in the
social structure that demands individual integrity but disinte-
grates the individual through labour and sexual exploitation. But
the movement of the novel is away from this inner contradiction
towards the rupture, open and articulate, of subject and the
world of the subject. In 'The Woman Pays' and 'The Convert'
we see on the one hand the body appropriated as a machine for
economic and sexual usage (Tess is compelled to become part of
the threshing machine and it is the episode in which this happens
which begins the sequence of events that precipitate her towards
prostitution). When Angel sees her after his return he is aware
that mind and body are separate in Tess. On the other hand,
though Tess has to withdraw from her body in order to sell it as a
commodity, she re-enters it to oppose the exploitation. During the
threshing episode she strikes Alec D'Urberville with her gauntlet,
and this foreshadows her most aggressive act, the murder of the
man who owns her which happens at the moment she is most
completely appropriated – as the kept woman.

Just as the process is double (complete appropriation as object/
complete aggression as subject), so is its consequence. By her act
she places herself beyond the reach of the ideology which
summons the subject to subject itself to its determinants, but
equally, she makes herself the object of its retaliation. Hardy

calls the last phase 'Fulfilment', and though it is heavy with irony since the fulfilment is the execution of Tess (the moving in to the kill of that which has had its 'sport' with Tess), it is also, quite genuinely, a flowering. Tess lives inside time, and time is on the side of the law which will destroy her for coming alive (repossessing her own body). But in the interval of time which is granted her, she lives outside its 'truth': 'I am not going to think outside of now' (LVIII). In one sense this is an evasion, and it is left to Angel to do everything to prolong the interval, but in another it is a triumph. In terms of attitude and tone, it is she who dominates, gently educating Angel to live in the now where they have space: she even welcomes its limits because she does not want to commit their love to duration. And Tess has created this out of a class and sexual killing. It is not a revolutionary act, and I would not want to argue that Hardy ever thought of the possibilities of revolution, whether sexual or political, but it is an act of the kind of which revolutions are made, and it gives us a novel which creates in itself a revolution in form. For it is finally the story of her biological growth and its inevitable break with the exploiting world: its subject is larger than a word like consciousness can account for. The 'human' Tess and the non-human forces that motivate her make of her a subject whose subjection is at war with its subjectivity. And we can only be aware of this because we see Tess not as in a flat picture masquerading as depth, but from all the angles that are possible. And that is why, whatever Hardy's own ideological commitment, no frame will hold his novel in place.

Tess of the D'Urbervilles is not the latest of the novels I have discussed, but I hope I have been able to indicate that it is formally the most advanced, and that at the same time, *because of this* it is the most politically advanced. And this is the whole intent of my article. The model I have proposed is clearly tentative and needs much more elaboration, but if it has demonstrated convincingly that we can only see the political importance of a text by attending to its formal identity as the object of an act of production, it has achieved its main intention. And this has clear consequences for any movement which attempts to rescue our way of seeing things from the ideology that structures our response.

8

Women in American Trade Unions: An Historical Analysis

ROSALYN BAXANDALL

The present-day women's movement in the United States has not paid a great deal of attention to the industrial and white-collar-labour force, nor to the particular problems of women employed there. There are a number of reasons for this. Earlier feminist movements tended to ignore questions of female psychology and biology and thus to underplay the personal and sexual aspects of our lives; to compensate for this contemporary feminism has stressed precisely these issues, frequently locating women's particular oppression in the creation of a feminine personality and seeing their inferior status in society as a result of being daughters and mothers in the nuclear family. As it is predominantly middle class if not in its politics, then in its origin, where it has focused on questions of employment the women's movement has largely promoted exceptional women to break through restrictive male barriers: the first woman nuclear physicist, orchestral conductor and so on.

On the other hand, there are strong reasons which are not in-herent within its own history why the women's movement has given scant attention to the question of working women and their organization. Traditional male-dominated trade union thinking places women in a particularly problematic and painful bind. Evoking and simplifying one aspect of Marxism, it is argued that once women join the paid industrial labour-force, become workers, they will be liberated from their particular oppression as women and instead be exploited along with, and no differently from, men until both together they are freed by their own activity in a socialist revolution. Yet against this, and apparently without awareness of the contradiction, it is constantly urged that it is a waste of time trying to organize women into trade unions. Often with a note of regret, the men who lead the unions and write the history books tell us of the difficulty in inducing women to organize at work. Women they suggest are 'conservative' compared with their labouring menfolk; they stop their providers from striking, intent only on the next pay cheque, their meal ticket. This apparently is because women are deferential to authority, are meek and mild and shy away from abrasive conflicts. In seeking psychic comfort rather than economic advancement, these males suggest, women identify and define themselves as wives and mothers instead of as a part of the working class. Pettiness, jealousy and narrowness prevent a class-consciousness and solidarity. In these arguments the fault is located in an innate character of women, rather than in the structure of the family and society, economic production or the trade unions themselves.

Although personally I am an advocate of a separate political movement for women, a feminist movement, I did for a long time take it for granted that men and women must join together at work to struggle against their bosses. But the more I have read of the history of the working class the more I have doubted that the present trade-union structure will serve the purpose of women or, for that matter, of men. At the present time, it seems indeed that only separate, women-only feminist caucuses within the trade unions might succeed in revitalizing the labour movement as a whole.

As for current arguments about priorities or basic causes of oppression within the women's movement, I consider that it is not necessary to deny the importance of opening up new and highly demanding careers to women, nor the significance of psychological and biological understanding of women's liberation, if we also insist that the whole of women's situation will not be comprehended, nor the freedom of all women be enabled, until the reality of participation in the mass work force by women is fully studied and the possibilities for organizing fundamental change in this setting are energetically explored.

Nonetheless, it is readily recognized that women are not a compelling factor in trade unionism today; only some 12 per cent of women employed in the United States are in trade unions. The present situation must be understood historically. To see why women's paid work can have come to be thought of as 'marginal' to their role of self-definition, we must go back at least to the seventeenth century when, with the advent of capitalism in England over a period of 200 years, industrial production was taken out of the home. This meant that the family no longer owned or controlled the means of production, nor was the work any longer the work of the family as a whole. Earlier, father, mother, and children had all contributed to the spinning and weaving processes, for example; now, father went off to the textile mills, earning a mite which his wife at home would eventually use to buy, among other items, garments for the children. The home was for women's work once the factory system commenced: it was the place for child-raising, relaxation while the production of commodities at the industrial plant focused the possibilities of organized struggle there.

To the present day, despite all changes in economic arrangements and predominant ideology, the notion of women as essential to the home and inessential to the work place remains. Women were too 'refined' or 'frail' to go into the coarse, ruthless world of outside work; or if they did, they were streetwalkers or not much better, or their husbands could not provide for them and it was a shame. 'Heavy' work would make a woman mannish or brutish; this argument became more common as the capitalist work place became more hellish, and the home was sought as a retreat. Or conversely, the male was unsuited for the peculiar tasks of the household: he wasn't delicate enough for many of its finer functions, and if he tried to adjust, he would be unmanned for the cruel struggles of the male world of work. In the eighteenth century it was thought that if women tried to apply their brainpower to men's tasks this would draw energy away from the womb and their child-bearing function would be withered.

Thus the present situation has its basis in the most fundamental organization of economic production and the manifold social and psychological relations that develop therefrom as implementation and rationalization. In the United States the situation evolved on lines superficially contradictory to those of classical capitalism in Europe, due to the later evolution of industry in the United States and also for some years the marginality of industry as a whole to the gross national product, in this vast agricultural colony of a European industrial power. The fact is that farmers' daughters were the earliest factory hands in the United States. Menfolk were occupied with making their farmlands produce. With few factories, and these devoted not to export but primarily to domestic requirements in cloth, a girl could profitably spend a few years employed and defer marriage according to the then socio-economic custom. Were it not for the evolved status of factories, easily borrowed from Europe, these daughters would have worked at spinning and weaving in the home as previously had been customary in agricultural societies. As soon as industry evolved in the United States to a level to compete for markets with Europe, women became less important and the speeded-up tasks were entrusted primarily to new immigrants from Ireland and Germany, males who could be driven hard for a poor wage, making American industry competitive on a world scale.

Even in the earliest periods of female predominance in American factory-work, women like Sarah Bagley and Harriet Robinson were active in creating labour associations. Like Bagley's Lowell Female Reform Association, these attempts were generally local or regional in scale; they seldom lasted long. If they did survive, as did Robinson's organizing initiative for the ten-hour day, they generally converged with male-directed utopian or reform movements. The female components lost any particularity, and female leadership became non-initiating. Males predominated in the new American industrial society as they did in Europe, and where an institution grew to significance (even when the organization stood for reform or revolution), the sexual hierarchy was reasserted.

Single women, and married women whose husbands provided poorly or not at all, continued in non-domestic employment and, therefore, often found motivation to join protective associations. Male organizations for mutual help generally were closed to them. They accordingly found solidarity within the structures extended to them by wealthy reformers, such as settlement houses and

YWCAs. These organizations could offer aid and some security to working women. They could not supply a power base in industry, capable of raising wages or improving work conditions, although they could issue pleas to the humane ideals of employers. Susan B. Anthony and Elizabeth Cady Stanton, founders of the women's suffrage movement in the United States, understood the importance of industrial employment in women's lives: they founded a Working Women's Association. Its efforts, however, were chiefly consumed in getting the women to support the effort to get the vote. This suffrage emphasis was political, in contrast to the usual reduction of demands to the purely economic plane (more wages, less hours) – but political in the definition provided by the battle for the vote, rather than political in a sense specifically arising from conditions of industrial employment. Their Working Women's Association was, in other words, political in a completely sex-defined dimension, with the labouring class left apart except for tactical organizing purposes of winning a constitutional amendment.

Male-organized associations, such as the National Labor Union, pledged in 1866 to support women workers specifically. They did not, however, hire female organizers of workers, nor did they allocate funds to organizing among women, and they often declared that women's rightful place was in the home.

For the first time, an all-female union local was founded when in 1869 Augusta Lewis, a typesetter, organized a women's section of the nationwide Typographical Union. Her early high hopes soon soured and she told the union's convention in 1871:

We refused to take the men's situation when they were on strike, and when there is no strike if we ask for work in union offices we are told by union foremen 'that there are no conveniences for us'. We are ostracized in many offices because we are members of the union, and although the principle is right, disadvantages are so many that we cannot much longer hold together . . . It is the general opinion of female compositors that they are more justly treated by what is termed 'rat' foremen, printers and employers than by union men.[1]

In 1878 this women's Typographical local which Augusta Lewis fought so hard to initiate disbanded, and thereafter the national union followed a policy of chartering no separate women's locals but of admitting women to membership on the same basis as men. Such a policy had pronounced disadvantages as women remained an unwelcome minority and could develop little leadership of their own.

Generally, women had to fight hard to become members of male-dominated unions and when they finally succeeded they were often resented and even specifically excluded from contract agreements. In 1921, Mabel Taylor wrote in a monthly magazine for working women:

The men in the shops are to blame for not taking the girls into their organization when they first entered the shops . . . [the men are] making the girls feel . . . that they are interlopers.[2]

The first negotiated agreement between the cloakmakers and their employees stated 'That no part of this agreement shall refer or apply to females employed by the Cloak Manufacturers' Association'.[3] Similar tales of being made to feel unwanted, and in time of need of betrayal by male unions, are related by Elizabeth Morgan, a radical reformer who organized a small group of Chicago clerks, book-binders, candy makers, typists, music teachers and gum makers into the Ladies Federal Union, by Kate Mullaney, a key organizer of the collar-workers' union in Troy, and by the Daughters of Saint Crispin, a female shoemakers' union.

The Knights of Labor, a short-lived labour union of the 1880s which was much feared by the bosses of industry, hired Leonora Barry to head a special Woman's Department which was to organize women workers as well as housewives. Her job was an impossible one since the employers would not allow her into the plants to investigate or organize. She had verbal backing from her male comrades, but nothing else. She wrote discouraging daily reports about problems she encountered:

Having no legal authority I have been unable to make as thorough an investigation in many places as I would like, and after the discharge of Sister Annie Conboy from the silk mill in Auburn, in February last for having taken me through the mill, I was obliged to refrain from going through establishments where the owners are opposed to our Order lest some members be victimized; consequently the facts stated in my report are not from actual observation but from authority which I have every reason to believe truthful and reliable.[4]

While male labour organizers also had difficulty in entering many work premises, Miss Barry's task was undoubtedly complicated by her lack of personal conviction that these women had any business doing factory work (a view of women's-place-is-in-the-home which was shared, incidentally, by the famous labour organizer Mother Jones). When Leonora Barry married she stopped working, and removed herself from the labour movement. Here she states her belief about women's ideal sphere:

> If it were possible, I wish that it were not necessary for women to learn any trade but that of domestic duties, as I believe it was intended that man should be the breadwinner. But as that is impossible under present conditions, I believe women should have every opportunity to become proficient in whatever vocation they choose or find themselves fitted for.[5]

Until the Second World War most women who worked were single. A married woman worked only if her husband were disabled, unemployed, dead or had deserted her. Marriage was the end of the working girl's career, which is why many unionists felt that to organize women was a wasted effort. Even the trade-union newspapers carried columns congratulating those women who had found marriage mates and left the rank-and-file.

It is difficult to say how many women worked for wages before 1900, because only full-time work was registered as work. Many women engaged in seasonal and home work. Much of women's work such as babyminding, or selling hand-made goods and foods, is still not recorded in the statistical index. On the basis of utilized indices, in 1900 women were only 18 per cent of the labour force, in 1920, 20 per cent, in 1930, 22 per cent.

Working for wages was considered unladylike and yet many women worked and couldn't be totally ignored. Labour organizing was an arduous task, but at least for men there were certain compensations. Within the union if you were successful you could rise. When your work was finished you came home and were soothed and comforted. For female organizers the task was more difficult. Elizabeth Gurley Flynn, a star organizer for the Industrial Workers of the World and later the Communist Party, jotted down in 1940 her envy of male organizers:

> I love my comrade organizers and speakers – but I don't envy
> their wives,
> I've been a wife myself and I'm a comrade too,
> I know the strain we are!
> The skipped meals, the broken dates, the unpaid bills,
> the hard lives . . .
> Yes I do envy them having someone to really care so much,
> I fear I envy you one thing only dear wives,
> Their love when I am lonely!
> and some one man – to do all that for me!
> I GUESS I NEED A WIFE![6]

Not only did the pioneer women labour organizers face hardships without the advancement opportunities or the creature comforts that their male comrades enjoyed, they often weren't given much respect. For Rose Schneiderman, a Polish immigrant girl who at the age of thirteen began working a sixty-four-hour week as a salesperson, the hardest part of rising to become an organizer was the discovery that her union leadership did not put any trust in her efforts. She nonetheless persevered, organizing at various times for the Cap Workers' Union, the Women's Trade Union League and the International Ladies Garment Workers' Union. Here is how she wrote to her fellow organizer and best friend, Pauline Newman, about the way her organizing was undermined:

> Three days before the strike [of shirtwaist makers], Schlesinger [President of the ILGWU] sent in Meyer Perlstein to manage it. I was furious because evidently Perlstein did not believe in my ability to see things through. I sent him a letter of resignation, but, of course I couldn't resign, for I still had the responsibility of getting the strike settled. Perlstein had nothing to do so he mixed up the leaflets which were all ready for the different shops and separated them all again.[7]

Rose Schneiderman finally quit her job as an organizer for the ILGWU and went to work with the Industrial Division of the Women's Suffrage Party, where she felt she'd be better appreciated. Leonora O'Reilly, Hannah Hennessey, and Clara Lemich, all working-class labour organizers, who are now forgotten because they didn't write skilfully or much and didn't have the education or time to learn, expressed similar frustration at working within male trade-union structures.

During the Depression, women had increasingly gone to work outside the home and by 1940 they were 25 per cent of the paid labour force. During the Second World War there was an upward lurch in the female-to-male ratio to 36 per cent in 1945, due not only to labour shortages during the war but also to a new scale of demand for the female-identified jobs in the clerical and service sectors. Did this lead to greater unionization of women to protect their interests through exercise of increased potential power? Certainly more women did enter unions and paid dues, but action on women's particular grievances was rare, and few women became activists or organizers. The great CIO organizing drives focused on men's work sectors – rubber, steel, auto – leaving aside the basically female industries and job categories. The CIO's few women unionists pleaded for more responsibility and warned their union brothers that with the war, if women weren't immediately trained for union leadership there would be no one prepared to take charge when the men were drafted into the army. The labour movement would suffer a paralysing blow. Anna Burlak, a Southern textile-mill worker and union organizer, in a report to the Communist Party at that time, said:

Especially with the coming danger of war and the possibility that a lot of our men comrades will be out at the front pretty soon, I feel that many of our party functionaries in the field still take the fact that it is necessary to develop women leaders with a grain of salt. It might not come out openly, but there is that hidden insinuation. And there is still scepticism as to the capabilities of women becoming leaders. I know that women although they are militant in strike struggles and demonstrations, are still hesitant to get up and speak in meetings; especially when they get the feeling from men that they don't know enough to get up and speak at a meeting. It is necessary for every one of our comrades, especially the men comrades, to devote more time to encouraging women to take leading parts in our trade union and party work. There is still a certain scepticism as to whether women can become district organizers of the Communist Party. I have heard this expressed by many comrades – 'she is a woman, how can she be a district organizer?'[8]

Numerous explanations have been offered for the decline of the power of unions in the United States, and particularly of the more left-wing unions, despite the new strengths developed in the thirties and apparently demonstrated right after the war. In this, as in so many instances, one major causal factor may be the *negative* one of the *failure* by labour-radical organizations to train female cadre to carry on during the war, and to double the leadership strength afterwards, when many pro-Communist male unionists were put on trial or quietly purged from unions.

It is well known that in the fifties and sixties the labour movement in the United States grew more conservative, bureaucratic and rigid in its procedures and goals. At the same time women's numbers in the labour force – having slipped back at the end of the war – mounted again, from their pre-war high of 25 per cent in 1940, to 29 per cent in 1950, and 33 per cent in 1960. By 1972, fully 42 per cent of the paid labour force in the United States was female. However, segregation of jobs remained the rule, with discrimination against women's pay scales as one result. One-third of all females were employed in 1968 in just seven kinds of jobs: secretary, waitress, domestic, elementary-school teacher, saleswoman, nurse, and book-keeper. This is how one worker on the Fisher Body assembly line in Detroit, Olga Domanski, recently described her department in terms of a 'harem':

The women were not scattered among men, doing jobs side by side with them. They were isolated in one corner of the shop in one department. They were treated as creatures apart – something very special – but special in a negative way. The 'specialness' of our department lay in the fact that the work we did had recently been reclassified by management from heavy work to light work; this is the way management distinguished 'men's work' from 'women's work'. It was apparent that the designation had nothing to do with heaviness or lightness, but only with rate of pay.[9]

Indeed little progress has been made by working women. Only a little over 12 per cent of women are organized, and one quarter of all unions have no women members. Women are not encouraged to become leaders in unions. Tokenism is a standard practice. One woman or sometimes two are appointed to the national executive board. Most unions have no special women's department. There is no maternity leave with pay, and pension benefits for women are lower. Only one union, Amalgamated Clothing Workers', provides day care, which its members pay for, and it was only in 1973 that the AFL–CIO (American Federation of Labor – Congress of Industrial Organizations) finally backed the Equal Rights Amendment.

Little budget is allotted for organizing the unorganized women workers. Some secretaries who have recently been organizing themselves at first sought union assistance and affiliation without success. Male unionists' attitudes on the whole remain primitive. This is how Mildred Sossi, the recording secretary of the United Telephone Answering and Communication Service Union, Local 789, tells of her problem in organizing workers:

> Married women refuse to join the union because their husbands – good union members – forbid it. These husbands, and we see a lot of it, are members of labor unions and they get pensions and benefits and good wages. They believe in the Union only for themselves.[10]

Conclusions

If it is worthwhile to pay attention to the condition of the ever-increasing number of women who work a good part of their lives outside the home, then it is important to see how women can gain a greater control over the benefits and the character of their paid work experience. This control, it is reasonable to believe, will benefit other areas of women's lives as well.

However, the record of women's relation to generally male-initiated and male-dominated labour unions is discouraging. Should other means than traditional labour-union affiliation be sought? Indeed can the existing union structures incorporate women's legitimate demands? Or should women try to achieve their demands through non-union organizations such as NOW, the National Organization for Women, which already presses equal-rights complaints before governmental agencies vigorously and with some significant results? Will 'guerrilla actions' by radical women's organizations against sexist employers, which get publicity but are of brief duration, serve the cause? Can individual women with raised feminist consciousness and acting on their own, who confront and explain to supervisors and employers, alter the basic situation if enough such women 'moving with the times' act thus?

In my view, all the above approaches to equalizing the condition of women at paid work can be considered useful, depending on the specific set of circumstances. Their combination, within a feminist-oriented organizational structure, seems potentially most effective. What does this say about the position of women towards the present male-dominated union structures? Should entirely new unions in the female-dominated fields, such as clerical work and domestic work, be launched? Should women's caucuses in the existing unions be established and their power fought for, as prelude to the further expansion of union activity in female-identified job fields?

Individual contacts and confrontations with industrial management and indeed with male workers on the one hand, and governmental regulation on the other, are clearly no substitute for the sustained, massed power of the (female) working class. I think no clear mandate can be discerned as between expansion of existing unions into unorganized female enclaves, and the launching of new all-women unions. The resources of the existing unions is formidable, as the recent confrontation between the Farm Workers' Union and the Teamsters for the organizing control in California agricultural-business shows. Rather, women must everywhere demarcate their specific demands. If all-women unions make good headway, women in potentially competitive unions will then be able to combat a 'fratricidal' tendency. Where all-women unions do not appear, existing unions with strong women's caucuses can organize around truly female demands.

It may be objected, on impressive evidence, that the present structure of unions on the whole is outmoded for purposes of struggle with corporate management. Clearly, the power of the rank-and-file within unions has diminished since the Second World War and that of management has grown. The ruling élite have become a multi-national power, while labour has lost efficacy, confined as it is within the national borders. Labour has been unable to prevent inflation, wage freezes, runaway shops, massive unemployment, the election of anti-labour candidates, compulsory overtime, speed-up, and unsafe and unhealthy conditions. Union officials may spend more time preventing 'wildcat' worker protest than they do in processing grievances through established channels.

The obsolescence of union structures has occurred in the past. Starting in the 1860s the growth of vertically integrated industry made it difficult for craft-organized unions to halt production and achieve demands. Unions within entire industries had to be organized. From 1900 to 1935 the more radical elements within the labour movement did strive for this restructuring, and after much bitter and heroic endeavour, it was done. The CIO, Congress of Industrial Organizations founded in the late thirties, is the coordinating body. Then after the Second World War with the United States emerging as the leading world power, industrial structuring became international and extremely difficult for those outside the managerial offices even to follow. Industry-wide unions found it almost impossible to cripple the production of the employers, since – for example – if the United Auto Workers stop production at every Ford Motor plant in the United States, production and profits will still continue unabated in the Ford Holdings at Düsseldorf or Caracas.

However, women's enclaves of work may have a largely unsuspected importance for labour as a whole in its apparently unequal struggle to contain and humble the international corporations. Why? Because the corporations may sprawl octopus-like around the world but their nerve-centres remain in the United States, and women, as clerical and administrative workers, are crucial to the operations. Government, management, and banking would come to a halt if women went out on strike. Or, like the Wobblies of a half-century ago, if they engaged in industrial sabotage. Merely because women in these positions of confidentiality and implementation have not to date acted in concert with the traditional trade-union movement, does not preclude that they will.

As for the existing trade-union structure, women certainly can achieve greater efficacy by organizing across trade-union lines, as women. An organization with this potential was recently founded; on 23–4 March 1974, 3,300 women came together from nearly every state and from fifty-eight unions to form the Coalition of Trade Union Women (CLUW). This organizing convention decided to form chapters within unions and also, depending on the community, without regard to the given union affiliation. From their separate female caucuses the women unionists will have a power base with which to relate to union bureaucracies. A priority of CLUW is to organize the unorganized. Moreover, women from unions in several countries outside the United States attended, and the Statement of Purpose says in part: 'We recognize that our struggle goes beyond the borders of this nation and we seek to link up with our working sisters and brothers throughout the world with concrete actions of worker solidarity.'

The organization of CLUW presents a breakthrough for women workers as well as the bourgeois feminist movement, which has been largely dominated by young professional women and represents their interests. At last there is a structural link and context for women workers and the women's movement to link forces and assert their demands.

In the past the labour movement has largely been concerned with demands relating to wages and conditions of production. Women workers are aware of their double role as workers and as consumers, and therefore might ultimately press their unions to negotiate national price as well as wage demands. A strong women's trade-union movement might moreover have more motivation to struggle for non-wage demands, as so many of the issues neglected by the male-led labour movement (such as the genuine humanization of labour, day-care, the end of compulsory overtime) may prove peculiarly sensitive issues for women workers.

On the one hand the infusion of women's consciousness may be the only remedy for the obsolescence of the increasingly ineffectual structure of unions as a means of struggle. On the other hand, the full emergence of the 'ghettoized' female values into the world of union struggle and of work may lend tangible substance to the goal which Marx and the socialists generally have expected all along, if not perhaps in these terms, of the *lutte dernière*: that the victory of working people will mean the unfolding of the most universal human values. It was the women in the Lawrence (Mass.) strike of 1912 who demanded roses as well as bread, a beautiful life as well as a living wage.

If unions can manage to incorporate the cultural (in the broad, anthropological sense), non-wage demands, they might to start with begin to provide a new social core to combat their members' alienation, which has not been averted within the nuclear family or in a home in a 'neighbourhood' apart from work. Before television and, in an earlier era, the union had filled the need among male workers for relaxation, culture and comraderie. To quote Marx in the *1844 Manuscripts*:

When communist *workmen* associate with one another, theory, propaganda, etc., is their first end. But at the same time, as a result of this association, they acquire a new need – the need for society – and what appears as a means becomes an end. You can observe this practical process in its most splendid results whenever you see French socialist workers together. Company, association, and conversation, which again has society as its end, are enough for them; the brotherhood of man is no mere phrase with them, but a fact of life, and the nobility of man shines upon us from their work-hardened bodies.

Perhaps when women take their rightful place within the unions, and introduce in a true guise the values of 'nobility', tenderness, nurture, etc., which have largely been attributed and segregated to them through the long agony of class society – perhaps when this occurs, the enriched social core of union activity may more truly resemble in embryo the future society.

9

Looking Again at Engels's 'Origins of the Family, Private Property and the State'

ROSALIND DELMAR

According to the materialistic conception, the determining factor in history is, in the last resort, the production and reproduction of immediate life. But this itself is of a two-fold character. On the one hand, the production of means of subsistence, of food, clothing and shelter and the tools requisite therefore; on the other, the production of human beings themselves, the propagation of the species. The social institutions under which men of a definite country live are conditioned by both kinds of production: by the stage of development of labour, on the one hand, and of the family on the other. The less the development of labour, and the more limited its volume of production and, therefore, the wealth of society, the more preponderantly does the social order appear to be dominated by ties of sex. However, within this structure of society based on ties of sex, the productivity of labour develops more and more; with it, private property and exchange, differences in wealth, the possibility of utilizing the labour power of others and thereby the basis of class antagonisms: new social elements, which strive in the course of generations to adapt the old structure of society to the new conditions until finally the incompatibility of the two leads to a complete revolution. The old society based on sex groups bursts asunder in the collision of the newly-developed social classes; in its place a new society appears, constituted in a state, the lower units of which are no longer sex groups but territorial groups, a society in which the family system is entirely dominated by the property system and in which the class antagonisms and class struggles, which make up the content of all hitherto *written* history now freely develop. (pp. 25–6)[1]

It is thus that Engels summarizes the main argument of his *Origins of the Family, Private Property and the State*, a text based on Lewis Morgan's *Ancient Society*[2]. What attracted Marx and Engels to Morgan's work was his skill at linking developments in the family form to alterations in the 'arts of subsistence' as he termed them. They shared his desire to establish the historicity of the family, and applauded his attempt to chart that history in a relation to material conditions of production rather than through philosophical speculation or the analysis of religion. The account given of the family in the *Origins* reflects Morgan's influence.

In the first section Engels outlines historical progression in the means of gaining subsistence and in the elaboration of instruments for the appropriation of nature. In the second he periodizes transformations in the form of family which, he remarks, 'proceeds concurrently with changes in the means of subsistence' (p. 39).

One of the foundations for this way of investigating the history of the family was Morgan's observation that amongst the Iroquois there existed a system of consanguinity which was in contradiction to actual family relationships. In other words, that the terms of expression of kinship, which implied rights, duties, obligations and prohibitions, were distinct from the visible relations in practice in the family. Further, Morgan claimed that in Hawaii there was in existence a form of family which corresponded to the Iroquois kinship system, but that again that family had a kinship system in contradiction to it.

The conclusion which was drawn from this was that the system of consanguinity and kinship was inherited from a form of family which had pre-existed the present one, and that there was, therefore, a sort of historic lag between changes in the family form and changes in systems of consanguinity. To put it differently, that kinship systems are a kind of ideological superstructure. 'Systems of consanguinity' (wrote Morgan) '. . . are passive, recording the progress made by the family at long intervals apart, and only changing radically when the family has radically changed.' 'And', adds Marx, 'the same applies to political, juridical, religious and philosophical systems generally.' (p. 46)

The question of whether or not this is actually the most fruitful way of understanding kinship systems is not at issue here. What is of more concern is what Engels was attempting to establish through a use of Morgan's researches. This was two-fold: (a) the existence of a form of family based on mother-right, a system where 'descent is traceable only on the *maternal* side, and thus the *female line* alone is recognized' (p. 55). If the existence of such a system could be proved, it would deal a powerful ideological blow against 'the absurd assumption which became inviolable in the eighteenth century, that the monogamian individual family, an institution scarcely older than civilization, is the nucleus around which society and the state gradually crystallized' (p. 103); (b) that this system historically preceded father-right and that the transition from one to the other coincided with the subordination of the female sex to the male sex. If this latter could be demonstrated then it would mean that not only did women's oppression have historic origins, but that it was also capable of historic resolution.

It is the second of these two preliminary propositions which is most hotly contended. I do not intend to go into the pros and cons of the dispute,[3] but rather to concentrate on the hypothesis of the transition which Engels puts forward. Even if it is merely a projection backwards from the situation of the modern monogamous family, which no scientific investigation will ever be able to verify in the past, it is an evocation which contains within it the elements of the socialist analysis of women's oppression and the preconditions of women's emancipation. That reason alone is sufficient to make it of interest.

The Hypothesis of the Transition

In the society where mother-right was the form of descent, Engels argues that there was a division of labour between the sexes, but no sex antagonism.

Women controlled the means of production inside the home, men those outside the home: 'According to the division of labour then prevailing in the family, the procuring of food and the implements necessary thereto, and therefore, also, the ownership of the latter, fell to the man; he took them with him in case of separation, just as the woman retained the household goods' (p. 66).

Engels then posits an intensification of production outside the home – 'the introduction of cattle breeding, of the working up of metals, of weaving, and finally field cultivation – and together with this the beginnings of slavery – according to the custom of society at that time, the man was also the owner of the new source of food-stuffs – the cattle – and later, of the new instrument of labour – the slaves' (p. 66).

This increase in the productivity of labour in the male sphere led to the creation of a surplus which could be appropriated as wealth, and gave men a new economic power over women.

Division of labour in the family had regulated the distribution of property between man and wife. This division of labour remained unchanged, and yet it now put the former domestic relationship topsy-turvy, simply because the division of labour outside the family had changed. The very cause that had formerly made the woman supreme in the house, namely, her being confined to domestic work, now assured supremacy in the house for the man: the woman's housework lost its significance compared with the man's work in obtaining a livelihood. (p. 521)

It was this new economic power, according to Engels, which gave men the strength to institute a political revolution against women, and overturn mother-right, replacing it with father-right. 'The reckoning of descent through the female line and the right of inheritance through the mother were hereby overthrown and male lineage and right of inheritance from the father instituted' (p. 67). What was thereby also instituted was the right to undisputed paternity. He adds that 'as to how and when this revolution was effected among the civilized peoples we know nothing', and depends for proof that such an upheaval did take place on both Morgan's demonstration of the existence of matrilineality and Bachofen's cultural researches into Greek myth and drama.[4] Bachofen had found, in the *Oresteia*, for example, an acting out of the rights of mother, father and son which culminated in an affirmation of the law of the father, and had interpreted in this the drama of a struggle between the old order and the new.

With this political revolution came a new form of family, the patriarchal family, tied to agriculture, which incorporates bondsmen into its structure, as a transitional form before the appearance of the monogamous family. The imposition of the patriarchy meant that women lost any right to separation. Leaving to one side for the moment Engels's characterization of the monogamous family, it is instructive to compare his hypothesis of the transition with that of the future liberation of women, in order to bring out what they have in common.

The emancipation of women and their equality with men are impossible and must remain so as long as women are excluded from socially productive work and restricted to housework, which is private. The emancipation of women becomes possible only when women are enabled to take part in production on a large, social scale, and when domestic duties require attention only to a minor degree. And this has become possible only as a result of modern large-scale industry, which not only permits the participation of women in production in large numbers, but actually calls for it and, moreover, strives to convert private domestic work also into a more public industry. (p. 152)

This is the kernel of Engels's conspectus of the future emancipation of women. Economic emancipation in socially organized production and the liberation of women from restriction to housework are the keys to sexual emancipation. On this all else rests.

Just as the subjugation of women coincided with the subjugation of one section of humanity into slavery, so women's future liberation will coincide with the abolition of wage slavery, for only when that happens will women finally have full freedom in marriage and regain the lost rights of separation: 'full freedom in marriage can become generally operative only when the abolition of capitalist production and of the property relations created by it, has removed all those secondary economic considerations which still exert so powerful an influence on the choice of partner'. (p. 88)

Engels thus locates women's oppression at the level of participation in production, links the conflict between the sexes to the appearance of private ownership of wealth, and posits the reconciliation of the sexes as possible only when private property has been abolished. The fortunes of women and of oppressed classes are intimately connected: neither can be free until economic formations based on private property have been abolished.

But although Engels has often, on account of this perspective, been accused of economic reductionism in his analysis of the family, he is in fact less of a reductionist than those who try to decipher the family solely in terms of its economic functions for capitalism and thus place the family in a one-to-one relationship with the mode of production. In distinction to this view Engels puts forward a conception of a form of family which can survive entire epochs, with modifications forced on it by the historical process.

The gist of Engels's argument is thus that changes at the level of the economy reverberate through the old social forms until a political and social transformation has been fully effected. The exposition rests on a synthesis of Morgan's anthropology and Bachofen's more idealist speculations. It also leans heavily on Marx's political theory of transformation, distilled in the *Preface to a Contribution to a Critique of Political Economy* (1859):

At a certain stage of their development the material forces of production in society come into conflict with the existing relations of production, or – what is but a legal expression of the same thing – with the property relations within which they had been at work before. From forms of development of the forces of production these relations turn into their fetters. Then occurs a period of social revolution. With the change in the economic foundation the entire immense super-structure is more or less rapidly transformed. In considering such transformations, the distinction should always be made between material transformations of the economic conditions of production, which can be determined with the precision of a natural science, and the legal, political, religious, aesthetic or philosophical – in short, ideological – forms in which men become conscious of this conflict and fight it out.[5]

The experience of socialist revolutions, which have to a certain extent acted out Engels's projections and applied his socialist theory in practice, are one means of verifying this approach. The experience of the Chinese revolution provides a case in point.

Women and Liberation in China

The traditional Chinese family was distinctively patriarchal.[6] The head of the family was usually the father, but could also be the grandfather, a paternal uncle, or an elder brother. Marriages were arranged between families, according to strict rules of exogamy. On marriage the woman entered her husband's clan, and her duties and obligations to her own clan were at the same time considerably diminished.

It was a paramount duty that a woman produce male offspring; even when concubinage was prohibited to the common people, an exception was made if the first wife did not give birth to a male child; in cases of divorce, which in practice was allowed only to the man, the woman was sent back to her family, and her male children remained with the husband. Women were strictly confined within the home, and footbinding was a symbol of restricted freedom, sexual bondage, and, simultaneously, sexual desirability.

Apart from the burden of oppression laid on the shoulders of women, the sexual problem had also a class aspect. When the Communist Party of China established the Kiangsi Republic in the early thirties, an investigation of the area revealed this aspect quite clearly. In a society where women were bought and sold, all the landlords and rich peasants had wives, some having concubines as well; 90 per cent of middle peasants had wives; 70 per cent of artisans and poor peasants; and, finally, 10 per cent of lumpen-proletarians and only 1 per cent of agricultural workers had wives.[7] Freedom of marriage was thus a necessity for the poorest strata of men as for women.

The revolutionary strategy against this was two-fold: land reform and marriage reform. Women received plots in the redistribution of land, and were to be educated (through the mediation of the women's associations) in agricultural skills. The new marriage laws prohibited purchase and sale of young girls, arranged marriages, polygamy and concubinage. Marriage between consanguineous relatives including cross-cousin marriages was also outlawed, and distinctions between legitimate and illegitimate children were abolished. Freedom of divorce was instituted, with the right of the woman to be supported after divorce. The effect of this latter provision was a phenomenal increase in the numbers of divorces.[8] Revolution in the relations of agricultural production was in this way linked to revolution in the relations of reproduction. Women's associations defended women's rights and gave expression to the needs and interests of women in the organs of political power.

The Chinese experience reflects in action an application of Engels's theories: it is this characteristic which makes the experience of socialist revolutions so important for women liberationists. A new economic reality has been accompanied by a new development in the family form. Economic emancipation of women in work outside the home and work-sharing within the home, together with freedom of marriage and the right of divorce are seen as central to its success. The old patterns of kinship relations remain, emerging, for example, in the handling of inheritance cases, where 'the influence of the feudal, ancestral classification of branches of the clan, and the system of succession based on it, is still widely spread among the masses'.[9] But these different elements open up specific problems.

Chinese women now participate in agriculture and industry on an impressive scale. The main slogan here is 'anything a man can do a woman can do'. This entry into social production however, itself gives birth to a new contradiction, that between social production and child-care. The accepted solution for this is socialized child-care (crèches, kindergartens and schools) although these are not yet available to all women. But this system of socialized child-care does not question the general sexual division of labour.

Further, the right of separation is one which is invoked less and less. The divorce rate in China has dropped enormously since the early years, and social pressure is exerted both for late marriage and against divorce. Chinese women I have talked to have been vehement in their declarations that the new marriage system is a response to the needs of women, and mainly a restriction on the sexual freedom of men. Antagonisms between men and women are by no means as marked in China as they are in capitalist societies, women are not sexual objects, and have an independence we could envy. But for what span of time a system of life-long monogamy could last in a dynamically changing society is open to doubt.

The final question arising from the Chinese experience is the treatment of male suprematism as a contradiction 'among the people' and hence as an object of ideological struggle. How is such an ideological struggle conducted? First and foremost, it is initiated and directed by the leadership of the Communist Party through the various organs of political power – the revolutionary committees at different levels, and through the mass organizations, trades unions, women's organizations, youth organizations and peasant organizations, which exist in the factories, communes and neighbourhoods. Mass propaganda is utilized, including wall newspapers, local and national newspapers, magazines, cartoons, discussion meetings, radio talks, plays, films. Of course, the most powerful ideological weapon is women's entry into all the diverse forms of social activity. Such a widespread counter-cultural exercise places extreme importance on understanding the mechanisms for the acquisition of culture, in particular the reproduction of ideology through the kinship structure.[10] But it is difficult to discern what weight the Chinese attach to this problem.

China provides an example of a society endeavouring to transform the family. The patriarchal family attached to agriculture is being replaced by the individual monogamous family. It could be argued that this experience has little relevance to feminists in monopoly capitalist countries, where the individual monogamous family has been dominant for generations. Modern feminism stands apart from Engels's theories and the socialist experience on two main issues – the monogamous family and the sexual division of labour.

The Monogamous Family

What is Engels's characterization of the monogamous family? It is 'the first form of the family based not on natural, but on economic conditions, namely, on the victory of private property over original, naturally developed, common ownership' (p. 74). Its appearance signals not 'the reconciliation of man and woman, still less the highest form of such a reconciliation. On the contrary, it appears as the subjection of one sex by the other, as a proclamation of a conflict between the sexes . . .' (p. 74). (In a similar vein Engels remarks that the emergence of the State betokens not the reconciliation of classes, but the irreconcilability of their interests.)

As a type of family organization monogamy stretches in time from the ancient Greeks to the present day, with variations in its structure effected by economic and historical change. It is above all the form of family of the ruling class. Engels points to two main contradictions, and two potentially unifying elements. The first contradiction is prostitution, arising from the male refusal to give up sexual freedom. 'Wage labour appears sporadically alongside of slave labour; and, simultaneously, as its necessary correlate, the professional prostitution of free women appears side by side with the forced surrender of the female slave' (p. 76). The prostitute in the sphere of sexual relations is analogous to the wage slave.

Capitalist commodity production, argues Engels, together with its intensification of wage slavery, intensifies prostitution, and, moreover, transfers the stamp of prostitution to bourgeois marriage itself 'sometimes on both sides, but much more generally on the part of the wife, who differs from the ordinary courtesan only in that she does not hire out her body, like a wageworker, on piecework, but sells it into slavery once and for all' (p. 79). Socially, this form of sexual exploitation is condemned, but this condemnation hits 'only the women; they are ostracized and cast out in order to proclaim once again the absolute domination of the male over the female sex as the fundamental law of society' (p. 76).

The second main contradiction produced is sexual rebellion of the woman, taking the form of adultery, and in those cases of monogamous marriage with a rebellious wife, says Engels 'we have a picture in miniature of the very antagonisms and contradictions in which society . . . moves, without being able to resolve and overcome them'.

Connected with adultery is the arousal of the first potentially unifying element in monogamy – individual sex love. Engels situates the appearance of individual sex love in the synthesis of the pairing family of the German tribes with the Roman form of monogamy, and locates its first cultural expression in the chivalrous love of the Middle Ages, and its first entry into the realm of human rights with the emergence of the capitalist class, which masked its desire for domination behind an appeal to human rights. But in proclaiming individual sex love a human right, the bourgeoisie, according to Engels, is confronted by yet a further contradiction.

Engels outlines the contradiction in this way: capitalism substituted the legal contract for traditional custom.

> But if real freedom to decide was demanded for all other contracts, why not for [the marriage contract]? Had not the two young people about to be paired the right freely to dispose of themselves, their bodies, and its organs? . . . if it was the duty of married people to love each other, was it not so much the duty of lovers to marry each other and nobody else? . . . In short, love marriage was proclaimed a human right; not only as man's right, but also, by way of exception, as woman's right.
> But in one respect this human right differed from all other so-called human rights. While, in practice, the latter remained limited to the ruling class, the bourgeoisie – the oppressed class, the proletariat, being directly or indirectly deprived of them – the irony of history asserts itself here once again. The ruling class continues to be dominated by the familiar economic influences and, therefore, only in exceptional cases can it show really voluntary marriages; whereas, as we have seen, these are the rule amongst the dominated class. (pp. 86–8)

There are several conditions which, in Engels view, make sex love the rule within the proletariat. First, complete absence of property. Second, the absence of bourgeois law in proletarian marriage relations. Third, the opportunity provided by modern industry for women to enter production on a mass scale, and thus gain economic independence, sometimes even becoming the bread-winner. Four, the right of separation which can thus be regained by the proletarian woman, given the first three conditions. The only vestige of male domination which Engels identifies within the proletarian family is the brutality of the proletarian man towards his woman. The main thrust of Engels's argument is that subjugation to male power is demanded more of the bourgeois woman than it is of the proletarian woman. That *as a woman* she is more oppressed. In order to verify this it is necessary to look at the actual condition of the working class woman.

The women's aid centres for battered women which women's groups have set up in response to the demands of working-class women are testimony enough to the continuation of brutality. But apart from this, in the last hundred years the proletarian family has itself undergone pressures and restraints the result of which suggest that the critique of the modern individual family can no longer just rest with the family of the bourgeoisie, but has to be extended to that of the working class.

In early capitalism women were in competition with men for factory employment. Their already existing inferiority was translated into a new economic inferiority – they were seized upon as a source of cheap labour and used to undercut male wages. But after the early phase of capitalist accumulation, the needs of industry for healthier and more skilled workers, together with the political need for a more stable and docile working class, turned the attention of the ruling class to the proletarian family. Ideologues found the explanation of a variety of social evils, including high infant mortality and an unhealthy work force, in the employed mother, and their solution was the attempt to form a proletarian family in the bourgeois image, that of an ideal family, where the man would be the 'bread-winner' and the woman a 'home-maker' attending to domestic tasks and child-care. Factory legislation restricted the work of both women and children, and industrial production became a male-dominated sector, the interests of male labour being protected by trades unions from which women were often openly excluded.

By the end of the nineteenth century a movement was in train to teach domestic economy to working-class women. Their other main alternative to factory work – domestic service – conveyed the 'proper' management of a modern monogamous family. In this century the teaching of domestic 'science' has increased rather than diminished, with women's magazines and courses in schools supplementing the training girls are supposed to receive at home.

Of course, the 'ideal' family has never been fully achieved. Wives of low-paid workers are still constrained to go out to work; their income is needed to maintain themselves and their families.

But during the development of British capitalism into its monopoly and imperialist phase, restrictions on female employment, combined with the penalization of employers who gave mothers work, the absence of nursery provision, the presence of education for domesticity, and a barrage of ideological interventions, effectively constituted the home as a centre of social life. The period before the First World War could be summarized as a period of the 'domestication of the working class', and the reassertion of women's economic dependence on men.

Equally as important has been the extension of State intervention in family relations, through the developing structure of the 'Welfare State', and, concomitantly, the extension of the law as a mechanism regulating the family of the working class. The right to divorce exists, but whether this represents a genuine right of separation is highly debatable. Women are still legally inferior to men, as they are economically.

In the position of the working-class woman of the present, it is hard to see any of the conditions mentioned by Engels as generally operative. Although the working class may not be caught up in the toils of property to the same extent and in the same way as the bourgeoisie, the house and the goods within it – and around for domestic production, recreation and transport – do represent an economic outlay on the maintenance of the family unknown in Engels's time. The post-Keynesian opening up of the working-class market has made the family a major unit of consumption. State regulation of the family through welfarism (family allowances etc.) and a generalized extension of marriage and family law means that the working class not only has the law available to them, but for some disputes (e.g. custody of children) has no recourse except to law. Finally, although women are certainly in production (often on a part-time basis) the female rate of pay is so much lower than the male rate that economic equality is still beyond the horizon. In these circumstances it is difficult to see how the working-class woman now has a greater right of voluntary separation than the middle-class woman. In fact, it is accurate to say that none of the distinguishing categories which Engels gives the proletarian family in capitalist conditions are discernible today.

Another sign of the distance travelled since Engels can be demonstrated by the way modern feminists understand the right to free disposal of one's body. The demand for free abortion and contraception not only indicates women's wish to control their own reproductive capacities but also implies a challenge to men's assumption that they have an automatic right to be fathers. Though the phrasing sounds similar, this is a very different matter from Engels's demand that both sexes should have the free disposal of their bodies by marrying for love.

Aside from this new emphasis, the women's movement has developed a critique of the oppressive nature of individual sex love. Individual sex love may have emerged as an advance in sex relations, but in the present situation, where romanticism prevails, it confronts us as a set of mystifications about what relations between men and women are really about and, as such, this has become a new terrain for struggle.

Finally, in a society that still discriminates against homosexuality, women's movements have proclaimed the full social and legal right to homosexuality. This is in sharp distinction to orthodox socialism which emphasizes the desirability of heterosexuality and defines homosexuality as a manifestation of the crisis of a decaying social order.

The Division of Labour

Marx and Engels conceived of a spontaneous sexual division of labour arising out of physiological difference and carried over into the social world: 'The first division of labour is that between man and woman for child-breeding' (p. 75). And again, writing of the American Indian organizations, Engels remarks that 'the division of labour was a pure and simple outgrowth of nature: it existed only between the sexes' (p. 149).

In the *Origins of the Family* Engels sees the division of labour as 'women in the home, men outside the home', a separation reflected in the division of property: men control the instruments of labour used outside the home, women those within it. But later anthropological findings have made it clear that there are no grounds for assuming such a clear and spontaneous division of labour, property and tasks of the kind Engels predicted, although a division of labour often of the most intricate kind, always does occur. This division, however, does not appear to be a 'simple outgrowth of nature', but rather, an element of the process of the transformation from nature to culture.

Engels's work does not contain any criticism of the sexual division of labour. Indeed this form of separation of responsibility is for him a question entirely outside of the problems of women's oppression. 'The division of labour is determined by entirely different causes than those which determine the status of women' (p. 61). His criticism is focused on the relative economic weighting which these forms of labour acquire, and the privatization of domestic labour. Whilst he envisages a future society where such labour will be transformed from private service into public industry, and where child-care will be socialized, there is no hint that in this future state of affairs such collective labour might cease to be performed exclusively by women.

This failure to criticize the sexual division of labour marks the break between Engels's analysis (and that of classical socialism) and the feminist perspective. Modern feminism implies a demand for reciprocity. Not only 'anything a man can do a woman can do', but also 'anything a woman can do a man can do'.

The argument that the main focus of women's oppression lies in women's confinement within a privatized domestic economy seems valid. But at the same time it is difficult to believe that work-sharing within the home (the abolition of housework as a category of labour performed by one person or by one sex) can be achieved if, in the social sphere, socialized domestic services and child-care continue to be performed exclusively by women.

The feminist critique of the division of labour between the sexes comes from the experience of women living within monopoly capitalist and imperialist countries. In these societies technology has developed to such an extent that any physiological difference between women and men (such as physical strength) can be rendered irrelevant by labour-saving machinery. At the same time the 'feminine' qualities of the heart, like nurturing and caring, have been recognized as cultural qualities rather than natural phenomena, and are not necessarily restricted to women alone. The recourse to arguments about an immutable female nature is often a defence of the status quo. Feminists question not only women's place in the social order, but that of men too.

Socialist feminists have developed a new analysis of the economic importance of women's work in the reproduction of labour power, and in the main have concentrated on the political economy of housework. More attention is now being paid to the implications and development of the sexual division in the world of employment. And various tendencies in the women's movement have encouraged the involvement of men in the care and education of small children. Both the emphasis on the economic and ideological importance of the reproduction of labour power and the demand that this cease to be women's work signal a radical shift from the socialist perspective.

If it is over the issues of the critique of monogamy and the division of labour that modern feminism goes beyond Engels, at the same time Engels did point his finger at some crucial questions which remain to be solved. First, Engels demonstrated that once capitalism is established, the contradiction arises for women between their work in social production and their work in the home. But although the attempted resolutions are different, this contradiction has appeared in socialist countries as well as in capitalist ones. Second, the *Origins of the Family* represents a sustained effort to demonstrate that the existence of sex conflict was bound up with particular historical phases in the development of the family. Such a perspective makes an appraisal of family organization central to an understanding of women's oppression. This is not to imply that Engels thought that the family was a totally autonomous structure. However, he does imply that the family has a relative autonomy, and that this family does not only *inherit* 'superstructures' (in the notable case of kinship relations), but also *produces* its own 'superstructures' – juridical relations (marriage and family law) and social-sexual mores. The terms of Engels's analysis are thus (1) the mode of production, (2) the form of family, (3) the kinship system, (4) juridical relations, and (5) social-sexual mores. What a revolutionary transformation of the form of family thus requires is, in the first place, the revolutionary transformation of the mode of production, a new set of legal guarantees, and the continuous transformation of social-sexual mores and kinship systems. The latter two require as a condition of their success a developed practice of ideological struggle.

Last, we should consider the step forward Engels's work represented. If the *Origins of the Family* constituted an achievement it was this – that it asserted women's oppression as a problem of history, rather than of biology, a problem which it should be the concern of historical materialism to analyse and revolutionary politics to solve.

10

Women in Revolutionary China*

DELIA DAVIN

Women revolutionaries during the Chinese Revolution, like
other women in other revolutions in history, were confronted
with the problem that contradictions arose between the interests
of women and the interests of the Revolution both nationalist and
socialist. Marriage reform for example, though proclaimed by
law in the Liberated Areas during the anti-Japanese War, was
certainly not pressed with great energy, for social disruption was
too dangerous in a war situation. Women, though feminists, had,
as revolutionaries, to make a united front with forces which
represented male chauvinism in the interests of another cause
which, by implication at least, took priority. These women as
Marxists were able to do this because they regarded the victory
of the revolution as a prerequisite to the liberation of women.
To them the contradiction was a temporary and non-antagonistic
one, which in the long term must disappear.

But in socialist construction the problem of priorities has
sometimes arisen again. It is difficult to liberate women in a poor
country, difficult to supply the necessary welfare, education and
health facilities when the overwhelming problem is to feed the
people; difficult to allocate scarce resources to social reform in a
developing country where economic growth is so vitally needed.
Yet too passive acceptance of other economic priorities may also
be an error, may lead to an under-achievement of potential.
Within the women's movement there were times when a tendency
emerged to accept stagnation or even retreat. Women were no
longer so greatly encouraged to work outside the home, and
women's traditional roles were glorified. These times coincided

*This paper was originally prepared for the IXth International Congress
of Anthropological and Ethnological Sciences held in Chicago in 1973.

with periods of slower economic growth, and such sacrifices were no doubt believed to further the interests of the Revolution as a whole. Since the Cultural Revolution this line has been condemned as a Liu Shao-ch'i policy contrary to the true interests of women. All this raises the problem of how to judge the real interests of the Revolution, and those of women and how to reconcile them with each other. If temporary contradictions arise, priorities must be chosen but by what criteria are they to be selected? As I trace the progress of the women's movement in China I will try to show how these problems have arisen and the tactics with which they have been met.

The patriarchal family system of traditional China restricted and oppressed women of all classes. Nor were women its only victims. Power was conferred not only by sex but also by age, and the family power structure subjected young men to the decisions of their seniors until a comparatively late age. Confucian family ideology was at its strongest amongst the élite who had the wealth, time and education to practise it, and it was in this class that the dependence of young people in general, and women in particular, was greatest.

The first women's movements in China, strongly influenced by foreign thought, drew their support mostly from women of the élite classes who claimed the rights of education and free-choice marriage that they heard their sisters in other countries enjoyed. They were able to draw on considerable male support at least in the earlier stages of their personal struggles, since their brothers and sweethearts could see in the struggle for women's emancipation, an idealistic justification for their own rejection of arranged marriages and their demands to make a romantic match. In time the struggle was perceived as a political one and in rather mechanistic emulation of the west, women demanding suffrage stormed the almost powerless parliament at Nanking in 1912.[1]

As men took part in the women's struggle so did women take part in general political struggle. Women were active in the early nationalist and republican movements, and women's armies fought in the 1911 Revolution. In 1924–5 during the Nationalists' northern expedition against the reactionary northern warlords, a fusion of women's military, revolutionary work, and feminist work amongst ordinary people took place for the first time. Women soldiers marched in the expedition and women propagandists from the political department of the army set up women's leagues amongst peasant women to fight for women's rights in each community they passed through. These, like the peasant leagues set up at the same time, were later crushed in the reaction of 1927-8. However, these inland southern areas were a short time later to be the scene of the Chinese Soviet areas, and the short-lived Central Soviet Republic (1931-4), so that some of the ex-members of these women's leagues must later have become members of the Communist women's movement on which I now propose to concentrate this article.

In this description of the Communist women's movement I will telescope the Soviet, anti-Japanese War and Civil War periods, but it must be remembered that the Communists were administrating quite large areas even in the late 1920s, that they set up the Chinese Soviet Republic in 1931 and that after the collapse of this stronghold and their long trek north, they built up new power bases during the anti-Japanese War, and in 1945 controlled a territory with a population of nearly twenty million before they swept on to gain control of the whole Chinese mainland by 1949. Thus they had, even before the establishment of the People's Republic, a very long period in which to develop and try out social policies, amongst them policies to alter the position of women.

Women played an important part in the revolution and in the revolutionary base areas. At times they fought on the front lines as regulars or irregulars. Far more often they played vital roles in their own villages because the majority retained their family responsibilities which made them less mobile than men. But in guerrilla warfare there is no true front line and no true rear. The combatant and the non-combatant are complementary and the former is aware of his absolute dependence on the latter. Both, therefore, have status and the division between them is less sharp than is sometimes imagined. Women laid mines, dug tunnels and organized tunnel warfare, besides acting as stretcher-bearers, nurses, scouts, messengers and food collectors. Food collecting was no mere routine job; the problem presented by the sudden arrival of a hundred hungry men in a village which practised a near subsistence agriculture would be a considerable one. It could only be solved by local people of tact who would know who might have the surplus food required, and how they could be persuaded to part with it. When the nature of the fighting changed during the Civil War (1946–9) and many men left the liberated areas as regular soldiers in the Liberation Army, women were again able to enlarge their role by taking a greater part than before in political and administrative work in the villages as well as in farm labour.

Land reform was carried out in 1946 in the old Communist base areas and by 1952 was complete over most of the country. It was a period of raw fierce class struggle which smashed the basis of landlord power. The movement had a very special significance for women since it was specifically laid down in the regulations for land reform that women should receive their share of land, and that their names should either be included as co-owners on a family title deed, or that title deeds should be issued to them as individuals. Women were not slow to realize the implications of this and indeed their reactions show an interestingly clear perception of the relation between their oppression and their economic dependence. For example, William Hinton recounts that women in Yellow Hill village, Hopei Province, said when they heard that they were to receive land, 'After we get our share we will be masters of our own fate'.[2] There is evidence that women sometimes used the threat of withdrawing themselves with their share of land from their husband's family to force a capitulation or at least a compromise when they felt themselves to be oppressed.

Women were everywhere urged to work outside the house as a means to achieving liberation, but land reform gave them more stake in doing so. At the same time it was a big political campaign in which they were expected to take part. For many the mass meetings at which it was decided what land should be confiscated and to whom it should be redistributed were the first occasions on which they appeared in public and spoke out in front of men. Often it was difficult for them to find the courage to do so. The Women's Federation, a mass organization for women led by the

Party, provided a closed women's forum where they could discuss, and the need to have such an organization with meetings attended only by women was recognized as a necessary preliminary to getting women to speak at mixed meetings. Often in the land reform team which came to each village to guide the course of land reform, there was a woman cadre who showed the peasant women that a woman could be an active and independent person, demanding and getting respect from her male colleagues as a true equal.

Local village activists were also of great importance in championing women's causes. Given an official capacity as the Women's Representative or as an office-holder in the Women's Federation, they had a power base from which to protect women's interests, and launch attacks on those who mistreated women. In the early years we find accounts of such women organizing struggle meetings against men whose wives complained they beat them, and even beating brutal husbands up themselves.[3] Such acts did not receive Party support. Contradictions in the ranks of the people were supposed to be solved by reason and persuasion rather than by violence, but were probably rather effective where they occurred. Chinese women had always used their menfolk's fear of loss of face as a weapon; in the new society they were able to do so to great effect.[4]

Not that village women were a united force in their struggle to change their place in society. One of the tragedies of the old family system was that it set woman against woman and made one woman the means of another's suffering. A bride entered her husband's home as a lonely figure, friendless and without allies in her new household. She took on the toughest domestic work, endured the resentment of her new family if the bride-price had been high, and became a convenient scapegoat when one was needed. She would normally have no affectionate ties with her husband at the start, and much militated against their developing, at least in the early years. The couple saw little of each other, did not speak together in public, and in quarrels between bride and mother-in-law the husband was as likely to intervene for his mother as for his wife.

Only by giving birth to children, preferably a son who would stay in the family, could a young woman ease her position and in time build up a circle of allies and thus a power base.[5] When her son was approaching adulthood a new young woman was introduced into the household as his wife. The mother's jealousy and concern that the newcomer should not disrupt her relationship with her son is understandable only when viewed against the investment she had made in her son and her dependence on him. Hence the notorious tension of the mother-in-law–daughter-in-law relationship in China.

The Marriage Law of the People's Republic of China promulgated in 1950, like the marriage laws of the liberated areas and the Soviet Republic before it, laid down a system of monogamous marriage, with free choice of marriage partners, the right of widows to remarry, the prohibition of bride-price and child-betrothal and the right to divorce by consent. The law was presented as being fundamental to the liberation of women, and the local branches of the Women's Federation were relied on heavily for its implementation. Yet there is much evidence that older women were amongst its most active opponents.

Older women 'rationalized' their opposition to the new law by saying that it was immoral for young unmarried men and women of different families to meet and become friendly – a necessary pre-condition to a system of free-love marriage, that young people 'were not good at' choosing their partners, and that it was not fair that the younger generation should have life so much easier than they themselves had done. However the fear of older women that the security they had gained over many years by raising sons whose primary loyalty was to their mothers might be shattered if love marriages took place, was clearly a strong factor in their opposition to the new law.

Since this division could sometimes split women's organizations down the middle, the issue had to be handled very carefully. Much of the advice given on the marital problems in the Press and in women's magazines is on how to get on with mother-in-law rather than her son. Furthermore, in spite of the great marriage law enforcement campaigns of 1950, 1951 and 1953, occasional reports in the Press show that old customs die hard, that marriages are still sometimes arranged in the old manner and, more rarely, bride-prices are paid. Probably in the countryside today, a compromise form of marriage is the most common in which, by the time of the ceremony the young couple and their families all know each other, and the young couple may indeed have been 'introduced' at the initiative of their parents or some other outsider, but have had a few chances to meet and make up their minds about each other. Certainly many books about marriage from the late 1950s onwards, advise young people to consult their parents over marriage, without of course obeying them blindly. These sort of 'semi-free marriages' as the Chinese term them, are probably a realistic institutional adjustment where good relations between the mother-in-law and daughter-in-law are very important to them both. For much as the face of peasant agriculture has been changed, mother- and daughter-in-law are still often workmates and in those areas where work is still strongly sextyped are likely to see more of each other than of their menfolk. Where work is less segregated between the sexes, it is likely to be the younger woman who joins the man in heavy outdoor work, and, if she has children, she may at times entrust them to her mother-in-law, which necessitates a reasonably amicable relationship. Where relations were not good, this arrangement could also raise the mothers-in-law's ire. When the young women formed a textile co-op in Chehu village, Hopei Province, their mothers-in-law not only lost their assistance in the kitchen, but even had to prepare their meals; they complained, 'Everything's turned upsidedown since the Communist Party came. Mothers-in-law have become daughters-in-law.'[6] But this problem was usually solved as the mother-in-law realized the material benefit to the whole family when the daughter-in-law took part in productive labour.

Other difficulties arose when women began to work in the fields. They lacked the necessary skills in all but their traditional tasks which, in fact, varied enormously from one region to another and if they included farm work at all, tended to be the least skilled jobs and almost never included such prestige-bearing tasks as ploughing. Indeed, judging from reports of the fierceness of opposition to women being allowed to plough, and the space that the press devoted to stories showing that they could do so successfully, I am inclined to believe that there may have been a superstitious taboo against it. These problems the Women's Federation overcame by running classes to teach agricultural skills, and by organizing women's pilot plots on which bumper crops were grown.

Collectivization of agriculture which took place in stages in China in the 1950s, gradually shifted the basis for income division from the ownership of land to the amount of labour contributed. Land was henceforth owned and farmed collectively and jobs were valued in the form of work points. When the crops were brought in they were divided according to the number of work points earned during the year. Furthermore since the work points, theoretically at least, were recorded in the names of individuals, the system increased general awareness of each individual's contribution to household income.

If women were to take full advantage of this, they had to solve various problems. The first of course was that of the demands on their time and energy made by housework, meal preparation and child-care, all of which tend to be particularly laborious in a backward rural economy. The canteens, nurseries, and sewing stations set up on a large scale under the communes have been much discussed in the West; the grain-husking and flour-milling centres less so, perhaps because, to those of us who are not accustomed to undertake these tasks for ourselves, they seem less of a new departure. Economically, however, they all represent the same process: the transfer of work from the household sector where it is unmeasured and unpaid, to the public sector where it is recorded and given an economic value. Once it has entered the market it also begins to confer a social prestige on the person who does it which, as household work, it lacked. Efficiently organized, this work can also be performed by fewer people if done on a large scale and therefore frees women to do other types of work.

Of course all this presupposes that worthwhile alternative occupations exist in the economy. And this has been the second great difficulty hampering women who wished to enter the labour force. China in the 1950s was still a very poor country, desperately short of capital and with an unfavourable man–land ratio. Job opportunities in the towns increased only slowly, and there was a danger that if the labour force in the countryside increased too fast, rapidly decreasing returns to labour would set in. In concrete terms in collective agriculture this would mean that the number of work points earned would increase more rapidly than the amount of grain produced, and that the remuneration of each work point in grain would fall. Such a fall obviously would be unpopular, and if associated with the entry of women into the work force would hardly bring them enhanced status.

Health has been another constraining factor on Chinese women's contribution to the work force. The countryside had almost no modern health facilities in 1949, and Chinese traditional medicine, useful though some of its practices have proved to be, was certainly not adequate to maintain all women in good health. The high value attached to big families meant frequent childbearing. Low nutritional levels, poor living conditions and complete ignorance of the nature of infections (traditional midwives did not sterilize their instruments) meant high infant and maternal mortality rates, and many chronic post-natal complications. Poor menstrual hygiene and ignorance caused vaginal infections. Menstrual pain seems also to be a problem for many Chinese women, at least if they are engaged in heavy manual work. It is a subject often discussed in the Women's Press, and many articles on agricultural management advise cadres to give women two or three free days during their periods. During the 1950s and 1960s, the Chinese did achieve a huge expansion of their health service. This however was somewhat urban-orientated until the Cultural Revolution. In the countryside maternal and infant mortality were greatly reduced long before this, by a huge programme of midwife-training, but minor gynaecological ailments seem to have remained rife.

Until very recently Chinese women continued to bear large numbers of children and thus spent a large proportion of their active lives pregnant or nursing.[7] The birth-control campaign has only been pressed with a proper degree of seriousness in recent years (incidentally the health and freedom of the mother are presented as the prime rationale for family planning), and, at the same time, public attitudes to it are becoming more receptive. People accustomed to a high infant mortality rate have many children to ensure the survival of two or three and even once infant mortality has fallen there is a credibility lag before the old practice is perceived as unnecessary. Yet a reduction in the birth rate is certainly, as it is presented in China, a prerequisite if women are ever to achieve equality with men in the economy and society.

Commune regulations decreed that men and women should receive equal pay for equal work. When men and women do the same type of work at piecework rates this is simple to apply. In other cases where the value of an hour's cotton-picking has to be calculated against an hour of carting fertilizer for example, it becomes complicated. Work evaluation, always one of the problems of collective agriculture, can be used to conceal pay discrimination against women, and women have waged many struggles against this practice.

What has been achieved in rural China seems to be that most able-bodied women work in the fields and in handicraft or minor manufacturing enterprises at least at busy times of year. Women's share of the total of work points earned certainly stands at less than a half. I would estimate it at something like a third, nor do they always in fact receive equal pay for equal work. Furthermore, crèches which may be either permanent or temporary, open only for rush work periods, though sometimes partly subsidized, are not free, and people in China, as elsewhere in the world, tend, in their minds at least, to discount the cost of childcare against women's earnings when evaluating their contribution to the household. Nevertheless as participants in the work force, women have at least the potential for independence necessary to gain any degree of self-determination and authority within the home. Their work also gives them a place and a voice in commune and village affairs where before they were largely confined to the women's community. And since women now have a productive economic value, the birth of a girl baby need not seem the crushing economic blow that it once was to a poor family. Furthermore, the campaign to encourage later marriage, which is partly to give girls more chance to train and develop independence before marriage, has been given a far greater chance of success by the fact that young unmarried women are no longer a burden but an asset to their families.

The women's movement is much further advanced towards its goals in the towns than in the countryside in China. Problems are fewer and more easily overcome. The problem of disbelief in women's capabilities has been largely overcome by the use of shock teams. The first women pilots were trained in 1950, a few years later the first all-woman train crew began to run one of the Peking–Tientsin expresses, women engineers and steel workers were employed at the great Anshan metalworks. In 1970 an all-woman oil-drilling team started work on the famous Taching oilfield and the first March 8th bridge-building team came into being. All this smacks perhaps of tokenism, but it has great psychological impact. Such women are given tremendous publicity in all the media, and no girl growing up in China today can believe herself disqualified by sex alone from scientific, or technical jobs. Even the incredulity of men has been shaken.

Work opportunities in the towns, like the towns themselves have expanded enormously. However, the population growth has been even faster and the problem of providing enough employment has proved severe. Rapid urban expansion has in fact caused other difficulties. Many towns have a severe housing shortage, and facilities such as schools and hospitals are also under strain. The expense of such provisions, as well as those of roads, shops and food supply – social overhead costs to use the economist's jargon – can be held down by large-scale introduction of women into the work force, since this by lowering the ratio of dependants to total population would make it possible to expand the labour force without a proportionate increase in the town's population. This should provide a long-run economic incentive to the State to get women into urban employment.

Since work is by its nature more permanent in the towns, canteens, crèches and other such collective facilities are more economic to develop. Enterprises are still sometimes accused of discrimination in their employment policies, and they clearly have some incentive to practise it since if they employ women they have to bear at least part of the cost of child-care facilities, and all the cost of maternity leave. The impact of such disincentives is presumably declining with the birth-rate in urban areas where young couples under heavy political pressure reinforced by the housing shortage and other practical factors, increasingly confine themselves to a family of two or three children.

Women in 1949 had a far lower literacy rate than men, and though the problem has been tackled by literacy classes, often run by the Women's Federation, and for the younger generation primary school in the cities is universal, older women are certainly educationally disadvantaged.

Many women, then, are unable to take factory jobs for which there is great competition, and men remain in the majority amongst factory workers who are themselves an élite minority amongst city-dwellers. Women are certainly more strongly represented in health and education, and probably also in service and distribution trades. Where women are certainly a majority is in the neighbourhood factories. These usually begin as *ad hoc* groups of housewives, making clothes or simple items for daily use, though the most successful now produce components for China's electronics industry. Like small workshops in Japan and Hongkong which do putting-out work and produce components for large enterprises, they give China's industry a valuable flexibility. Their equipment is simple and versatile, and because they depend on housewives' labour they can raise or decrease production and employment without too much social disturbance. They usually work on a largely self-financing, cooperative basis, and do not offer medical insurance. They therefore involve no financial risk to the state and have low overheads and therefore low unit costs.

The implications of such enterprises for women are mixed. Their workers earn less and enjoy fewer welfare benefits than true industrial workers. On the other hand neighbourhood factories demand low levels of skill and literacy, offer work close to the home often with flexible hours, and expand the demand for labour. Thus housewives who would otherwise be unemployed gain employment and with it an individuality independent of family identification, an independent source of money, and a new self-respect. Nor does this self-respect spring only from their earning power. The wish to build up the country and to strengthen the Revolution is deeply felt and is particularly well satisfied in these small enterprises where there is a greater feeling of personal involvement than is possible in big factories. In this they also differ sharply from the workshops of Japan and Hongkong, for the involvement is not produced only by the scale of the enterprise, but also the fact that it has been set up by and is usually run by the women who work in it.

Street committees, which are in effect basic level organs of government, and welfare agencies have also given women a real vehicle for achievement. At street level they depend on volunteers, and these are most often housewives. The day-to-day tasks of such women include mediation in family disputes, hygiene inspections to check that privies are covered, courtyards swept and breeding-grounds for flies eliminated, the distribution of ration tickets to the unemployed, the registration of new arrivals in the area and the reading of newspapers to the illiterate. Street committees also have close contacts with neighbourhood factories, and often run nurseries for women who travel to work but prefer to leave their children near home. Obviously these women have power. Petty power perhaps, but power as it impinges on ordinary people's lives. And, importantly at least in the early years, this was a power that women could exert directly over men if, for example, they were the culprits in breaches of the hygiene rules.

The Marxist proposition that women's liberation can come only through their participation in socially productive labour has always formed the theoretical basis of the Chinese Communist Party's policy on women, but the effort expended on this goal and the comparative emphasis on it and on other strategies for women's liberation have in fact varied considerably over the years.

In 1942, in the revolutionary capital, Yenan, during the rectification movement, certain women intellectuals were attacked for 'narrow, divisive feminism' which attempted to solve women's problems by attacking their family situations without reference to economic factors. A Central Committee resolution claimed 'we have not given enough attention to economic work amongst women' and presented productive work for women almost as a panacea.[8] During these years the greatest effort was at first devoted to getting women to work in textile handicraft production; later, coinciding with the departure of many men in the army, came the campaign to get women to work in the fields. At this time, however, a Central Committee resolution admitted that productive labour was not in fact the only and ultimate solution to the women problem, that remnants of feudal ideas about women would remain for some time, and that a prolonged period of education would be necessary to overcome them.[9]

The campaign to get women to take part in productive work gathered momentum and was applied on a national basis in the fifties, but suffered a strange lull in 1954 and again in 1957. It revived briefly in 1956 with the cooperative movement and again in 1958 during the Great Leap Forward, only to suffer another, though apparently slighter, eclipse in the early 1960s. During the Cultural Revolution involvement in productive work was once more presented as the major goal for women and this line has since been maintained. The *People's Daily* editorial for Women's Day 1973, entitled 'Working Women a Great Revolutionary Force',[10] quoted Lenin on the importance of getting women to 'take part in socially productive labour, to liberate them from "domestic slavery", to free them from their stupefying and humiliating subjugation to the eternal drudgery of the kitchen and the nursery'.[11]

Lenin's words contrast strangely with the mood of 1955 when under the slogans 'Housework is Glorious Too' and 'Let's be Pretty', a positive cult of the housewife was fostered, women were urged to seek fulfilment through raising a socialist family, and the pages of women's magazines were filled with recipes and dress patterns. The reaction of the 1960s, perhaps to avoid rousing the indignation of women cadres again, was less overtly anti-career woman, but still laid great stress on the joys of marriage and motherhood.

The Chinese explanation of fluctuations of policy towards women is that they reflect the struggle between the two lines. During the Cultural Revolution the editor of *Chinese Woman*, the organ of the Women's Federation, was attacked for having followed the revisionist line of Liu Shao-ch'i. The cynical economist would fit policy fluctuations to changing economic policies and conditions and relate the volume of encouragement for women to work at a given time to the current demand for labour. These explanations are not of course incompatible since we know that the Chinese define the periods which we see were lulls in the recruitment of women as periods when the Liu-ist line was in control of the economy and prevented more radical expansionist policies.

Whether we accept either or both of these explanations, it seems to me that the Chinese experience raises some problems of international relevance for women. What is the relation between women's participation in the work force and the status of women? Clearly it is not a simple one, for we know of many societies where women slave, and are despised. The existence of the work ethic is crucial: where work is considered a mug's game, hard workers are mugs. What other factors count?

How can we make judgements on the aims and achievements of the women's movements in other countries? If the family reforms which the Chinese women's movement advocated seem limited, and its sexual morality repressive to women in western movements, do we conclude that they have been duped or are such differences a natural and desirable consequence of culture and history? Can we criticize compromises if they were forced by harsh economic and political reality and how do we judge if they are truly forced? How can we evaluate the great achievements of the Chinese women's movement against its clear shortcomings? Dispassionate study seems impossible but cross-cultural criticism is dangerous. Here surely the context is vital. Chinese women fought an oppression blacker and more absolute than women of the west. The official institutions of traditional China were male-dominated to a degree unsurpassed in the world. Chinese women once dealt with this situation with a combination of passivity and covert sabotage. In a few decades they changed their strategy to one of open struggle and in alliance with the forces of national and socialist revolution, have demolished much of the social framework of their oppression.

These developments have taken place under a state which officially guarantees full sex equality, but still lacks the resources to provide all the necessary material conditions for it. Nor is the ideal of the equality of men and women entirely accepted by the people. Old ideas die hard. Such limitations are inevitable. Mao

Tse-Tung himself has acknowledged that women's liberation is not yet complete,[12] and as long as the Chinese women's movement itself does not accept the *status quo* as satisfying its ultimate aspirations we can surely salute its achievements without ignoring its problems.

11

The Rights and Wrongs of Women: Mary Wollstonecraft, Harriet Martineau, Simone de Beauvoir

MARGARET WALTERS

Each of the three writers I am considering is, in a different way, important for the woman's movement today. Each spells out very clearly some of the dilemmas that face us in writing and thinking about ourselves. Their lives spread over two centuries; Mary Wollstonecraft lived at the end of the eighteenth century, and spoke out of the wave of radical-intellectual enthusiasm engendered by the revolutions in America and France. Harriet Martineau had a considerable reputation as an intellectual in Victorian England. And Simone de Beauvoir emerged out of the political and philosophic ferment of forties Paris to write *The Second Sex*, the classic study of women that is still the basis, or at least an essential reference point, for so much present feminist thinking.

I have not chosen them at random: all three belong to the same bourgeois feminist tradition. All three fought alone. There was no possibility of a women's movement in Wollstonecraft's time, Martineau felt her individual example was more important than any movement, and de Beauvoir – though she has allied herself with the present movement – worked out her ideas long before it emerged. Though all three use very different vocabularies and concepts, their analysis of women's problems is essentially the same. *The Second Sex* is a development and culmination of ideas that Mary Wollstonecraft had formulated in *The Vindication of the Rights of Woman*.

The Vindication was certainly the first great feminist statement in English. It crystallized, in a single powerful protest, ideas that had been aired in one form or another for more than a century –

arguments that women as much as men were God's creatures, pleas that they be educated more seriously and allowed to develop their moral and intellectual capacities. Fired by the French Revolution, Wollstonecraft extended these pleas to the political sphere: if bourgeois man was breaking down centuries-old traditions, then women could do likewise. *The Vindication* is basically a plea for equality with bourgeois man – educational, legal and political equality. (Wollstonecraft saw that a better education alone was not enough, and attacked those upper-class bluestockings who used their privileged status in a man's world as a way of provocatively emphasizing their femininity.) *The Vindication* is also, and just as essentially, an attack on the idea of *femininity*. For during the eighteenth century, when some women were beginning to articulate their rights, the distinction between the sexes was in fact becoming harder and sharper. In an increasingly middle-class society women were paradoxically in a more anomalous position, more firmly excluded from public affairs and the world of work. A leisured femininity was becoming the mark and proof of gentility, and there were endless handbooks and educational manuals designed to reassure the new middle classes by codifying the rules of proper feminine behaviour. Wollstonecraft – like most feminists who came after her – spent a lot of time pointing out the absurd contradictions of this prescribed femininity. She argued that even a writer like Rousseau, who had deeply influenced her own thinking about social injustice, was part of this contradictory process – his cult of the 'natural' woman, his romantic and idealized femininity, was designed to keep her in her proper place. It was easy to fight open contempt, less easy to fight this new myth of morally ennobling womanhood.

Dismissing, then, those pretty feminine phrases, which the men condescendingly use to soften our slavish dependence, and despising that weak elegancy of mind, exquisite sensibility, and sweet docility of manners, supposed to be the sexual characteristics of the weaker vessel, I wish to show that elegance is inferior to virtue, that the first object of laudable ambition is to obtain a character as a human being, regardless of the distinction of sex, and that secondary views should be brought to this simple touchstone.[1]

De Beauvoir's position, though more sophisticated, is hardly any different.

But Wollstonecraft not only wrote the *Rights of Woman*, she was trying to finish at the time of her death a novel called *The Wrongs of Woman, or Maria*. Her point was partly that the oppression of women is personally experienced, that their protest springs out of a deep personal sense of injustice and wrong. She was also struggling with a more difficult problem. She, like her heroine, attacks the way conventional feminine stereotypes confine and imprison us, and demands her rights as a human being. But both author and character find that woman's problems go deeper than that, that her sexual feelings and affections somehow escape her rational understanding, that there is a gap between the demand for her rights and her overwhelming sense of her wrongs. There's an odd sense that even if she got her rights, a sense of wrong would persist.

In each of the writers I am considering, there seems to be a gap between the theory and the lived experience, between feminism and femininity. Wollstonecraft admitted it, in words and in her life, most easily and openly. She struggled all her life to fulfil both parts of her nature, to work and live like a man, but like a woman as well. She refused to suppress one side of herself, though she found her refusal to compromise brought her pain and disillusion. Her attack on femininity did not mean she wanted to become a man. Martineau – living in Victorian England – tended to adopt a more simply masculine role. She wrote with a tone of impersonal authority and consistently asserted that the discussion of women's wrongs had no place in the struggle for women's rights. She then wrote a remarkable autobiography and a novel in which she explored the price she had paid for her 'human' equality. And I think there is the same kind of dislocation in de Beauvoir, though it is harder to pin down because she denies it. Her attack on artificial femininity leads her to confound all differences between the sexes. She drains all meaning from the terms masculine and feminine, and ends up recommending a curiously abstract humanity. She only occasionally reveals, as it were accidentally, the difficulties that face a woman living and writing in a male world.

It is remarkable, incidentally, to see what similar reactions the work of all three met. Wollstonecraft and de Beauvoir were both accused of indecency, exaggeration, of being unfeminine and too feminine at the same time. All three were alternately praised and blamed for being 'masculine', then criticized for not writing with 'masculine' objectivity. Even Mary Wollstonecraft's husband, William Godwin, writing a courageous and loving *Memoir* after her death felt he had to apologize for the masculine or 'amazonian' vigour of her style in the *Vindication*, and he assures the readers that her *Letters from Sweden*, written after an unhappy love affair, are full of softness and sensibility. How different is Sartre's praise of de Beauvoir for combining the 'intelligence of a man' with the 'sensibility of a woman'?[2]

Each of these three writers suggests the problems of developing a consciousness of our own that is neither stereotyped femininity nor a secondhand masculinity. Each of them is trapped between the 'masculinity' and 'femininity' she tries so hard to disentangle. Each insists on her rights to equality with man – and finds, at some level, the poverty of that equality. Each suggests what a woman can achieve, and the price, in this society, she may pay for that achievement.

Mary Wollstonecraft (1759–97)

All the world is a stage, thought I; and few are there in it who do not play the part they have learnt by rote; and those who do not, seem marks set up to be pelted at by fortune; or rather as sign-posts, which point out the road to others, whilst forced to stand still themselves amidst the mud and dust.[3]

Mary Wollstonecraft's fame has always rested on her life as well as her writings. In 1798, a year after she died, her husband William Godwin published his *Memoirs* of her along with her love letters to Gilbert Imlay, father of her first daughter. Godwin's account of her life is both loving and honest – and he was publicly pilloried for his frankness. Ever since, Wollstonecraft has been regarded as the archetypal feminist, monster or angel. A contemporary reviewer exclaimed in horror that she was subversive in practice as well as theory – 'she lived and acted as she wrote and thought'. Moralists pointed to her death in childbirth as fitting end to a misspent life, while various women novelists smugly caricatured her learning, her radical politics and her unhappy love affairs. Nineteenth-century feminists felt she was something of an embarrassment to the cause. Harriet Martineau condemned her, and in 1890 Mrs Fawcett, reprinting the *Vindication of the Rights of Woman*, uneasily discounted Wollstonecraft's 'sickening' personal life.

Ironically, the reverse is true today. Her unconventional life has attracted a lot of attention, but her ideas are very little discussed. Wollstonecraft is important because of her passionate and life-long struggle to live out the implications of her ideas, and her courage in confronting her own inconsistencies. Her inevitable confusions and failures – and her efforts to articulate them – are as illuminating as her achievements. Taken together, her many surviving letters, her two semi-autobiographical novels (*Mary, a Fiction* and *The Wrongs of Woman, or Maria*), provide, along with the *Vindication*, an extraordinary insight into the difficult relationship between feminism and femininity.

Mary Wollstonecraft was born in 1759 of a middle-class family that was going down in the world. Her grandfather had been a successful Spitalfields manufacturer, her father squandered a fortune in various unsuccessful ventures as a gentleman farmer. The family moved around so often – London, Essex, Yorkshire, London again, Wales – that Wollstonecraft was never sure of her own birthplace.[4]

But she was preoccupied with her childhood to the point of obsession, continually re-living the same basic drama in her conversation, and trying to understand it in both her novels. She was bitterly critical of both her parents. Her father was feckless, tyrannical, contemptuous of women. As Maria, her autobiographical heroine describes him, sarcastically:

His orders were not to be disputed; and the whole house was expected to fly, at the word of command, as if to man the shrouds, or mount aloft in an elemental strife, big with life or death. He was to be instantaneously obeyed, especially by my mother, whom he very benevolently married for love; but took care to remind her of the obligation, when she dared, in the slightest instance, to question his absolute authority.[5]

Wollstonecraft told Godwin that she often threw herself between her parents to deflect her father's rage from her mother, and would lie awake whole nights fearing some outburst of violence. She pitied her mother's sufferings. Her dying words, 'A little patience and all will be over' were to haunt Wollstonecraft for the rest of her own life. But she despised her as well – for her passivity, for her feminine sentimentality – and most of all for her open preference for the oldest son, Ned. ('Such indeed is the force of prejudice, that what was called spirit and wit in him was cruelly repressed as forwardness in me', Maria complains bitterly, of her brother.) Ned had inherited money in his own right; he was to become a successful lawyer. Wollstonecraft was never to forgive him – 'the representative of my father, a being privileged by nature – a boy'.

Lonely, deprived, angry at the pointless restraints imposed on her, Wollstonecraft seems to have coped by creating a compensatory world of her own, first in religion, then in reading and finally in friendship. Her love for Fanny Blood was crucial in her development away from her immediate family. It is perceptively described in the novel *Mary*, where Fanny is renamed Ann. The heroine not only takes Ann as a model – she is a little older, accomplished, elegant – but looks to her for all the love she lacks at home. Inevitably, she is disappointed; Ann is in love with a man, and keeps a certain distance from the younger girl. So Mary cultivates her own greater ardour, treasuring her disillusion as a sign of sensitivity; she asserts her superiority, revealed in her intense sensibility. She literally turns herself into a romantic heroine.

By chance, some letters survive from this period of Wollstonecraft's life, addressed to another fifteen-year-old schoolgirl called Jane Arden. They read as high comedy – but they give some insight into her difficult adolescence. Wollstonecraft converts a storm in a teacup – over who is best friends with whom – into tragic drama. She strikes poses, insists on her own superiority, flourishes her own sufferings, and tries to blackmail Jane into giving her the love she desperately needs. The high-flown romantic talk about love and jealousy is cover for sheer childish rage at not getting what she wants. Yet the silly melodramatics are also an exercise in self definition. This is the way most of us grow up, though we mostly lack Wollstonecraft's naïve but impressive openness about the process.

> If I did not love you I would not write so; – I have a heart that scorns disguises, and a countenance which will not dissemble: – I have formed romantic notions of friendship. – I have once been disappointed: – I think if I am a second time I shall only want some infidelity in a love affair, to qualify me for an old maid, as then I shall have no idea of either of them. – I am a little singular in my thoughts of love and friendship; I must have the first place or none. – I own your behaviour is more according to the opinion of the world but I would break such narrow bounds. I will give you my reasons for what I say; – since Miss C– has been here you have behaved in the coolest manner. – I once hoped our friendship was built on a permanent foundation . . .[6]

She is even on the verge of a real insight into the way we all slip into patterns that may trap us for life. Many of her later letters to men have the same mixture of entreaty and self-righteousness. All through her twenties, she seems to have fallen in love with a series of men who were scared off by her vehemence. She was, she wrote, 'too apt to be attached with a degree of warmth that is not consistent with a probationary state'. The whole problem was to be spelled out most clearly in her love-affair with Gilbert Imlay, whom she met when she was thirty-four, and an established writer. She was still tormented by her need for an impossibly satisfying love, still as contemptuous of anyone who disappointed her. And there are flashes of the same tone even in the notes she wrote to Godwin, though because he genuinely loved her and sought her happiness, he seemed to be able to calm her anger, distrust, and self-doubt.

At fifteen, Wollstonecraft claimed, 'I resolved never to marry for interested motives or to endure a life of dependence'. She was oversimplifying – her feelings towards men and marriage were very complicated – but she showed an impressive determination to strike out on her own. Like so many skimpily educated girls, she found it hard to earn a living. At nineteen, she went to Bath as companion to an old lady. After returning home to nurse her mother through her last illness, she stayed for a time with Fanny Blood and survived by taking in needlework. Then – showing exceptional energy – she started a school at Newington Green, hoping to find independence not only for herself but for her two younger sisters Eliza and Everina. Fanny married and went to Portugal; in 1785 Wollstonecraft travelled there alone to nurse her friend, who died in childbirth. When she returned, she found that her sisters had been unable to keep the school going, so she went as governess to Lord Kingsborough's family in Ireland.

They were the only jobs available to a middle-class girl – and she hated them all. A lady's companion

is above the servants yet considered by them as a spy, and ever reminded of her inferiority when in conversation with her superiors . . . A teacher at a school is only a kind of upper servant, who has more work than the menial ones. A governess to young ladies is equally disagreeable.[7]

Mary Wollstonecraft managed to struggle to a freer life as a writer. Eliza and Everina were to remain teachers all their lives.

Though she had left home at the first opportunity, Wollstonecraft stayed tied to her family. She resented her father's failure to provide for his daughters to the end of her days, but she actually took over his chaotic business affairs. She assumed the role of mother to her two younger sisters, and spent a lot of time organizing, not only her own family, but Fanny Blood's as well. Godwin praised her as 'victim of a desire to promote the benefit of others'; her beneficiaries sometimes felt they were her victims. She bullied her family and friends for their own good, blackmailed them, cast them in a scenario of her own making. Though she had a genuine feeling for their problems, she tended to impose her own fantasies on them. When, inevitably, they acted independently, she reproached them bitterly. 'I looked for what was not to be found' is a complaint that echoes through her letters.

Thus, not long after her mother died, Wollstonecraft went to take care of her sister Eliza who had married a man called Bishop, had a baby daughter, and broken down. It is hard to tell exactly what was happening, as we only have Wollstonecraft's version in letters to Everina. She was desperately anxious to help Eliza out of her hysterical depression; but, partly because she was acting out some drama of her own, she probably did more harm than good. (Eliza was certainly bitterly resentful of her sister in later life.) Initially, Wollstonecraft explains, she had some sympathy for the husband. 'My heart is almost broke with listening to B. while he reasons the case', but she fairly rapidly cast him as the villain of the piece. Even his concern for the baby was described as a mere 'plausible tale', a cover, she hints darkly, to his determination to 'gratify the ruling passion'. Wollstonecraft finally smuggled Eliza out of the house and hid her away in obscure lodgings. Her letters combine genuine love and sympathy for the wretched Eliza with an unacknowledged sexual hostility towards Bishop. She thoroughly enjoys her role as Eliza's saviour and protector, and seems proud that the world will condemn her as a 'shameful incendiary'. She is as thrilled as a child by the excitement and intrigue: 'I hope B. will not discover us, for I could sooner face a lion; yet the door never opens but I expect to see him panting for breath.' And at a moment when she is fairly obviously acting out some of her deep distrust of marriage, and her parents' unhappy marriage in particular, she adds as a postscript, 'I almost wish for a husband, for I want someone to support me'.[8]

The letters Wollstonecraft wrote all through her difficult twenties show her trying out a remarkable variety of roles. Without stint, without fear of absurdity, she throws herself into a bewildering succession of parts – romantic heroine, protective parent, poor invalid, teacher, business woman, and finally, writer. In the letters written from the Kingsborough household, for example, she is usually the suffering, sensitive heroine. ('I am a poor melancholy wretch – and at night half mad'.) She reads Rousseau, and cultivates intense and sentimental friendships with various young clergymen, and demonstrates with every sigh and flutter her superiority over the pretty, frivolous Lady Kingsborough. Yet she sometimes sounds like a cynical woman of the world, apparently even flirting with Lord Kingsborough. More frequently, she is the severe intellectual, judging the upper classes and finding them wanting; or the teacher, speaking of her charges in tones of high moral seriousness. When she writes to Fanny Blood's brother George, she is Lady Bountiful; he called her the 'princess', and she revelled in it. With Eliza and Everina, she is a nagging but affectionate mother. She is contradictory and absurd, self-pitying, self-dramatizing. But I think her preoccupation with *herself* makes her so compelling, so curiously modern. In a society where a woman was not really expected to have a self, except insofar as she was daughter, wife, mother, what choice did Wollstonecraft have but to playact, experiment, try to invent herself?

Her restless energy finally found a more satisfactory outlet in writing. Her first book – *Thoughts on the Education of Daughters* – was undertaken because she needed money, typically, not for herself but for the Blood family. She was introduced to the radical publisher Joseph Johnson by some of the Dissenting intellectuals whom she had met at Newington Green, and she wrote about the only thing she knew – teaching. Feminist writing all through the eighteenth century had concentrated on the issue of education, and Wollstonecraft's book is squarely in that tradition. Her fairly mild plea that girls be allowed to develop their God-given faculties is given a certain bite by her own difficulties in picking up an education where and as she could. Though she strives hard for an impersonal tone, there is a lively, personal undercurrent in her writing, that issues, for example, in her protests about the few jobs available to women, her sad remarks on the miseries of being in love, and her attack, far more pointed than in earlier writers, on the artificiality of 'feminine' refinement.

The book was not much noticed, though it gave her a great deal of personal satisfaction. 'I hope you have not forgot that I am an Author' she wrote grandly to Everina. But for the time being she had to swallow the bitter pill of accepting employment as a governess. Her second book, *Mary, a Fiction*, is an effort to compensate for her sense of being declassed and humiliated. The fictional Mary is no mere governess, but the daughter of a well-off landed family. (And the satirical portrait of Mary's mother owes as much to Lady Kingsborough as to Mrs Wollstonecraft.) But Mary has all the qualities her creator cultivated to prove her superiority to the aristocrats who devalued her: intelligence, religious fervour, intense feelings. In short, Mary is full of *sensibility*. The word remains one of Wollstonecraft's highest terms of praise, though in the *Vindication* and elsewhere she satirized the more absurd manifestations of the eighteenth century cult of fine feelings. Mary's true sensibility and capacity for passion set her above the conventionally feminine ladies of fashion, whose affected sensibility covers cold hearts.

In *Mary*, Wollstonecraft reveals herself as a thoroughly romantic writer, one of the first of the English romantics. She insists on the importance of individual perception. Personal experience and passion have their own truth, which may differ from conventional wisdom. Though her novel is often clumsy, she feels towards a new notion of the individual self as struggling towards growth and fulfilment sometimes in opposition to society. And this romanticism is a crucial element in her feminist protest against what society imposes on women.

When Wollstonecraft was sacked by Lady Kingsborough, Joseph Johnson came to her rescue by offering her regular work on his new *Analytical Review*. Justly proud of the financial independence and status this brought her, she told her sister that 'I am then going to be the first of a new genus . . .' The exaggeration is understandable – it was still very rare for a woman to live as a professional writer. Wollstonecraft literally educated herself as she wrote, learned French and German as she translated. Moreover, the political education that had begun in conversations with her Dissenting neighbours at Newington Green was rapidly broadened. Through Johnson, who became a close and paternal friend, she came to be accepted on equal terms by most of the important radical intellectuals of the day – Priestly, Paine, Godwin, William Blake. She was still often lonely and depressed, and she fell passionately – though, she insisted, platonically – in love with the painter Fuseli, a friend of Johnson's and a married man. He seems to have encouraged her for a time, then retreated back to wedded safety; Wollstonecraft went so far as to suggest to his wife that they live as a threesome – and was thrown out of the house. Her love became a torment to her, a continual reminder of her 'comfortless solitude'.

Nevertheless, after only two years in London, she felt confident enough to tackle the masculine world on its own terms. Novels and books on education were acceptable enough from a woman.

But her reply to Edmund Burke, *The Vindication of the Rights of Man* (1790) took exceptional boldness. In response to his attacks on the French Revolution and its effect on English intellectuals, she reiterates arguments long familiar in Dissenting circles. The laws of England protect property, not liberty, and deny the 'natural rights' all men derive from God. Wollstonecraft pleads for justice, not privilege, an open society not one constricted by inherited rights. Her imagination is fired by what is happening in France – the struggle against moribund tradition to create a new society based on principles of equality. Though her book is not an original contribution to the major political and philosophical debate of the day, it did well because it was forceful, deeply felt, and occasionally eloquent. And it was an essential step in her development into a feminist.

*

Less than two years later, Wollstonecraft published her *Vindication of the Rights of Woman* (1792). She sets out to describe the condition of women in general terms – she speaks 'for my sex, not for myself'. Its motive power is her personal history, the sense that 'most of the struggles of an eventful life have been occasioned by the oppressed state of my sex'.[9] It brings together the separate strands of her previous books – the demand for better education for girls, the new romantic stress on individual feeling, and the concept of natural as against property rights – and fuses them into a new kind of protest. It takes the simple but crucial step of extending the rights of *man*, to include woman. In retrospect it seems obvious; in fact it was a genuine breakthrough (in England at least) on which feminist thinking still depends.

Wollstonecraft was writing out of excitement at the possibilities for political change suggested by the French Revolution; and from her personal confidence at being accepted by a group of radical writers. But both the revolution and her fellow radicals were threatening to let her down. Even those like Godwin or Paine who were not unsympathetic to women were not particularly concerned with their problems. The French National Assembly had not extended the new political and civil rights to women, and another of Johnson's authors, Thomas Christie, had defended this exclusion of women 'from the cares and anxieties of State affairs, to which neither their frame nor their minds are adapted'. So the *Vindication* is a polemic addressed to the French statesman Talleyrand, and by implication to English radicals, as well as a plea to women themselves.

> If the abstract rights of man will bear discussion and explanation, those of woman, by a parity of reasoning, will not shrink from the same test . . . Who made man the exclusive judge, if woman partake with him of the gift of reason?[19]

Written in six weeks, the *Vindication* is circular and often confused. It is exploratory, and often falls back on rhetorical repetition or sarcasm instead of argument. Wollstonecraft's language has an unmistakable personal bite. She is obviously angry, at men, at women, and I suspect at possibilities she sees in herself. Though she has shrewd things to say about specific aspects of woman's situation – her political and legal disabilities as well as her lack of education and job opportunities – Wollstonecraft digs beneath these to the basic anomalies of her role in society. Femininity is something imposed on us by men; and the very concept is full of contradictions.

In the present state of society, Wollstonecraft argues, women *are* inferior. Anyone who is oppressed from birth will be weak, ignorant, lazy and irresponsible, hardly human. She has a sharply satiric eye for feminine folly, and for the masculine attitudes that encourage and exploit that folly. Gallantry is mere condescension, a way of keeping inferiors happy. Woman is at once protected and deprived, idolized and despised. Told that she is a goddess or a queen, she discovers that she is treated like a domestic servant or, if she is unlucky, a slave. And lacking any real power, women learn to cash in on their weaknesses. They are cunning, coquettish, and demanding. 'Told from their infancy and taught by the example of their mothers' that they must find a man to support them, they soon learn to exploit their looks. So – though women cultivate their sensibilities and live in a cloud-cuckoo land of romantic dreams – they manage not to 'fall in love' till they meet a wealthy man.

Wollstonecraft claims that women are selfish and narcissistic.

> Taught from their infancy that beauty is woman's sceptre, the mind shapes itself to the body and roaming round its gilt cage, only seeks to adore its prison.[11]

But they are not expected to have real selves at all. Never properly educated and insulated from the real world, they rarely think – and feel very little either. Rather, they learn to arouse feelings in others, for 'it is only through their address to excite emotion in men that pleasure and power are to be obtained'. All possibility of individuality is lost; 'all women are to be levelled, by meekness and docility, into one character of yielding softness and gentle compliance'. And with so much importance placed on externals, seeming is more important than being, and a woman must always playact at being a woman. The most impeccably feminine woman is in a sense the most masculine, for she consumes her life in fulfilling male fantasies. She exists only in and for male admiration.

Any woman who tries to escape this absurd trap and act like a human being runs the risk of being hunted out of society for being 'masculine'. (This point recurs again and again through the *Vindication;* it obviously springs from Wollstonecraft's own experience.) If behaving in a masculine way means attaining genuine virtue, Wollstonecraft recommends that we all 'grow more and more masculine'. But she admitted that the fear of being thought unwomanly runs very deep, affecting even the most intelligent. A woman like Mrs Piozzi, the well-known bluestocking, uses her mind to 'burnish rather than to snap' her chains. 'All our arts', wrote Mrs Piozzi, 'are employed to gain and keep the hearts of men.' That, replies Wollstonecraft, is a 'truly masculine sentiment', the repetition parrot-fashion, of the very attitudes that 'brutalize' us. It is worth noting that women were some of the *Vindication*'s severest critics. Hannah More refused even to read it as the title was fantastic and absurd, while Hannah Cowley protested coyly that 'politics are *unfeminine*'. It is hardly surprising that Wollstonecraft felt isolated, and complained that history discloses only inferiority, 'how few women have emancipated themselves from the galling yoke of

318 The Rights and Wrongs of Women

sovereign man'. She admits, half-joking, that she sometimes wonders if the few extraordinary women who manage to achieve anything are not 'male spirits confined by mistake in female frames'. And it is hardly surprising that though she sets out to persuade women to think for themselves, she often falls back on an appeal to men to exercise their generosity and set us free.

Indeed, Wollstonecraft herself anxiously affirms her own respectability. She reassures readers that she would not dream of seducing women away from their domestic roles, their womanly duties. At moments, she simply reiterates the familiar eighteenth-century argument: women must prove themselves capable of self-discipline and reasoned moral chance, so as to become more responsible wives and mothers. She sketches an 'ideal' woman, a monster of self-denial: a widow, '. . . raised to heroism by misfortunes, she represses the first dawnings of a natural inclination, before it ripens into love . . . her children have all her love and her brightest hopes are beyond the grave, where her imagination often strays.' Both in her earlier and later writings (*Mary* and *Maria*, for example), Wollstonecraft argued woman's right and need to express her feelings and desires. But in the *Vindication* she stresses duty and principle; she is as severely puritanical as some of those Victorian feminists who would impose stricter moral controls on men and women alike, and who felt, half-consciously, that a woman struggling towards fuller humanity might be forced to suppress her sexuality.

Though the *Vindication* is less daring than Wollstonecraft's life or her novels, it defines with brutal clarity an idea central to later feminism – that femininity is an artificial construct. We learn to be women from the day we are born – and in the absence of any alternative, we exploit it for all we are worth. Yet – and this is the crucial double-bind – this artificially created state is supposed to be *natural* and therefore immutable. Wollstonecraft indignantly quotes Rousseau's claims that women are naturally modest or naturally fond of dress or naturally vain.

I have, probably, had an opportunity of observing more girls in their infancy than J. J. Rousseau. I can recollect my own feelings, and I have looked steadily around me; yet . . . I will venture to affirm, that a girl, whose spirits have not been damped by inactivity, or innocence tainted by false shame, will always be a romp, and the doll will never excite attention unless confinement allows her no alternative . . . I will go further, and affirm, as an indisputable fact, that most of the women, in the circle of my observation, who have acted like rational creatures, or shown any vigour of intellect, have accidentally been allowed to run wild . . .[12]

Wollstonecraft herself learned from Rousseau that an appeal to nature and natural rights could be a subversive tactic, a way of undermining an unjust society. But as a woman she saw how often the word is used to uphold the *status quo*. She spots its dangerous ideological content. Women, she insists, are no more naturally inferior than the poor are naturally ignorant. In both cases, the word is used by the powerful and privileged to hold the poor in their proper station, women in their proper sphere. Property and propriety alike, pretending to be natural and therefore universal values, are in fact the expression of what she calls 'partial' interests.[13]

At moments, Wollstonecraft has real insight into the way sexual oppression of women is connected with larger social inequalities. Sexual relations are *power* relations, each partner manoeuvring for advantage. Sometimes she simply denounces men as tyrants and oppressors. At other times she glimpses the way society's authoritarian structures are reflected in the family; like men who are 'subjected by fear', women in their turn become petty tyrants, oppressing their servants and children. Even – or especially – among the deprived, there is a pecking order. In her later *Letters from Sweden*, she developed this notion in her description of how servants, treated almost as slaves, still perpetuate the larger injustices. The men

stand up for the dignity of man by oppressing the women. The most menial, even the most laborious offices are therefore left to these poor drudges . . . In the winter, I am told, they take the linen down to the river to wash it in the cold water; and though their hands, cut by the ice, are cracked and bleeding, the men, their fellow servants, will not disgrace their manhood by carrying a tub to lighten the burden.[14]

She recognizes, at moments, that the femininity she satirizes in the *Vindication* is class based. Extreme femininity is a proof of gentility, women are always struggling to be 'ladies'. And she developed this point in her unfinished novel, *Maria*. There are two heroines, the unhappy middle-class wife, and the working-class girl, Jemima. Wollstonecraft genuinely tries to understand Jemima's situation – her miserable childhood, her desperate struggles merely to survive, her fears of losing her job. Though Jemima has worn herself out working as a servant, as a washer-woman, and finally, in despair, as a prostitute, she has managed to pick up some education – but can find no use for it. According to Wollstonecraft, wife and prostitute are equally oppressed, and she tries to work out the connection between the two, however sentimentally. She is not a good enough novelist to do more than sketch their friendship, but she does manage to justify her claim that the book will show 'the wrongs of different classes of women equally oppressive, though from differences in education neces-sarily various'. And that is a remarkable feminist – and radical – advance.

Wollstonecraft's feminism was basically a demand for equality with bourgeois man. She was no economist, and saw only dimly that relations between the sexes were involved, not just with abstract power but with money. In *Maria* she argues that mar-riage is a contract based on property interests, and that while a woman has to depend on man for maintenance, marriage is a form of legal prostitution. She wants the vote for women, but reminds us that in England, what she calls 'hard-working mechanics' are deprived as well, that the whole system of repre-sentation is just a 'handle for despotism'. On her Scandinavian trip she tried to analyse the different countries in economic as well as political terms – she comments on wages, land tenure and trade. And she foresees a time not so far in the future, when the middle class will no longer be the progressive class.

England and America owe their liberty to commerce which created a new species of power to undermine the feudal system. But let them beware of the consequences; the tyranny of wealth is still more galling and debasing than that of rank.[15]

It is also worth noting that she did not just demand better education for women. She pleaded for universal education to the age of nine – something almost unheard of in her day. Until nine, boys and girls of all classes would receive free public schooling; after nine, those 'intended for domestic employments or mechanical trades' will be segregated for vocational training, while those of 'superior abilities, or fortune' go on to liberal studies. She saw very clearly how sex affects ability; she had not fully thought out the connections between ability and 'fortune'. But though education was a major concern all her life, she admitted its limits. Social pressures will always outweigh formal education.

I do not believe that a private education can work the wonders which some sanguine writers have attributed to it. Men and women must be educated in a great degree, by the opinions and manners of the society they live in.[16]

So she comes to the conclusion, again and again, that without a general reorganization of society there will be no real 'revolution in female manners'.

*

Wollstonecraft had already discovered, in her own life, how hard it is to escape from the bonds of this 'artificial' femininity. Her own feelings oscillated violently from one extreme to another, and she was continually surprising herself by turning into what she most hated. In the year after the *Vindication* was published, she apparently found less and less satisfaction in her career. She wrote very little, and brooded over her lonely, frustrated passion for Fuseli. Eventually she decided to go to Paris, to get away from him, and to see for herself what was happening there. But she had hardly arrived when she fell hopelessly in love with another unsatisfactory man, the American adventurer Gilbert Imlay.

She struggles to understand her contradictory self. Having insisted that love should be subordinate to reason, she was at the mercy of her passion for Imlay. She flouted conventional morality and bore his child, then lapsed into anxious 'feminine' respectability. She withdrew from her success as a writer into the familiar role of betrayed and suffering woman. Taking full adult control of her life, she regressed to a frightened child demanding an impossible security. Yet somehow, in her letters and novels, she kept on trying to articulate and so partly understand her confused needs. 'What a long time it requires to know ourselves', she wrote sadly, 'and yet almost every one has more of this knowledge than he is willing to own, even to himself.'[17]

Wollstonecraft realized that an understanding of childhood is central to any self-knowledge. To understand what we are, and what we might become, we must go back to our earliest days. But this is particularly true for women, who are deprived of a real childhood then imprisoned in an artificial one; 'made women of when they are mere children, and brought back to childhood when they ought to leave the go-cart forever'. Women are not expected to grow, or grow up. Femininity is a matter of arrested development – and she experienced that as fact, not metaphor. Her letters suggest that she was an adolescent, constantly experimenting with herself, until she was almost thirty. Then, just when she was beginning to make her name as a writer, she was overwhelmed by helpless depression which she tried to describe to her fatherly publisher Johnson. Her letter is itself a childish complaint, and an effort to understand how and why the child persists in the adult:

There is certainly a great defect in my mind – my wayward heart creates its own misery – Why I am made thus I cannot tell; and till I can form some idea of the whole of my existence, I must be content to weep and dance like a child – long for a toy, and be tired of it as soon as I get it.

We must each of us wear a fool's cap; but mine alas! has grown so heavy, that I find it intolerably tiresome. Goodnight! I have been pursuing a number of strange thoughts since I began to write, and have actually both laughed and wept immoderately. – Surely I am a fool.[18]

And a few months before she died she wrote in the same vein to Godwin: 'my imagination is forever betraying me into fresh misery, and I perceive that I shall be a child to the end of the chapter'. But her 'childishness' was also a sign of strength, of capacity for growth. Her strident and hysterical complaints sometimes sound like birth pangs. Wollstonecraft pushes herself to extremes, lets herself return to the irrational, uncharted violence of earliest childhood, to the period before we are 'made women', so as to find out what else a woman might be.

I have already referred to her novel *Mary* as a thinly fictional-ized account of her own girlhood. But it is interesting not just as a source of information, but as a serious attempt at understand-ing the difficult process of growing up. As a girl, Mary rejects both her parents. She has no models, no one to identify with, so she has, literally, to invent herself. Gradually she half-recognizes that her parents are not just monsters outside her, but have a permanent hold on her imagination. She is horrified to discover that she shares her father's violent temper, for example, and she certainly has her mother's capacity for depressed suffer-ing. She rebels angrily against male domination, only to dream of an all-protecting fatherly love. She both pities and resents her mother, then acts as mother towards her closest friend and lover. Wollstonecraft uses the rather conventional story to explore her ambivalent feelings towards both men and women, and to express her sense that we may, all through our lives, re-enact dramas rooted in childhood. She fails to develop her insights dramatic-ally; she writes sketchily, indulges in naïve wish fulfilment, or falls back on novelistic clichés. (For example, she marries her heroine off very young to a husband who never appears in the story, and whose only function is to ensure that Mary will have even less chance of happiness.) But her real, if half-conscious, perceptions are enough to infuse the skimpy story with an odd urgency.

The most original and curious section is the one based on Wollstonecraft's love for Fanny Blood. Though Mary looks up to Ann at first, taking her as a model, she quickly becomes the dominant one in the relationship. Disappointed in Ann because her friend's love for her is less intense and complete than her own, she becomes increasingly critical – and increasingly maternal. She nurses Ann, supports her through an unhappy love affair, dreams of protecting her against the whole world. She contrasts her own love with the rather lukewarm devotion of Ann's absent lover.

Ill-fated love had given a bewitching softness to [Ann's] manners, a delicacy so truly feminine that a man of feeling could not behold her without wishing to chase her sorrows away.[19]

Gradually this 'romantic friendship' 'occupied her heart and resembled a passion'. (The only men who interest her at all, Mary tells us, are 'past the meridan of life and of a philosophic turn'.) She adopts the classic masculine role towards Ann – protecting and patronizing. When Ann finally marries the man who had kept her dangling all this time, Mary follows her to Portugal to nurse her on her deathbed. The husband is hardly mentioned; when Ann dies, it is Mary who is left bereft, in a world that is suddenly a desert.

At this point in the novel, the heroine turns back to her own 'feminine' side. Her sensitivity, heightened by her grief, attracts the admiration of an ugly but romantic man called Henry, who offers to love and cherish her as if she were his own child.

His child! What an association of ideas! If I had had a father, such a father! She could not dwell on the thoughts, the wishes which obtruded themselves. Her mind was unhinged, and passions un-perceived filled her whole soul.[20]

But within a few pages, Mary is travelling alone back to England, unhappy, but almost ecstatic in her sense of her own independent self, her potential power. When she meets Henry again, the two imperceptibly change places. Henry has already proved rather inadequate in his role of protector, even before he falls ill; Mary again finds herself as nurse and protector to her love. Again she has to call on her own maternal – and masculine – strength; when Henry, too, dies, Mary is left once again mourning for her love, like an abandoned child. At the end of the novel, Mary decides to live with her almost forgotten husband, though she cannot bear to think about his caresses. She decides to devote herself to living for others – a reduced, dutiful, 'feminine' life that is a sad echo of her mother.

The need for love was the heart of the problem. Wollstone-craft had always argued that love should be controlled by reason. In her first book, *Thoughts on the Education of Daughters*, she insisted that marriage should be based not on love but on friendship and respect. 'A woman cannot reasonably be unhappy, if she is attached to a man of sense and goodness, though he may not be all she could wish.' But she admits sadly that people of 'sense and reflection' are most likely to fall prey to 'violent and constant passions', and speaks feelingly of the unhappiness of loving someone of whom your reason disapproves. She also suggests that it is very easy to prolong feelings beyond their natural course, 'to gratify our desire of appearing heroines'. In the *Vindication* she takes a harder line. Women are obsessed by love simply because their lives are so empty, and she spoke sharply of those wives who

waste their lives in *imagining* how happy they should have been with a husband who could love them with a fervid increasing affection every day, and all day.[21]

But she had already eaten out her heart over Fuseli, and in the letters to Gilbert Imlay, the American adventurer she met in Paris, she explores the extremes of misery and desperation. Because they were so often separated – by political barriers in Paris, by Imlay's business trips, later by his affairs – the letters tell a fairly continuous story. They begin easily, warmly, affectionately. Wollstonecraft is both playful and passionate, obviously delighting in the release of her long repressed sensuality. She makes jokes about her growing dependence on him, and even about her moments of reserve and withdrawal. When she gets pregnant, she is delighted. (She had obviously half-wanted to be a mother before – mothering her own sisters, and at one point adopting an orphan, a little girl, who was dropped rather callously when Wollstonecraft grew tired of her.) As the months of her pregnancy pass, she occasionally complains of inexplicable low spirits, but avoids thinking about Imlay's absences and what they might mean. Fanny's birth affords her some respite. She enjoys breast feeding her and playing with her, and is both surprised and pleased at the strength of her love. But she grows more and more depressed, her happy sensuality gradually eroded by doubt, suspicion and anger. Imlay has, fairly obviously, abandoned her. Though Wollstonecraft sees that she must end the relationship, she struggles to maintain it, both because she needs help with the child, but also because the further Imlay recedes, the more obsessed she becomes. One moment she is a child, cajoling him, promising to be good, within the same sentence she sets up as his judge, his superior. Her real sense of hurt and betrayal – and she was, after all, left with an illegitimate child in a foreign country – are pitched as high as she can. ('Yes; I could add with poor Lear – What is the war of elements to the pangs of disappointed affection?') She praises herself at Imlay's expense.

> It is my misfortune, that my imagination is perpetually . . . lending you charms, whilst the grossness of your sense, makes you ... overlook graces in me that only dignity of minds and the sensibility of an expanded heart can give.[22]

She reasons herself out of love, then lapses into hysteria; she attacks him, then threatens suicide. She promises to make no more demands, the very promise a demand; endlessly, she ends the relationship, then refuses to believe it's over till he ends it.

> Why am I forced thus to struggle continually with my affections and feelings? . . .Why are those . . . the source of so much misery, when they seem to have been given to vivify my heart and extend my usefulness? . . . Will you not endeavour to cherish all the affection you can for me! What am I saying? Rather forget me, if you can – if other gratifications are dearer to you . . .
>
> I never suffered in my life so much from depression of spirits – from despair. – I do not sleep – or, if I close my eyes, it is to have the most terrifying dreams, in which I often meet you with different casts of countenance . . .
>
> I have lived in an ideal world, and fostered sentiments that you do not comprehend – or you would not treat me thus. I am not, I will not be, merely an object of compassion – a clog, however light, to teize you. Forget that I exist; I will never remind you . . .
>
> My complaints shall never more damp your enjoyment – perhaps I am mistaken in supposing that even my death could, for more than a moment . . .
>
> My image will haunt you. – You will see my pale face – and sometimes the tears of anguish will drop on your heart, which you have forced from mine.[23]

Round and round she goes, caught in the trap of her own conflicting desire, torn between her sense and her sensibility, between her emotions and her intelligence. Some of her earlier biographers found the letters simply embarrassing: tedious, hysterical and self-dramatizing. And of course, even granting her objectively difficult situation, they are all those things. But I suspect that most women will find them absurd, painful – and familiar. Almost inadvertently, Wollstonecraft was struggling to express an experience that seems to be central to many of us. Mary Wollstonecraft never fully understands what is happening to her. She remains immersed in her misery, and her efforts to reason with herself and adopt an adult control of her obsession, only feed back into the vicious circle of agony and reproaches. She had claimed that passion could be educative; she was hardly prepared for the return of her repressed feminine side, her oscillation between cruelty and self-destruction. She found herself living inside a 'frightful dream', in which no one, including herself, behaved according to the script. She attempted suicide, jumping into the Thames off Putney Bridge – and was furious that she could not even manage to die. But, somehow, she recorded the state, and that is an achievement we cannot afford to neglect.

And she picked herself up out of her suicidal despair, struggling to put her life and her career together again. While she was pregnant and uncertain of Imlay, she was still working hard on her *Historical View of the Origin and Progress of the French Revolution* (1794), and at the depth of her misery she went to Scandinavia with Fanny and a nurse, and wrote a lively and thoughtful account of her travels – the *Letters from Sweden* (1796). She seemed to be on the verge of a genuinely stable and fulfilling relationship with William Godwin when she died, in great pain, a few days after the birth of her second daughter Mary.

In her last, unfinished novel, *The Wrongs of Woman, or Maria*, she had tried to come to grips with these shattering experiences and assimilate them to a more general account of women's sufferings. As in *Mary* the basic situation is both melodramatic and schematic. Maria has been imprisoned in a madhouse by her husband, and she and Wollstonecraft brood over the idea that the whole world is a prison and women are the slaves. Every other woman Maria comes in contact with has had experiences nearly as hair-raising as her own. Wollstonecraft obviously exaggerated, partly because she felt embattled. Men minimize the 'misery and oppression peculiar to women, arising from the partial laws and customs of society', and even women usually write from a masculine point of view.

A friend called George Dyson had criticized the manuscript, and Wollstonecraft retorted.

I am vexed and surprised at your not thinking the situation of Maria sufficiently important, and can only account for this want of – shall I say it? delicacy of feeling – by recollecting that you are a man.[24]

But her basic point is a serious one. Women must talk for themselves, tell their own life-stories, however absurd and trivial they may seem to men. It is only by articulating their denied feelings, their wrongs, that they will find the strength to protest. The projected climax of the novel was to be a courtroom scene where Maria finds the courage to make a public protest – about her own particular sufferings, and the oppressed situation of all women. Partly because she has talked with Jemima and other women, she sees that her own unhappy marriage reflects a wider situation: that marriage is an economic contract designed for the protection of property, and not for the needs of the individual. She opposes a morality of *feeling* to society's hypocritical materialism. The judge responds predictably: A woman's wrongs can never excuse any violation of the marriage vow. 'What virtuous woman thought of her feelings?' She should 'love and obey the man chosen by her parents and relations'.

But – and again something interesting emerges through all her under- and over-writing – the feeling on which Maria bases her protest is itself obscure, ambiguous. Wollstonecraft insists that women too have sexual passions and needs; at one point Maria confesses that she controls her behaviour only because she cannot flirt with a man without feeling strongly attracted to him. Society punishes Maria for an adulterous love, and demands that she obey her husband. But Wollstonecraft is obsessed by the idea that love, by its very nature, is doomed. Maria, despite herself, despite all her courage and intelligence, is in some sense the source of her own unhappiness.

She falls in love, in the madhouse, with a man called Henry. Their love is an idyll that fulfils some of Maria's deepest needs, and gives her courage to fight her oppressors. Yet from the start it is shot through with unhappiness, with rumours of madness. It can only flower in impossible circumstances, with an impossible man. For Wollstonecraft has flashes of remarkable insight into the way her heroine literally conjures her lover out of her own loneliness and need. Like Mary in the earlier novel, Maria is the moving force. 'Fancy, treacherous fancy, began to sketch a character congenial to her own . . . He was then plastic in her impassioned hand and reflected all the sentiments which animated and warmed her.' Maria notices, and refuses to notice, their incompatibility; she both foresees, and invites, his desertion.

The end was to be a series of unmitigated disasters. One set of notes reads 'Divorced by her husband – Her lover unfaithful – Pregnancy – Miscarriage – Suicide.' There is also the sketch of an alternative where Maria attempts suicide, and lives to devote herself to the child who has been restored to her, forgetting any hope of personal happiness or fulfilment.

Those two alternatives seem to sum up her deepest fears about women. Neither the conventionally melodramatic plot, nor her generalizations about the oppression of women seem adequate to the pervasive and inconsolable sadness, the feeling of something lost before it is gained. The liberation of feeling, of sexuality, may further imprison you. You may struggle for years to be an active, independent human being, to be overwhelmed in the end by a need for love that is rooted in earliest childhood, that is impossibly demanding, unappeasable, destructive of the 'self' that has been so carefully constructed. In the first novel Mary had asked, angrily, 'Have I desires implanted in me only to make me miserable? Will I never be gratified? Shall I never be happy?' The answers seem to be, not in a world hopelessly divided by sex, not in a world where a woman is helplessly divided against herself.

Harriet Martineau (1802–76)

The best friends of that cause are women who are morally as well as intellectually competent to the most serious business of life, and who must be clearly seen to speak from conviction of the truth and not from personal unhappiness. The best friends of the cause are the happy wives and the busy, cheerful single women, who have no injuries of their own to avenge, and no painful vacuity or mortification to relieve.[25]

Harriet Martineau is much less immediately appealing than Mary Wollstonecraft. High-minded, rigorously principled, didactic, she exactly fits popular notions of the typical Victorian. She herself admitted that she was 'too solemn, too rigid, and prone to exaggerations of differences and to obstinacy'. Her self-righteous rectitude and appeals to Duty to justify her most trivial acts could infuriate even close friends. (Jane Carlyle once exploded: 'She feels it her duty (Varnish!) to set this example, etc, etc. I felt it my duty (without varnish!) to tell her that I considered the whole uproar *unworthy* of her.') Martineau was easily shocked, and never slow to express heavy disapproval of other people's sex lives. She severed all connections when George Eliot went to live with her lover, G. H. Lewes, and even disapproved when her friend Elizabeth Barrett married fellow-poet Robert Browning. Charlotte Brontë was desolated by Martineau's criticisms of *Villette* for its excessive passions.

Martineau's comments on Mary Wollstonecraft are revealing. The latter, she wrote, was

with all her powers, a poor victim of passion, with no control over her own peace, and no calmness or content except when the needs of her individual nature were satisfied.[26]

She felt strongly that Wollstonecraft and women like her actually harm the cause; a preoccupation with personal wrongs can only set back the fight for women's rights. So Martineau consistently subordinated her own needs and emotions to her principles. Her work became her life. 'My business in life,' she said, 'has been to think and learn, and to speak out with absolute freedom what I have thought and learned.' Given the period, the statement was a remarkable one, and so was her achievement. Harriet Martineau was a widely read and respected writer on politics and economics; that is, on emphatically 'masculine' topics. What makes her even more remarkable is her insight, almost despite herself, into the cost of her own achievement.

Martineau's literary reputation was based on her first major undertaking, the 'Illustrations of Political Economy'. They began to appear in 1832 when she was thirty, an unknown girl from the provinces. Her only previous writing had been for an obscure Unitarian magazine, the *Monthly Repository*, and she had to battle hard to get her idea accepted by a London publisher. The 'Illustrations' were a series of didactic stories simplifying and explaining the 'science' of political economy that had been developed by writers like Adam Smith, Riccardo, Malthus and James Mill. Martineau was not an original thinker but she was a superb popularizer, and her tales exactly met a huge public appetite for books explaining the tremendous social changes of the 1820s and 1830s. The Napoleonic Wars had drastically affected the English economy; technological advances were changing older patterns of industrial employment; there was great working-class unrest – machine breaking, strikes – and the beginnings of serious working-class organization. She saw herself as an educator speaking to both middle- and working-class audiences, and instructing them in the social laws that would ensure a stable society based on harmony between different class interests.[27]

It is easy to forget that this was a genuinely audacious role for a woman. Reviews in some of the important periodicals – later she was to be a regular contributor to them – give some idea of what she was up against. The *Quarterly*, for example, was predictably sarcastic about her story on population control.

Poor innocent! She has been puzzling over Mr Malthus's arithmetical and geometric ratios, for knowledge which she should have obtained by a simple question or two of her mamma.

But as they further contemplated the horrors of what Martineau had done, the patronizing tone slipped into something close to hysteria:

A *woman* who thinks child-bearing a *crime against society*! An *unmarried woman* who declaims against *marriage*!! A *young woman* who deprecates charity and a provision for the *poor* ! ! !

A woman should be a Lady Bountiful, and not wear herself out trying to understand social questions – which were, by definition, beyond her. The *Edinburgh Review*, on the face of it more polite, concurred. It laughed uneasily at her visionary millennium when 'the ladies will have taken out of our monopolizing hands the cares of Parliament and public life'. But the reviewer managed to calm his 'horror of the Amazons of politics' by a splendidly contorted piece of reasoning. Political economy is to do with the poor; women are traditionally charitable to the poor; *therefore* a woman may express interest in political economy – with the proviso that 'the less women usually meddle with any thing which can be called public life out of their village, we are sure the better for all parties'.[28]

The public did not agree. Martineau's tales – which appeared monthly for two years – averaged around ten thousand sales an issue. The Chancellor, Lord Brougham, is reported to have said that an insignificant girl from Norwich was doing more good than any man in the country, and politically, Martineau became a voice to be reckoned with. For the rest of her long life, she worked hard as a professional writer, pouring out a stream of articles, pamphlets, books on social problems, histories, travel accounts, as well as an autobiography, novels, and children's stories. The sheer range of her interests is extraordinary.

She was a serious and lifelong feminist. Her first published article (in the *Monthly Repository* 1821) was a survey of 'Female Writers of Practical Divinity' whose example, she felt, might inspire other women to write, and it was followed by a plea for better education for girls. She returned to the question of education all through her life in *Society in America* (1837) and *Household Education* (1849), as well as various articles and newspaper leaders, and her arguments are essentially the same as Wollstonecraft's. Girls should be educated to their fullest capacities, taught to think and work in an orderly and sustained way. Like Wollstonecraft, she reassures her readers that even the most advanced education – in Latin or mathematics, say – need not unfit us for womanly duties.

Her long theoretical statement about women is in *Society in America*. In some ways, she felt that women in America were better off than in England. Marriage laws were less heavily weighted in favour of men, and a few more professions were open to women. Nevertheless most women led lives as confined, as frivolously feminine as in England, and educated women, with little outlet for their talents, had as dangerous a tendency towards pedantry or religious obsession. But the anomaly of woman's position is more obvious in America, because it is such a blatant contradiction of the constitution which guarantees rights to all men. Martineau's point is the same as Wollstonecraft's: *human* rights cannot exclude women. The comparison between women and slaves, a rhetorical device for Wollstonecraft, had precise meaning for Martineau, who had travelled widely in the States and worked with the Abolitionists. In the case of women as of slaves

justice is denied on no better plea than the right of the strongest. In both cases the aquiescence of the many and the burning discontent of the few of the oppressed, testify, the one to the actual degradation of the class, and the other to its fitness for the enjoyment of human rights.[29]

Martineau constantly uses the American situation to make points about women in England – where the situation is more difficult because the contradictions are concealed. Instead of a constitution, the English have law and tradition, and most people never realize that women have 'never actually or virtually assented' to those laws that govern their lives.

Most of Martineau's feminist writings are scattered through periodicals and newspapers. She was a well-informed and pungent journalist, well placed to publicize specific abuses and inequalities and she wrote often and fully about the difficulties of working women; there are articles on women in prison, women and emigration, the problems of women with violent husbands. She was a friend of Florence Nightingale and helped publicize her work on nursing and the army; and towards the end of her life she wrote cogently and effectively for the campaign against the Contagious Diseases Act.

But this scattered work takes on great urgency because she recognized that the situation of women was changing. More and more women, middle class and working class, had no choice but to go out to work. The whole concept of 'earning one's bread' is, she argues, a fairly recent one, for men as well as women. It only arose with the complicated shift from a feudal and domestic economy, to a commercial and industrial one where the middle class is dominant. The idea and reality of work has changed, for men as for women. But despite the drastic social changes of the last fifty years

> our ideas, our language, and our arrangements have not altered in any corresponding degree. We go on talking as if it were still true that every woman is, or ought to be, supported by father, brother or husband . . . A social organization framed for a community of which half stayed at home while the other half went out to work, cannot answer the purposes of a society, of which a quarter remains at home, while threequarters go out to work.[30]

Many of her articles deal with the actual situation of women workers, forced to earn their living, but handicapped because they are untrained, excluded from many jobs by male jealousy, poorly paid and expected to put up with appalling conditions. She made a special study of domestic servants, and wrote several training guides for the Poor Law Commissioners. She has the detached benevolence of the Victorian philanthropist – but her feminism gives her work edge and insight. And her memories of the time when her family lost its money and she had had to earn her living by taking in sewing are never too far away.

Most of her journalism reached a very wide audience. After the appearance of *Society in America*, dozens of women wrote to her complaining of how the 'law and custom' of England oppressed them.

> Some offered evidence of intolerable oppression, if I could point out how it might be used. Others offered money, effort, courage in enduring obloquy, everything, if I could show them how to obtain, and lead them in obtaining, arrangements by which they could be free in spirit, and in outward liberty to make what they could of life.[31]

But she let the opportunity evaporate. Deeply attracted to other women and sympathetic to their troubles, she was nervous about identifying with them. Though at one point she was involved with plans for a periodical to further the cause of women, she held the emerging women's movement at arm's length. She would work for women's rights, but only as an individual. Like Florence Nightingale, like many other Victorian women who had struggled free of stereotyped femininity, she was alarmed by and sarcastic about 'Women's Missionaries'.

Often as I am appealed to speak, or otherwise assist in the promotion of the cause of Women, my answer is always the same: – that women, like men, must obtain whatever they show themselves fit for . . . Whatever a woman proves herself able to do, society will be thankful to see her do, – just as if she were a man.[32]

Her argument is familiar to this day: if I did it, anyone can. The fact that she was so successful in an exclusively male province led her to minimize the depth of sexual distinctions. She refuses to confront the fact that inequality is one of the bases of bourgeois society. For all her knowledge of economics, she ends up with an oversimple and idealistic view of the relationship between the individual and society. Wollstonecraft's belief in the future has hardened into a rigid moral optimism that denies the bitterness of class and sexual divisions.

Unlike many respectable Victorians, Martineau was not unsympathetic to working-class organizations. She knew the work of the Saint Simonians, for example, and Robert Owen's communities, and even suggested that women might make use of their ideas about the 'economy of association'. But she was virulently hostile to strikes, indeed to social conflict of any kind. Progress towards an 'equality of human rights' could only come through reason, cooperation, the recognition by any single group that its best interests coincided with the good of society as a whole. She hoped to press on the rich 'a conviction of their obligations' and induce the poor 'to urge their claims with moderation and forbearance, and to bear about with them the credentials of intelligence and good sense'. She was a manufacturer's daughter – and the best, most intelligent kind of nineteenth-century liberal. She never really questioned the categories of rich and poor – any more than, in the last resort, she questioned the categories masculine and feminine.

Men, like the rich, must recognize their obligations to women who, like the poor, have an unanswerable case. Women must *prove* themselves rational and dispassionate; they, like the poor, must cultivate forbearance and put their case in reasoned and impersonal terms.

I have no vote at elections, though I am a tax-paying housekeeper, and responsible citizen; and I regard the disability as an absurdity, seeing that I have for a long course of years influenced public affairs to an extent not professed or attempted by many men. But I do not see that I could do much good by personal complaints, which always have the suspicion or reality of passion in them.[33]

Her tone towards many contemporary advocates of women's rights is the one she uses to put down strikers and working-class rabble rousers. Caroline Norton, who made her own miserable marriage public in an effort to change marriage laws 'violates all good taste' and displays 'an epicurean selfishness'. The writer Anna Jameson always strikes one monotonous note, 'the ill usage that women with hearts have received from men who had none'. Less of herself and her experiences would have doubled the effect of Jameson's pleas for equality.

All through her work, Martineau sets up an impassable division between the personal and the impersonal, between – on the one hand – discipline, principle, duty, the rational mind; and on the other, passion. Wollstonecraft was in her eyes a 'poor victim of passion'. Charlotte Brontë's heroines love 'too readily, too vehemently' and are saved only because they 'do their duty and are healthy in action, however morbid in passion'. Martineau tells us that she herself made a conscious decision to dwell on things that are 'hopeful, lovely, bright and honest' as opposed to the 'dark and foul' passions. Passion is always dark, unhealthy, self-destructive. It springs from a sense of being wronged, and issues in a desire for vengeance; it is an egotistic demand for satisfaction. The word obviously sums up a whole disturbing area of experience – irrational, infantile, *feminine* – that would threaten Martineau's independence and dutiful self-denial.[34]

Like Wollstonecraft, Martineau denied that reason was the exclusive possession of men; she denied that there were 'masculine' or 'feminine' virtues. Men should be gentler and women bolder. But in her struggle to break free of conventional feminine stereotypes, she ended up equating rationality with men and passion with women. Some of her anonymous periodical writing is quite explicitly written from an authoritative and impersonal masculine perspective – *we* think such and such about *them*, women. Martineau saw her career as a writer in terms of a masculine choice, a masculine persona – and so, I suspect, did many of the other Victorian women who wrote under male pseudonyms. Harriet Martineau's *Autobiography* reveals very clearly the psychological as well as the practical reasons why the choice posed itself in those terms.[35]

*

For the remarkable thing is that while overtly denying passion and personal experience, Martineau managed to write a very personal and honest account of growing up in Victorian England. Ironically, it was criticized in the very terms she used to blast Wollstonecraft. Lord Russell of Liverpool contrasted the 'generous flow of truth in all her public writings' with the 'acrid dribblings of the private pen'. She should not have brooded over her unhappy childhood, but shown a 'manly reticence. The woman who has got rid of the customary mental sterility of her sex ought to make short work of frailties of mood and temper.'

Born in Norwich in 1802, she was the sixth of eight children. Her father, a member of a well-off Unitarian family, was a cloth manufacturer. He was a mild, intelligent and considerate man, but he seems to have influenced Martineau far less than her brothers, or, indeed, two of her teachers. When he died in 1826, she was horrified by her inability to express her feelings – or her inability to feel. Mrs Martineau dominated the household, and Harriet sought her love with a desperate anxiety that rendered her fearful and awkward – and resentful. She was apparently slow and sickly, and was overshadowed by her livelier brothers and sisters.

Maria Chapman, one of her closest friends, says that Martineau 'not only remembered the feelings of her own childhood but felt them over again, through life'. Certainly her accounts of the anxiety she felt when she was hardly more than a baby have a dizzying truth to them.

Sometimes the dim light of the windows in the night seemed to advance till it pressed upon my eyeballs, and then the windows would seem to recede to an infinite distance. If I laid my hand under my head on the pillow, the hand seemed to vanish almost to a point, where the head grew as big as a mountain. Sometimes I was panic struck at the head of the stairs, and was sure I could never get down; and I could never cross the yard to the garden without flying and panting, and fearing to look behind, because a wild beast was after me. The starlight sky was the worst; it was always coming down to stifle and crush me and rest upon my head.[36]

This could hardly be bettered as a description of anxiety that distorts and dislocates the world. The tiniest details come alive with inexplicable horror – the 'awful large gay figures' in chintz curtains, the moving lights from a magic lantern, the 'waves flowing and receding below and great tufts of green weeds swaying to and fro' as she walks with her father on a broken jetty. She is constantly ill, with fear, with her inability to express the fear, with rage and guilt.

Martineau's modern biographers have naturally enough described her as neurotic. R. L. Wolff, for example, in an interesting essay in his *Strange Stories*, describes the *Autobiography* as a case history. But he actually tells us very little that Martineau herself is not perfectly aware of. She sees as well as we can the nervous roots of her illness and depression, how her anger and remorse issue in fantasies of suicide and martyrdom, how she seeks compensation for her inadequacy first in religion then in reading. Moreover, she recognizes that her life is a whole, that what she was as a child partly determines her adult life, that we never fully escape from the emotional patterns of childhood.

Partly because she was shy and delicate, partly because she had so many older brothers and sisters, partly because her mother was not very affectionate, she felt unloved and neglected. In compensation, she developed a passionately protective love towards her younger brother, James, and her sister. She tried to guide and teach them, put part of herself into them. Yet she still had an 'unbounded need for approbation and affection', particularly from her mother, and was desperately jealous of her sister Rachel, eighteen months older.

When we were little more than infants, Mr Thomas Watson, son of my father's partner, one day came into the yard, took Rachel up in his arms, gave her some grapes off the vine, and carried her home across the street, to give her Gay's *Fables*, bound in red and gold. I stood with bursting heart, beating my hoop, and hating every body in the world. I always hated Gay's *Fables*, and for long could not abide a red book.[37]

On one occasion she actually dared protest to her mother, angrily complaining that 'everything that Rachel said and did was right and everything that I said and did was wrong', but though the two girls were treated more impartially afterwards, some forty years later Martineau still resented the way she was silenced and sent upstairs. Forty years later she was still complaining that a bit more warmth and openness from her mother might have transformed her whole life.

The more resentful and inward-turned she became, the more she was teased for being 'dull and unobservant and unwieldy'. She was painfully conscious of her lack of feminine charm, and once told Maria Chapman that

I never had but one civil speech about my looks, and that was a compliment to my hair. As a child I used to take the matter into consideration. What did I take myself to be? Not pretty, certainly. But was it a hopeless matter altogether? . . . But at fifteen a saucy speech of a satirical cousin – 'How ugly all my mother's daughters were, Harriet in particular' – settled the question for me. I never doubted my ugliness after that.[38]

Miserable, miserly, she brooded endlessly over her sense of being deprived and damaged. She made common cause with the servants, who were treated coldly, rudely; they, like children, were oppressed and denied status as human beings. Her closest childhood friendship was with a little girl whose leg had been amputated, and so could not run around to play hide-and-seek with the other children. Martineau found herself spending all her free time 'with cold feet and a longing mind, with E. leaning on my arm, looking on while other children were at play'. She was embarrassed when people stared at the two of them in the street, and even more embarrassed when her mother, with what seems to have been characteristic disregard for her children's feelings, decided that E.'s 'constant tugging' on Harriet's arm was making her grow crooked – and sent her daughter to explain as much to E.'s mother. Martineau was trapped – between resentment at her mother for not rescuing her from an intolerable situation, a deep identification with E.'s sufferings, hostility to E., and guilt at deserting her. For the rest of her life, she was haunted by images of maiming. It was shortly after this, she tells us, that she became deaf – and she herself attributes it partly to the dreams of martyrdom that she wove around E. Her best-known school story *The Crofton Boys* is about a little boy who loses his foot, one of the heroines of her novel *Deerbrook* is badly crippled, and when she underwent mesmeric trances in the 1840s, Martineau talked repeatedly about her left arm being crushed and amputated.

Martineau says that the strongest passion in all her life was for her brother James. In later years they quarrelled bitterly, and because she cannot bring herself to discuss it fully in the *Autobiography*, the relationship remains obscure. Even the best biography – by R. K. Webb – explains it away far too easily as a sign of her 'latent homosexuality'. According to Webb, love for her brother based on shared intellectual interests was an effective defence against sexual feelings. That surely discounts the strength of passions between brothers and sisters. It certainly underplays the bitterness of their eventual quarrel. James reviewed his sister's book on her conversion to free thought in highly personal terms, scoffing at her admiration for her young co-author, Henry Atkinson. After she died, he publicly attacked her account of their mother and childhood – in terms, by the way, that unconsciously confirm her description. An ostensibly intellectual disagreement was obviously rooted in love and jealousy going back to earliest childhood.

As a very young child, Martineau had poured all her loneliness and frustrated love on to James. She adored him, protected him, and guided his education. Like many Unitarians, the Martineaus took education seriously for the girls as well as the boys. At eleven, Martineau was sent to an excellent day school, at sixteen to a boarding school in Bristol where she studied under the well-known Unitarian Dr Carpenter. Within the family circle, books and newspapers were freely available, and Martineau retreated into a world of books. Even the fact that her older brothers teased her about her precocious interest in politics and the National Debt must have, obliquely, encouraged her. Her parents took her seriously enough to take her advice on James's education, and he followed her to Bristol. For years, they read and studied and talked together.

But at nineteen, she was confronted by the realities of her situation as a young lady. James went away to college, leaving her wretched and 'widowed' and suggested that she 'take refuge' in a new pursuit like writing. So she tried it, in compensation, and in competition. Eventually, of course, she was far more successful than he ever was, which must have posed problems for both of them. Certainly the brief but rambling paragraph where Martineau dismisses the strongest passion of her life suggests that she is still struggling to free herself from the intolerable conflict of need and resentment that he arouses in her.

The fact, the painful fact, in the history of human affections is that, of all natural relations, the least satisfactory is the fraternal. Brothers are to sisters what sisters can never be to brothers as objects of engrossing and devoted affection . . . Sisters are bound to remember that they cannot be certain of their own fitness to render an account of their own disappointments, or to form an estimate of the share of blame which may be due to themselves on the score of unreasonable expectations.[39]

As a middle-aged woman, Martineau worked out some of her feelings for James in her intense friendship with Henry Atkinson, whom she met during her experiments with mesmerism. Much younger than her, he was probably homosexual, an intellectual dilettante; Martineau idolized him, leaning on his support through her very public conversion to free thought. Yet she always retained the dominant role, treating him as if he were a woman, charmingly illogical but not really up to serious political matters. James jeered at her for prostrating herself at the feet of a nonentity; but it seems fairly clear that in some odd unacknowledged way, Martineau was taking some kind of revenge, through Atkinson, on her loved – and hated – brother.

A conflict between 'masculine' and 'feminine' roles underlies her difficult relations with James, and comes to the surface in every major crisis in her life. The *Autobiography* shows in great detail how the distinction was enforced, even within this comparatively enlightened family. The boys were encouraged in study and business, the girls in study and household cares. Harriet, who had an excellent business head, was both proud and resentful of her domestic skills. She dreaded being thought unwomanly. Whenever she discusses a woman writer whom she admires, she automatically praises her housekeeping as well: Charlotte Brontë's family knew her skill with the needle before they recognized her talent with the pen, and the mathematician Mrs Somerville kept one of the best tables in England. 'A woman of science knows no wrongs,' she insists; yet her life of Mrs Somerville (in *Biographical Sketches*) is a bitterly ironic comment on how devotion to family ruined the scientist. And her life of Mrs Wordsworth, whose only claim to fame was her self-sacrificing devotion to the poet, is full of barely concealed distaste.

Martineau is always anxious to explain 'for my mother's sake'

that I could make shirts and puddings, and iron and mend, and get my bread by my needle, if necessary (as it once was necessary for a few months), before I won a better place and occupation with my pen.[40]

She also describes, with cold precision, the difficulties she overcame to become a writer. It took thirteen years from the time she left school before she emerged as a writer and independent woman. All through those years she had to fight for time to think and work; she got up early in the morning, sat up over her books at night. She was continually interrupted, for

it was not thought proper for young ladies to study very conspicuously; and especially with pen in hand. Young ladies (at least in provincial towns) were expected to sit down in the parlour to sew, – during which reading aloud was permitted, – or to practise their music; but so as to be fit to receive callers, without any signs of blue-stockingism which could be reported abroad.[41]

When Martineau's first piece was published in the *Monthly Repository*, her older brother praised it without realizing it was her work. She confessed, and he replied gravely, calling her 'dear' for the first time,

'Now dear, leave it to other women to make shirts and darn stockings and do you devote yourself to this.' I went home in a sort of a dream ... That evening made me an authoress.[42]

But it was not so easy to reconcile the 'authoress' with the dutiful daughter. Like many Victorian girls, Martineau got stuck in a protracted adolescence. A woman could be a daughter, or a wife and mother; what, after all, were the alternatives? (Florence Nightingale is a case in point, hysterically angry at her inability to escape from the meaningless round of daughterly duties; while Mary Carpenter, the daughter of Martineau's old teacher in Bristol, said that her childhood lasted till she was fifty, and her mother died.) Martineau was luckier, for when she was twenty-seven, there was an unexpected turning point. Her father had died two years before, and in 1829 his business collapsed, leaving his widow and unmarried daughters almost penniless.

> I who had been obliged to write before breakfast, or in some private way, had henceforth liberty to do my own work in my own way; for we had lost our gentility ... but for that loss of money, we might have lived on in the ordinary provincial method of ladies with small means, sewing, and economizing, and growing narrower every year ...[43]

Even so, her problems were not immediately resolved. She began to look for money for the reviewing she had done in an inevitably dilettante way for the *Monthly*, and she went to stay in London while she looked for more hack work. But her mother sent 'peremptory orders' that she return home.

> I rather wonder that, being seven and twenty years old, I did not assert my independence, and refuse to return, so clear as was in my eyes, the injustice of remanding me to a position of helplessness and dependence, when a career of action and independence was opening before me ... the instinct and habit of old obedience prevailed, and I went home, with some resentment, but far more grief and desolation in my heart.[44]

She resigned herself, sweetly, submissively, angrily, to the feminine work of sewing and basket making, but continued to slog away at her writing. At about this point, she began to formulate the idea for her political economy series. The project was put to various publishers, and tentatively accepted. Learning that it was in acute danger of collapsing, she wanted to do 'what a man of business would do in my case' – go to London and sort things out. 'My dear, you would not think of doing such a thing alone, and in this weather,' her mother replied. But Martineau shrewdly referred the question to an older brother and when he 'said oracularly "GO"', she went. Ironically, this brother Henry was a ne'er-do-well whom Martineau later took into her own house. But male authority is male authority, however weak its vessel and even strong self-willed women like Mrs Martineau and her daughter were nervous of acting without it.

As a successful writer, Martineau's internal conflicts only increased. She loved having a home of her own, being free to write undisturbed. Some of the most attractive pages in the *Auto-biography* are alive with her almost physical pleasure in making her own decisions, setting her own routines. But her mother came to visit, and not only stayed, but installed an elderly aunt as well. At the point when Harriet was succeeding at her 'masculine' work, she was back playing the dutiful daughter. She wrote to her mother with some anxiety.

I fully expect that both you and I shall occasionally feel as if I did not discharge a daughter's duty, but we shall both remind ourselves that I am now as much a citizen of the world as any professional *son* of yours could be. My hours of solitary work and of visiting will leave you much to yourself.[45]

Martineau's account of her troubled relations with her mother – something central to the way any girl becomes a woman – is sad and perceptive. (Wollstonecraft never had to face it in such an acute form; she managed to leave home early, and her mother died when she was twenty-three. She struggled all her life with the memory, the image, which may have been worse; but she did not live with the ageing and unhappy reality as Martineau did.)

It is fairly clear that – though neither woman would admit it for a moment – mother and daughter were very alike. Both were strong-willed, stubborn, ambitious, moralistic. Maria Chapman commented that Mrs Martineau's 'strong consciousness of the hidden *man* in her own heart' made her sympathetic to her daughter's work. She was also very envious, and worked out some of her frustrated energy on Harriet.

My mother, who loved power, and had always been in the habit of exercising it, was hurt at confidence being reposed in me, and distinctions shown, and visits paid; and I, with every desire to be passive and being in fact wholly passive in the matter was kept in a state of constant agitation . . .[46]

Martineau obviously needed and enjoyed her mother's anxious concern for her health. She liked being nursed and guarded against intruders. Moreover her self-respect depended on maintaining an image of herself as dutiful, self-denying, silently forbearing.

> I was not allowed to have a maid, at my own expense, or even to employ a workwoman; and thus, many were the hours after midnight when I ought to have been asleep, when I was sitting up to mend my clothes.[47]

The formidable intellectual is hardly to be recognized in this good little mouse afraid to assert herself. But matters were even more complicated because she was in fact the man of the house, responsible for two old ladies and for Henry as well. They constantly pressed her to earn more so that they could move to a bigger house and entertain in style. Martineau found the situation more and more intolerable. She had fainting fits whenever they quarrelled; she dreamed, obsessively, that her mother 'had fallen from a precipice or over the banisters or from a cathedral spire; and that it was my fault'.

At thirty-five, Martineau was overwhelmed with a double crisis. Her anxiety at home reinforced her doubts about the work she was doing so successfully. She was offered the editorship of a new periodical dealing with economics; it would bring prestige, money, the culmination of all her literary ambitions. It would also, she pointed out, advance the cause of women, proving finally that they were the equals of 'men of business'. But when she had to decide, she panicked.

> The realities of life press upon me now. If I do this I must brace myself up to do and suffer like a man. No more waywardness, precipitation and reliance on allowance from others! Undertaking a man's duty, I must brave a man's fate.[48]

While she was still dithering, a letter from her brother James settled the question. He disapproved, she turned the project down – saved by masculine authority from her own authoritative masculine self. Instead she turned to the 'liberty' of fiction in

Deerbrook – it was acceptable for women to write novels – and finally collapsed into bed. She stayed there for the next five years. With her usual unsparing honesty about her own tangled motives, she herself describes it as a retreat from the pressures of work and family, into the most helplessly feminine role of all. Characteristically though, she kept some control over her own life, taking solitary lodgings in Tynemouth, and continuing to write, though at a lower pitch. After 'expecting an early death till it was too late to die early', she was dramatically cured by mesmerism. Her own description – a curious mixture of scientific interest and mysticism – makes it clear that this was a primitive form of psychotherapy. Submitting her will to her female mesmerist and to her maid was a crucial element in her cure, and gave her intense pleasure. It is also worth noting that her mother, who often visited her while she was an invalid, virtually cut off relations after Martineau's much publicized recovery.

*

Martineau had mixed feelings towards 'that matter which is held to be all important to woman – love and marriage'. On the one hand she pays lip-service to conventional ideas of womanly fulfilment, on the other she hints at the 'serious and irremediable' evils of married life. She insists, probably truthfully, that she is completely happy and satisfied as a single woman. She also admits that the 'deepest springs' of her nature have never been touched. Her tragedy is that work and fulfilment as a woman should be posed as irreconcilable alternatives.

Though she could not afford to look too closely at her own defences, though she never recognized the depth of her attraction to women like Maria Chapman or faced the implications of her hysterical self-righteousness about sex, she still makes a great effort to write honestly about her feelings. When she was twenty-four she was briefly engaged to a friend of her brother James. Thirty years later she can hardly bring herself to think about her distress and indecision.

I was ill, – I was deaf, – I was in an entangled state of mind between conflicting duties and some lower considerations; and many a time did I wish, in my fear that I should fail, that I had never seen him.[49]

She tried to force herself into appropriate feelings, was obviously appalled by what she discovered in herself, then reacted violently to the opposite extreme of ruthless self-preservation. (She speaks disingenuously of 'unaccountable insults' from his family. Apparently she refused to see him and demanded the return of his letters when he was gravely ill.) She acted with a callousness born of panic – and all those years later could not see what she was saying. 'It was happiest for us both that our union was prevented by any means': and goes on to explain, with obvious relief, that her suitor 'became suddenly insane' and died shortly after.

Yet a curious and complex passage goes beyond self-justification to explore the roots of her feelings.

If I had had a husband dependent on me for his happiness, the responsibility would have made me wretched. I had not faith enough in myself to endure avoidable responsibility. If my husband had *not* depended on me for his happiness, I should have been jealous. So also with children. The care would have so over-powered the joy, – the love would have so exceeded the ordinary chances of life, – the fear on my part would have so impaired the freedom on theirs, that I rejoice not to have been involved in a relation for which I was, or believed myself unfit. The veneration in which I hold domestic life has always shown me that the life was not for those whose self respect had been early broken down, or had never grown.[50]

Her account of this tangle of ambiguous and conflicting feelings is very sophisticated. She recognizes that she cannot separate love from anxiety and jealousy, that she only experiences love as possessive fear. What she is as a woman can only be explained in terms of her family history. And the aggressive, unappeased child is so strong in the adult woman that she can survive only by guarding her separate and single state as if her life depended on it – which in a sense it did. As I mentioned earlier, she is usually classified as a latent homosexual, and that may be true – as far as it goes. But it does not go far in helping us understand her dilemma in a society where the whole of life is rigidly polarized in sexual terms. Her homosexuality – along with her ambivalence to her own work, her mixed attitudes to marriage, her fear of sexuality, her painful mixture of need and resentment towards her mother – have to be seen in the light of the long series of destructively simplified choices forced on her, forced on us all, between 'masculine' and 'feminine' roles.

Her novel *Deerbrook*, written just before her long illness, when she was most deeply troubled about her choices, should be read along with the *Autobiography*. She tells us that writing the book was a 'relief to my pent-up sufferings, feelings and convictions, and I can truly say that it was uttered from the heart'. The characters reflect the sexual divisions that plagued Martineau all her life. The hero, Edward Hope, is a doctor, and he carries the novel's main theme – a scientist's struggle against superstition and wilful obscurantism. The women – two sisters, Margaret and Hester, the lame governess Maria, and the villain of the piece, Mrs Rowland – are wholly concerned with their emotional lives, and more particularly love. Yet only the women come alive; and the only really convincing relationships are those between the women. Martineau seems to pour her own feelings into them, and through them explores various aspects of her own denied femininity.

The governess Maria, relegated by poverty and lameness to an observer's role, makes the most powerful statement in the novel. Love, she insists to her friend Margaret – and she speaks on the basis of her earlier experiences as well as her present detachment – is invariably agonizing, even if there is a happy outcome. Worst of all, it has to be endured in silence, for women almost never find the courage to discuss their pain with each other.

Every mother and friend hopes that no one else has suffered as she did . . . some conclude, at a distance of time, that they must have exaggerated their own sufferings or have been singularly rebellious and unreasonable. Some lose the sense of anguish in the subsequent happiness . . .

So the young girl is totally unprepared for her misery.

It seems a mere trifle has plunged her there. Her friend did not come when she looked for him, or he is gone somewhere, or has said something that she did not expect. Some such trifle reveals to her that she depends wholly upon him – that she has for long been living only for him, and on the unconscious conclusion that he has been living only for her . . . The universe is, in a moment, shrouded in gloom. Her heart is sick, and there is no rest for it, for her self respect is gone.[51]

Unrequited love is the worst agony, and all a woman can do is pray to emerge morally stronger after her struggle with herself. But the perception underlying Martineau's rather melodramatic prose is more radical and disturbing than that. She sees love – whatever its outcome – as a kind of death. It is the sign of a complete change in our existence, as a free, untroubled girl is turned into a woman. A part of the grown woman has died with her girlhood.

As R. L. Wolff has pointed out in his perceptive analysis of the novel, each of the women characters represents an aspect of Harriet Martineau's own feminine self. Hester is a terrifying emotional possibility, Maria the repressed and limited reality, and Margaret the ideal. Hester particularly is a remarkable study of obsessive jealousy, drawing on Martineau's own feelings towards her sister Rachel, and dramatizing her insights into the possessiveness that might have been released in her had she married. Hester is restless, irritable, self-pitying. She can never accept that she is loved or lovable; she broods over the idea that her dead father used to prefer Margaret, or that a brother who died as a baby *might* have loved Margaret better. Even after she marries the man she loves, she remains wretched, insecure, and demands impossible proofs of affection. Compulsively, she goes through the same routine: she explodes in angry jealousy, then collapses in hysterical sobbing, and ends in remorse promising never to do it again. The next day, or week, she starts back on the same sterile, self-destructive cycle. Even when she has a baby, she is jealous of Margaret's love for the child, and tries to interfere with her sister's friendship with Maria. And of course, like many jealous people, she tends to create what she dreads. People *do* prefer Margaret, and Hester's own husband is secretly in love with her sister.

For Margaret represents something that Hester, like Martineau dreamed of becoming. She is submissive, gentle, long-suffering – wholly feminine. But more important, she is never plagued by Hester's agonized self doubts. Even when she is unhappy, believing that the man she loves has turned against her, her central being is never shaken. As Hope describes her, she is what Hester, like most neurotics, longs to be: 'pure existence without question, without introspection, without hesitation or consciousness'.

Unlike Hester, Maria is calm and thoughtful, despite her unhappy situation. An accident that killed her father and left her lame and penniless has ruined her dreams of a home and husband of her own. So she earns her living as a governess, and sits by the schoolroom window watching the others wander in the summer meadows. Maria finds her satisfaction in curiosity and concern for others, in doing her duty. She has to learn to repress her own needs and jealousies – she had loved the man Margaret eventually marries, and finds what satisfaction she can in her disciplined intelligence, in the fact that she sees more than any of the other characters. She is a morally impressive woman – and a sad and revealing image of some of Martineau's fears and fantasies about her own choice in life.

And I think Woolf is right to argue that a fourth character represents a further aspect of Martineau's 'feminine' feelings. In the figure of Mrs Rowland, a neighbour to the others, she works out some of her own aggression towards her domineering mother. Mrs Rowland, full of 'ill will, selfish pride and low pertinacity about small objects' brings unhappiness to each of the other women. She sacks Maria, damages Hester's marriage, and nearly succeeds in putting an end to Margaret's romance with her brother. And – with great satisfaction – Martineau pays her back. Purely because of her own stupidity, her small daughter falls ill and dies; she is left permanently chastened.

Martineau was not a particularly skilful novelist. Having set up a fascinating psychological situation, she never really develops its implications. Hester never has to face the fact that her husband really loves Margaret, and she is reformed – not very convincingly – by suffering and poverty. Martineau evades the full force of the story she has created, by falling back on external melodrama (a plague epidemic) and a morality that insists on the value of suffering. But given these limits, the novel is an impressive achievement that deserves to be better known.

Martineau lived to be an old woman. After she got up from her sickbed in 1845, she resumed a full professional life until at least 1866. No longer young, the sexual tensions that had nearly destroyed her were more easily resolved. She planned and built her own house in the Lake District, and lived in happy control of a large household, always full of friends, nephews and nieces, and young girls whom she trained as servants, but who seem to have been genuinely attached to her. She organized and lectured her neighbours for their own good, established a Building Society, travelled to Egypt, and wrote endlessly. She is a comic but very impressive figure, the complete matriarch, smoking her cigars like any 'man of business'.

Simone de Beauvoir (b. 1908)

... far from suffering from my femininity, I have, on the contrary, from the age of twenty on, accumulated the advantages of both sexes; after *L'Invitée*, those around me treated me both as a writer, their peer in the masculine world, and as a woman; this was particularly noticeable in America: at the parties I went to, the wives all got together and talked to each other while I talked to the men, who nevertheless behaved towards me with greater courtesy than they did towards the members of their own sex. I was encouraged to write *The Second Sex* precisely because of this privileged position. It allowed me to express myself in all serenity.[52]

Just because Simone de Beauvoir is so much closer to us in time, it is harder to see her clearly. When I first read *The Second Sex* – about fifteen years ago, before the present women's movement – it struck me with the force of genuine revelation. It helped me make some sense of my confused and isolated depression. Since the book appeared in 1949, de Beauvoir has received thousands of letters from women all over the world, grateful for the way her book helped them to see their personal frustrations in terms of the general condition of women.

She has also written in very great detail about her own life as a woman. There are four long volumes of autobiography (the first appeared in 1958, the last in 1972). Her main purpose, she says, 'has been to isolate and identify my own particular brand of femininity'. She presents and interprets her life in the terms that she outlines and develops in *The Second Sex*. Autobiography and theory are two aspects of a lifelong preoccupation. Her most interesting critic, Albert Memmi, has argued in his book *The Dominated Man* that, taken together, they tell 'the story of a single journey: one woman's journey towards real emancipation', and this unity makes her work 'the most important feminist project ever to have been attempted'.

I want to concentrate here on the relationship between the autobiographies and *The Second Sex*. The four autobiographical volumes (*Memoirs of a Dutiful Daughter*, *The Prime of Life*, *The Force of Circumstance*, and *All Said and Done*) for all their total recall of rich detail covering over sixty years of a crowded, active life, are no haphazard accumulation of memories, no outpouring of personal confession. They are very carefully structured to demonstrate a thesis about her own life.

When I was about fourteen I identified with Louisa M. Alcott's Jo and with George Eliot's Maggie; I longed to assume that imaginary dimension which made these story-book heroines and the writer who projects herself into them so fascinating, and to assume it before an audience . . . Later I did try to recount my life, endowing my experience with artistic necessity.[53]

She presents her life as an achieved project, unified by her childhood ambition to know and write as honestly as possible. She has always insisted that she is satisfied with what she has made of her life – indeed, that she has never had to ponder over any important decision. There is a very real sense in which she presents herself as an *exemplary* figure. Not that she is a model to be followed, and not, as Memmi suggests, that she offers a solution to the feminine dilemma. But she offers her own life as an *example*, a successful example, of how one girl escaped that dilemma, rejecting the feminine part of 'object, Other', and choosing to create and assert her liberty.

The Second Sex, she tells us, was written from a position of strength, not weakness. In fact, she is slightly apologetic about concentrating on women's problems at a time when 'some of us have never had to sense in our femininity an inconvenience or an obstacle'. Since 1949, de Beauvoir has modified her optimism about the general situation, admitting that equality is not so easily achieved. But – despite the vicious attacks on her own book that sometimes led her to reassess male friends – she continues to insist that her own femininity has never been a burden of any kind. At one point, she does admit that

In France if you are a writer, to be a woman is simply to provide a stick to be beaten with. Especially at the age I was when my first books were published. If you are a young woman they indulge you with an amused wink. If you are old, they bow to you respectfully. But lose the first bloom of youth and dare to speak before acquiring the respectable patina of age: the whole pack is at your heels![54]

In a recent interview, she suggested that women today may even have a more difficult time than she did, simply because so many more of them challenge men on their own terms, and the men are therefore more hostile. But she continues to insist that she has no personal experience of women's wrongs, that she has escaped the burden of oppression that she analyses so brilliantly in *The Second Sex*.[55]

She argues that she was never in any danger of losing her independent freedom, and that she has never felt hostility towards men. In a world where personal relationships are difficult and dangerous, especially for women, her relationship with Sartre is the great success of her life, and since she met him, aged twenty-one, she has never felt lonely. She is no simple-minded optimist, of course. Personal doubts and political events have often forced her to reassess her earlier attitudes. She sees that her youthful freedom was an illusion, based on petty bourgeois privilege, and *Force of Circumstance* ends on a note of bitter disillusion about the passing of youth, the dishonesty of a bourgeois society that promises everything to its children and conceals the harsh political facts of advanced capitalism. But it is hard to see how that disillusion has touched her personal sense of herself. She once wrote, in criticism of the young girl she was, that

nothing, I believed, could impede my will, I did not deny my femininity, any more than I took it for granted. I simply ignored it.[56]

But there is some curious sense in which she continues to ignore it.

De Beauvoir is sometimes attacked for writing too personally. I think the opposite is true: if anything, she does not write personally enough: the superb consistency of her life and work is also its limitation. In order to keep it up, she has to reject great areas of experience. She finds it difficult to write about childhood, except as an apprenticeship to adult life; she is uneasy with sexuality, and she keeps her distance from dreams, madness, extreme states of any kind. My problem with the autobiographies is that they fit only too neatly into the intellectual framework of *The Second Sex* – and help pinpoint the final inadequacy of that framework. Whereas Martineau, for example, somehow faces the price she paid for her achievements, and manages at least occasionally to confront some of what she had to suppress, de Beauvoir denies that any suppression has taken place. She is capable of extraordinary frankness – within carefully set limits.

> ... I feel no resistance to speaking frankly about my life and myself, at least insofar as I place myself within my own universe. Perhaps my image projected in a different world – that of the psychoanalysts – might embarrass me. But as long as it is I who paint my own portrait nothing daunts me.[57]

But when I read the autobiographies, and even more the novels, I am always bothered by a shadow behind the clear outlines of her self-portrait, feelings denied or kept strenuously at bay. Her rigorous self-examination can be a kind of self-evasion.

*

In *The Second Sex*, de Beauvoir approaches the situation of woman from 'the perspective of existential ethics'. We are human because we transcend nature. To be human is to create, to invent, to find meaning for life not in mere living but in projects of ever-widening scope. Man 'remodels the face of the earth, he creates new instruments, he invents, he shapes the future' – and that is what distinguishes him from the animals. Our activities and aspirations define us. We are human insofar as we *produce*, not merely reproduce. Man chooses to break the cycle of meaningless biological repetition, and frees himself through the constant struggle towards further freedoms. 'The present finds its only justification in its expansion into an indefinitely open future'. Someone who rejects this struggle and lapses back into the 'brutish life of subjection to given conditions' is morally at fault, inauthentic. Someone who is denied the freedom to struggle, is oppressed.

Woman's tragedy throughout history is that she has been denied this right to aspiration – denied full humanity. According to de Beauvoir the dualism between the self and the other is crucial to human consciousness. 'We find in consciousness itself a fundamental hostility to every other consciousness; the subject can be posed only in being opposed – he sets himself up as the essential, as opposed to the other, the inessential, the object.' But women have been refused reciprocity. She is always *and* archetypally Other, seen by and for men, always the object and never the subject. (So she comes to stand for Nature, Mystery, the non-human; what she represents is more important than what she experiences.) And of course, women have colluded in this, perpetuating their alienation from themselves. As long as she clings to her femininity she is denying her human possibilities.

There is no doubt that this intellectual schema is very effective. It helps de Beauvoir to synthesize previous work on women, gives consistency to her brilliant analysis of the figure of woman in myth and literature, and lends bite and clarity to her anatomy of woman's lived experience from childhood to old age. She still stands by her account, though in *Force of Circumstance* she admitted that it needed a more materialist basis. She would found 'the notion of woman as other and the Manichean argument it entails not on an idealistic and *a priori* struggle of consciences but on the facts of supply and demand'. In fact the real weakness of her argument is not just that it is idealistic, but that it is, indeed, Manichean. It works polemically; as a superb tactic for attacking the feminine mystique, and systematically exposing the contradictions on which the whole notion of femininity rests. But de Beauvoir claims to be writing philosophically, not polemically; to be helping us understand our possibilities as women, and not just fighting against our limits. And her existential ethic actually prevents her from doing that.

She begins by attacking the assumption, hidden in all culture, that the masculine is the absolute human type, the norm against which women are measured and defined. The first half of her book is a brilliant analysis of that masculine bias. And – like Wollstonecraft before her – de Beauvoir protests at the way any woman who struggles to be a human being is labelled 'masculine'. But she is continually on the edge of slipping into the very attitudes she attacks.

Her argument is – her own word – Manichean. Her cool, unhesitating authoritative prose sets up a whole series of absolutely rigid oppositions – masculine vs feminine, culture vs nature, human vs animal, production vs reproduction, activity vs passivity. The first term is always good, the second bad. De Beauvoir herself reflects and sustains the absolute sexual division whose concrete effects she attacks. She attacks the mystique of femininity – by accepting a masculine mystique. In the end, it is *she* who equates the human with the male sex, who idealizes male values, sees life from a masculine perspective. 'The devaluation of femininity has been a necessary step in human evolution', and the 'androgynous' world of the future will be a 'brotherhood'. Again,

it is male activity that in creating values has made of existence itself a value; this activity has prevailed over the confused forces of life; it has subdued Nature and Woman.[58]

De Beauvoir rightly points out that the idealizing of 'feminine' virtues is often a ploy to imprison women in their difference. She does not recognize that those virtues are not in themselves bad. 'Femininity' cannot be discarded; rather, it has to be incorporated in a fuller kind of humanity.

In a recent interview she argued that

Culture, civilization, universal values have all been the work of men, since it is they who have stood for universality. Just as the proletariat, challenging the bourgeoisie as the dominant class, does not throw out the whole bourgeois heritage, in the same way women have to use, on an equal basis with men, the instruments men have created, not reject them totally.[59]

This is obviously true. If we throw out culture because it is 'masculine', we throw the baby out with the bathwater, and are left with nothing, not even the language to express our rejection. De Beauvoir herself has done very valuable work in disentangling the 'masculine' bias of our civilization from what she calls its universal values. I still have an uneasy suspicion that she drastically oversimplifies the class and sexual bias of those abstract and universal ideas. In fact, I wonder if the very notion of universality – rationality, objectivity – is not more limited than she recognizes. If there were genuine shifts in class and sexual relations, men would change as drastically as women. We might have to rethink – reimagine – our whole notion of culture, of *human* values.

For de Beauvoir's definition of what it means to be human – indeed her whole existential philosophy – is loaded with unacknowledged class and intellectual assumptions. This emerges most clearly when she moves from the general to the particular, and outlines the possibilities open to individual women today. (She admits, of course, that no individual can solve the problem alone, and that women will never be free without a radical transformation of society.)

The emancipated woman wants to be active, a taker, and refuses the passivity man means to impose on her. The 'modern' woman accepts masculine values; she prides herself on thinking, taking action, working, creating on the same terms as man.[60]

It is surely a bleak prospect. The emancipated woman sounds just like that familiar nineteenth-century character, the self-made man. (And isn't that the model underlying all her philosophic sophistication? Early capitalist man, dominating and exploiting the natural world, living to produce, viewing his own life as a product shaped by will, and suppressing those elements in himself – irrationality, sexuality – that might reduce his moral and economic efficiency. His moral and emotional life is seen in capitalist terms – as de Beauvoir tends to see hers. She sees childhood as an apprenticeship, a time for amassing, acquiring, accumulating knowledge. Experience is often a matter of debts or credits – the image of the balance sheet recurs in her work. And the French title of her latest autobiography is *Tout compte fait* (not quite the same as the English translation, *All Said and Done*). De Beauvoir argues that the emancipated woman will seek professional autonomy and financial independence; that she will avoid marriage, and probably children as well. She sees little hope for the woman of, say, thirty-five, who has four children and no professional qualifications. And de Beauvoir has little understanding, either, of the girl who is bored to death in a factory and office, and who may be desperate to escape into marriage and maternity. She writes brilliantly about women's problems in general terms, but she seems to have very little sense of other women as individuals who may differ from her. There is little warmth towards other women in the autobiographies, and even in the novels, where she often writes about wives and mothers, her writing has an almost clinical coldness. She is presenting case studies, and not deeply imagined individual characters.

De Beauvoir asserts the importance and the possibility of emancipation, but it remains a very abstract quality. She is free only because she denies very important areas of experience. In *The Prime of Life*, she admits that the freedom she and Sartre enjoyed was in many ways abstract and illusory, possible only because they had no family ties or responsibilities except to themselves. She points out that there were two available disciplines – dialectical materialism and psychoanalysis – which might have helped them see how limited their choices were, how their freedom was in fact class privilege. But I am not sure that de Beauvoir ever really modifies her idealistic view of liberty. She gives an interesting account, for example, of her own terror when Sartre was badly depressed, scared that he was going crazy.

To me he stood for pure mind and radical freedom; I would not consider him as a sport of obscure circumstances, a mere passive object. I preferred to think that he produced these fears and delusions of his because of some perverse streak in his character, and his breakdown I found more irksome than alarming.[61]

She is frank about how cowardly and short-sighted she was; but adds 'if I had shared his anxiety I most certainly would have been no help at all to him; so no doubt my anger was a healthy reaction'. That is, she sees her own limitations only to rationalize them and so manages to keep any genuinely disrupting experience at a distance. In the last volume of autobiography, her concept of liberty has not changed in the slightest, despite her references to class conditioning; she still reviews her life in terms of a very simple dichotomy between chance and choice, insisting on the primacy of will.

Towards the end of *The Second Sex*, de Beauvoir briefly looks at the possibility that freedom may be hard to attain – at least for a woman. The would-be emancipated woman may be caught in an insoluble dilemma, her choices drastically limited.

> The advantage man enjoys, which makes itself felt from his childhood, is that his vocation as a human being in no way runs counter to his destiny as a male ... Whereas it is required of woman that in order to realize her femininity, she must make herself object and prey, which is to say she must renounce her claims as sovereign subject. It is this conflict that especially marks the situation of the emancipated woman. She refuses to confine herself to her role as female, because she will not accept mutilation; but it would also be a mutilation to repudiate her sex. Man is a human being with sexuality; woman is a complete individual, equal to the male, only if she too is a human being with sexuality. To renounce her femininity is to renounce part of her humanity.[62]

This raises more problems than I can adequately discuss in this context. As usual, I think she sets a far too absolute barrier between the sexes. A man's sexuality may be at odds with his humanity too; we all, men and women alike, act out 'masculine' and 'feminine' roles; and passivity is not always and automatically bad. As she often does, de Beauvoir has argued herself into a corner. She is so determined to prove that there is no such thing as a 'feminine' nature, that she is at a loss when she has to confront the real differences – and similarities – between men and women.

But beyond that, she seems to be making an interesting admission: in our present society, a woman faces the possibility of mutilation either way, whatever her choices. It is precisely that dilemma that she usually denies, whether in her theory or in her personal writings. De Beauvoir's achievement – like that of Harriet Martineau – is a triumph; but she pays a great price for it. Her own life – like her view of human history – depends on a 'devaluation of femininity'. And that means the loss of something real in herself, not just escape from an artificial stereotype.

Her work would have been even more valuable if she had managed to confront the contradictions she glosses over.

*

The first volume of the autobiography, *Memoirs of a Dutiful Daughter*, is a remarkably full and vivid account of her childhood. She conjures up the taste and texture of her early life: the Paris flat, the summers she spent at her grandfather's estate, the Catholic schooldays. Like many stories about growing up, it's exciting and coherent. The story is shaped towards the conditions of its own existence – the emergence of an independent woman. And she dramatizes her struggle with, and within, her bourgeois environment. It is a portrait of the artist as a young woman. But underlying the sense of triumphant progress is a more painful story. She doesn't underestimate her difficulties, and she tells the story of her adolescent conflict with her parents, for example, with painstaking honesty. But she sidesteps the anxiety implicit in the family situation by being good at school work and using that as a key to the future. From very early on de Beauvoir got into the habit of using the future to compensate for the present.

She was born in Paris in 1908. Her father was a lawyer but refused to take his profession very seriously. Despising the bourgeois virtues of thrift and hard work, he aspired to an aristocratic mode of life which he could not afford. He was sceptical, cultivated, an accomplished amateur actor. His wife, on the other hand, was conventionally pious; naturally lively but increasingly subdued within the marriage, first by her husband's casual infidelities, later by their comparative poverty. De Beauvoir tells us she was a secure and happy child – though she was shaken by fits of violent and inexplicable rage. She was bossy, competitive, humourless; she passionately resented being treated as a *child*, though she insists she didn't mind being a girl. ('The boys I knew were in no way remarkable. The brightest one was little Rene . . . and I always got better marks than he did.') Getting better marks became more and more important in her life. Her father, whom she adored, encouraged her to study.

Papa used to say with pride: 'Simone has a man's brain, she thinks like a man; she *is* a man.'

Yet in her adolescence she saw more clearly that she didn't have the freedom of her cousin Jacques and his male friends.

> But I did not give up all hope. I had confidence in my future. Women, by the exercise of their talent or knowledge, had carved out a place for themselves in the universe of men.[63]

Her work for competitive exams gave structure and meaning to her life. But her father, from whom she derived her respect for culture, turned on her. He allowed her to work towards a profession so that she could support herself. But she became a constant reminder of his failure to provide well for the family, and he resented the fact that she was not pretty and feminine. It must have been a difficult relationship, and as soon as she could she left home.

Through the story of her own progress towards an emancipated life as a student she weaves the lives of her closest friend Zaza and her cousin Jacques. In some sense Zaza is de Beauvoir's other self, her feminine, defeated side. Zaza also wanted to write, to live independently. When they first met she was actually the stronger, more defined personality. But she was more deeply involved with her family, hating her father and tied to her mother. She was nostalgic about her childhood, and she dreamed of having her own children. She fell in love with a friend of de Beauvoir's, but when the man proved evasive and her mother too demanding, Zaza fell ill and died. De Beauvoir admits that for a long time she felt that Zaza's death was the price of her own freedom – though I'm not sure how fully she realizes that in writing about her friend she is also writing about her own darker possibilities. In writing about Jacques she works out some of her unacknowledged resentment against men. Even as a small girl she admired Jacques and it was he who introduced her to modern literature and helped emancipate her from the stultifying Catholic respectability of her home. Later they thought of marrying, but Jacques went off and married a richer girl. While she describes his later life – the failure of his marriage and his business, his drunkenness and early death – with calm detachment, I get a strong impression that she is taking her revenge.

The first volume ends with de Beauvoir free of her family –

she is completely happy in the world of students and young intellectuals. They accept her as an equal; men, she tells us, 'were my comrades, not my enemies'.

Far from envying them I felt that my own position, from the very fact that it was an unusual one, was one of privilege. One evening Pradelle invited to his house his best friends and their sisters. Poupette went with me. All the girls retired to Mlle Pradelle's room; but I stayed with the young men. Yet, I did not renounce my femininity . . .[64]

Even more important, she had begun her lifelong relationship with Sartre; he was, she tells us, the dream companion she had longed for ever since she was fifteen, the partner

a little stronger and more agile than myself, who would help me up from one stage to the next . . . someone who would guarantee my existence without taking away my powers of self determination.

Sartre was her 'double', in whom she found her 'burning aspiration raised to the pitch of incandescence. I should always be able to share everything with him.'[65]

Sartre provides her, she tells us, with the 'sort of absolute unfailing security that I had once had from my parents, or from God'. He 'guarantees' her happiness, and justifies the world for her – though, she admits, 'there was nothing that could perform the same service for him'.

There are real problems in discussing her relationship with Sartre. De Beauvoir herself puts it at the centre of her life, continually writing in terms of what 'we' did or thought, yet in one sense tells us very little about it. I am not sure that she really confronts either her dependence, *or* her very real independence; she is oddly vague about the shifts and adjustments that allowed them to continue as a couple while both had affairs with other people. She insists, for example, that she followed Sartre 'joyfully because he led me along the paths I wanted to take; later, we always discussed our itinerary together'. But

philosophically and politically the initiative has always come from him. Apparently some young women have felt let down by this fact; they took it to mean that I was accepting the relative role I was advising them to escape from. No. Sartre is ideologically creative, I am not . . .

the real betrayal of my liberty would have been a refusal to recognize this particular superiority on his part; I would then have ended up a prisoner of the deliberately challenging attitude and the bad faith which are at once an inevitable result of the battle of the sexes and the complete opposite of intellectual honesty. My independence has never been in danger because I have never unloaded any of my own responsibilities onto Sartre.[66]

All this sounds perfectly reasonable – but is it true? I have the uneasy feeling that, while rightly insisting on her own independent work, de Beauvoir carefully avoids the least danger of competing with her man, and gives an odd, sophisticated new twist to the old doctrine of 'separate but equal'. I am not sure that her own work is not in some ways more creative and original than Sartre's – and that she has always been terrified to admit it.

Albert Memmi has pointed out, too, that she tells us almost nothing about their sexual life as a couple. This is partly, I suppose, the familiar problem of autobiography: you may expose yourself, but do you have the right to expose other people as well? But I get the same feeling that I do when Martineau refuses to discuss her relations with her brother. To speak freely might be too disrupting, too disturbing. For she does not, after all, hesitate to speak freely about other people in her life – Nelson Algren, for example, or Camille.

De Beauvoir defends herself against this kind of query by describing it as gossipy and 'cannibalistic'. But she *is* writing an autobiography, asking for our sympathetic identification with her life.

If any individual – a Pepys or a Rousseau, an exceptional or a run-of-the-mill character – reveals himself honestly, everyone, more or less, becomes involved.[67]

But what is honesty? Both Pepys and Rousseau speak far more frankly, present themselves in far more unpleasant postures, than de Beauvoir is prepared to do. Obviously it is far easier for a man to write openly about his sexual feelings. De Beauvoir tells us that one of her models was Michel Leiris's *Manhood* – one of the best accounts of individual sexuality that I have ever come across. But Leiris succeeds partly because there are myths, images external to him, round which he can organize his fantasies. (He takes two paintings of nudes by Lucas Cranach – the *Lucretia* and the *Judith* – and they serve to focus and unify his dreams and fears about women. As de Beauvoir proved conclusively in *The Second Sex*, these images do not work in the same way for a woman. If we imagine ourselves as Lucretia or Judith, we only perpetuate our alienation from ourselves; and patriarchal erotic art does not provide us with images in which we can discover our own feelings about men.) Nevertheless, the attempt to write about sexuality is crucially important for women. Violette Leduc, for example, makes a brave and moving effort to confront her own pain and chaos – and it is to de Beauvoir's credit that she recognized the quality of Leduc's writing, and encouraged her to continue. Nevertheless she tries to assimilate Leduc to her own scheme of values, and in her introduction to *Les Ravages*, underplays its sheer *sexual* honesty. She complains elsewhere that too many modern women writers concentrate exclusively on sexuality – though without specifying names – and she certainly retreats from it in her own writing – even in the novels, where presumably she would be less nervous of telling tales.

In fact, there is only one place in the autobiography where she talks openly about adult sexuality. She explains that she 'had surrendered my virginity with glad abandon' to the man she loved. For 'when heart and body are all in unison, there is high delight to be had from the physical expression of that oneness'. But when she and Sartre were separated – posted to different schools in the provinces – she was appalled by the split between her body and mind. She missed Sartre, and wanted a man, any man.

The idea of any discrepancy between my physical emotions and my conscious will I found alarming in the extreme: and it was precisely this split that in fact took place. My body had its own whims and I was powerless to control them; their violence overrode all my defences. I found out that missing a person physically is not a mere matter of nostalgia but an actual *pain*.[68]

Yet this is the only place I can find – at least until she faces the rather different problems of old age – where she sees that sexuality may not be amenable to the will.

She admits openly to jealousy. When she was teaching in Rouen, she and Sartre became friendly with a young student called Olga, and the couple became a trio. De Beauvoir describes it as Sartre's idea; it met his needs and not hers, and she was terrified, overwhelmed with jealous insecurity.

Sartre . . . let himself go, to the great detriment of his emotional stability, and experienced feelings of alarm, frenzy and ecstasy such as he had never known with me. The agony which this produced in me went far beyond mere jealousy: at times I asked myself if the whole of my happiness did not rest upon a gigantic lie.

The same panic was to recur later. Sartre visited America after the war and fell in love with a girl referred to as M. De Beauvoir was again devastated, wondering whether the new love was not more important; she brooded over the thought that there was

a harmony between them at a depth – at the very source of life, at the wellspring where its very rhythm is established – at which Sartre and I did not meet, and perhaps that harmony was more important to him than our understanding.[69]

Any woman will sympathize with what she's saying; the situation sounds appallingly familiar. Yet the whole drive of her writing, in each case, is to minimize what she has admitted, to defuse it, to see it as incidental – an important, a disturbing incident, agreed – in the even course of her life. (The situation with Olga was the subject of her first novel, *L'Invitée*. In that sense it was of major importance and altered her life; it held the seeds of the real freedom that she was to discover in her own work.) Despite this, there seems to me to be considerable tension underlying her coolly rational prose; she has an extraordinary ability to simultaneously admit and deny something:

I persuaded myself that a fore-ordained harmony existed between us on every single point. 'We are,' I declared, 'as one.' This absolute certainty meant that I never went against my instinctive desires; and when, on two occasions, our desires clashed, I was completely flabbergasted.[70]

Yet she never really explains how her sense of the word 'we' changes – or indeed, if it does. She and Sartre remain a couple – but what *kind* of couple?

She also gives the impression – in hints and hardly acknowledged sentences buried in the books – that though she may have
dominated Sartre in day-to-day matters, it was he who called the
tune emotionally. In the relationship with Olga, it is clear enough
– de Beauvoir frankly admits that she wanted nothing of what he
had created and went along with it because she was terrified of
asserting her own independent vision. The account of her reaction to his affair with M. – this was after the war, when she was
working independently and successfully – is even more disturbing.
Her own love-affair with Nelson Algren, she explains, began
when Sartre phoned and asked her to stay longer in America as
M. was staying longer with him in Paris.

> I'd had enough of being a tourist; I wanted to walk about on the
> arm of a man who temporarily would be mine. I thought first of my
> New York friend, but he didn't want either to lie to his wife or to admit
> such an affair to her; we decided against it. I called Algren.[71]

Exactly the same thing happened the following summer. De
Beauvoir had arranged to go to the States for four months while
M. again visited Sartre in Paris. When M. rang to say she was not
coming, de Beauvoir decided to cut short her own stay with
Algren by two months. When she got back from the States, M.
decided to come after all, and she thought of going back to
Algren. None of this necessarily calls in question the depth or
authenticity of her feelings for Algren. It does suggest that – like
most intense feelings – they had complicated and murky roots in
anger, fear, anxiety.

In *Force of Circumstance*, de Beauvoir describes a time she
spent living alone on the outskirts of Paris while Sartre was with
M. She was paralysed by anxiety and physical despair, in a state
that 'bordered on mental aberration'. She attributes this, a little
disingenuously, to the aftermath of the war, or the first dread of
coming middle age. She then dismissed the subject, plunging
into a long account of the books she was reading, the people she
saw, what was happening politically, her conversations with
Sartre, who had 'kept me in touch with what was happening in
life by letter'. She tries to calm her panic by immersing herself in
external activities, and asserts the importance and persistence of

a life that M. could never share. But on a trip to Scandinavia undertaken after M.'s departure, she is haunted by appalling dreams, constantly on the edge of hallucination.

I had nightmares. I can remember a yellow eye at the back of my head which was being pierced by a long knitting needle. And my anxiety states came back. I tried to conjure these crises away with words: 'The birds are attacking me – must drive them away; it's such an exhausting struggle keeping them off, day and night . . .'[72]

She is never quite able to admit her dreams, her anxiety states, her fantasies, into full consciousness. In *All Said and Done*, she devotes a long section to dreams; but she describes them just as if they were films she had seen, entertaining, curious, but remote from her real life. In several of them, Sartre refuses her something, or rejects her; but her only explanation is that she is playing out something that has never happened in fact. Reading them, I was driven back to her original account of why they never married or had children. Both are decisions that I respect and even agree with; both seem to me far more difficult decisions than she claims. Memmi has argued that her account indicates that it was basically Sartre's decision not hers, and I think he may be right.

I would have regarded it as highly artificial to equate Sartre's absence with my own freedom – a thing I could only find, honestly, within my own heart and head. But I could see how much it cost Sartre to bid farewell to his travels, his own freedom, his youth – in order to become a provincial academic, now finally and forever grown up. To have joined the ranks of the married men would have meant an even greater renunciation. I knew he was incapable of bearing a grudge against me; but I knew, too, how vulnerable I was to the prick of conscience . . .[73]

And again, 'Sartre could not resign himself to going on to the "age of reason" to full manhood . . . (he) had thrown himself so wholeheartedly into the business of being young that when his youth would finally leave him he would need strong enchantments indeed to afford him consolation'.

Her explanations of why she never had a child are carefully rational – though she occasionally admits to some deeper fear. Even as a small child, she was repelled by babies – 'red-faced, wrinkled, milky-eyed'. As a student she met one of her closest friends, Nizan, with his wife and child, and her only reaction was horror at the way he was submerged and tied down. (His wife never even registered on her consciousness.) When she met Sartre

> my happiness was too complete for any new element to attract me. A child would not have strengthened the bonds that united Sartre and me; nor did I want Sartre's existence reflected and extended in some other being.[74]

As long as Sartre was her 'double', her other self, a child was probably a genuine impossibility. A child would have forced a completely different kind of relationship; inevitably it would have polarized them, divided the 'human' back into 'masculine' and 'feminine' elements. So she discovers a whole series of reasons for not having a child. She did not need a baby as an extension and fulfilment of herself, as Sartre provided all she needed. She was so hostile to her own family that she would expect hostility or indifference from her own children; motherhood seemed incompatible with a writer's life.

> I was shocked by Zaza's declaration – we were both fifteen at the time – that having babies was just as important as writing books: I still fail to see how any common ground could be discovered between two such objects in life. Literature, I thought, was a way of justifying the world by fashioning it anew in the context of the imagination – and, at the same time of preserving its own existence from oblivion. Childbearing, on the other hand, seemed no more than a purposeless and unjustifiable increase of the world's population.[75]

This is convincing in its own terms – and completely inadequate. It is a piece of rationalization that tells us almost nothing. The feelings she describes are very common in fifteen-year-old girls; it is much harder to maintain them intact beyond that age. True, women find it very difficult to combine maternity with creative work. (Mary Wollstonecraft found pain and desperation, as well as pleasure, in her experience as a mother.) It is equally true that the decision *not* to have children is intensely difficult. (As Martineau half-realized.) Having a baby and writing a book are obviously very different experiences; but at a *fantasy* level, for men as well as for women, they are surely very close, and we may dream or imagine one in terms of the other. For all her psychological sophistication and insight, de Beauvoir seems to have missed the real point of what she is writing about.

De Beauvoir returns again and again to the question of how her relationship with Sartre has survived intact all these years. One question has always recurred, she tells us, and never been solved. 'Although my understanding with Sartre has lasted for more than thirty years, it has not done so without some losses and upsets in which the "others" always suffered.' In her own case, her important sexual affairs were always conducted at a distance. Algren 'belonged to another continent, Lanzman to another generation'. The affair with Lanzman, nearly twenty years younger, was immensely important: she 'rediscovered her body', found that she was a young woman again. She and Sartre had always kept their emotions under control – in fact, they addressed each other as 'vous' – and Lanzman satisfied some nostalgia for childish violence and fury. Though she had never lived with Sartre, she and Lanzman shared her flat for several years. For a time she says she wondered about her relationship with Sartre:

Of course we would always remain intimate friends, but would our destinies, hitherto intertwined, eventually separate? Later I was reassured. The equilibrium I had achieved, thanks to Lanzman, to Sartre, to my own vigilance, was durable and endured.[76]

I suppose my main difficulty is that we never really know quite what it is that endured; we accept that it is important, but never really understand why. We see that she has spent a lifetime working out and on her relationship with one man, – but that relationship is an absence at the heart of her life story.

I sometimes wonder if the extraordinary detail with which she writes is not a way of holding us at a distance; it gives the illusion, but only the illusion, of intimacy. At times, she seems to fall between two stools; she is unclear whether she is writing a chronicle of events and people, or an autobiography that will clarify the pattern, the underlying meaning, of her own existence. Often the two go together. She communicates vividly how a journey, a friendship, or a love-affair mark a stage in her inner life.

She explores some new possibility in herself as she extends her knowledge of the outer world. But at other points in her story, de Beauvoir shies away from this conjunction of inner and outer. Her catalogue of books and films and conversations often reads like an evasion of what was really happening. Alternatively, some of her apparently objective accounts of other people, particularly of other women, seem to reveal more about her than about them. The projection of her own hidden fears on to Zaza gives that story its intensity; on the other hand, the descriptions of Camille and Lise are cold, categorizing, full of suppressed anger.

This odd separation may have something to do with her intense distrust of any kind of psychoanalytic thinking. Though she formally recognizes its values – she stresses the importance of childhood, for example – it never seems to affect her perspective on herself. In *The Second Sex* she complained that

the language of psychoanalysis suggests that the drama of the individual unfolds within him. But a life is a relation to the outside world, and the individual defines himself by making his own choices through the world around him.[77]

The dichotomy is surely a false one. Determined to maintain the notion of life as a series of free choices, de Beauvoir misses the real connections between inner and outer. She angrily rejects, for example, the suggestion that Sartre is some kind of father figure to her, or that the student Olga might have taken the place of the child she never had. Obviously that kind of comment can be crude and simplistic; it neither explains, nor explains away, a relationship or an emotion. But a sense of similarities, connections, identifications can enrich present relationships. Through dreams, fantasies, images that work below the level of conscious thought, we can glimpse the deeper patterns that animate all our lives. De Beauvoir claims that she can see the child she was at five, in the adolescent, in the adult woman. But that is precisely what she never manages to communicate. Her own childhood is simply as a period of apprenticeship, a time in which she acquired the knowledge and experience needed by the adult woman. Her childhood has meaning only in relation to what she became later; as an adult, she never feels childish, never needs to regress, or needs to act out what was denied or suppressed in her childhood. Having rejected both her mother and father, she never feels them as a burden or a presence inside her head. With one important exception. In some ways, her account of her mother's last illness, the short book called *A Very Easy Death*, is the most moving thing she has written. And it is moving partly because she finds herself confronted with emotions she cannot rationalize away, a desperate love and sense of identity in which she rediscovers her own childhood and forsees her own death.

I had understood all my sorrows until that night: even when they flowed over my head I recognized myself in them. This time my despair escaped from my control: someone other than myself was weeping in me. I talked to Sartre about my mother's mouth as I had seen it that morning and about everything I had interpreted in it . . . And he told me that my own mouth was not obeying me any more: I had put Maman's mouth on my own face and in spite of myself, I copied its movements. Her whole person, her whole being, was concentrated there, and compassion wrung my heart.[78]

*

Like Wollstonecraft, like Martineau, de Beauvoir used her novels to explore more freely these aspects of her life minimized in her other writing. Her novels are varied in subject matter – *The Blood of Others* is set in occupied Paris, *All Men are Mortal* is a historical novel set in the reign of Charles V, *The Mandarins* examines French political and intellectual life in the years following the Second World War. All of them are structured according to clearly articulated philosophical and moral themes. Yet the most memorable and living things in all of them are the studies of women in love, women unhappily in love.

L'Invitée was her first published work, and de Beauvoir is very frank about its origins in the unhappy relationship between herself, Sartre and Olga. Its subject is autobiographical, and she tells us that she worked out her own jealous fantasies to their bitter end. At the start of the novel, the heroine, Françoise, is settled and secure, happy in her long-standing relationship with Pierre, and contented in her work for the theatre that Pierre runs.

The novel traces the way she is gradually undermined and forced to call her whole life in question. Xavière, the girl whom she has adopted, maternally, possessively, gradually becomes more and more important in her life. Like a cuckoo in the nest, Xavière displaces her with Pierre, and destroys Françoise's confident self-image. De Beauvoir manages to catch some of the terrifying complexity of jealousy. Françoise is as obsessed with Xavière as she is with Pierre; all the uncertainties that she has kept hidden even from herself are exposed one by one. Françoise becomes more and more like the minor character, Elizabeth, whose whole life is an act to conceal from others, if not from herself, her own emptiness and inability to feel anything. The book moves to a minor climax half way through when Françoise falls ill. Unable to cope with her conflicting feelings towards both Xavière and Pierre, she retreats into delirium. Yet the illness is dramatically ambiguous. It is both a withdrawal from combat, and an attack on the other two. Françoise masochistically leaves the field free to their loves, but appeals to their sympathy by demonstrating her distress. Predictably, it fails to solve anything and Françoise is drawn back into the emotional trap she has helped create, to the point where she can do and feel nothing except in relation to the claustrophobic trio.

She has an affair with a young actor called Gerbert, a friend of all three, and someone in whom Xavière has expressed interest. To Françoise, it is an escape and a fresh start; until she realizes that Xavière sees it as an act of betrayal and revenge. In the last chapters of the novel, Pierre is away and the conflict narrows down to the two women. Françoise is increasingly unable to see anything except from Xavière's point of view; eventually, to destroy her own image in Xavière's eyes, she turns on the gas and leaves the girl to die in her sleep. Françoise – and the author as well – see it as an act of self definition.

Alone. She had acted alone. As alone as in death. One day Pierre would know. But even his cognizance of this deed would be merely external. No one could condemn or absolve her. Her act was her very own. 'It is I who will it.' It was her own will which was being accomplished, now nothing at all separated her from herself. She had at last made a choice. She had chosen herself.[79]

De Beauvoir later admitted that Françoise had defended herself against Xavière's invasion of Françoise's personality by an 'equally brutal and irrational act', but added that the rights and wrongs of the case were irrelevant. But there is a split here that runs all through the novel. I agree with de Beauvoir when she claims that the murder is no melodramatic afterthought, that the whole story, everything that Françoise has been, tends to this point. But the story exists on two levels. There is the philosophical framework about the Self and the Other within which the character and the author discuss and contain what is happening. And there is a very powerful and psychologically complicated study of love and hate and jealousy, that eludes the rational, rationalizing structure. The novel could have ended on a frightening paradox: Françoise can only assert herself through an act of destruction and self-destruction. But de Beauvoir seems too close to her heroine, not so much in her hostility to Xavière, but in her intellectual rationalizations – and her blindness to her feelings about Pierre.

Pierre, significantly, is hardly a presence in the novel. De Beauvoir recognizes this, explaining that because she was 'loathe to offer the public a portrait of Sartre as I knew him' she created neither an accurate portrait nor an original character. But beyond this, I get the impression that she is *protecting* Pierre. Part of Françoise's tragedy is that she never really confronts her feelings for her lover, never recognizes her own rage and hostility. She refuses to see that Pierre behaves childishly and selfishly. (It is interesting that we never know if he and Françoise have any sexual connection; they share a bed on occasion but that seems to be all. Yet the affair between Pierre and Xavière is platonic – which leaves one wondering what was wrong with them all.) There is an undercurrent of fury and frustration running all through Françoise's cool analysis of herself and the other two, that finally explodes in murder. When Françoise turns on Xavière, she is acting out her self-hatred and her hatred of Pierre, as well as her resentment of the younger girl. Yet even pushed to this extreme, she manages to throw up a smokescreen of words to conceal her real motives.

At its best, *L'Invitée* is a powerful study of jealousy. It is less powerful than it might have been because de Beauvoir, like her heroine, never fully admits the complexity of what is happening, never admits that the ending calls in question the whole basis of the relationship between Pierre and Françoise.

The Mandarins is a much more assured book, far more public and wide-reaching in its concerns. But despite its wealth of fascinating political detail, its emotional centre is the story of a woman destroyed by love. There is a sharp line drawn between Henri and Anne, the hero and heroine. Henri is a writer, wrestling with political and literary problems. Plagued by a worn-out love affair when we first meet him, he frees himself with comparative ease and after a series of trivial but enjoyable liaisons he ends up as a reasonably contented husband and father. His loves are always marginal to his real preoccupations, and marriage seems to renew his creative drive.

The heroine, Anne Dubreuilh, lives very differently. She is a psychoanalyst, but her work never touches her very deeply. Her life centres on her writer husband Robert, and her daughter Nadine. She had married Robert, who is much older than she, as a student: they long ago ceased to sleep together, and Anne feels lonely, useless, old. In the course of the novel, she goes to America and has a passionate and idyllic love affair with a writer called Lewis Brogan. But though for a time at least she rediscovers her youth and a sensuality, this affair too ends painfully, and she comes close to killing herself. She refuses to stay with Lewis, for her real life is in Paris. Yet we get the impression that she *could* only have loved someone at a great distance, who would never really disrupt her life. The underlying implication of the book is that a woman cannot integrate her sexuality in the rest of her life as men do. It is a superb, and depressing, study of the way women are divided against themselves. This is equally true of the minor characters. Henri's mistress, Paule, pins her whole life to that one affair and goes half-crazy when it ends. Paradoxically she seems most tragic and vulnerable when she is 'analysed' out of her fantasies into a normal active life. Anne's daughter Nadine, on the other hand, is completely promiscuous. Having lost her real love in the war, she cannot feel deeply for anyone. Though she is happier at the end, less angry and destructive, there seems little chance that she will find lasting fulfilment in her marriage to Henri. There is some suggestion that Nadine is repeating the kind of marriage her mother made twenty years earlier, and though she is very different from Anne, she may find herself, in middle age as lonely and troubled.

Anne's affair with Brogan, de Beauvoir has pointed out, is closely based on her own affair with Algren, though she reminds us that Anne is not herself.

It was mainly the negative aspects of my experience that I expressed through her: the fear of dying and the panic of nothingness, the vanity of earthly diversions, the shame of forgetting, the scandal of living. The joys of existence, the pleasure of writing, all those I bestowed on Henri. He resembles me at least as much as Anne does, perhaps more.[80]

She rightly defends herself against criticisms that she did not choose a more 'positive' heroine; a woman who 'assumed an equal role with men in the realm of professional and political responsibilities'. Yet I think she may be glossing over a real problem. Even today it is curiously difficult for women novelists to portray women *except* in terms of their emotions, their private lives. (One of the few exceptions that springs to mind is Doris Lessing's *The Golden Notebook*. It is not that her heroine Anna is any less unhappy and divided. The point is that she is *also* the focus for the novel's very considerable political and social interests.) De Beauvoir goes on to explain that she depicted women 'as for the most part, I saw them, and as I still see them today: divided'.

My point is simply that the division within women – or rather the division between the sexes – is such a powerful theme in this book, and in most of her novels, that it is hardly possible to believe that she is simply reflecting on something external to herself. The unhappiness of love and its inevitable frustrations seems to engage the deepest part of her imagination, though she continues to insist that she was never in any personal danger of dependence.

The same themes recur in her last two pieces of fiction. *Les Belles Images* is about an attractive young wife and mother, Laurence, with a fashionable job in advertising, who gradually realizes how shallow all her relationships are, how empty of meaning her whole life. She sees no hope for herself but is determined, somehow, to see that things are different. Monique, the heroine of the title story in the collection *The Woman Destroyed* is older, even more hopeless. Her husband leaves her for another woman, and she realizes in horror how long she has been deluding herself about her marriage, how she has pretended that time stands still and love stays the same forever. Both characters are sympathetically seen, but the stories read more like cautionary tales, examples of what can happen to women. De Beauvoir's cool style keeps them at a distance from herself and from us; they remain rather flat, one dimensional. (The difference is obvious if you compare, say *Les Belles Images*, with a recent novel by Doris Lessing, *The Summer Before The Dark*, which is also about a middle-aged woman trapped by the comfortable domestic life that has been her whole life. We feel for her, and with her; she comes alive, with an imaginative depth that seems to elude de Beauvoir.)

The only exception in these later stories is the heroine of *The Age of Discretion* – a successful woman academic who finds that her work, to which she is totally committed, begins to lose its meaning in the face of old age. In the last few years de Beauvoir has been increasingly concerned with the problems of ageing, and some of her most disturbing work has come out of that preoccupation. The idea and experience of old age in some ways undermines her whole definition of what it is to be human. It destroys the concept of self definition through willed exploits, of life as a continued transcendence of nature, of the future as the only justification for the present. Her long theoretical work *Old Age* is both moving and paradoxical, because de Beauvoir continues to maintain her limited rational perspective against the last enemy. It is both a triumph and, as it has to be, a defeat.

*

Each of the three writers I have been considering, though widely separated in time, was fighting essentially the same battle. Though Martineau disapproved of Wollstonecraft, though de Beauvoir's direct sources are French not English, they all belong to the same bourgeois feminist tradition – the centuries old struggle for equality with man. All three argue for our right to escape from an artificial and degrading femininity and to be fully human. As Wollstonecraft put it with typical aggressiveness, if understanding and virtue are defined as masculine, women should 'every day grow more and more masculine'. Or as she said elsewhere: 'I do earnestly wish to see the distinction of sex confounded in society, unless where love animates the behaviour.'

It is an interesting qualification. Wollstonecraft spent much of her life trying to reconcile love and motherhood – the difficult life of the emotions – with being an intellectual. Her clear and forceful demand for equal rights was increasingly complicated. She came to see, on the one hand, the profound injustice of the society in which she was seeking equality; and on the other, the chaos of her own feelings, of woman's psychology. She is an extraordinarily open and suggestive writer who speaks directly to us today. Many of her insights were lost in the nineteenth century. Feminists like Harriet Martineau had to fight so hard to win a place for themselves in a man's world that they exhausted all their energies. Martineau, with her tough, consciously masculine intellect and her puritan respectability, is characteristic of many nineteenth-century feminists. But she was striking because she managed to confront the fact that she had been able to develop only part of herself, that she had lost as well as gained. De Beauvoir, like Martineau, made a powerful attack on the masculine ideology of femininity – but at the cost of adopting that ideology herself. She has developed and refined Wollstonecraft's first fumbling attempts to explore the social and economic significance of woman's oppression; but she has not confronted the deeper contradictions of women's psychological life.

All three writers seem to me most illuminating, most thought-provoking, just where they are most confused; where they try to envisage those parts of themselves that elude their rational constructs and polemical demands. The problems facing women who are trying to redefine themselves and their possibilities may be insoluble at the moment. We are inevitably torn between masculine and feminine identities. But feminism cannot afford to throw out the whole notion of femininity, however mystifying and limiting it is. We need to redefine both masculinity and femininity, and not deny all meaning to the terms in the name of an abstract humanity. The demand for equality as human beings and the attack on the feminine mystique remain crucial tactics for the women's movement, but there are signs we are moving beyond them. Wollstonecraft, Martineau and de Beauvoir are our feminist past, and we need to fully recover and understand their lives and work before we can reimagine ourselves.

12

Women and Equality*

JULIET MITCHELL

As a number of people, such as Charles Fourier and Karl Marx, have commented, the position of women in any given society can be taken as a mark of the progress of civilization or *humanization* within that society. There may be slave societies, like that of the Ptolemies, in which there is an élite of privileged women, but it is not such an élite that we are talking about when we consider the position of women in general as the index of human advance: men and women actually become human in relation to each other and if one sex is denigrated as a sex then humanity itself is the loser. I do not mean this in the simple sense that any exploitation or oppression diminishes the dignity of the whole society – though that is, of course, the case – but in the rather special sense that it is precisely in his transformation of the functions of sexuality and reproduction and communication into emotional relationship and language that at a basic level man as an animal becomes man as a human being. If we consider that within this process women as a social group have been oppressed, then we can see the depth of the problem. However, rather than hesitating at the edge because the question is too large for contemplation, it is obviously worth considering smaller, specific aspects. In this essay I shall present a selective history of the conscious protest that women have made against their position.

Biological differences between men and women obviously exist but it is not these that are the concern of feminism. Society in its preliminary organization distinguishes the sexes as social groups in many different ways. But, so far as it is known, what-

*A slightly different version of this essay was delivered as The Sixteenth T. B. Davie Memorial Lecture at the University of Cape Town in 1975 and published in *Partisan Review*.

ever the way, women are always disadvantaged in this distinction. Opposition to this situation is always a possibility, but I think that it is important to separate conscious from unconscious opposition. Modern feminism, particularly in America, is anxious to trace its own history and in doing so has identified medieval witches, among others, as its ancestors. Witches defended female crafts and medical skills against encroaching male professionalism and a violently patriarchal church. Witchcraft is one cultural form of female protest and a history of this and other forms would be very interesting. But my argument is that feminism as a conscious political ideology is not trans-historical, it cannot be generalized as just any form of female protest. That is to say that it is not produced by the general conditions of all societies which for their functioning (indeed for their existence) divide men and women as social groups. Instead feminism arises only in very particular historical circumstances. An exemplary instance of these circumstances would seem to be found in England in the seventeenth century.

There are several implications to the thesis that feminism arises in the type of historical conditions found in England in the seventeenth century. I think that not the least of these is the suspicion that I am discussing what is known in the women's movement as 'bourgeois feminism'. Not only am I ignoring, for the reasons just stated, the heroic struggles of women in other social contexts, but in claiming that feminism, if it is to be given any precise meaning, starts as an awareness by middle-class women I am ignoring the massive contribution of working-class women to its formation. I seem to be confirming the current media myths that it is only privileged women who protest. But some distinctions here are mandatory.

'Bourgeois feminism' in the mid twentieth century must indicate a tendency within the women's movement that believes that its demands can be met within the context of the present capitalist society. It is not that the feminists in the seventeenth century were not largely from the bourgeois class – they were – but that such a perspective had a very different meaning in that period. Of course working-class women, ex-slave women, women from the *lumpen*-proletariat and so on contributed to, reshaped and developed feminism, but in its essential meaning it seems to me to have been the conception of middle-class women or, at least, a conception that initially spoke to and for them. If we look at the moment in which they first formulate it I suggest that even the most ardent socialist feminist will have nothing to be ashamed of in her origins. However, such a demonstration does involve a very selective history. In trying to pinpoint this bourgeois tradition I shall select those who demonstrate it best. Furthermore I have elicited one aspect of bourgeois thought that seems to me to make the connection between the rise of feminism and the ideology of capitalism most clearly – this aspect is the concept of equality.

All democratic countries have as one of their highest aspirations the attaining of equality among their citizens, but in no democratic country in the world do women have equal rights with men. England has been a democratic country for over three hundred years, equality has been a guiding principle; yet this is how the authors of a recent survey of women's rights in Britain introduce their researches:

At no level of society do [women] have equal rights with men. At the beginning of the nineteenth century, women had virtually no rights at all. They were the chattels of their fathers and husbands. They were bought and sold in marriage. They could not vote. They could not sign contracts. When married, they could not own property. They had no rights over their children and no control over their own bodies. Their husbands could rape and beat them without fear of legal reprisals. When they were not confined to the home, they were forced by growing industrialization to join the lowest levels of the labour force. *Since then, progress towards equal rights for women has been very slow indeed.* (My italics)[1]

The authors go on to document how in work, education, social facilities and under law women are treated as men's inferiors and, despite such appearances as equal pay acts, equality is never attained.

Equal rights are an important tip of an iceberg that goes far deeper. That they are only the tip is both a reflection of the limitation of the concept of equality and an indication of how profound and fundamental is the problem of the oppression of women. The position of women as a social group in relation to men as another social group goes far deeper, then, than the question of equal rights, but not only are equal rights an important part of it but they have the most intimate connection with the whole history of feminism as a conscious social and political movement.

What then could be seen to be the strengths and limitations of the concept of equality? I plan to give a parallel account: first, the meaning of the concept of equality followed by an attempt to relate it to the history of feminism and then some suggestions on how we must, while never undervaluing it, go beyond equality. In using England one is fortunate in that England does present something of a model – an exemplary case – of the historical connections I want to make. But, with obviously important variations, all capitalist and later industrial capitalist countries have crucial similarities and it should be possible to slot another particular example into the general framework provided by English history.

The economic development of capitalism is always uneven and the ideological world view that goes with economic development will likewise be uneven and not necessarily develop in a parallel manner. I do not intend to consider, except cursorily, the material economic and social base either of the development of capitalism or of the position of women, but only some particular ideologies and politics that go with it. One consequence of the uneven development of any ideological world view has an effect intrinsic to the presentation of this argument here: as I am tracing a continuity in ideas, the discontinuities will get short shrift. The material position of women and the attitudes towards them have zigzagged like a cake-walk or the proverbial snail up the side of a well – two slithers up and one slither down, sometimes one up and two down, as the authors quoted earlier record:

. . . progress towards equal rights for women has been very slow indeed. There have even been times when the tide seemed to turn against them. The first law against abortion was passed in 1803. It imposed a sentence of life imprisonment for termination within the first fourteen weeks of pregnancy. In 1832 the first law was passed which forbade women to vote in elections. In 1877 the first Trades Union Congress upheld the tradition that women's place was in the home whilst man's duty was to protect and provide for her.[2]

Certainly both the history of feminism and the ideology of equality in general and for women in particular offer a monument to the law of uneven development. It is a monument I shall largely pass by in selecting the continuous track.

Equality as a principle – never as a practice – has been an essential part of the political ideology of all democratic capitalist societies since their inception. In being this it has expressed both the highest aspiration and the grossest limitation of that type of society. The mind of liberal and social democratic man soars into the skies with his belief in equality only to find that it must return chained, like the falcon, to the wrist whence it came. For it is not only that capitalist society (which produces its own version of both liberal and social democratic thought) cannot produce the goods or practise what it preaches but that the premise on which it bases its faith in equality is a very specific and a very narrow one. The capitalist system establishes as the premise of its ideological concept of equality the economic fact of an exchange of commodities: a commodity exchanged for another of roughly equal value. In overthrowing the noble landlords of a preceding period the newly arising and revolutionary bourgeoisie made free and equal access to the production and exchange of commodities the basis of man's estate: individual achievement replaced aristocratic birth.

In England in the late fifteenth century, the absolutist monarchy first overcame the multiplicity of feudal lords and the multifariousness of competing jurisdictions of secular and temporal powers. As happened later in France, for example, the central power of the still largely feudal monarch created and integrated large economic areas and established an equality of duties. The notion of equality of duties stands midway between a system of privilege asserted by feudal landlords and the concept of equality of rights propounded by the capitalist middle classes in the seventeenth century in England and the late eighteenth century in France. The legal edifice which enshrined the new equality of rights replaced the harmony between a law of privilege and economic privilege with a complete disjuncture between legal equality and economic disparity – if disparity is not too mild a word to fit the bill.

In bourgeois ideology everyone has access to the dominant entrepreneurial class; in the capitalist economy that it expresses, of course, the majority of the people do not. For the accumulation of capital – which is the rationale of capitalism – profits must be made; for profits to be made there is one particular commodity that cannot be equally exchanged and it is the only commodity that the majority of the population possess – the commodity of labour power. In a capitalist system the person who has only one commodity to sell (his labour power) is thought to be doing this in a free and equal way – no one enforces his labour and he is paid a 'fair' wage for the job. But in fact, if profits are to be made and capital to accumulate, there is no way in which a wage could be *equal* to the proferred labour-power – the labour-power must produce *more* than the wage answers for, else where is the profit to come from? (The worker's labour-power, which is in a sense himself, produces a surplus.) The freedom to work is little more than the freedom not to go hungry: the equal bargaining power of employer and employee is the right of the employer to hire or dismiss the employee and the right of the employee to be dismissed or go on strike – without a wage.

Under capitalism 'equality' can only refer to equality under the law. Because it cannot take into account the fundamental inequities of the class society on which it is based, the law itself must treat men as a generalizable and abstract category, it must ignore not only their individual differences, their different needs and abilities, but the absolute differences in their social and economic positions. Since the seventeenth century the law has expressed this, its precondition.

Bourgeois, capitalist law is a general law that ensures that everybody is equal before it: it is abstract and applies to all cases and all persons. As the political theorist Franz Neumann writes: 'A minimum of equality is guaranteed, for if the law-maker must deal with persons and situations in the abstract he thereby treats persons and situations as equals and is precluded from discriminating against any specific person.'[3] In writing further of the concept of political freedom with which the bourgeois concept of equality is very closely linked, Neumann continues to analyse this particular capitalist notion of law in these terms:

The generality of the law is thus the precondition of judicial independence, which, in turn, makes possible the realization of the minimum liberty and equality that inheres in the formal structure of the law.

The formal structure of the law is, moreover, equally decisive in the operation of the social system of a competitive-contractual society. The need for calculability and reliability of the legal and administrative system was one of the reasons for the limitation of the power of the patrimonial monarchy and of feudalism. The limitation culminated in the establishment of the legislative power of parliaments by means of which the middle classes controlled the administrative and fiscal apparatus and exercised a condominium with the crown in changes of the legal system. A competitive society requires general laws as the highest form of purposive rationality, for such a society is composed of a large number of entrepreneurs of about equal power. Freedom of the commodity market, freedom of the labour market, free entrance into the entrepreneurial class, freedom of contract, and rationality of the judicial responses in disputed issues – these are the essential characteristics of an economic system which requires and desires the production for profit, and ever renewed profit in a continuous, rational capitalistic enterprise.[4]

The law, then, enshrines the principles of freedom and equality – so long as you do not look at the particular unequal conditions of the people who are subjected to it. The concept 'equal under the law' does not apply to the economic inequities it is there to mask. The law is general, therefore, as *men* – employer and employee – are equal, the law does not consider the inequality of their position. Equality always denies the inequality inherent in its own birth as a concept. The notions of equality, freedom or liberty do not drop from the skies; their meaning will be defined by the particular historical circumstances that give rise to them in any given epoch. Rising as the slogan of a bourgeois revolution, equality most emphatically denies the new class inequalities that such a revolution sets up – the equality exists only as an abstract standard of measurement between people reduced to their abstract humanity under the law.

Those seem to me to be some of the limitations of the concept of equality – what of its strengths? When a rising bourgeoisie is struggling against an old feudal order, that is, before it has firmly constituted itself as the dominant class, in its aspirations it does in some sense represent all the social classes that were subordinate previously: its revolution initially is a revolution on behalf of all the oppressed against the then dominant class – the nobility. The ideological concepts that the bourgeoisie will forge in this struggle are universalistic ones – they are about *most* people and the society most people want. New formulations about 'human nature' will jostle with old ones and eventually set themselves as permanent truths. New values, such as a belief in the supremacy of reason, will be treated as though they have always been the pinnacle to which men try to ascend. These ideas will seem to be not only timeless but classless. Equality is one of them. Equality is the aspiration of the bourgeoisie at the moment when as the revolutionary class it momentarily represents all classes.

The liberal universalistic concept of equality, encapsulating the highest and best aspirations of the society, is represented by these words of Jeremy Taylor's:

> If a man be exalted by reason of any excellence in his soul, he may please to remember that all souls are equal, and their differing operations are because their instrument is in better tune, their body is more healthful or better-tempered; which is no more praise to him than it is that he were born in Italy.[5]

Taylor recognizes that there are differences but these should not count. It is this universalistic aspect of the concept that has continued in the most ennobled liberal and social-democratic thought within capitalism; because it is instituted as a demand of the revolutionary moment it soars above the conditions that create it, but because this revolution is based on these conditions – the conditions of creating two new antagonistic 'unequal' classes – to these conditions it must eventually return trapped by the hand that controls even its flight.

A history of the concept of equality would run in tracks very similar to a history of feminism. First introduced as one of the pinnacles of the new society's ideology in revolutionary England of the seventeenth century, the notion of equality next reached a further high in the era of enlightenment in the eighteenth century and then with the French Revolution. Feminism likewise has both the continuity and the fits and starts of this trajectory. Feminism as a conscious, that is self-conscious, protest movement, arose as part of a revolutionary bourgeois tradition that had equality of mankind as its highest goal. The first expressions of feminism were endowed with the strengths of the concept of equality and circumscribed by its limitations. Feminism arose in England in the seventeenth century as a conglomeration of precepts and a series of demands by women who saw themselves as a distinct sociological group and one that was completely excluded from the tenets and principles of the new society. The seventeenth-century feminists were mainly middle-class women who argued their case in explicit relation to the massive change in society that came about with the end of feudalism and the beginning of capitalism. As the new bourgeois man held the torch up against absolutist tyranny and argued for freedom and equality, the new bourgeois woman wondered why she was being left out.

Writing on marriage in the year seventeen hundred, Mary Astell asked:

... If Absolute Sovereignty be not necessary in a State how comes it to be so in a Family? or if in a Family why not in a State; since no reason can be alleg'd for the one that will not hold more strongly for the other,

and:

If *all Men are born free*, how is it that all Women are born slaves? As they must be if the being subjected to the *inconstant*, *uncertain*, *unknown*, *arbitrary Will* of Men, be the perfect Condition of Slavery? [6]

How could men proclaim social change and a new equality in the eyes of the Lord and consistently ignore one half of the population? It is to the values of the revolutionary society and against those of the old that the feminists appealed. The old society was represented by arbitrary rule, superstition, irrational custom and pointless pedantry of argument – more problematic were the continued use of two otherwise respected sources – Aristotle and the Bible.

Aristotle's contribution to the debate on the status of women can be summarized by his comment: '... and woman is, as it were, an impotent male, for it is through a certain incapacity that the female is female' and the arguments the women made against this were organized around a thorough refutation of any *natural* inferiority: there was no physical, 'bodily' difference in men and women's minds (it was left to the nineteenth century to try and prove by measurement that there was a physiological sexual defect here). The power of reason was the mark of mankind's superiority over the beasts, if women were deficient in this it could only be as a result of their lack of educational and social opportunities for improving their minds.

Considerable ingenuity was spent reinterpreting the assumed mysogyny of the Bible. Mary Astell demonstrated that St Paul in crucial passages was arguing not literally but allegorically, yet beneath the sophistication of her own argument there is a simple appeal to the new common-sensical aspect of reason:

For the Earthly *Adam's* being *Form'd* before *Eve*, seems as little to prove her Natural Subjection to him, as the Living Creatures, Fishes, Birds and Beasts being Form'd before them both, proves that Mankind must be subject to these Animals.[7]

The feminists ask for the equal status that they insist any reasonable person must grant they should have by right of all the professed values of the society. As the anonymous author of 'An Essay in Defence of the Female Sex' writes in her dedication to Princess Ann of Denmark: 'I have only endeavour'd to reduce the Sexes to a Level, and by Arguments to raise Ours to an Equality at the most with Men.'[8] The arguments for equality are still valid in all democratic societies and few of these feminist demands for equal rights (mainly to education and professional employment) have been adequately met. But the demands for equality are permeated with something more radical still.

I want to select three aspects of the seventeenth-century feminists' arguments that make it clear this was the beginning of political feminism. First, in rejecting women as naturally different from men they are forced to define women as a distinct *social* group with its own socially defined characteristics. Second, as a result of this they see that men *as a social group* oppress women as a social group – they are not against men as such but against the social power of men; women's oppression as they put it is due to 'the Usurpation of Men, and the Tyranny of Custom'. Finally while they want to be let into men's privileged sphere they also want men to learn something from women; though they wouldn't have used exactly these terms the feminization of men is as important as the masculinization of women – they do not undervalue female powers only their abuse. In the quotation from the anonymous author that I have just cited we should note that there are two clauses: she wants to be equal to men *and* her arguments have endeavoured 'to reduce the Sexes to a Level'. There is a current Chinese slogan that says 'anything a man can do a woman can do too'; feminism in the seventeenth century, as today, would add: 'anything a woman can do a man can do too' – though the seventeenth-century terms for this sexual 'levelling' are slightly different.

The mental agility of women is valuable. 'I know' (writes our anonymous author) 'our Opposers usually mis-call our Quickness of Thought, Fancy and Flash, and christen their own Heaviness by the specious Names of Judgement and Solidity: but it is easy to retort upon 'em the reproachful ones of Dulness and Stupidity with more Justice',[9] and she goes on to claim that potentially the women's world of care-for-others could be as much a repository of the highest values of civilization as the men's world of pursuing material gain – there is nothing in itself wrong with domesticity; it is only women's enforced exclusive confinement thereto and men's self-imposed exclusion therefrom that creates the evil; but given this exclusiveness then indeed it is evil. As the Duchess of Newcastle somewhat fancifully wrote in 1662:

... men are so unconscionable and cruel against us, as they endeavour to Barr us all Sorts or kinds of Liberty, as not to suffer us Freely to associate amongst our own sex, but, would fain Bury us in their houses or Beds, as in a Grave; the truth is, we live like Bats or owls, Labour like Beasts, and Dye like worms.[10]

The early feminists do not consciously congregate as a political movement but they do propose to establish female groups usually for educational and self-educational purposes – they want to develop 'friendship' among women. (The urge for female friend-ship bears a resemblance to the desire for sisterhood as it is advocated in the Women's Movement today.) Clearly a larger rebellion crossed their minds:

> . . . women are not so well united [writes Mary Astell] as to form an Insurrection. They are for the most part Wise enough to Love their Chains, and to discern how very becomingly they sit. They think as humbly of themselves as their Masters can wish, with respect to the other Sex, but in regard to their own, they have a Spice of Masculine Ambition, every one would Lead, and none will Follow . . . therefore as to those Women who find themselves born for Slavery, and are so sensible of their own Meanness to conclude it impossible to attain to anything excellent, since they are, or ought to be, the best acquainted with their own Strength and Genius, She's a Fool who would attempt their Deliverance and Improvement. No, let them enjoy the great Honor and Felicity of their Tame, Submissive and Depending Temper! Let the Men applaud, and let them glory in, this wonderful Humility![11]

It was left to later generations of women to try and devise a way of solving the problem of the masculine ambition to lead and of overcoming the apathy of feminine contentment – both are struggles that still continue. But less ironic and more strident than Mary Astell, the Duchess of Newcastle could wish she 'were so fortunate, as to persuade you to make a frequentation, association, and combination amongst our sex, that we may unite in Prudent consuls, to make ourselves as Free, Happy and famous as Men . . .'[12] In fact a number of groups were formed and though they lacked the larger political unity and range of reference, such 'frequentations' do bear some resemblance to the small groups which are the distinctive unit of organization within feminism today.

The seventeenth-century feminists are today frequently criticized for only wanting the liberation of the women of their own social class. Certainly whenever they explicitly thought of the labouring classes, it did not occur to them to consider that their own demands for access to education, the world of business and the professions were strikingly inappropriate for women (or men) of a lower class. When they talked of freeing 'half the world' they were oblivious of class differences. Yet I think to criticize them for being blinkered by their bourgeois vision is ahistorical and inaccurate. In so far as they came from the revolutionary class of that epoch and that they pointed out the oppressions that still existed, they did speak for all women. I said earlier that at the point where it is challenging an old order a revolutionary class speaks a universalistic language initially on behalf of all oppressed groups. If this is true in general it must be true for women – the seventeenth-century feminists appealed in a universalistic language on behalf of women to the highest concepts of freedom and humanity of which their society was capable. Even the very precepts of a revolutionary change, in any era, cannot transcend the social conditions that give rise to them. In demanding entry into a male world, the end of men's social oppression of women and equality between the sexes, the women were truly revolutionary. They had explanations but they did not have a theory of how women came to be an oppressed social group, but still today we lack any such full theoretical analysis. They understood clearly enough that in their own time they were being made to live like bats and they saw the contradictions between this oppression and the ideology of liberty and equality; at that historical point to go beyond such insight and such forceful protest could only be millenianism – as they well knew. In a final dedication to Queen Anne of her book on marriage, Mary Astell addresses the future: 'In a word, to those Halcyon, or if you will *Millennium* Days, in which the Wolf and the Lamb shall feed together, and a Tyrannous Domination which Nature never meant, shall no longer render useless if not hurtful, the Industry and Understanding of half Mankind!'[13]

When feminism next really reached a new crescendo, with Condorcet and Mary Wollstonecraft and the French Revolution, it was the hurtfulness not the uselessness of the oppression of women that was uppermost in the writers' minds. The principles were clear, Condorcet was emphatic in stating them. 'Either no member of the human race has real rights, or else all have the same; he who votes against the rights of another, whatever his religion, colour or sex, thereby adjures his own.'[14] It is as bad to be tyrants as to be slaves, men and women are degraded by the oppression of women. But what is new to the argument, and best expressed in Mary Wollstonecraft's *A Vindication of the Rights of Women* (1792) is the constant analysis of the damage done to women and therefore to society by conditioning them into inferior social beings. The theme is present in the seventeenth century, but a hundred years of confirmation has made its mark: 'femininity' has been more clearly defined as fragility, passivity and dependence – economic and emotional. Wollstonecraft inveighs against such false refinement:

In short, women, in general ... have acquired all the follies and vices of civilization, and missed the useful fruit ... Their senses are inflamed, and their understandings neglected, consequently they become the prey of their senses, delicately termed sensibility, and are blown about by every momentary gust of feeling. Civilized women are therefore so weakened by false refinement, that, respecting morals, their condition is much below what it would be were they left in a state near to nature.[15]

Between the end of the seventeenth and the end of the eighteenth century it would seem that among the middle classes the social definition of sexual differences had been more forcefully asserted; the behavioural characteristics of 'masculinity' and 'femininity' had drawn further apart. Behind Wollstonecraft's energetic analysis is a dilemma with which we are still familiar: if a woman strives not to fall for the lure of feminine subservience she is labelled 'masculine', in which case what happens to her legitimate femininity or 'femaleness'? How can one be a woman, indeed womanly, and avoid the social stereotypes? The answer is a concept of humanity which more urgently unifies the social characteristics of men and women:

A wild wish has just flown from my heart to my head, and I will not stifle it, though it may excite a horse-laugh. I do earnestly wish to see the distinction of sex confounded in society, unless where love animates the behaviour.[16]

In fact Wollstonecraft, while asserting equality as a human right, has to some degree moved away from what I have characterized as an essentially liberal position into one that we might describe as radical humanism. Though like the seventeenth-century writers her highest good is reason and she demonstrates that women are inferior because they have been subjugated – not as is usually argued that they are subjugated because they are inferior – yet there is a new political dimension to her feminism. Where her English predecessors were demanding the practice consistent with the revolutionary values of their society, Wollstonecraft, living in the double context of by then reactionary Britain yet having the inspiration of the French Revolution, wanted not a change *within* society but a change *of* society:

> I do not believe that a private education can work the wonders which some sanguine writers have attributed to it. Men and women must be educated, in a great degree, by the opinions and manners of the society they live in . . . It may . . . fairly be inferred, that, till society be differently constituted, much cannot be expected from education.[17]

and,

> Rousseau exerts himself to prove that all *was* right originally: a crowd of authors that all *is* now right: and I, that all *will be* right.[18]

In Wollstonecraft the millennium has come down firmly from heaven to earth.

The writer to whom I wish to refer finally in this sketch of the relationship between feminism and the concept of equality is John Stuart Mill. To offer a somewhat sweeping generalization, after Mill, in England the feminist struggle moves from being predominantly the utterances of individuals about a philosophical notion of equality to being an organized political movement for the attainment, among other things, of equal rights. Of course, the one does not exclude the other, it is a question of emphasis.

In a lucid and powerful manner, Mill's essay, 'The Subjection of Women' (1869), written at the height of the Victorian repression of women, resumes with a new coherence the arguments with which we have become familiar. Thus he has a clear perspective on the argument that maddened the earlier writers, that women's characteristics and social status were 'natural': 'What is now called the nature of women is an eminently artificial thing – the result of forced repression in some directions, unnatural stimulation in others'[19] and, 'So true is it that unnatural generally means only uncustomary, and that everything which is usual appears natural. The subjection of women to men being a universal custom, any departure from it quite naturally appears unnatural'.[20] Mill also looks back with clarity on the history of democracy and of women's rights – or rather lack of them.

Where the seventeenth-century women looked to their own new society for change and Wollstonecraft, with the example of the first radical years of the French Revolution at hand, looked to change her society, Mill, writing from within an industrial capitalism that had hardened into fairly extreme conservatism had to stand aside and argue from the best of the past and the hope of the future. Most importantly, the justice and morality he wants have not yet been found in the world: 'Though the truth may not yet be felt or generally acknowledged for generations to come, the only school of genuine moral sentiment is society between equals'[21] and – 'We have had the morality of submission, and the morality of chivalry and generosity; the time is now come for the morality of justice.'[22]

But Mill's lucidity, unlike Wollstonecraft's exuberance, forces him to constrict his own vision. Although at one moment he speculates that the reason why women are denied equal rights in society at large is because men must confine them to the home and the family, he does not pursue the implications of this insight and instead programmatically demands these rights. When it comes down to it, his equality is, quite realistically, equality under the law:

... on women this sentence is imposed by actual law, and by customs equivalent to law. What, in unenlightened societies, colour, race, religion or, in the case of a conquered country, nationality, are to some men, sex is to all women; a peremptory exclusion from almost all honourable occupations, but either such as cannot be fulfilled by others, or such as those others do not think worthy of their acceptance.[23]

and

... the principle which regulates the existing social relations between the two sexes – the legal subordination of one sex to the other – is wrong in itself, and now one of the chief hindrances to human improvement.[24]

I am not arguing against Mill's position but trying to indicate a lack that is implicit in this perspective. Mill's concept of human beings that are freed from the artificial constraints of a false masculinity or femininity is somehow more abstract than that of the earlier feminists. The seventeenth-century women thought if men and women were equal they could gain some quality from each other. Mary Wollstonecraft's vision combined in one being the best of a female world with the best of a male world. Mill correctly argues that we cannot know what men and women will be like when released from present stereotypes but out of this correctness comes an elusive feeling that Mill, seeing so accurately women's miserable subordination, failed to see their contribution. This turns on the question of the importance of the reproduction and care of human life – Mill does not see, as Wollstonecraft does, that there might be a gain in men really becoming fathers (instead of remote, authoritarian figureheads) as well as in women being freed to pursue the so-called 'masculine' virtues. That Mill's concept of humanity is abstract, that he did not seem to consider the contribution of 'femaleness' once freed of its crippling exclusiveness to oppressed women, may have been because he was a man; it may just as easily have been because of the different social circumstances from which he wrote. Because he was not living at the moment when the bourgeoisie was the revolutionary class, the universalistic aspect of such thought of which I spoke earlier must turn to abstraction, there is no other way in which it can refer to all people.

John Stuart Mill in a sense expresses the best and the last in the high liberal tradition. His ideals represent the best his society is capable of but they can no longer be felt to represent that society – as a consequence there is a sort of heroic isolation to his philosophy. Because of his isolation, because of his abstraction, in this field Mill's thought pinpoints and 'fixes' the essence of liberalism:

The old theory was, that the least possible should be left to the individual agent; that all he had to do should, as far as practicable, be laid down for him by superior powers. Left to himself he was sure to go wrong. The modern conviction, the fruit of a thousand years of experience, is that things in which the individual is the person directly interested, never go right but as they are left to his own discretion; and that any regulation of them by authority except to protect the rights of others, is sure to be mischievous. This conclusion, slowly arrived at, and not adopted until almost every possible application of the contrary theory has been made with disastrous result, now (in the industrial department) prevails universally in the most advanced countries, almost universally in all that have pretensions to any sort of advancement. It is not that all processes are supposed to be equally good, or all persons to be equally qualified for everything; but that freedom of individual choice is now known to be the only thing which procures the adoption of the best processes, and throws each operation into the hands of those who are best qualified for it.[25]

Mill's philosophy is an overriding belief in the individual and in the right of the individual to fulfil his or her maximum potential, Mill's concept of equality is therefore an equality of opportunity. As a politician he fought for equal rights for women under the law.

Since Mill wrote there has, I think, been, in an uneven way, a decline in the tradition of liberal thought. Today, exactly three quarters of the way through the twentieth century, 'equality' would seem to have become a somewhat unfashionable concept. Equal rights are still strenuously fought for but equality as the principle of a just and free society rarely elicits the eloquent support it once received. I am neither a philosopher nor a political scientist and I am ill-equipped to analyse why this should be the case. I can, however, point to some observations we all might make.

The concept of equality as a high ideal flourishes as a revolutionary aspiration when it is confronted with two types of conservatism – as Mill's was in Victorian England. One type of conservatism is a direct reflection of the economic conditions of a society once the society had settled down after its revolutionary open-endedness. When class distinctions have rigidified, then the conservative ideology of capitalism can bear a striking resemblance to the old order the revolutionary bourgeoisie once overthrew. In its naked crudity this conservatism is found in Arthur Young's statement: '... everyone but an idiot knows that the lower classes must be kept poor, or they will never be industrious'[26] or in a verse of a hymn popular in England in the years before the First World War:

> The rich man in his castle,
> The poor man at his gate,
> God made them high or lowly
> And ordered their estate.[27]

The best liberal traditions of liberty, equality and individualism such as those represented by Mill rarely engaged directly with conservatism of this sort, but their presence as an alternative *within* the same society hopefully acts to circumscribe the possible power of such reactionary stances.

There is another conservative tradition that is more testing for the liberal conception of individualism and equality and that is Tory radicalism. Where conservative conservatism argues that there are generic differences which must be the basis of inequalities between groups of people, Tory radicalism, like liberalism and, for that matter socialism and communism, argues that there are differences between individuals. The litmus test here for establishing a distinction between the political philosophies is to see what happens to these individual differences. Tory radicalism always offers a place in the past, a romantic golden age when society was small enough for all these differences to flourish – merely as differences, be they handicaps or advantages. The liberal concept that I have presented here, argues that we are all different but these differences can only be realized in their infinite variety if we are given equal opportunities to make what we individually and differently can of them – they cannot be the basis of different treatment. The socialist and communist perspective suggests that 'equality' in capitalist society is based on class inequality; in a classless society there will still be differences or inequalities, inequalities between individuals, strengths or handicaps of various kinds. There will be differences between men and women, differences among women and among men; a truly just society based on collective ownership and equal distribution would take these inequalities into account and give more to he who needed more and ask for more from he who could give more. This would be a true recognition of the individual in the qualities that are essential to his humanity.

When the liberal concept of equality – the ideal of a revolutionary bourgeoisie – has to oppose not conservatism, as it did in Mill's case, but a system of thinking such as that of socialism which looks to a new future, then its own radicalism is weakened and that is what has been happening in a somewhat sporadic fashion since the last part of the last century.

A crisis in the history of the concept of equality can, I think, be marked by one book that epitomizes the problem: the publication of the Halley Stewart lectures that the socialist historian, R. H. Tawney gave in 1929. The book, entitled *Equality*, is a most moving document – a humanitarian plea for equality as, quite simply, a correct, indeed *the* correct principle of civilization. The framework within which Tawney argues for equality is that of moral and ethical philosophy, the terms in which he assesses the progress of equality are those of poverty and disparity of opportunity particularly in education. There is no underlying analysis of a class-antagonistic society and even in the lengthy epilogue written in 1950 the racial minorities in Britain are not mentioned, the position of women is not hinted at. Yet Tawney's own recommendations transcend the limitations of his belief in equality: he must argue for redistribution of wealth and for more collective provision of social services. His argument follows the liberal tradition but starts to look beyond it and sees that the freedom of privilege must be controlled; that freedom in a class society is ultimately freedom for one class to exploit another.

It was not malicious oversight that made Tawney fail to see women as a deprived group – when he was writing women were simply not seen as a group at all. Ten years before he wrote and roughly fifteen years after his epilogue they were seen as a group once more. Feminism had in both cases pointed to the fact. In 1974, using the very criteria by which Tawney estimated the march of equality – poverty – a survey carried out in Britain found that women were the single most impoverished social group. The survey was not carried out by feminists, but feminism had made the investigators conscious of this category: women were found both to be a distinct social group and an underprivileged one.

The fight for equal rights for women today takes place against this weakening of the liberal conception of equality. It is important both to remember that ideal and to realize its limitations. Too many revolutionary groups would skip the present and think that given both a falseness in the conception and its ultimate unrealizability, 'equality' is not something to be fought for: too many not-so-revolutionary groups think that equal rights are attainable under class-antagonistic systems and are adequate. Equal rights will always only be rights before the law but these have by no means been won yet nor their possible extent envisaged. A new society that is built on an old society that, within its limits, has reached a certain level of equality clearly is a better starting point than one that must build on a society predicated on privilege and unchallenged oppression.*

*I am greatly indebted to Hilda Smith of the University of Maryland, Washington D.C. for introducing me to the seventeenth-century feminists, and for letting me read her excellent work on the subject prior to its publication.

Notes

1. Wisewoman and Medicine Man: Changes in the Management of Childbirth

1. Helen Gideon, 'A Baby is Born in the Punjab', *American Anthropologist*, 64, 1962, p. 1223.
2. See Ann Oakley, *Housewife*, Allen Lane, 1974, especially chapters 4, 7 and 8.
3. To say that in most non-industrialized cultures reproductive care systems are female-controlled is clearly a generalization. Although this generalization is not based on a systematic sample of small-scale societies, it emerges out of an extensive reading of the ethnographic literature. Exceptions to it may exist and various permutations on the basic theme may be found (for example, the 'shaman' or medicine man may play an advisory role); nevertheless, it does appear to be the case that in most human societies the major part of the control and practice of reproductive care rests with the women.
4. The information on the Navajo Indians comes from Clay Lockett, 'Midwives and Childbirth among the Navajo', *Plateau*, 72, 1939, pp. 15–17; that on the D'Entrecasteaux Islanders from Edward Ford, 'Notes on Pregnancy and Parturition in the D'Entrecasteaux Islands', *The Medical Journal of Australia*, 2, 1940, pp. 498–501. This whole area abounds in methodological difficulties. Most of the historical and anthropological accounts we have are written by men; the question that has to be asked is how far their reports of the situation tally with reality as experienced by the women in any particular culture or during any particular period. A specific problem is that men are often denied access to detailed knowledge of how female-controlled reproductive care systems operate.
5. See Hilary Rose and Jalna Hanmer, 'Radical Feminism and the Technological Fix', paper presented to the British Sociological Association Annual Conference, *Sexual Divisions and Society*, Aberdeen, Scotland, 7–10 April 1974.
6. Joan Haggerty, 'Childbirth Made Difficult', *Ms*, January 1973.
7. See Eliot Freidson, *Profession of Medicine*, Dodd, Mead and Company, New York, 1971, and A. M. Carr-Saunders and P. A. Wilson, *The Professions*, Clarendon Press, 1933.
8. Judging by the contemporary sources quoted by historians; for

example in Keith Thomas's *Religion and the Decline of Magic*, Weidenfeld and Nicholson, 1971. In the witchcraft literature, women are more often mentioned than men in connection with a healing role. See, for example, Christina Hole, *A Mirror of Witchcraft*, Chatto and Windus, 1957 and Alan Macfarlane, *Witchcraft in Tudor and Stuart England*, Routledge and Kegan Paul, 1970. Richard H. Shryock has some information about lay medicine in colonial America and later periods in his *Medicine in America: Historical Essays*, John Hopkins Press, Baltimore, 1966. See also Joseph F. Kett, *The Formation of the American Medical Profession*, Yale University Press, New Haven, 1968, chapter I, 'The Weak Arm of the Law'.

9. Alice Clark, *Working Life of Women in the Seventeenth Century*, Frank Cass, 1968.

10. Almost all the herbs which composed the typical medieval garden have been found to contain some property of value to modern medicine. See Muriel Joy Hughes, *Women Healers in Medieval Life and Literature*, Morningside Heights, New York, 1943.

11. Both these quotes are taken from M. J. Hughes, op. cit., p. 50.

12. A. Clark, op. cit., p. 269.

13. '... midwifery existed on a professional basis from immemorial days ... The midwife held a recognized position in society and was sometimes well educated and well paid ... it is certain that women of a high level of intelligence and possessing considerable skill belonged to the profession.' A. Clark, op. cit., pp. 265, 268.

14. Barbara Ehrenreich and Deidre English's pamphlet, *Witches, Midwives and Nurses* (Glass Mountain Pamphlets), makes the connection between healing, midwifery and witchcraft roles, but does not present precise evidence about the degree of overlap. Thomas Forbes's *The Midwife and the Witch* (Yale University Press, New Haven, 1966) asks the question whether midwives were witches but fails to provide an answer. Keith Thomas (op. cit.) simply says that 'popular magicians' went under a variety of names, including 'wisewoman', 'sorcerer' and 'witch' (p. 178). The sexual hostility interpretation of witchcraft is offered for Continental witchcraft especially, see Mary Douglas (ed.), *Witchcraft Confessions and Accusations*, Tavistock Publications, 1970. Accusations of sexual perversions and orgies with the devil are not found very often in English witchcraft material.

15. John Demos, 'Underlying Themes in the Witchcraft of Seventeenth-Century New England', *American Historical Review*, 1970, pp. 1311–26.

16. Quoted in Geoffrey Parinder, *Witchcraft: European and African* Faber, 1958, p. 51.
17. See for example Norman Dennis, Fernando Henriques and Clifford Slaughter, *Coal is Our Life*, Eyre and Spottiswoode, 1956; Michael Young and Peter Willmott, *Family and Kinship in East London*, Pelican, 1962.
18. See M. J. Hughes, op cit., chapter 4, 'Academic Medicine'. On the exceptions to the rule banning women from the universities see Kate Campbell Hurt-Mead, *A History of Women in Medicine*, London, 1938.
19. See Iago Galdston (ed.), *Historic Derivations of Modern Psychiatry*, McGraw Hill, New York, 1967, p. 50.
20. Noel Poynter, *Medicine and Man*, C. A. Watts and Co, 1971.
21. Mary Douglas suggests this is, in part, because the baby – unborn or newly born – is a marginal being. On sex-differentiation and pollution beliefs generally see chapter 9, 'The System at War with Itself' in *Purity and Danger*, Routledge and Kegan Paul, 1956.
22. This example comes from James Frazer's *The Golden Bough* and is quoted by Peter Lomas in 'Childbirth Ritual', *New Society*, 31 December 1964.
23. John E. Gordon, Helen Gideon and John B. Wyon, 'Midwifery Practices in Rural Punjab, India', *American Journal of Obstetrics and Gynaecology*, 93, 1965, p. 735.
24. Brian Abel Smith, *The Hospitals: 1800–1948*, Heinemann, 1964, p. 23.
25. *Minority Report of the Royal Commission on the Poor Laws*, 1909.
26. Joint Committee of the Royal College of Obstetricians and Gynaecologists and the Population Investigation Committee, *Maternity in Great Britain*, Oxford University Press, 1949, p. 78.
27. For this reason, histories of midwifery written by male obstetricians tend to be over-concerned with the emergence of male midwives and the application of surgical procedures to childbirth; the traditional female midwife barely gets a reference (and if she is mentioned, it is usually in derogatory terms). H. R. Spencer's *The History of British Midwifery* (John Bale, Sons and Danielsson, 1927) is a classic example of this approach.
28. Like other modern delivery techniques there are indications of episiotomy being used by midwives in small-scale societies.
29. Quoted in Jean Donnison, 'The Development of the Profession of Midwife in England from 1750–1902', unpublished Ph.D. thesis, University of London, 1974, p. 62.
30. See the essay by Sally Alexander in this volume.

31. On the decline of breastfeeding see J. C. Drummond and A. Wilbraham, *The Englishman's Food*, Cape, 1958.

32. On the growth of the infant welfare movement in Britain and elsewhere see the works of C. F. McCleary, *The Early History of the Infant Welfare Movement*, H. K. Lewis and Co., 1933, and *The Maternity and Child Welfare Movements*, P. S. King and Son, 1935.

33. *Report of the Proceedings of the National Conference on Infantile Mortality*, President John Burns, published in London by P. S. King and Son, 1906, pp. 41–2.

34. See Leonore Davidoff, *The Best Circles: Society, Etiquette and the Season*, Croom Helm, 1973.

35. *Report of the Proceedings of the National Conference on Infantile Mortality*, op. cit., p. 20.

36. C. F. McCleary, op. cit., 1933, p. 127.

37. C. F. McCleary, published a book with this title in 1945 (*Race Suicide*, Allen and Unwin), but literature on the theme of national depopulation abounded in the early years of the century.

38. See Anna Davin, 'Imperialism and the Cult of Motherhood', paper presented to the British Sociological Association Annual Conference, *Sexual Divisions and Society*, Aberdeen, Scotland, 7–10 April 1974.

39. See C. F. McCleary, op cit., 1935, p. 89.

40. ibid., pp. 89–90.

41. My own father, born in 1907, was wet-nursed, but I know of no data on the general incidence of wet-nursing during this period. From the mid to the late nineteenth century doctors continued to recommend wet-nursing, but after 1900 this became less common. See Anne Roberts, 'Feeding and Mortality in the Early Months of Life; Changes in Medical Opinion and Popular Feeding Practice 1850–1900', unpublished Ph.D. thesis, University of Hull, 1973.

42. Quoted in C. F. McCleary, op. cit., 1935, p. 92.

43. John B. McKinlay, 'Some Aspects of Lower Working-Class Utilization Behaviour', unpublished Ph.D. thesis, University of Aberdeen, 1970.

44. M. S. G. Moller, 'Bahaya Customs and Beliefs in Connection with Pregnancy and Childbirth', *Tanganyika Notes and Records*, 50, 1958, pp. 112–17.

45. William Farr, *Vital Statistics*, Edward Stanford, 1885, p. 279.

46. *Report of an Investigation into Maternal Mortality*, HMSO, 1937, p. 11.

47. This is one explanation of the curious fact that, according to the *Report of an Investigation into Maternal Mortality* (op. cit.),

maternal mortality was highest in social classes I and II. In 1930–32 in England and Wales, puerperal sepsis was 20 per cent higher in social classes I and II than in social class V (p. 108).

48. The Westminster figures are cited in Donnison, op cit., p. 56; the second set of figures comes from W. Farr, op. cit., p. 274.

49. J. E. Gordon, H. Gideon and J. B. Wyon, op. cit.

50. This figure is quoted by C. F. McCleary, op. cit., 1935, p. 177. The report was the *Final Report of the Departmental Committee on Maternal Mortality and Morbidity*, 1932.

51. *Maternal Mortality in New York City*, report of the New York Academy of Medicine, 1933. The results are cited in the British *Report of an Investigation into Maternal Mortality*, op. cit., pp. 26–7.

52. Sidney and Beatrice Webb, *The State and the Doctor*, Longmans, Green and Co., 1910, pp. 58–9.

53. *Maternity in Great Britain*, op. cit., pp. 48–9. The 1972 British figure comes from the *Department of Health and Social Security Annual Report 1972*, HMSO, p. 21.

54. *Report of the Proceedings of the National Conference on Infantile Mortality*, op. cit., p. 310.

55. 'Memories of Seventy Years' by Mrs Layton in Margaret Llewellyn Davies (ed.), *Life as We Have Known it*, Co-operative Working Women, Hogarth Press, 1931.

56. ibid., pp. 30–31.

57. *Report of an Investigation into Maternal Mortality*, op. cit., p. 253.

58. *Department of Health and Social Security Annual Report 1970*, HMSO, p. 199 and *Annual Report 1973*, HMSO, p. 27.

59. Quoted in C. Fraser Brockington, *The Health of the Community*, J. and A. Churchill, 1954, p. 163.

60. Frances E. Kobrin, 'The American Midwife Controversy: A Crisis of Professionalization', *Bulletin of the History of Medicine*, July–August 1966, p. 358.

61. Quoted in B. Ehrenreich and D. English, op. cit., p. 24.

62. See F. E. Kobrin, op. cit.

63. As an example of this criticism see Ellen Frankfort, *Vaginal Politics*, Bantam Books, New York, 1973.

64. See Margaret Mead and Niles Newton, 'Cultural Patterning of Perinatal Behaviour', in Stephen A. Richardson and Alan F. Guttmacher (eds.), *Childbearing – its Social and Psychological Aspects*, Williams and Wilkins, Baltimore, 1967, pp. 210–15.

65. There is, however, a substantial amount of evidence that all drugs administered during labour and delivery have some kind of effect on the mother and/or the baby. See M. P. M. Richards, 'Some

Recent Research on the Effects of Obstetric Anaesthetics and Analgesics', Unit for Research on Medical Applications of Psychology, unpublished paper, February 1975.

66. See for example Jane Hubert, 'Belief and Reality: Social Factors in Pregnancy and Childbirth', in M. P. M. Richards (ed.), *The Integration of a Child into a Social World*, Cambridge University Press, 1974; Hazel Houghton, 'Problems of Hospital Communication', in Gordon McLachlan (ed.), *Problems and Progress in Medical Care*, third series, Oxford University Press, 1968.

67. See for example Joan Emerson, 'Behaviour in Private Places: Sustaining Definitions of Reality in Gynaecological Examinations', in H. P. Dreitzel (ed.), *Recent Sociology*, vol. II, Collier-Macmillan, 1970; Ann Oakley, 'Aspects of the Doctor–Patient Relationship in Obstetrics and Gynaecology: Some Preliminary Observations', forthcoming paper.

68. On the connections between social ideologies concerning women and medical treatment in another culture see Ian Young, *The Private Life of Islam*, Allen Lane, 1974.

69. See Sally McIntyre, 'Who Wants Babies: The Social Construction of Instincts', paper presented to the British Sociological Association Annual Conference, *Sexual Divisions and Society*, Aberdeen, Scotland, 7–10 April 1974.

70. In the history of midwifery, the importance of experience is a constant theme. It was a customary requirement that a practising midwife should have had children herself.

71. Again, female resistance to male control over women's bodies is a theme that crops up recurrently in issues to do with childbirth or child-care over the centuries.

72. Quoted in M. J. Hughes, op. cit., p. 91.

73. See J. Emerson, op. cit.; Phyllis Chesler, *Women and Madness*, Allen Lane, 1974, chapter 5, 'Sex Between Patient and Therapist'.

74. P. Lomas, op. cit., p. 14.

75. See the excellent *Our Bodies, Our Selves* produced by the Boston Women's Health Book Collective, Simon and Schuster, New York, 1972.

76. *Ms*, February 1973, p. 118.

2. Women's Work in Nineteenth-Century London: A Study of the Years 1820–50

1. For a lucid statement of the purpose and need for a feminist history, see Anna Davin, 'Women and History', in Michelene Wandor (ed.), *The Body Politic*, Stage 1, 1971.

2. For accessible contemporary accounts of the breakdown of the family, see Leon Faucher, *Manchester in 1844*, Frank Cass, 1969, pp. 47–8; Frederick Engels, 'The Condition of the Working Class in England', *Marx and Engels on Britain*, Moscow, 1962, pp. 162–3, 174–82; for Marx's view of the material effects of modern industry on the family, see *Capital*, Dona Torr (ed.), vol. 1, Allen & Unwin, 1971, pp. 495–6.

3. Lord Shaftesbury was an Evangelical Tory and social reformer. His speech to the House of Commons, 7 June 1842, is cited in Ivy Pinchbeck, *Women Workers and the Industrial Revolution, 1750–1850*, Frank Cass, 1969, p. 267.

4. For contemporary views of the effects of density of population, see for example, John Simon, *Report on the Sanitary Condition of the City of London 1849–50*, p. 86.

> It is no uncommon thing, in a room of twelve foot square or less, to find three or four families *styed* together (perhaps with infectious diseases among them) filling the same space day and night – men, women and children, in the promiscuous intimacy of cattle. Of these inmates, it is mainly superfluous to observe, that in all offices of nature they are gregarious and public, that every instinct of personal or sexual decency is stifled, that every nakedness of life is uncovered.

5. Mrs Austin, *Two Lectures on Girls' Schools, and on the Training of Working Women*, 1857, p. 12. Hannah More (education), Elizabeth Fry (prisons), Mary Carpenter (Ragged Schools), Louisa Twining (workhouses), Octavia Hill (housing and charity reform) all advocated 'industrial training' in the form of housework and needlework for their 'fallen' sisters. These women opened up social work as an appropriate activity for middle-class women. Mrs Jameson's lecture, 'The Communion of Labour', 1855, was the most influential expression of the sentiments embodied in such activities. The links between evangelicalism, respectable philanthropy and early feminism have yet to be elucidated.

6. Charles Dickens, *Bleak House*, Household Ed. p. 56.

7. 1851 Census, vol. 3, Parliamentary Papers (PP), 1852–3, LXXXVIII, table 2, p. 8.

8. For seasonality and irregularity in the London trades in the nineteenth century, see Gareth Stedman Jones, *Outcast London*, Oxford University Press, 1971, chs. 1–5; H. Mayhew, *London Labour and the London Poor*, 4 volumes, vol. 2, 1861, pp. 297–323. On p. 322, Mayhew wrote, 'I am led to believe there is considerable truth in the statement lately put forward by the working

classes, that only one third of the operatives of this country are fully employed, while another third are partially employed, and the remaining third wholly unemployed'.

9. The preface to the 1841 Census stated that,

the number of women about 20 years of age, without any occupation returned, consists generally of unmarried women living with their parents, and of the wives of professional men or shopkeepers, living upon the earnings, but not considered as carrying on the occupation of their husbands. (PP, 1844, XXVII, p. 9).

10. E. Thompson and E. Yeo, *The Unknown Mayhew*, The Merlin Press, 1971, p. 394. (Pelican, 1973). Henry Mayhew was a nineteenth-century journalist and friend of the poor. See footnote 78.

11. H. Mayhew, op. cit., vol. 3, p. 344.

12. E. Thompson and E. Yeo, op. cit., p. 407.

13. H. Mayhew, op. cit., vol. 3, p. 221 : 'As a general rule I may remark that I find the society men of every trade comprise about one tenth of the whole ... if the non-society men are neither so skilful nor well-conducted as the others, at least they are quite as important a body from the fact that they constitute the main portion of the trade.' See E. Thompson and E. Yeo, op. cit., pp. 218–19, 409–10; Iorwerth Prothero, 'Chartism in London', *Past and Present*, no. 44, 1969; and E. Thompson, *The Making of the English Working Class*, Pelican 1968, p. 277.

14. H. Mayhew, op. cit., Vol. 2, p. 155. Mudlarks are

compelled, in order to obtain the articles they seek, to wade sometimes up to their middle through the mud left on the shore by the retiring tide ... They may be seen of all ages from mere childhood to positive decrepitude, crawling among the barges at the various wharfs along the river ... mudlarks collect whatever they happen to find, such as coal, bits of old iron, rope, bones, and copper nails ... They sell to the poor.

15. Humphrey House, *The Dickens World*, Oxford University Press, 1961, p. 146.

16. Charles Dickens, *Our Mutual Friend*, Household Ed., p. 17.

17. Hector Gavin, *Sanitary Ramblings in Bethnal Green*, 1848, p. 11. See also Dr Mitchell's *Report on Handloom Weaving*, PP, 1840, XXIII, p. 239 for a description of housing in Bethnal Green.

18. Charles Dickens, *The Old Curiosity Shop*, Household Ed., p. 35.

19. Edwin Chadwick, *Report on the Sanitary Conditions of the Labouring Population of Great Britain*, 1842, p. 166.

20. *The Population Returns of 1831*, 1832, p. 14. These figures refer to the City within and without the walls.

21. Quoted in G. S. Jones, op. cit., p. 164 and see ch. 8. *passim*. See also K. Marx, op. cit., p. 674.

> Every unprejudiced observer sees that the greater the centralisation of the means of production, the greater is the corresponding heaping to-gether of the labourers, within a given space; that therefore the swifter capitalistic accumulation, the more miserable are the dwellings of the working people. 'Improvements' of towns, accompanying the increase of wealth, by the demolition of badly built quarters, the erection of palaces for banks, warehouses &c, drive away the poor into even worse and more crowded hiding places.

22. 'Report of the Statistical Society on the Dwellings in Church Lane, St Giles's', *Journal of the Statistical Society of London*, vol. xi, 1848.
23. This estimate was constructed from R. Price-Williams, 'The Population of London 1801–1881', *Journal of the Royal Statistical Society of London*, 1885, no. 48, pp. 349–432.
24. J. Hollingshead, *Ragged London in 1861*, 1861, p. 143.
25. E. Thompson and E. Yeo, op. cit., p. 122.
26. Charles Dickens, *Old Curiosity Shop*, Household Ed., p. 57.
27. Derek Hudson (ed.), *Munby, Man of Two Worlds*, J. Murray, 1972, p. 99.
28. D. George, *London Life in the Eighteenth Century*, Kegan Paul, 1930, p. 170.
29. 'Report of an Investigation into the State of the Poorer Classes of St George's in the East', *Journal of the Statistical Society of London*, August 1848, p. 203. Of the women's occupations only one gunpolisher, one yeast maker, and one coal wharf keeper fall out-side the conventional category of 'women's work'.
30. Handicraft guilds excluded division of labour within the workshop by their refusal to sell labour power as a commodity to the mer-chant capitalist. See K. Marx, op. cit., pp. 352–3.
31. ibid., p. 341. 'The collective labourer, formed by the combination of a number of detail labourers, is the machinery specially character-istic of the manufacturing period.'
32. ibid., pp. 342–3.
33. A. Clark, *Working Life of Women in the Seventeenth Century*, Frank Cass, 1968, especially pp. 154–61.
34. K. Marx, op. cit., p. 646.
35. See P. Laslett, *The World We Have Lost*, Methuen, 1971, ch. 1; A. Clark, op. cit., p. 156, for women and marriage. Spinning for example, women's most important industrial work in the manu-facturing period was ideal 'employment for odd minutes and the mechanical character of its movements which made no great tax

on eye or brain, rendered it the most adaptable of all domestic arts
to the necessities of the mother'. (ibid., p. 9.)

36. K. Marx, op. cit., p. 419.
37. Select Committee on Handloom Weavers, PP, 1834, X, q. 4359.
38. G. S. Jones, op. cit., ch. 4; Arthur Redford, *Labour Migration in
England, 1800–50*, Manchester University Press, 1964, pp. 48–9,
137–9. In times of good trade, for instance in the Spitalfields silk
industry, whole families were employed, and

> from the metropolis, the demand for labour goes into the country. All
> the old weavers are employed with their wives and families; agricultural
> labourers are engaged on every side, and everyone is urged to do all he
> can. Blemishes for which at other times a deduction from the wages
> would have been claimed, are now overlooked. Carts are sent round to
> the villages and hamlets, with the work, for the weavers, that time may
> not be lost in going to the warehouse to carry home or take out work.
> (PP, 1841, X, p. 18.)

39. Under- or un-employment was one of the features of the industrial
reserve army of labour, since the demand for labour-power followed the fluctuations of the trade cycle. See Marx, op. cit., ch. 25,
section 3. In those trades which had not been transformed by the
factory system and machinery, lengthening of the working day and
the reduction of wages below subsistence were the only means of
increasing the productiveness of labour and hence surplus value.
See ibid., pp. 302–3, 475, 484, 658–9.
40. H. Mayhew, op. cit., vol. 2, p. 312.
41. H. Mayhew, op. cit., vol. 2, p. 314.
42. An analysis of the role of women in these struggles is to be found
in Barbara Taylor, *Women Workers and the Grand National Consolidated Trades' Union*, unpublished paper, 1974.
43. Statistical Society Journal, op. cit., p. 203.
44. K. Marx, op. cit., p. 179.

> The distinction between skilled and unskilled labour rests in part on
> pure illusion, or, to say the least, on distinctions which have long since
> ceased to be real, and that survive only by virtue of a traditional con-
> vention; in part on the helpless condition of some groups of the working
> class, a condition that prevents them from exacting equally with the rest
> the value of their labour power.

45. E. Thompson and E. Yeo, op. cit., p. 518–9.
46. House of Lords Sessional Papers, 1854–5, vol. 5, p. 27.
47. E. Thompson and E. Yeo, op. cit., p. 525.
48. Mins. of Evidence, Children's Employment Commissioner, PP,
1843, XIV, f. 29.

49. E. Thompson and E. Yeo, op. cit., p. 528.
50. C. Dickens, *Sketches by Boz*, ch. III, 'Shops and Their Tenants', p. 28.
51. I. Pinchbeck, op. cit., vol. 1, p. 290.
52. H. Mayhew, op. cit., vol. 1, p. 363.
53. E. Thompson and E. Yeo, op. cit., p. 363.
54. ibid., p. 452.
55. PP, 1843, XIV, op. cit., ff. 242–3.
56. J. Grant, *Lights and Shadows of London Life*, vol. 1, 1842, p. 196.
57. PP, 1843, XIV, ff. 241–2, and following quotes from same source.
58. G. Dodds *Days at the Factory*, 1843, pp. 370–71, and following quotes from same source.
59. E. Thompson and E. Yeo, op. cit., p. 534.
60. J. R. MacDonald, *Women in the Printing Trades*, 1904, chs. 1 and 11. Summarizing the reasons why women replaced men, MacDonald wrote: 'The advantages of the woman worker are:

1. That she will accept low wages; she usually works for about half the men's wages.

2. That she is not a member of a Union, and is, therefore, more amenable to the will of the employer as the absolute rule of the workshop.

3. That she is a steady worker (much emphasis must not be placed upon this, as the contrary is also alleged), and nimble at mechanical processes, such as folding and collecting sheets.

4. That she will do odd jobs which lead to nothing.

Her disadvantages are:

1. That she has less technical skill than a man, and is not so useful all round.

2. That she has less strength at work and has more broken time owing to bad health and, especially should she be married, domestic duties, and that her output is not so great as that of a man.

3. That she is more liable to leave work just when she is getting most useful; or, expressing this in a general way, that there are more changes in a crowd of women workers than in a crowd of men workers.

4. That employers object to mixed departments.'

61. G. Dodd, op. cit., p. 139, and following quotes from same source.
62. Dr Mitchell, *Report of Hand-Loom Weaving*, PP, 1840, XXIII, p. 271.
63. *Household Words*, 1852, vol. V, pp. 152–5.
64. 'Transfer Your Custom', London, 1857, p. 16.
65. C. Booth, *Life and Labour of the People of London*, 17 vols., 1902,

1st series, vol. 4, p. 299. Clara Collett wrote of women workers, 'the position of the married woman is what her husband makes it, whereas her industrial condition may depend largely upon her position and occupation before marriage'. (ibid., p. 298), and see ibid. for married women's lack of freedom of movement.

66. H. Mayhew, op. cit., vol. 1, p. 151.

67. PP, 1843, XIV, op. cit., f. 298.

68. H. Mayhew, op. cit., vol. 1, p. 466.

69. H. Mayhew, op. cit., vol. 1, p. 39.

70. *The City Mission Magazine*, vol. 10, 1836, p. 127.

71. H. Mayhew, op. cit., vol. 3, p. 307.

72. H. Mayhew, vol. 1, pp. 463–4. Kensal Green was apparently 'the paradise of laundresses', Mary Bayley, *Mended Homes and What Repaired Them*, 1861.

73. 'Transfer Your Custom', op. cit., 1857, p. 22.

74. H. Mayhew, op. cit., vol. 2, p. 496.

75. I have filled out Mayhew's list. H. Mayhew, op. cit., p. 457.

76. ibid., pp. 43–4.

77. H. Mayhew, op. cit., vol. 1, pp. 385–6.

78. Mayhew's investigations are invaluable because he allowed working people to describe their own lives, but he did promote the notion that women and children should be the economic dependents of their menfolk, as a solution to the 'superfluity' of casual labour. England was producing sufficient wealth to support all her population, he argued, but not enough employment. Women should therefore return to the home. This underlying assumption lead him to concentrate on men's casual labour rather than women's. His methods of investigation were very thorough however; see E. Thompson and E. Yeo, op. cit., pp. 61–2 for the detailed questions he asked of trade organizations etc., and read their introductory essays for an assessment of his work.

79. E. Thompson and E. Yeo, op. cit., p. 463.

80. ibid., p. 139.

81. Appendix to *Report on Condition of Hand-Loom Weavers*, PP, 1840, XXIV, p. 77.

82. E. Thompson and E. Yeo, op. cit., pp. 142–3.

83. 'Transfer Your Custom', op. cit., p. 11.

84. E. Thompson and E. Yeo, op. cit., pp. 525–6.

85. According to the vestry-clerk of the Stepney Union; in a letter to the Poor Law Commissioners: 'The Commissioners are probably aware that the indoor female paupers within this and the neighbouring unions, for many years past, have been principally em-

ployed in needlework, such as shirtmaking or slopwork, which is almost the only kind of employment open generally to females out of doors within this district, in which there are no manufactories employing female labour. To this resource they are almost invariably driven whenever deprived of husbands or of parents. PP, 1843, XIV, op. cit., p. 124.

86. E. Thompson and E. Yeo, op. cit., p. 159.

87. PP, 1843, XIV, f. 270.

88. H. Mayhew, op. cit., vol. 1, p. 45.

89. ibid., p. 372.

90. ibid., pp. 464–5.

91. PP, 1840, XXIII, op. cit., p. 270. According to the 'Investigation into the Poorer Classes of St George's in the East', op. cit., p. 198, the children observed by the Society were 'apparently very healthy' and sent as early as possible to school, 'though sometimes into little, filthy, smokey, dame schools'; others were 'clean and fairly ventilated, and kept by persons with habits of order and propriety'.

92. H. Mayhew, op. cit., vol. 1, pp. 462–3.

93. ibid., vol. 3, p. 410.

94. Mins. of Evidence, Select Committee on Police of the Metropolis, PP, 1828, vol. 6, p. 31.

3. Women and Nineteenth-Century Radical Politics: A Lost Dimension

1. For a discussion of this question which does rather overstate the 'independence' of working women in this period, see Neil McKendrick 'Home Demand and Economic Growth: a New View of the Role of Women and Children in the Industrial Revolution', in *Historical Perspectives: Studies in English Thought and Society in Honour of J. H. Plumb* (1974).

2. Samuel Bamford, *Passages in the Life of a Radical*, (1844), Cass reprint, 1967, p. 164.

3. ibid., p. 200.

4. Percival Percival, *Failsworth Folk and Failsworth Memories*, Failsworth, 1901, plate.

5. Don Manuel Alvarez Espriella (R. Southey), *Letters from England*, 1808, pp. 46–7.

6. *Nottingham Review*, 11 September 1812. For examples of women's participation in food riots in the eighteenth-century and a discussion of its significance, see E. P. Thompson, 'The Moral Economy of the

English Crowd in the Eighteenth Century', *Past and Present*, no. 50, February 1971, pp. 115–18.

7. Wanda F. Neff, *Victorian Working Women*, Allen and Unwin, 1929, p. 35. For examples of women's friendly and radical societies in two industrial districts during this period, see two Birmingham University BA dissertations, K. Corfield, *Some Social and Radical Organizations among Working-Class Women in Manchester and District 1790–1820*, 1971, and E. Nicholson *Working-Class Women in Nineteenth-Century Nottingham 1815–1850*, 1974.

8. James Burland, *Annals of Barnsley*, MS in Barnsley Public Library.

9. John Wade, *History of the Middle and Working Classes*, cited in W. F. Neff, op. cit., p. 32. Card setting was usually done by women or children, Benjamin Wilson (in *The Struggles of an Old Chartist*, Halifax, 1887, p. 13) earned ½d. for every 1,500 cards he set as a young child in the 1820s.

10. 'Lodges of Industrious Females shall be instituted in every district where it may be practicable; such lodges to be considered in every respect, as part of, and belonging to, the GNCTU.' Rule XX of Rules and Regulations of the GNCTU, in S. and B. Webb, *History of Trade Unionism*, 1920, p. 725.

11. From the obituary notice of Thomas Lingard, *Barnsley Chronicle*, 7 November 1875.

12. *Demagogue*, 5 July 1834. William Lovett, *The Life and Struggles of William Lovett* (1877), Fitzroy, 1967, p. 50. Joel Weiner, *The War of the Unstamped*, Cornell University Press, 1969.

13. See Cecil Driver, *Tory Radical, a Biography of Richard Oastler*, 1946, for the best account of both movements.

14. Pitkeithly to Broyan, 28 December 1838, HO/40/47.

15. F. H. Grundy, *Pictures of the Past*, 1879, p. 98 (my italics).

16. Benjamin Wilson, op. cit., pp. 1–3.

17. HO/20/10.

18. W. E. Adams, *Memoirs of a Social Atom*, 1903, p. 163. The 'Sacred Month' was a proposal for a month's general strike which was put forward in the early days of the Chartist movement. The Chartists were never in fact called upon to observe it, as the idea was abandoned by the leadership.

In his article on 'Working-Class Women in Britain 1890–1914', (in *Workers in the Industrial Revolution: Recent Studies of Labour in the United States and Europe*, Transaction Books, New Brunswick, New Jersey, 1974), Peter Stearns points to the fact that few of the working-class autobiographies of the period mention the mother of the author. For the Chartist period the exact opposite is the case. The writers of autobiographies in this early part of the century nearly all seem to have been brought up by widowed mothers or other female relatives.

19. *Ashton Reporter*, 30 January 1869.

20. *London Despatch*, 1 April 1838.

21. C. Aspin (ed.), Angus Benthune Reach, *Manchester and the Textile Districts in 1849*, Helmshore, 1972, p. 107. In July 1848, the secretary of the Hyde branch of the Land Company, John Gaskell, registered the birth of twin daughters Mary Mitchel and Elizabeth Frost, *Northern Star*, 15 July 1848.

22. *Northern Star*, 17 March 1838 and *passim*.

23. ibid., 3 February 1838.

24. ibid., 23 June 1838.

25. ibid., 13 April 1839.

26. Henry Vincent to John Minikin, 4 September 1837. (MS letters in Transport House collection.)

27. Henry Vincent to John Minikin, 10 June 1838.

28. Henry Vincent to John Minikin, 18 June 1838.

29. Henry Vincent to John Minikin, 17 August 1837.

30. Henry Vincent to John Minikin, 2 October 1838.

31. Henry Vincent to John Minikin, 17 November 1838.

32. *Northern Liberator*, 5 January 1839.

33. *Northern Star*, 30 March 1839.

34. *Sheffield Telegraph*, 6 April 1839.

35. *Northern Star*, 3 February 1839.

36. Benjamin Wilson, op. cit., p. 8.

37. As, for example, the two shopkeepers in Ashton-under-Lyne who gave evidence against Joseph Rayner Stephens in 1839, and were forced out of business by the subsequent boycott of their shops.

38. Rev. F. Close AM, *A Sermon Addressed to the Female Chartists of Cheltenham*, 1839, p. 21.

39. *Social Pioneer*, 16 March 1839.

40. ibid., 6 April 1839.

41. For the best account of Owenism see J. F. C. Harrison, *Robert Owen and the Owenites*, Routledge and Kegan Paul, 1969.

42. *Social Pioneer*, 30 March 1839.

43. *Northern Star*, 2 February 1839. (The whole address is reprinted in my *The Early Chartists*, Macmillan, 1972.) The Chartist demand 'no women's labour, except in the home and the schoolroom' seems to have been widely accepted.

44. Edward Haymer, *A Brief Account of the Chartist Outbreak in Llanidloes*, Llanidloes, 1867. Reprinted in *The Early Chartists*.

45. Frank Peel, *The Risings of the Luddites, Plug-Drawers and Chartists*, 1880, 4th ed., Frank Cass, 1968, pp. 333–4.
46. F. H. Grundy, op. cit., p. 100.
47. Rev. Francis Close, op. cit., p. 23.
48. MS letter Elizabeth Pease to Wendell and Ann Phillips, 29 March 1842. (In Library of Society of Friends, London.)
49. R. J. Richardson, *The Rights of Woman*, 1840. Reprinted in *The Early Chartists*.
50. William Lovett, op. cit., p. 32.
51. ibid., p. 141n.
52. *The National Association Gazette*, 12 March 1842.
53. ibid., 7 May 1842.
54. Benjamin Wilson, op. cit., pp. 9–10.
55. *Peoples' Paper*, 29 November 1856.
56. *Notes to the People*, 1851–2, reprinted 1967, vol. II, p. 515.
57. ibid., p. 709.

4. Landscape with Figures: Home and Community in English Society

1. M. Weber, *The Theory of Social and Economic Organization*, Glencoe, Illinois, 1947, pp. 341–2. For an elaboration of the theoretical arguments covered in this paragraph, see H. Newby, 'The Deferential Dialectic', *Comparative Studies in Society and History*, vol. 17, no. 2, 1975, pp. 139–64.
2. H. Perkin, *The Origins of Modern English Society, 1780–1880*, Routledge and Kegan Paul, 1968, p. 51.
3. The way part of this tension was handled by a sexual division of labour is discussed in L. Davidoff, *The Best Circles: Society Etiquette and the Season*, Croom Helm, 1973, chapters 1 and 2; J. Forster, *Class Struggle and the Industrial Revolution*, Weidenfeld and Nicolson, 1974, chapter 6; see also 'The Idea of Locals and Cosmopolitans', in R. K. Merton, *Social Theory and Social Structure*, Glencoe, Illinois, 1957.
4. 'Ideology' in *International Encyclopedia of the Social Sciences*, vol. 7, New York, 1968, p. 69.
5. For the way such 'maps' can be built up from childhood see P. Gould and R. White, *Mental Maps*, Pelican, 1974.
6. Cassell's *Book of the Household: A Work of Reference on Domestic Economy*, vol. 1, p. 27.
7. 'It is important to stress how difficult it is for anyone in any social or moral context to say what they mean by "natural" and why it

recommends itself as good. Two distinct steps are involved here: defining what is meant by "natural" and arguing that what is natural is good.' Christine Pierce, 'Natural Law Language and Women', in V. Gornick and B. K. Moran (eds.), *Woman in Sexist Society*, New York, 1971, p. 243.

8. There is an underlying tone of much that has been written on this theme concerning rural society; workers are viewed as contented cows – happiness is abetted by a bovine intelligence. See some of the contributions to E. W. Martin (ed.) *Country Life in England*, Macdonald, 1966. Elsewhere the position of women has been directly compared with that of horses. 'I believe we must have the sort of power over you that we're said to have over our horses. They see us as three times bigger than we are or they'd never obey us.' Virginia Woolf, *The Voyage Out*, Penguin, 1970, p. 210.

   Of course the word 'pet' has similar connotations when used as a term of endearment towards wives and children.

9. See the introduction to section one of C. Bell and H. Newby (eds.) *The Sociology of Community*, Allen and Unwin, 1974; also H. Newby, 'The Dangers of Reminiscence', *Local Historian*, vol. II, no. 3, 1973, pp. 334–9.

10. G. Best, *Mid-Victorian Britain, 1851–75*, Panther, 1973, p. 85.

11. R. Glass, 'Conflict in Cities', in CIBA Foundation Symposium, *Conflict in Society*, London, 1966, p. 142.

12. J. C. Loudon, *A Treatise on Forming, Improving and Managing Country Residences*, 1806, p. 5.

13. R. Glass, op. cit., p. 142.

14. R. Williams, *The Country and the City*, Chatto and Windus, 1973, p. 120.

15. W. B. Pemberton, *William Cobbett*, Penguin, 1949, p. 139.

16. A. Chandler, *A Dream of Order: The Medieval Ideal in Nineteenth-Century English Literature*, Routledge and Kegan Paul, 1971.

17. *Political Register*, 14 April, 1821.

18. Cited by R. Williams, *Culture and Society, 1780–1850*, Penguin, 1961, p. 34.

19. P. Laslett, *The World We Have Lost*, Methuen, 1965, p. 25.

20. The chief importer into the sociological tradition is Ferdinand Tonnies. This has been well exemplified by McKinney and Loomis in their introduction to *Gemeinschaft und Gesellschaft*, pp. 12–29 (Harper and Row). See also R. Glass, op. cit.; R. E. Pahl, 'The Rural-Urban Continuum', in R. E. Pahl (ed.), *Readings in Urban Sociology*, Pergamon Press, 1969; R. J. Green, *Country Planning: The Future of the Rural Regions*, Manchester University Press, 1971.

21. Cited by R. Gill, *Happy Rural Seat*, New Haven, 1972, p. 4.

22. E. Percy, *Some Memories*, Eyre and Spottiswoode, 1958, cited by D. Spring, 'Some Reflections on Social History in the Nineteenth Century', *Victorian Studies*, vol. IV, 1960–61, p. 58. Also H. Newby, op. cit., 1975.

23. W. Peck, *Home For the Holidays*, Faber, 1955. Many middle-class memoirs speak of the custom of renting vicarages or even school houses in the country for family holidays.

24. Mrs Sarah Stickney Ellis is one of the best known writers of these advice books. For a fuller list see J. A. and O. Banks, 'The Perfect Wife', in *Feminism and Family Planning in Victorian England*, Liverpool University Press, 1964, pp. 58–70.

25. A mother and mistress of A. Family, *Home Discipline – Or Thoughts on the Origin and Exercise of Domestic Authority*, 1841, p. 106.

26. Cassell's *Book of the Household*, op. cit., p. 31.

27. 'The front fence . . . gives no real visual or acoustic privacy but symbolizes a frontier and a barrier.' Amos Rappoport, *House Form and Culture*, Princeton, N.J., 1969, p. 133.

28. Augustus Mayhew, *Paved With Gold*, 1858, p. 8, quoted in Myron Brightfield, *Victorian England in its Novels*, vol. IV, Los Angeles, 1968, p. 349.

29. 'One curious feature of Victorian houses is the increasingly large and sacrosanct male domain . . .' M. Girouard, *The Victorian Country House*, Oxford University Press, 1971. On the social meaning of physical separation see E. T. Hall, *The Hidden Dimension: Man's Use of Space in Public and Private*, Toronto, 1966.

30. A new category of paintings, *Domestic Pictures*, was created by the Royal Academy in 1852. 'The return of the man from work, from war, from the sea or from a journey was a very popular theme.' Helene E. Roberts, 'Marriage, Redundancy or Sin? The Painter's View of Women in the First Twenty-Five Years of Victoria's Reign' in M. Vicinus, (ed.), *Suffer and Be Still: Women in the Victorian Age*, Bloomington, Indiana, 1972, p. 51.

31. Economists, sociologists and historians have continued to use the concept of *the household* assuming identity of interests up to the present day; an identity which greatly benefits the superordinate. See J. K. Galbraith's recent critique in *Economics and the Public Purpose*, Deutsch, 1974.

32. Anon., 'Out of the World', *Cornhill Magazine*, VIII, September 1863, p. 374.

33. 'In our traditional and largely subconscious opinion, what the marriage ceremony does is to consecrate a woman and a house-

mistress.' Lord Raglan, *The Temple and the House*, Routledge, 1964, p. 34.

34. J. Ruskin, *Sesame and Lillies*, 1868, p. 145.

35. R. Gill, op. cit., p. 201.

36. Keith Thomas, 'The Double Standard', *Journal of the History of Ideas*, April 1959.

37. Richard Steele in *The Spinster* (1719) recalls that the word was not originally opprobrious but referred to the laudable 'industry of female manufacturers'.

38. Jane Collier in her *Essay on the Art of Ingeniously Tormenting*, 1753.

39. Jean L'Esperance, *Woman in Puritan Thought*, MA thesis, McGill University, 1955.

40. R. P. Utter and G. Needham, *Pamela's Daughter*, New York, 1972.

41. *Meliora*, vol. 7, 1858, p. 75. Patrick Colquoun in his treatise on the *Police of the Metropolis* (1797) refers to prostitutes as brazen lower-class hussies who should be kept from the sight of respectable women by the police. The classification of 'good' and 'bad' women is, of course, made by men in the masculine interest.

42. 'The details of a control over prostitution need not form the subject of a separate bill' argued the *British and Foreign Medical Chirurgical Review* in January 1854, 'any more than the Commissioners of sewers require a new clause for each clearage. The object would be completely accomplished by its being enacted that prostitution, meaning the demanding or receiving money for sexual intercourse, is a criminal act; and that as a punishment, the individual shall be placed under the control and surveillance of a commission, and that the commission be authorized to make such arrangements as may be considered necessary for the public safety.'

43. *The Magdalen's Friend and Female Homes Intelligences*, June 1860, p. 93.

44. Charles Kingsley 'Woman's Work in a Country Parish', *Sanitary and Social Lectures and Essays*, 1880, p. 13.

45. 'Lights and Shadows of London Life', *Meliora: A Quarterly Review of Social Science*, 1867, p. 270.

46. For a discussion of the attempt – and its failure – see, G. S. Jones, 'The Deformation of the Gift: The Problem of the 1860s', *Outcast London*, Oxford University Press, 1971.

47. Elizabeth Burton, 'Gardens', *The Early Victorians at Home, 1837–1861*, Longman, 1972.

48. Edward Hyams, *The English Garden*, Thames and Hudson, 1966, p. 273.

49. Robert Kerr, *The Gentleman's House or How to Plan English Residences from the Parsonage to the Palace*, 3rd ed., 1871, p. 66.

The most influential builder of country houses of the period was also a Scotsman, William Burn. The influence of Scotsmen in architecture and landscape gardening was part of the growth of these pursuits; a separation of the expert and the consumer. M. Girouard, op. cit.

50. J. C. Loudon, *An Encyclopaedia of Cottage, Farm and Villa Architecture and Furniture, Containing Designs for Dwellings From the Cottage to the Villa*, 1833, chapter II, pp. 780–82.

51. R. Gill, op. cit., p. 112.

52. Sir Gilbert Scott, *Secular and Domestic Architecture*, 1857, quoted in M. Girouard, op. cit., p. 2.

53. R. Gill, op. cit., p. 15.

54. F. M. L. Thompson, *Hampstead, Building a Borough, 1650–1964*, Routledge and Kegan Paul, 1974, pp. 91–2.

55. One of the most famous and enduring was Mrs Sherwood's *The Fairchild Family* which was first published in 1818, ran to fourteen editions before 1847, and was still in print in 1913. The book begins: 'Mr and Mrs Fairchild lived very far from any town; their house stood in the midst of a garden . . .' The Fairchild rural paradise is inhabited by the family of parents and children, the devoted servants and assorted loyal villagers.

56. A few well-known examples from the nineteenth century are, Samuel Butler, *A Way of All Flesh*, Penguin, 1947; Florence Nightingale, 'Cassandra' in Ray Strachey, *The Cause*, London, 1928; Betty Askwith, *Two Victorian Families*, Chatto and Windus, 1971; Ruth Borchard, *John Stuart Mill*, London, 1957; Cynthia White cites the year-long correspondence in the *Englishwoman's Domestic Magazine* in the 1850s on the subject of corporal punishment of children 'in the course of which the corrective measures employed were fully described, throwing a new and sadistic light on the concept of the "pious" Victorian mother.' *Women's Magazines: 1693–1968*, Michael Joseph, 1970, p. 46.

57. Joyce Cary, *To Be a Pilgrim*, Michael Joseph, 1942, quoted in R. Gill, op. cit., p. 204.

58. Quentin Bell, *Virginia Woolf: A Biography*, Vol. I, *1882–1912*, Hogarth Press, 1972; P. and T. Thompson, 'Family and Work Experience Before 1918', Social Science Research Council Project, interviews.

59. 'At Home and At School', *All the Year Round*, 8 October 1859, p. 572.

60. Hence the banning of women from underground work in the mines and field work in agriculture, and the attempt to ban them from work in factories can be seen as part of this attempt at control (as well as in the humanitarian progress usually emphasized by historians). Angela John, 'Pit Brow Lasses – a Test Case for Female Labour', unpublished paper, 1974.

61. T. J. Barnardo, 'Something Attempted, Something Done', published by the offices of the Barnardo Institution, 1889, p. 30.

62. *The Magdalen's Friend*, no. 4, July 1860, p. 113.

63. W. Greg, 'Why are Women Redundant?', *Literary and Social Judgements*, London, 1862, pp. 73–4.

64. Brian Harrison, 'For Church, Queen and Family: The Girl's Friendly Society, 1874–1920', *Past and Present*, November 1973.

65. Not to speak of the variations produced by the continued existence of domestic manufacture and craft. For the difficulty of evaluating this response see, E. P. Thompson, *The Making of the English Working Class*, Gollancz, 1963, p. 414–17. (Pelican, 1968.) R. Q. Gray, 'Styles of Life, the "Labour Aristocracy" and Class Relations in Later Nineteenth-Century Edinburgh', *International Review of Social History*, vol. XVIII, 1973. Ralph Samuel, 'Home and Work', *Ruskin History Workshop Pamphlet*, forthcoming.

66. Not political or economic reform are his solution but, like Mrs Gaskell, greater love between the classes. Martha Vicinus, 'Literary Voices of an Industrial Town, Manchester, 1810–70'; H. J. Dyos and M. Wolff, *The Victorian City: Images and Realities*, Routledge and Kegan Paul, 1973, p. 756.

67. Ben Brierly, 'Out of Work', *Lancashire Stories*, VI, 1884, pp. 77–8, quoted in ibid., p. 755.

68. Mr Steel-Maitland, *Royal Commission on the Poor Laws*, 1909, vol. 43, p. 182.

69. W. Peterson, 'The Ideological Origins of British New Towns', *American Institute of Planners Journal*, vol. XXXIV, 1968. D. Thorns, *Suburbia*, MacGibbon and Kee, 1972 and 'Planned and Unplanned Communities', *University of Auckland Papers in Comparative Sociology*, no. 1, 1973.

70. P. J. Schmitt, *Back to Nature: An Arcadian Myth in Urban America*, Oxford University Press, New York, 1969, p. xvii and see John Betjeman's poem on Letchworth.

71. Eugene A. Clancy, 'The Car and the Country Home', *Harper's Weekly*, IV, 6 May, 1911, p. 30; cited by P. J. Schmitt, op. cit., p. 17.

72. William Smythe, *City Homes on Country Lanes*, New York, 1972, p. 60.

73. E. Howard, *Garden Cities of Tomorrow*, quoted in B. I. Coleman, *The Idea of the City in Nineteenth-Century Britain*, Routledge and Kegan Paul, 1973, p. 197–8.

74. A. Jackson, *Semi-Detached London: Suburban Development, Life and Transport, 1900–1939*, Allen and Unwin, 1973, p. 136.

75. ibid., p. 143; L. Hanson, *Shining Morning Face: The Childhood of Lance*, Allen and Unwin, 1949.

76. C. White, op. cit., pp. 99–100.

77. D. Paterson, *The Family Woman and the Feminist: A Challenge*, Heinemann, 1945, p. 37.

78. P. Berger and H. Kellner, 'Marriage and the Construction of Reality', H. P. Dreitzel (ed.), *Recent Sociology* (Patterns of Communicative Behaviour), no. 2, Collier-Macmillan, London and New York, 1970.

79. Domestic servants, agricultural labourers and married women were the last categories (bar children) to gain citizenship rights in the twentieth century. Married women are not quite full citizens to this day, see, L. Davidoff, 'Mastered for Life: Servant and Wife in Victorian England', *Journal of Social History*, Summer 1974.

80. J. C. Loudon, op. cit.

81. ibid., p. 797.

82. Kirk Jeffries, 'The Family as Utopian Retreat from the City: The Nineteenth-Century Contribution', *Sounding: An Interdisciplinary Journal*, Spring 1972.

83. W. E. Houghton, *The Victorian Frame of Mind, 1830–1870*, Yale University Press, 1957, p. 393.

84. For example in a writer like Dylan Thomas, middle-class and middle-aged women are seen as life *denyers*: men are perpetual boys, escaping their moral strictures, glorying in sexual and alcoholic adventures. See *Under Milk Wood*. This is simply a variation of the 'woman as saviour' theme; whichever is emphasized, women embody in themselves the moral order.

85. 'It should be noted that the particular and peculiar pairing of "passivity" and "responsibility" may account for many aspects of the behaviour of adult women.' Harriet Holter, *Sex Roles and Social Structure*, University of Oslo Press, 1970, p. 60.

5. Femininity in the Classroom: An Account of Changing Attitudes

1. 'Why are We Educating Our Boys and Girls?', *Parent's Review*, vol. XXXIV, no. 8, August 1923.

2. Such an education is supposed to develop a rational mind, critical faculties and an ability to grasp concepts. See, for instance, Paul Hirst in *Journal of Curriculum Studies*, vol. I, no. 2, 1968 and 1969.

3. The earliest I have been able to find date from 1865 and are not very satisfactory. In 1898 the *Return of the Pupils in Public and Private Secondary and Other Schools in England* published by the Stationery Office, simply said that the figures did not exist.

4. See for example V. W. Hughes, *A London Family 1870–1900*, Oxford University Press, 1953; 'A Ladies' School Seventy Years Ago' by an octogenarian in *Treasury*, February 1905; 'An Enquiry into the State of Girls' Fashionable Schools', *Frazer's Magazine*, June 1945.

5. *Secondary Education in the Nineteenth Century*, Cambridge University Press, 1921.

6. Quoted in Dorothea Beale's edition of the *Schools' Enquiry Commission*, 1869, p. 31.

7. See 'Landscape with Figures: Home and Community in English Society', pp. 139–75.

8. Figures are hard to come by, but the Census of 1861 shows that of nearly six million adult English women, there were 3,488,952 wives, 756,717 widows and 1,537,314 spinsters.

9. J. and O. Banks in *Feminism and Family Planning in Victorian England* (Liverpool University Press, 1964), estimated that in 1851 there were 25,000 governesses in England.

10. For details of provision of schools for the working classes, see H. Silver, *The Concept of Popular Education: A Study of Ideas and Social Movements in the Early Nineteenth Century*, MacGibbon and Kee, 1965.

11. *Report from the Select Committee on the Education of the Poorer Classes*, 1838, p. 13.

12. Frances Buss, who had been a governess, founded the North London Collegiate School in Camden Town in 1850, where she introduced a 'Boys'' curriculum and a system of external examination for girls. Emily Davies, daughter of an evangelical family, became Principal of Girton College, Cambridge in the 1870s.

13. Anne Clough became Principal of Newnham College, Cambridge. F. D. Maurice was a member of the Christian Socialists. His sister was a governess. In 1848 he founded Queen's College for women and girls in Harley Street.

14. Dorothea Beale taught at Queen's College, and became Head-

mistress of Cheltenham Ladies College in 1858. She was supposed to have little understanding of the problems of unsupported spinsters as she was 'comfortably off'.

15. For interesting discussions of changes in the education of boys see D. V. Glass, 'Education and Social Change in Modern England', in A. H. Halsey, J. Floud and C. A. Anderson (eds.), *Education, Economy and Society*, (Free Press, U.S., 1965), and R. Williams, *The Long Revolution* (Penguin, 1965), chapter, 'Education and British Society'.

16. E. M. Sewell, *Principles of Education Drawn from Nature and Revelation and Applied to Female Education in the Upper Classes*, Longman, Roberts and Green, 1865, vol. II, p. 219.

17. J. Fitch, 'Women and the Universities', *Contemporary Review*, August 1890, p. 252.

18. H. Spencer, 'Principles of Biology', *Lancet*, no. 2, 1886, p. 315.

19. Alice Zimmern, *Renaissance of Girls' Education in England*, Longman, 1898.

20. ibid. Advertisement inside the back cover.

21. In 1880 attendance at the elementary school was made compulsory up to the age of ten, and in 1893 it was raised to eleven and in 1918 to fourteen.

22. James Booth, *Female Education of the Industrial Classes*, Bell and Daldy, 1855.

23. Edith Sellers, *An Antedeluvian on the Education of Working-Class Girls: Nineteenth Century and After*, August 1916, p. 337.

24. S. A. Burstall and M. A. Douglas (eds.), *Public School for Girls*, Longmans Green and Co., 1911, quote from p. 26.

25. See for instance in the *Journal of Education – a Monthly Review and Record*, vol. XXXII, 'Science Teaching in Girls' Schools', by four Girton and Newnham tutors, January 1910, pp. 36–8.

26. Alice Ikin, 'Education for Womanhood', in *Education – Primary, Secondary and Technical*, vol. XLVII, April 1926, p. 358; V. M. Hughes, *A London Family 1870–1900*, Oxford University Press, 1954, p. 179.

27. Meyrick Booth, 'The Present Day Education of Girls – an Indictment', in *Nineteenth Century and After*, August 1927, pp. 259–69.

28. See for instance W. Felter, 'The Education of Women', *Educational Review*, vol. XXXI, 1906, pp. 351–63.

29. *Report of the Central Advisory Council for Education '15–18'*, Ministry of Education, HMSO, 1959, The Crowther Report, para 51.

6. The Education of Girls Today

1. See Audrey Hunt, *A Survey of Women's Employment*, Government Social Survey, H M S O, 1968.

2. There are difficulties in distinguishing cause and effect in interpreting evidence of this kind. It is of course possible that the reason the women are inactive and unemployed is because of their pathological problems.

3. See J. Newsom, 'The EducationWomen Need', *Observer*, September 1964.

4. J. Newsom, *The Education of Girls*, Faber, 1948.

5. See Josephine Kamm, *Hope Deferred* (Methuen, 1965), for a history of girls' education.

6. For example an emphasis on spoken or conversational English; 'the ability to speak well is . . . a desirable accomplishment . . . An attractive voice is also a positive help in the business of acquiring a husband and will endure longer than more obvious but more temporary charms' (Newsom, 1948).

7. The government consultative document *Equal Opportunities for Men and Women* states that the Department of Education and Science is to begin discussions with the universities 'to establish how they could best respond to the need to avoid any discrimination on grounds of sex in their admissions policy'. The universities' memorandum in response to the document also rejects any suggestion that there is discrimination against women: 'the process of selection operates impartially without regard to the sex of the applicant' (Committee of Vice Chancellors and Principals, London, 1974). In a speech opening a United Nations Conference on the position of women, Margaret Thatcher (Secretary of State for Education) claimed that there is no discrimination against women or girls in British education (July, 1973).

8. A substantial number of local authorities now forbid caning in primary schools, and its use in secondary schools appears to be less and less frequent. However, residual differences in the type of social control applied to girls and boys probably remain. The practice of using sex as a criterion for grouping children is, for example, widespread – instances are 'boys get your milk first', 'girls line up on the right hand side'.

9. See for example, J. W. B. Douglas, *The Home and the School*, MacGibbon and Kee, 1964.

10. ibid.

11. See M. Wisenthal, 'Sex Difference in Attitudes and Attainment in Junior Schools', *British Journal of Educational Psychology*, 35, 1965, pp. 79–85.

12. See J. W. B. Douglas, J. M. Ross and H. R. Simpson, *All Our Future*, Peter Davies, 1968.

13. 'A National Survey of the Ability and Attainment of Children at Three Age Levels', *British Journal of Educational Psychology*, 30, 1960, pp. 124–34.

14. Fifteen until 1973, when it was raised to sixteen.

15. The inclusion of independent schools would increase this difference rather than reduce it, since girls in such schools leave earlier than their male contemporaries in independent boys' schools. According to unpublished data from the Medical Research Council National Survey on Health and Development, 14 per cent of boys in independent or direct-grant schools left at eighteen or later compared with 8 per cent of girls.

16. See Celia Phillips, *Changes in Subject Choice at School and University*, Weidenfeld and Nicolson, 1969.

17. See Tessa Blackstone and Oliver Fulton, *Sex Discrimination among University Teachers: a British–American Comparison*, forthcoming.

18. The effect of the onset of puberty on motivation to study and interest in academic work may well be stronger for girls than for boys, and may explain why the gap in average performance is closed or even reversed between the ages of eleven and fifteen. For a discussion of the importance of physiological and psychological changes during puberty on achievement motivation, see J. Bardwick, E. Douvan, M. Horner and D. Gutmann, *Feminine Personality and Conflict* (Wadsworth, Brooks Cole, 1970), especially the papers by Bardwick and Douvan.

19. See Jane Zorza, *Sex-Role Socialization*, unpublished dissertation, University of Sussex, 1973, and Crescy Cannan, 'Female from Birth', *Times Educational Supplement*, no. 2956, 14 January 1972, p. 20.

20. See A. H. Halsey, *Trends in British Society Since 1900: a Guide to the Changing Social Structure of Britain*, Macmillan, 1972, and the 1971 Advance Census Analysis, HMSO, 1973.

21. See J. W. B. Douglas, *The Home and the School*, MacGibbon and Kee, 1964.

22. See R. Rosenthal and L. Jacobson, *Pygmalion in the Classroom: Teacher Expectation and Pupils' Intellectual Development*, Holt, Rinehart and Winston, New York, 1968 and D. Hargreaves, *Social Relations in Secondary Schools*, Routledge and Kegan Paul, 1966.

23. See J. Bardwick, E. Douvan, M. Horner and D. Gutmann, op. cit., for the American evidence for this, in particular the paper by Horner.
24. It is interesting that the most profound difference in the educational treatment of boys and girls is where education relates most closely to the world of work.
25. See Harriet Holter 'Sex Roles and Social Change', in Hans Peter Dreitzel (ed.), *Family, Marriage and the Struggle of the Sexes* (*Recent Sociology no. 4*), Collier-Macmillan, 1972.
26. *Projections*, Ward Lock, 1972.
27. The official report where this argument is best developed is *Half Our Future*, of which Newsom was the chairman. For example the report stated that 'the progress from the child's first lump of plasticine at home to the housewife furnishing her home with conscious taste is a progress through primary and secondary ways of learning'. (Central Advisory Council for Education, HMSO, 1963, p. 112.)
28. Until such latent differentiation has disappeared in home and school, it is difficult to determine whether any of the differences in girls' and boys' performance or behaviour in the educational system can be ascribed to innate differences.

7. Woman and the Literary Text

1. In this introductory section there are a number of influences, both negative and positive, that inform my thinking. For instance, the concept 'the literariness of a literary text' is the term Ramon Jakobson uses to define the preoccupation of Russian Formalist critics, whose work in turn permeates this essay, as I think the formalists showed the possibility of a science of literary criticism. A crucial secondary source for rethinking this basic question is Pierre Macherey's *Pour une theorie de la production literaire* (Paris, 1966). On the other hand, the influences I am opposing can be exemplified by the notion of a 'literary response' as it is used, for instance, by Kate Millett in her book *Sexual Politics* (Sphere, 1972). Despite its many excellences and despite its explicit opposition to traditional modes of academic criticism, I find Millett's book makes use of some of the most dangerous of Anglo-Saxon literary ortho-doxies. It identifies the author with a character who then becomes a spokesman, it thus reduces literature to a response to social or ideological questions and forgets that literature transforms the material on which it is based, it forgets, in fact, that it is literature.

2. Mrs Eliza Lynn Linton (1822–98) was the author of many novels. Her book *The Girl of the Period* (Two vols. 1883) is a collection of essays originally published in the important weekly, the *Saturday Review*. It is a book well worth reading for its transparency. Some of the essays are 'Modern Mothers' (an argument against nurses on the grounds that they teach children 'class coarseness'), 'What is Woman's Work?', 'The Shrieking Sisterhood', 'Womanliness' and 'The Sweets of Married Life' ('a wife's first treat, and her greatest, is when her husband begins to leave off this kind of fervid lovemaking and settles down into the tranquil friend' – II, 128).

   All quotations are from this edition and the reference in parenthesis is to volume and page.

3. Harry Quilter, *Is Marriage a Failure?*, 1887. The preface states that it is a selection from the 27,000 letters received by the *Daily Telegraph* about an article by Mona Caird in the *Westminster Review* which argued that marriage should be a contract whose terms are drawn up by the agreement of both parties.

   'Glorified Spinster's' letter is on pp. 53–5. The quotation from the preface is on p. 10.

4. It will no doubt be noted with some scepticism that seven of the eight novels chosen as examples in this essay are by men. This had not struck me when I chose them but it may well not be accidental. But generally in the nineteenth century there is an important problem raised by the fact that a number of serious writers, the Brontës, George Eliot, Olive Schreiner (who used the name Ralph Iron when she published her remarkable *The Story of An African Farm* in 1883) and Vernon Lee (Violet Paget) used male pseudonyms. Of course, there is a simple enough explanation of this: it is a way of avoiding being classed among the writers of what George Eliot called 'Silly Novels by Lady Novelists'. But the effect of it on the narrative rhetoric would repay careful attention, especially in the cases of *Shirley*, *Adam Bede* and Schreiner's book. At the same time, the number of writers who created popular success as women novelists servicing the mythology of the feminine – Mrs Henry Wood (*East Lynne*), M. E. Braddon (*Lady Audley's Secret*), Mrs Humphrey Ward (*Robert Elsmere*), Marie Corelli, Mrs Oliphant and Mrs Craik, are the most obvious examples – is enormous, and clearly an important area of research.

5. Margaret Oliphant (1828–97) is best known as the author of *The Chronicles of Carlingford* (1863–76) one of which, *Miss Majoribanks* has recently been reissued (Chatto, 1969) with an editorial accolade by Q. D. Leavis. She was also a prolific reviewer for *Blackwood's*

Magazine and wrote a review of *The Woman Who Did* and *Jude the Obscure* called 'The Anti-Marriage League'. There is an account of her fascinating career in V. and R. A. Colby, *The Equivocal Virtue: Mrs Oliphant and the Victorian Literary Market Place*, Archon, 1966.

Madam was serialized in *Longman's Magazine* between January 1884 and January 1885, and published in three volumes in 1885. Quotations are taken from the serial version and references are to chapters.

6. Henry James, *The Portrait of A Lady* (1881). Quotations are from the Penguin edition (1963) which is based on a later, revised text, but this is not important for the purposes of my argument. The original edition ended with what is now the penultimate paragraph of the novel and was thus slightly more ambiguous.

   James's extensive use of the female protagonist makes him a writer of first importance in any consideration of literature in this area. One should mention especially *The Bostonians* (1886) which is concerned partly with the feminist movement in New England in the 1870s.

7. Henry James, *The Art of the Novel*, R. P. Blackmur (ed.), 1934, pp. 48–51.

8. Mrs Linton's logic seems absurd, though this is partly because I am juxtaposing different parts of the book. Nevertheless it is worth noting that such women are frequently presented as sexually ambiguous. In Meredith's *The Ordeal of Richard Feverel* (1859), the hero's other woman, Bella Mount, dresses up as a dandy as part of their sexual game, and she remains as 'cold as ice' (i.e. unromantic). Hedda Gabler's pistols are part of the same complex, and some of Moreau's versions of Salome are androgynous.

9. George Macdonald (1824–1905) was a Scottish Congregationalist Minister who retired at the age of twenty-six to write books. Between 1851 and 1897, he wrote more than fifty books, some of them for children. His first adult fantasy, *Phantastes* was published in 1858. The best account I know of the background to *Lilith* is an unpublished doctoral dissertation at the University of Reading by R. McGillis (1973).

10. By 'humanism' I mean a strictly agnostic commitment to the belief that the human mind can work out its own answers. Lilith is not a humanist – on the contrary, she exhibits a kind of Nietzschean will. By linking this with her commitment to liberty, Macdonald is clearly simplifying his task.

11. H. Rider Haggard (1856–1925) scored his first success with *King*

Solomon's Mines (1886). *She* followed in 1887. Together with Robert Louis Stevenson, he opened up a vein of exotic romance which became one of the dominant forms of the eighties and nineties. He is also the first of the Imperialist writers, to be followed by Kipling and John Buchan. Both *King Solomon's Mines* and *She* have reached Hollywood. *Nada the Lily* is another of his novels that will be found relevant to this theme.

12. I have tried to show in the first two sections that the use of a woman as a centre of consciousness does not necessarily constitute her being sited as the subject of her own experience, since often her own nature as a woman is seen to be given. But I would not like to underestimate the importance of the female centre of consciousness in the history of fiction. The major instances – Richardson, Austen, Gaskell, Eliot – seem however to be exploiting the special aptitude of woman for registering the social limitations on the apparently free mind, and most of the narratives concern a movement towards accommodation. There are texts in which this accommodation is so precarious as to invite a radical questioning (for example, *Persuasion* and Gaskell's remarkable novel, *Sylvia's Lovers*), and Charlotte Brontë, as Kate Millett shows, uses her heroines in a much more radical way. What happens in our period is that a largely legalistic logic poses the question of woman's freedom as unanswerable by concepts of 'nature'.

13. Grant Allen (1848–99) was a popular novelist and writer on biology who dabbled in various branches of radical thought. One of his earliest novels, *Philistia*, contains a fictional portrait of Marx.

14. I think that *Shirley* and *Villette*, though there is no question of denying that they are much more serious works than *The Woman Who Did*, should be seen in the light of this discussion too. For though they are both 'feminist' texts, they are also very limited by the bourgeois conceptions of freedom that are revealed by Allen's novel. Which is why Charlotte Brontë can seem so reactionary when she is also so radical.

15. The conflation of the two is clearly a favourite myth of conservative ideology. We have seen it there in *The Girl of the Period*, and it is also very marked in James's *The Bostonians*. Lawrence also resorts to it, though it should not be forgotten that Clara Dawes, in *Sons and Lovers*, who makes possible the hero's sexual adulthood, is bound up with the suffragettes.

16. It is important to make this distinction, because, unlike Mill, Meredith uses nature as an affirmative concept. The point is that for him the 'nature of woman' is as eminently artificial as it is for

Mill. Nature in Meredith always appears as a disruptive and radical force. I wouldn't argue that this is not an ideological concept, but it is very different from the idea that it is natural to behave according to social prescription. It means, for one thing, that one's 'nature' is not defined by the group (sexual, social etc.) of which one happens to be a member.

Interestingly enough, in view of the first two sections, Percy Dacier who falls in love with Diana, and who tries in a sophisticated way to subordinate her to his own self-realization, dilates on her charms in a passage of absurd romantic rhetoric, in exactly the terms I have used to define the two aspects of the woman-object: 'She was dear past computation, womanly, yet quite unlike the womanish woman, unlike the semi-males courteously called dashing, unlike the sentimental' (XXVI). This is immediately after he has decided he can count on 'making the dear woman his own in the eyes of the world'. For the elaboration of male subjectivity, see *The Egoist*.

17. Gissing wrote a number of novels and stories which focus on the situation of woman in various ways. Most notable are *The Unclassed*, *A Life's Morning*, *Thyrza* and *The Emancipated*.

The eighties and nineties saw the publication of several of more or less 'naturalist' fictions which are relevant to this section. We should mention George Moore's *Esther Waters*, and, although 'naturalist' is hardly an accurate classification, the stories of Mark Rutherford, *Miriam's Schooling*, *Catherine Furze* and *Clara Hopgood*. Ian Fletcher's *Selections from British Fiction 1880–1900* (1973) is a valuable anthology and guide.

The best account of *The Odd Women* in its historical context is by Maria Chialant, *Annali*, vol. X, 1967, p. 155.

18. Herbert Spencer (1820–1903) was truly the originator of what has come to be known as 'Social Darwinism', although his major sociological principles were published before *The Origin of Species*. He it is who originated the phrase 'survival of the fittest'.

19. Stokes, *Resistable Theatres*, Elek, 1972, p. 155.

The issue here is between two ways of describing Darwin's law of evolution. In the first edition of *The Origin of Species*, he used the phrase 'natural selection' and only later added Spencer's term 'survival of the fittest'. The first description, though it identifies an *immediate* cause of evolution by no means presupposes an overall pattern and a law of progression – but Spencer's phrase clearly does. Darwin's original idea could not be turned into a social programme since it tended if anything to deny any purpose in nature. The growth of Tess, though it is predictable to the extent that a 'phase' is clearly a recurrent period in life, has no social purpose. On the contrary it is anti-social.

8. Women in Trade Unions in America: An Historical Analysis

1. G. A. Stevens, New York Typographical Union 6, *A Study of a Modern Trade Union and its Predecessors*, Albany, 1913, p. 437.
2. Mabel Taylor, 'Where Are the Men to Blame?', *Life and Labor*, June 1921.
3. Louis Levine, *The Women Garment Workers, a History of the International Garment Workers*, Theubsch, New York, 1924, p. 54.
4. Proceedings of the General Assembly of the Knights of Labor, Minneapolis, 1877, p. 1581, in Catholic University, Washington DC.
5. *Report of the General Instructor and Director of Woman's Work*, Proceedings of the General Assembly of the Knights of Labor, Atlanta, 1889, p. 1, in Catholic University, Washington DC.
6. Unpublished poem in a manuscript of the Elizabeth Gurley Flynn Collection, in the American Institute for Marxist Studies, New York City.
7. From a letter to Pauline Newman from Rose Schneiderman, Taminent Library.
8. Anna Burlak, 'The Work of the Textile Unions', *Party Organizer*, 5–6, vol. 7, May–June 1934, p. 54.
9. Olga Domanski, 'Pages from a Shop Diary', *Notes on Women's Liberation, We Speak in Many Voices* (*News and Letters*), Detroit, 1970.
10. Claudia Dreyfus, 'Trade Union Women's Conference', *The Nation*, 10 March 1974.

9. Looking Again at Engels's 'Origins of the Family, Private Property and the State'

1. There are many editions of Frederick Engels's *Origins of the Family, Private Property and the State*. The edition which I have used is published by the Pathfinder Press, 1972, with an introduction by Evelyn Reed. Page references given after quotations are to that edition.
2. Lewis Morgan, *Ancient Society*, Macmillan, London, 1877. It is interesting to note that Engels's sub-title to the *Origins* is 'In the light of the researches of Lewis H. Morgan', and that the text of

his book is partly based on Marx's notes on Morgan, which have not yet, to my knowledge, been published in English, but which are available in Russian and German.

3. Wilhelm Reich took up the banner of defence of Engels's historical reading of the importance of the mother-right, father-right shift in his article 'The Imposition of Sexual Morality' (in *Sex-Pol*, *Essays 1929–34*, Lee Baxandall (ed.), Vintage Books, New York, 1972). The essay is intended to counter the Freud of *Totem and Taboo*, with its implications of universal patriarchy. Basing himself on the material collected in Malinowski's *The Sexual Life of Savages*, Reich attempts to locate in the maternal uncle (the mother's brother) and his structural position a transformational mechanism from mother-right to father-right. When Engels himself deals with the relation son–maternal uncle, he treats it as a vestige of the old mother-right family form. On the Germans, for example, he comments on Tacitus' description thus:

> The mother's brother regards his nephew as his son; some even hold that the blood tie between the maternal uncle and the nephew is more sacred and close than that between father and son, so that when hostages are demanded the sister's son is considered a better pledge than the natural son of the man whom they desire to place under bond. Here we have *a living survival of the mother-right, and hence original, gens...* (pp. 131–2, my italics).

4. Johann Jacob Bachofen, *Myth, Religion and Mother-Right, Selected Writings*, Routledge and Kegan Paul, 1967.

5. Karl Marx and Frederick Engels, *Selected Works*, 1 vol., Lawrence and Wishart, 1970, pp. 181–2.

6. cf. M. J. Meijer, *Marriage Law and Policy in the Chinese People's Republic*, Hong Kong University Press, 1971.

7. For an explanation of these categories see 'How to Differentiate the Classes in the Rural Areas', *Selected Works of Mao Tse-tung*, vol. 1, Peking, 1965, p. 137.

8. Chi-Hsi Hu ('Mao Tse-tung, la revolution et la question sexuelle', *Revue française de science politique*, Vol. XXIII, no. 1 February 1973.) cites these figures:

> According to statistics established by the local soviets of Yiyang and Hengfeng, districts in the extreme north-east of the Soviet zone of Kiangsi, 3,783 marriages and 4,274 divorces in toto were registered in the course of the period from 6 March to 25 June 1932. These statistics reveal that in 82 per cent of the cases divorce was demanded unilaterally by one of the spouses and that nine couples got married and then

divorced on the same day ... by way of comparison, one can signal that, throughout the entire year of 1930, there were no more than sixty-two cases of divorce in Peking, and 853 cases in Shanghai, the great 'westernized' city with many millions of inhabitants.

9. Meijer, op. cit., appendix XII.
10. For an assessment of the importance of kinship structures to the analysis of women, see 'Patriarchy, Kinship and Women as Exchange Objects' in Juliet Mitchell, *Psychoanalysis and Feminism*, Pelican, 1975.

10, Women in Revolutionary China

1. For a brief account of the movement for women's suffrage and rights, see Roxanne Wilke, 'Woman as Politician: 1920s', in Marilyn B. Young (ed.), *Women in China: Studies in Social Change and Feminism*, Center for Chinese Studies, University of Michigan, 1973. This book contains the fullest record of women in revolutionary China and also provides a long and useful bibliography on women in Chinese history.
2. William Hinton, *Fanshen*, Monthly Review Press, New York, 1966, p. 397. (Pelican, 1972)
3. Jack Belden, *China Shakes the World*, Pelican, 1973, p. 402.
4. For a very interesting description of the manipulative power developed by women, see Margery Wolf, *Women and the Family in Rural Taiwan*, Stanford University Press, 1972, p. 40.
5. Margery Wolf has observed this process with great insight and describes this important but neglected family grouping whose focus is 'mother' as the 'uterine family', ibid., pp. 32–41.
6. Liu Heng, 'Chehu, the Village Where Cloth is Produced in Every Home', in *The Production Campaign of Village Women in the Liberated Areas of China*, New China Publishing House, 1949, p. 17 (in Chinese).
7. This could be so even in urban China. A sample survey carried out in a Shanghai factory in the early 1950s showed that 17 per cent of the women workers were pregnant twice within a year, and 53 per cent once within the year. *Economist*, 23 March 1957, p. 986.
8. 'Resolutions of the Central Committee of the Chinese Communist Party on the Present Orientation of Work Amongst Women in the Anti-Japanese Base Areas, 1942', in *Documents of the Women's Movement of the Liberated Areas*, New China Publishing House, 1949 (in Chinese).
9. Resolutions of the Central Committee of the Chinese Communist

Party on the Present Orientation of Work Amongst Women in the Countryside of the Liberated Areas', 1948, in *Documents of the Women's Movement of the Liberated Areas*, New China Publishing House, 1949.
10. *People's Daily*, 8 March 1973.
11. V. I. Lenin, 'International Women's Day', *Pravda*, March 1920. Reprinted in V. I. Lenin, *Women and Society*, International Publishers, New York, 1938.
12. André Malraux, *Antimemoirs*, Bantam, New York, 1970, pp. 463–5. (Penguin, 1970)

11. The Rights and Wrongs of Women: Mary Wollstonecraft, Harriet Martineau, Simone de Beauvoir

1. *Vindication of the Rights of Woman*, p. 82. All quotations are from the edition by Miriam Kramnick, Penguin, 1975.
2. William Godwin, *Memoirs of the Author of a Vindication of the Rights of Woman*, 1798. Quotations from the edition by W. C. Durant, 1927. See pp. 54–5, 84–5.

There is a useful account of reactions to Wollstonecraft's work in R. M. Wardle, *Mary Wollstonecraft*, Kansas, 1951, pp. 158–62 on the *Vindication*, and pp. 317–22 generally.

Sartre is quoted in a summary of de Beauvoir's life by D. Desmarquest, at the end of *Tout compte fait*, Paris, 1972.
3. Wollstonecraft, *Letters Written During a Short Residence in Sweden, Norway and Denmark*, 1796, p. 242.
4. In some ways, Godwin's *Memoir* remains the most interesting account of her life. Wardle's biography is thorough and scholarly. Claire Tomalin, *The Life and Death of Mary Wollstonecraft* (Weidenfeld and Nicolson, 1974), is readable, and her attempt to piece together Wollstonecraft's early loves is interesting. But easily the best biography is Margaret George, *One Woman's Situation*, Illinois, 1970. None of these writers, however, take her ideas very seriously. One of the best short accounts of her intellectual development is in K. N. Cameron, *Shelley and his Circle*, 4 vols., Harvard University Press, 1961–70, especially vol. I (1961), pp. 46–65.
5. *The Wrongs of Woman, or Maria*, in *The Posthumous Works of the Author of the Vindication of the Rights of Woman*, 1798, vol. I, p. 142.
6. Wollstonecraft's letters have unfortunately never been collected. This is from a well-edited selection in Cameron, II, 955. Her letters to Godwin have been edited by R. M. Wardle. Others are available

in C. Kegan Paul, *William Godwin, His Friends and Contemporaries*, 1876.

7. *Thoughts on the Education of Daughters*, 1787, p. 70.

8. C. Kegan Paul, *William Godwin, His Friends and Contemporaries*, vol. I, pp. 166–70.

9. *Letters from Sweden*, p. 214.

10. *Vindication*, p. 87.

11. ibid., p. 131.

12. ibid., p. 129.

13. References to 'nature' are to be found throughout the *Vindication*. The crucial comparison with the poor is on p. 154; but on p. 81 Wollstonecraft herself uses the word 'nature' ideologically; she is she explains, addressing women in the middle class, 'because they appear to be in the most natural state'.

14. *Letters from Sweden*, p. 27.

15. ibid., p. 170. See also p. 244.

16. *Vindication*, p. 102. For her ideas on education, see especially pp. 286–7.

17. *Letters from Sweden*, p. 117.

18. *Posthumous Works*, vol. IV, pp. 76–8.

19. *Mary, A Fiction*, 1788, p. 34.

20. ibid., p. 97.

21. *Vindication*, p. 116. And see the whole discussion of love in *Thoughts on the Education of Daughters*, esp. pp. 81–6.

22. R. Ingpen (ed.), *The Love Letters of Mary Wollstonecraft to Gilbert Imlay*, 1908, pp. 131, 133.

23. ibid., pp. 114, 116, 145, 160, 167.

24. K. N. Cameron, op. cit., vol. IV (1970), p. 887.

25. Harriet Martineau, *Autobiography, with Memorials by Maria Weston Chapman*, 3rd ed., 1877, vol. I, p. 401.

26. ibid., vol. I, p. 133.

27. See R. K. Webb, *Harriet Martineau, A Radical Victorian*, Heinemann, 1960; this is a thorough and useful account of her intellectual and social background.

28. *Quarterly Review*, XLIX, 1833, pp. 141, 151; *Edinburgh Review*, LVII, 1833, p. 1.

29. *Society in America*, III, pp. 106–7.

30. *Edinburgh Review*, CIX, 1859, p. 298.

31. *Autobiography*, vol. II, p. 104.

32. ibid., vol. I, p. 401.

33. ibid., vol. I, p. 40.

34. Martineau refers to Caroline Norton though without naming her, in *Autobiography*, vol. I, pp. 400–401. See the lives of Anna Jameson and Charlotte Brontë in the 1855 enlarged edition of *Biographical Sketches*. Her review of *Villette* is reprinted in Vera Wheatley, *The Life and Work of Harriet Martineau*, 1957.

35. Her piece on 'Female Industry', *Edinburgh Review*, CIX, 1859, is written as if by a man.

36. *Autobiography*, vol. I, p. 10.

37. ibid., vol. I, p. 19.

38. ibid., vol. III, p. 39.

39. ibid., vol. I, pp. 99–100.

40. ibid., vol. I, p. 27.

41. ibid., vol. I, p. 100.

42. ibid., vol. I, p. 120.

43. ibid., vol. I, p. 142.

44. ibid., vol. I, p. 149.

45. ibid., vol. III, pp. 43–5.

46. ibid., vol. I, p. 249.

47. ibid., vol. II, pp. 150–51.

48. ibid., vol. II, p. 110.

49. ibid., vol. I, p. 131.

50. ibid., vol. I, p. 132.

51. *Deerbrook*, 1839, vol. I, pp. 305, 308–9.

52. *Force of Circumstance*, Penguin, 1968, p. 199. (All quotations from the first three volumes of de Beauvoir's autobiography are from the Penguin editions.)

53. *All Said and Done*, 1974, p. 463.

54. *Force of Circumstance*, p. 661.

55. Interview with Alice Schwartzer, *Le Nouvel Observateur*, 14 February 1974, p. 51.

56. *Prime of Life*, 1965, p. 367. The comments on Sartre are in *Force of Circumstance*, p. 659, and in the *Nouvel Observateur* interview.

57. *Force of Circumstance*, p. 7.

58. *The Second Sex*, 1972, p. 91. See also pp. 676 and 687.

59. *Le Nouvel Observateur*, p. 53.

60. *The Second Sex*, pp. 674–5.

61. *Prime of Life*, pp. 212–13.

62. *The Second Sex*, p. 643, but see the whole of the chapter on the independent woman and the *Nouvel Observateur* interview.

63. *Memoirs of a Dutiful Daughter*, 1970, p. 121.

64. ibid., p. 295.

65. ibid., pp. 145–6, 345.

66. *Force of Circumstance*, pp. 660–61.

67. *Prime of Life*, p. 8.

68. ibid., p. 63.

69. On the affair with Olga, *Prime of Life*, p. 261; with M., *Force of Circumstance*, p. 78.

70. *Prime of Life*, p. 143.

71. *Force of Circumstance*, p. 135.

72. *Force of Circumstance*, p. 143.

73. *Prime of Life*, p. 77.

74. ibid., p. 77.

75. ibid., p. 78.

76. *Force of Circumstance*, p. 309.

77. *The Second Sex*, p. 75.

78. *A Very Easy Death*, Penguin, 1969, p. 28.

79. *She Came to Stay*, Penguin, 1966, p. 416.

80. *Force of Circumstance*, p. 280. See also p. 278.

12. Women and Equality

1. Anna Coote and Tess Gill, *Women's Rights: A Practical Guide* Penguin, 1974, pp. 15–16.

2. ibid., p. 16.

3. Franz Neumann, 'The Concept of Political Freedom', in *The Democratic and the Authoritarian State*, The Free Press of Glencoe, New York, 1964, p. 167.

4. ibid., pp. 167–8.

5. Quoted in R. H. Tawney, *Equality*, Allen and Unwin, 1964, p. 48.

6. Mary Astell, *Reflections Upon Marriage*, 1700 (no pagination).

7. ibid.

8. Anon., *An Essay in the Defence of the Female Sex*, 1696.

9. ibid., p. 17.

10. Margaret Lucas, Duchess of Newcastle, 'Female Orations', in *Orations of Divers Sorts*, 1662, pp. 225–6.

11. Astell, op. cit.

12. Lucas, op. cit.

13. Astell, op. cit.

14. Caritat, Marquis de Condorcet, 'Sur l'admission des femmes au droit de cite', 1790, quoted in Tomalin, *The Life and Death of Mary Wollstonecraft*, Weidenfeld and Nicolson, 1974, p. 104.

15. Mary Wollstonecraft, *A Vindication of the Rights of Women* (1792), Everyman Library, 1970, p. 67. (Penguin, 1975)

16. ibid., p. 63.

17. ibid., p. 25.
18. ibid., p. 18.
19. John Stuart Mill, *The Subjection of Women* (1869), Everyman Library, 1970, p. 238.
20. ibid., p. 230.
21. ibid., p. 259.
22. ibid., p. 259.
23. ibid., p. 316.
24. ibid., p. 219.
25. ibid., pp. 234–5.
26. Arthur Young, quoted in R. H. Tawney, op. cit., p. 94.
27. From the hymn 'All Things Bright and Beautiful'.

FOR THE BEST IN PAPERBACKS, LOOK FOR THE

In every corner of the world, on every subject under the sun, Penguin represents quality and variety – the very best in publishing today.

For complete information about books available from Penguin – including Pelicans, Puffins, Peregrines and Penguin Classics – and how to order them, write to us at the appropriate address below. Please note that for copyright reasons the selection of books varies from country to country.

In the United Kingdom: Please write to *Dept E.P., Penguin Books Ltd, Harmondsworth, Middlesex, UB7 0DA*

If you have any difficulty in obtaining a title, please send your order with the correct money, plus ten per cent for postage and packaging, to *PO Box No 11, West Drayton, Middlesex*

In the United States: Please write to *Dept BA, Penguin, 299 Murray Hill Parkway, East Rutherford, New Jersey 07073*

In Canada: Please write to *Penguin Books Canada Ltd, 2801 John Street, Markham, Ontario L3R 1B4*

In Australia: Please write to the *Marketing Department, Penguin Books Australia Ltd, P.O. Box 257, Ringwood, Victoria 3134*

In New Zealand: Please write to the *Marketing Department, Penguin Books (NZ) Ltd, Private Bag, Takapuna, Auckland 9*

In India: Please write to *Penguin Overseas Ltd, 706 Eros Apartments, 56 Nehru Place, New Delhi, 110019*

In Holland: Please write to *Penguin Books Nederland B.V., Postbus 195, NL–1380AD Weesp, Netherlands*

In Germany: Please write to *Penguin Books Ltd, Friedrichstrasse 10–12, D–6000 Frankfurt Main 1, Federal Republic of Germany*

In Spain: Please write to *Longman Penguin España, Calle San Nicolas 15, E–28013 Madrid, Spain*

In France: Please write to *Penguin Books Ltd, 39 Rue de Montmorency, F-75003, Paris, France*

In Japan: Please write to *Longman Penguin Japan Co Ltd, Yamaguchi Building, 2–12–9 Kanda Jimbocho, Chiyoda-Ku, Tokyo 101, Japan*

FOR THE BEST IN PAPERBACKS, LOOK FOR THE

A CHOICE OF PENGUINS AND PELICANS

The Literature of the United States   Marcus Cunliffe

The fourth edition of a masterly one-volume survey, described by D. W. Brogan in the *Guardian* as 'a very good book indeed'.

The Sceptical Feminist   Janet Radcliffe Richards

A rigorously argued but sympathetic consideration of feminist claims. 'A triumph' – *Sunday Times*

The Enlightenment   Norman Hampson

A classic survey of the age of Diderot and Voltaire, Goethe and Hume, which forms part of the Pelican History of European Thought.

Defoe to the Victorians   David Skilton

'Learned and stimulating' (*The Times Educational Supplement*). A fascinating survey of two centuries of the English novel.

Reformation to Industrial Revolution   Christopher Hill

This 'formidable little book' (Peter Laslett in the *Guardian*) by one of our leading historians is Volume 2 of the Pelican Economic History of Britain.

The New Pelican Guide to English Literature   Boris Ford (ed.)
Volume 8: The Present

This book brings a major series up to date with important essays on Ted Hughes and Nadine Gordimer, Philip Larkin and V. S. Naipaul, and all the other leading writers of today.

FOR THE BEST IN PAPERBACKS, LOOK FOR THE 🐧

A CHOICE OF PENGUINS AND PELICANS

Adieux Simone de Beauvoir

This 'farewell to Sartre' by his life-long companion is a 'true labour of love' (the *Listener*) and 'an extraordinary achievement' (*New Statesman*).

British Society 1914–45 John Stevenson

A major contribution to the Pelican Social History of Britain, which 'will undoubtedly be the standard work for students of modern Britain for many years to come' – *The Times Educational Supplement*

The Pelican History of Greek Literature Peter Levi

A remarkable survey covering all the major writers from Homer to Plutarch, with brilliant translations by the author, one of the leading poets of today.

Art and Literature Sigmund Freud

Volume 14 of the Pelican Freud Library contains Freud's major essays on Leonardo, Michelangelo and Dostoyevsky, plus shorter pieces on Shakespeare, the nature of creativity and much more.

A History of the Crusades Sir Steven Runciman

This three-volume history of the events which transferred world power to Western Europe – and founded Modern History – has been universally acclaimed as a masterpiece.

A Night to Remember Walter Lord

The classic account of the sinking of the *Titanic*. 'A stunning book, incomparably the best on its subject and one of the most exciting books of this or any year' – *The New York Times*

FOR THE BEST IN PAPERBACKS, LOOK FOR THE

A CHOICE OF PENGUINS AND PELICANS

The Second World War (6 volumes)   Winston S. Churchill

The definitive history of the cataclysm which swept the world for the second time in thirty years.

1917: The Russian Revolutions and the Origins of Present-Day Communism
Leonard Schapiro

A superb narrative history of one of the greatest episodes in modern history by one of our greatest historians.

Imperial Spain 1496–1716   J. H. Elliot

A brilliant modern study of the sudden rise of a barren and isolated country to be the greatest power on earth, and of its equally sudden decline. 'Outstandingly good' – *Daily Telegraph*

Joan of Arc: The Image of Female Heroism   Marina Warner

'A profound book, about human history in general and the place of women in it' – Christopher Hill

Man and the Natural World: Changing Attitudes in England 1500–1800
Keith Thomas

'A delight to read and a pleasure to own' – Auberon Waugh in the *Sunday Telegraph*

The Making of the English Working Class   E. P. Thompson

Probably the most imaginative – and the most famous – post-war work of English social history.

A CHOICE OF PENGUINS AND PELICANS

The French Revolution   Christopher Hibbert

'One of the best accounts of the Revolution that I know . . . Mr Hibbert is outstanding' – J. H. Plumb in the *Sunday Telegraph*

The Germans   Gordon A. Craig

An intimate study of a complex and fascinating nation by 'one of the ablest and most distinguished American historians of modern Germany' – Hugh Trevor-Roper

Ireland: A Positive Proposal   Kevin Boyle and Tom Hadden

A timely and realistic book on Northern Ireland which explains the historical context – and offers a practical and coherent set of proposals which could actually work.

A History of Venice   John Julius Norwich

'Lord Norwich has loved and understood Venice as well as any other Englishman has ever done' – Peter Levi in the *Sunday Times*

Montaillou: Cathars and Catholics in a French Village 1294–1324
Emmanuel Le Roy Ladurie

'A classic adventure in eavesdropping across time' – Michael Ratcliffe in *The Times*

The Defeat of the Spanish Armada   Garrett Mattingly

Published to coincide with the 400th anniversary of the Armada. 'A faultless book; and one which most historians would have given half their working lives to have written' – J. H. Plumb

FOR THE BEST IN PAPERBACKS, LOOK FOR THE

PENGUIN HEALTH

The Prime of Your Life Dr Miriam Stoppard

The first comprehensive, fully illustrated guide to healthy living for people aged fifty and beyond, by top medical writer and media personality, Dr Miriam Stoppard.

A Good Start Louise Graham

Factual and practical, full of tips on providing a healthy and balanced diet for young children, *A Good Start* is essential reading for all parents.

How to Get Off Drugs Ira Mothner and Alan Weitz

This book is a vital contribution towards combating drug addiction in Britain in the eighties. For drug abusers, their families and their friends.

Naturebirth Danaë Brook

A pioneering work which includes suggestions on diet and health, exercises and many tips on the 'natural' way to prepare for giving birth in a joyful relaxed way.

Pregnancy Dr Jonathan Scher and Carol Dix

Containing the most up-to-date information on pregnancy – the effects of stress, sexual intercourse, drugs, diet, late maternity and genetic disorders – this book is an invaluable and reassuring guide for prospective parents.

Care of the Dying Richard Lamerton

It is never true that 'nothing more can be done' for the dying. This book shows us how to face death without pain, with humanity, with dignity and in peace.

FOR THE BEST IN PAPERBACKS, LOOK FOR THE

A SELECTION OF PEREGRINES

The Uses of Enchantment   Bruno Bettelheim

Dr Bettelheim has written this book to help adults become aware of the irreplaceable importance of fairy tales. Taking the best-known stories in turn, he demonstrates how they work, consciously or unconsciously, to support and free the child.

The City in History   Lewis Mumford

Often prophetic in tone and containing a wealth of photographs, *The City in History* is among the most deeply learned and warmly human studies of man as a social creature.

Orientalism   Edward W. Said

In *Orientalism*, his acclaimed and now famous challenge to established Western attitudes towards the East, Edward Said has given us one of the most brilliant cultural studies of the decade. 'A stimulating, elegant yet pugnacious essay which is going to set the cat among the pigeons' – *Observer*

The Selected Melanie Klein

This major collection of Melanie Klein's writings, brilliantly edited by Juliet Mitchell, shows how much Melanie Klein has to offer in understanding and treating psychotics, in revising Freud's ideas about female sexuality, and in showing how phantasy operates in everyday life.

The Raw and the Cooked   Claude Lévi-Strauss

Deliberately, brilliantly and inimitably challenging, *The Raw and the Cooked* is a seminal work of structural anthropology that cuts wide and deep into the mind of mankind. Examining the myths of the South American Indians it demonstrates, with dazzling insight, how these can be reduced to a comprehensible psychological pattern.